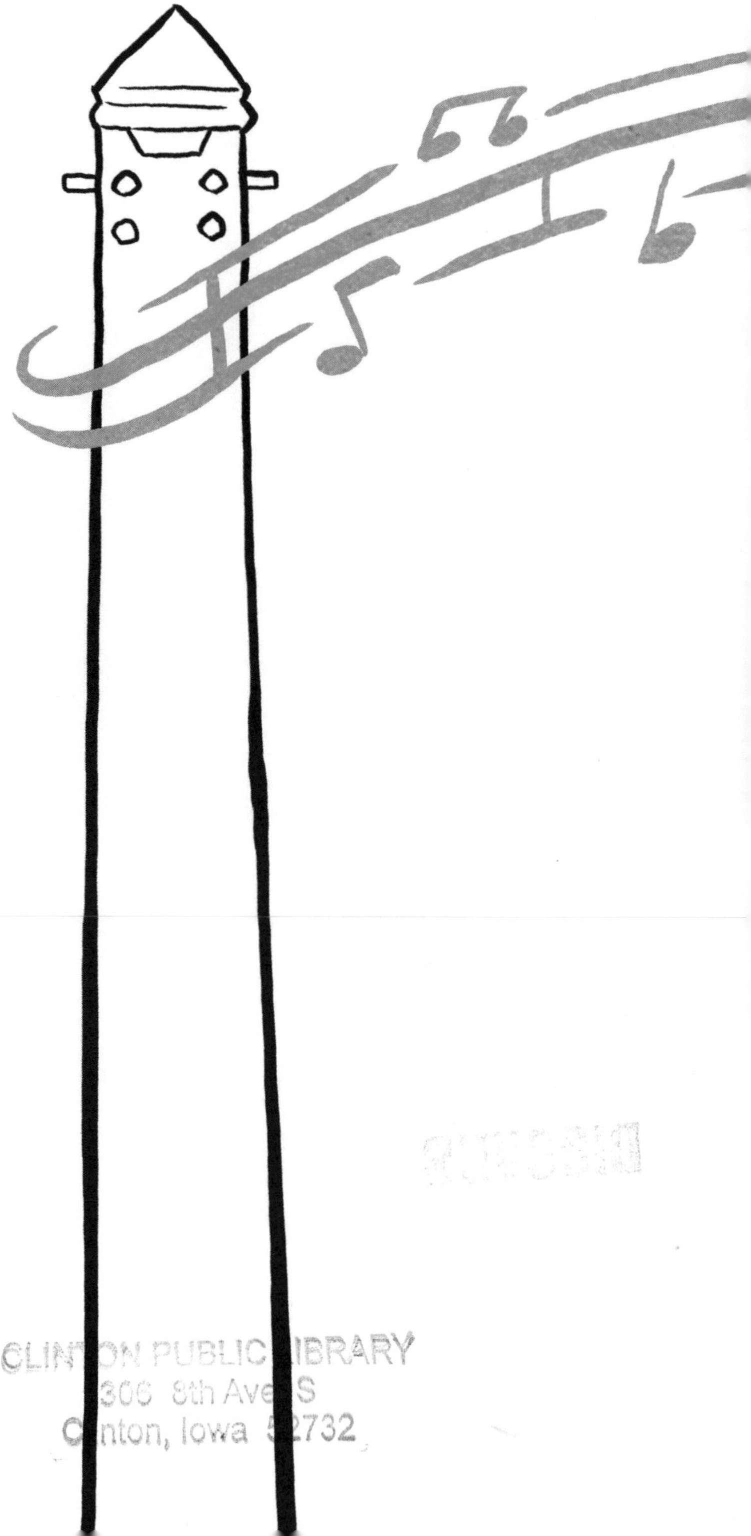

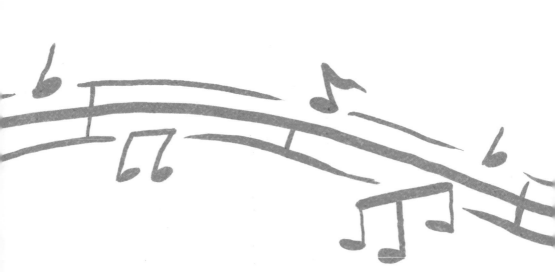

JARED K FLETCHER - LOGO AND COVER DESIGN

JEFF POWELL - INTERIOR DESIGN

TKO STUDIOS

SALVATORE SIMEONE - CEO & PUBLISHER

TZE CHUN - PRESIDENT & PUBLISHER

JATIN THAKKER - CHIEF OPERATING OFFICER

SEBASTIAN GIRNER - EDITOR-IN-CHIEF

DJELIYA

Published by TKO Studios, LLC.
Office of Publication: 1325 Franklin Avenue, Suite 545, Garden City, NY 11530.
 Printed in China.
ISBN: 978-1-952203-24-4

TKOPRESENTS.COM

djeliya

BY

JUNI BA

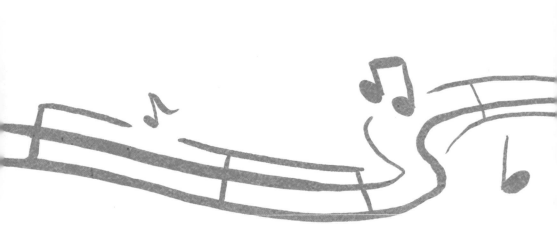

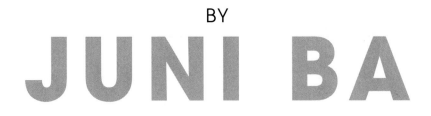

To my families.
The one from Dakar, and the
one from the bookshop.

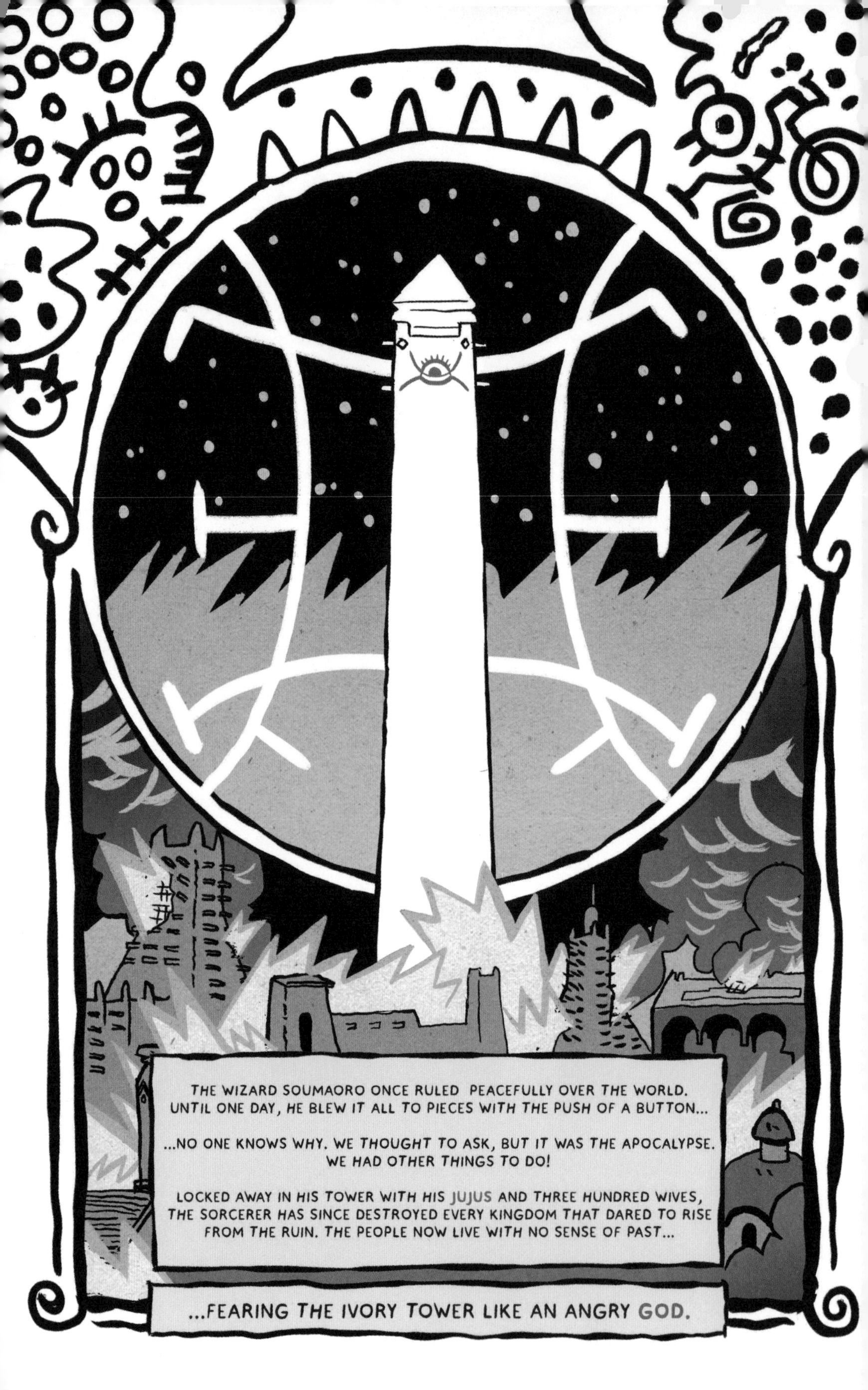
THE WIZARD SOUMAORO ONCE RULED PEACEFULLY OVER THE WORLD. UNTIL ONE DAY, HE BLEW IT ALL TO PIECES WITH THE PUSH OF A BUTTON...
...NO ONE KNOWS WHY. WE THOUGHT TO ASK, BUT IT WAS THE APOCALYPSE. WE HAD OTHER THINGS TO DO!
LOCKED AWAY IN HIS TOWER WITH HIS JUJUS AND THREE HUNDRED WIVES, THE SORCERER HAS SINCE DESTROYED EVERY KINGDOM THAT DARED TO RISE FROM THE RUIN. THE PEOPLE NOW LIVE WITH NO SENSE OF PAST...
...FEARING THE IVORY TOWER LIKE AN ANGRY GOD.

I

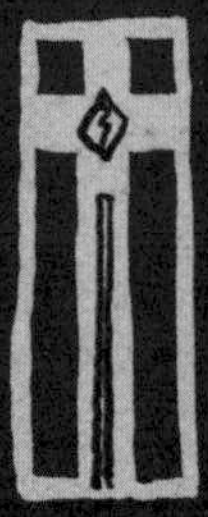

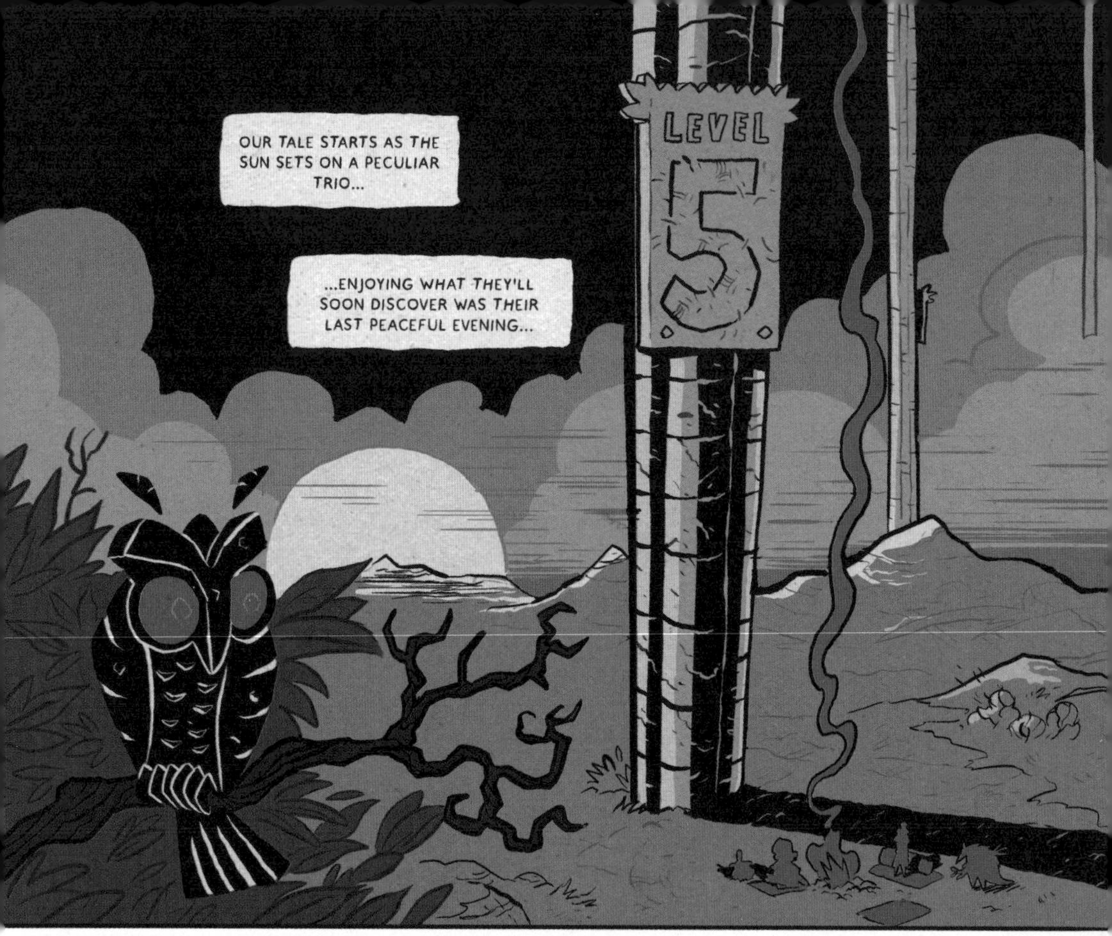
OUR TALE STARTS AS THE SUN SETS ON A PECULIAR TRIO...
...ENJOYING WHAT THEY'LL SOON DISCOVER WAS THEIR LAST PEACEFUL EVENING...
LEVEL 5

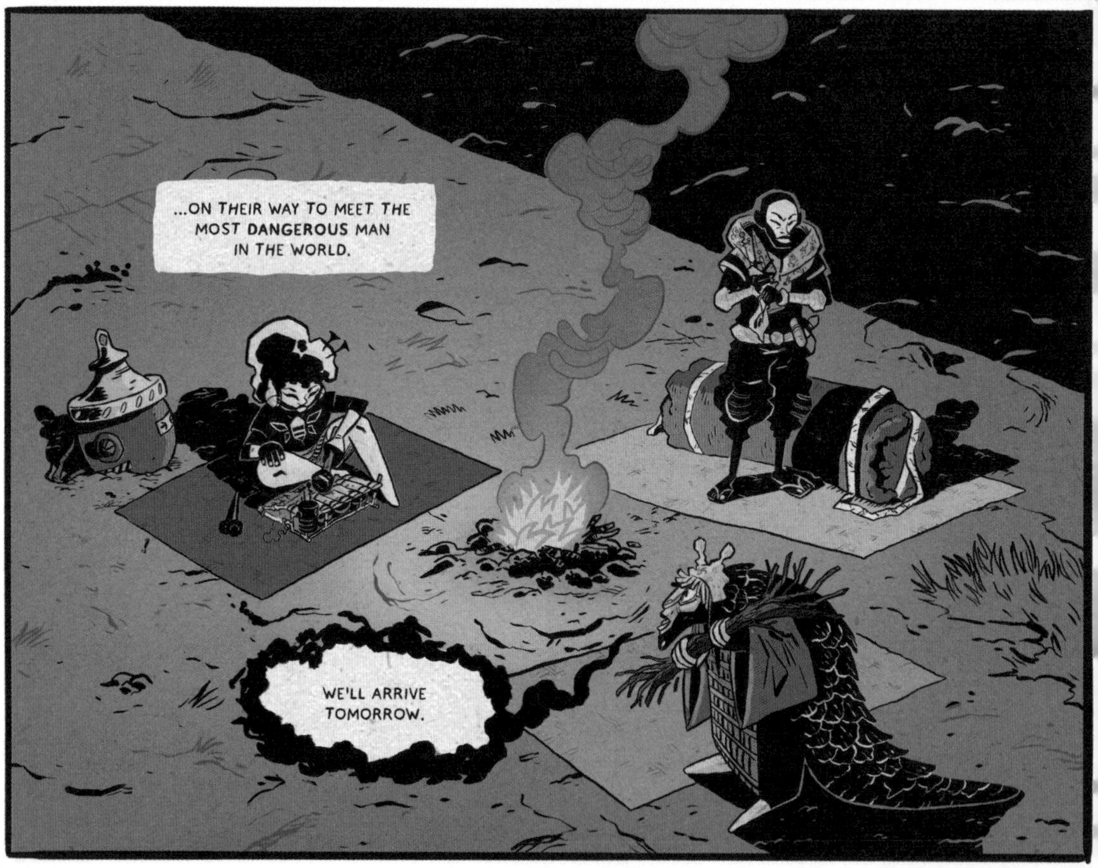
...ON THEIR WAY TO MEET THE MOST DANGEROUS MAN IN THE WORLD.
WE'LL ARRIVE TOMORROW.

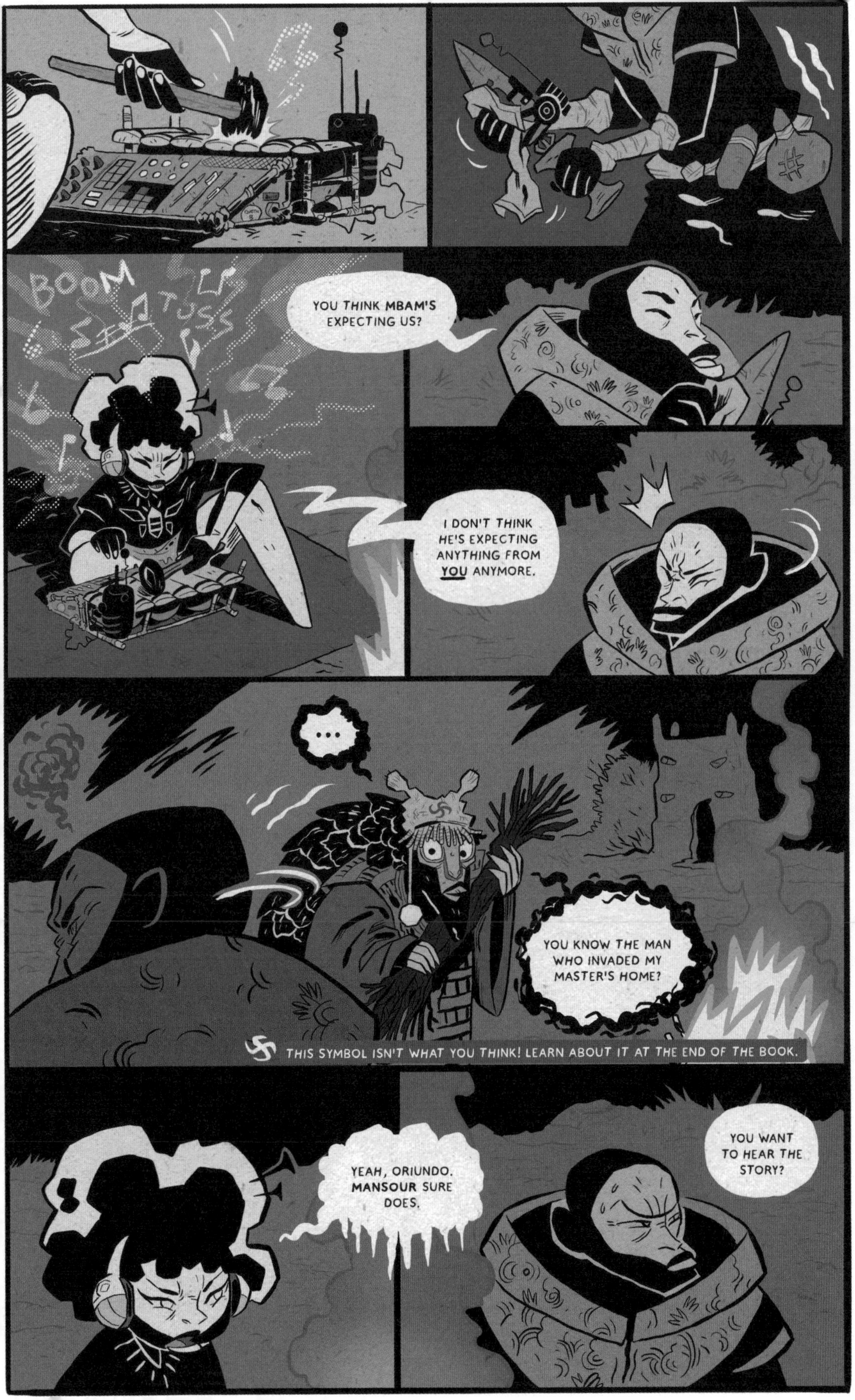
BOOM
TUSS
YOU THINK MBAM'S EXPECTING US?
I DON'T THINK HE'S EXPECTING ANYTHING FROM YOU ANYMORE.
...
YOU KNOW THE MAN WHO INVADED MY MASTER'S HOME?
THIS SYMBOL ISN'T WHAT YOU THINK! LEARN ABOUT IT AT THE END OF THE BOOK.
YEAH, ORIUNDO. MANSOUR SURE DOES.
YOU WANT TO HEAR THE STORY?

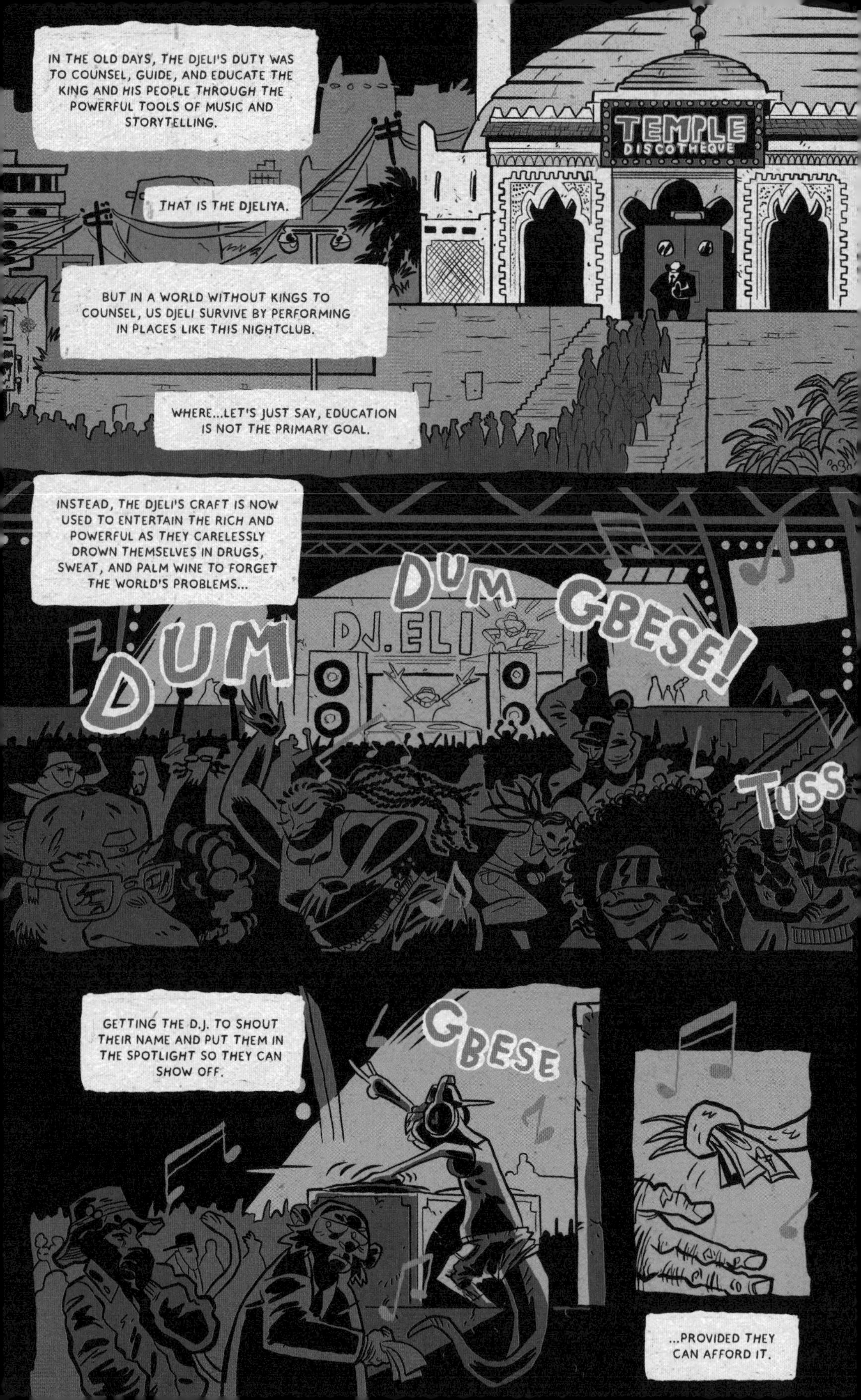
IN THE OLD DAYS, THE DJELI'S DUTY WAS TO COUNSEL, GUIDE, AND EDUCATE THE KING AND HIS PEOPLE THROUGH THE POWERFUL TOOLS OF MUSIC AND STORYTELLING.
TEMPLE
DISCOTHEQUE
THAT IS THE DJELIYA.
BUT IN A WORLD WITHOUT KINGS TO COUNSEL, US DJELI SURVIVE BY PERFORMING IN PLACES LIKE THIS NIGHTCLUB.
WHERE...LET'S JUST SAY, EDUCATION IS NOT THE PRIMARY GOAL.
INSTEAD, THE DJELI'S CRAFT IS NOW USED TO ENTERTAIN THE RICH AND POWERFUL AS THEY CARELESSLY DROWN THEMSELVES IN DRUGS, SWEAT, AND PALM WINE TO FORGET THE WORLD'S PROBLEMS...
DUM
DUM
DJ.ELI
DUM
GBESE!
TUSS
GETTING THE D.J. TO SHOUT THEIR NAME AND PUT THEM IN THE SPOTLIGHT SO THEY CAN SHOW OFF.
GBESE
...PROVIDED THEY CAN AFFORD IT.

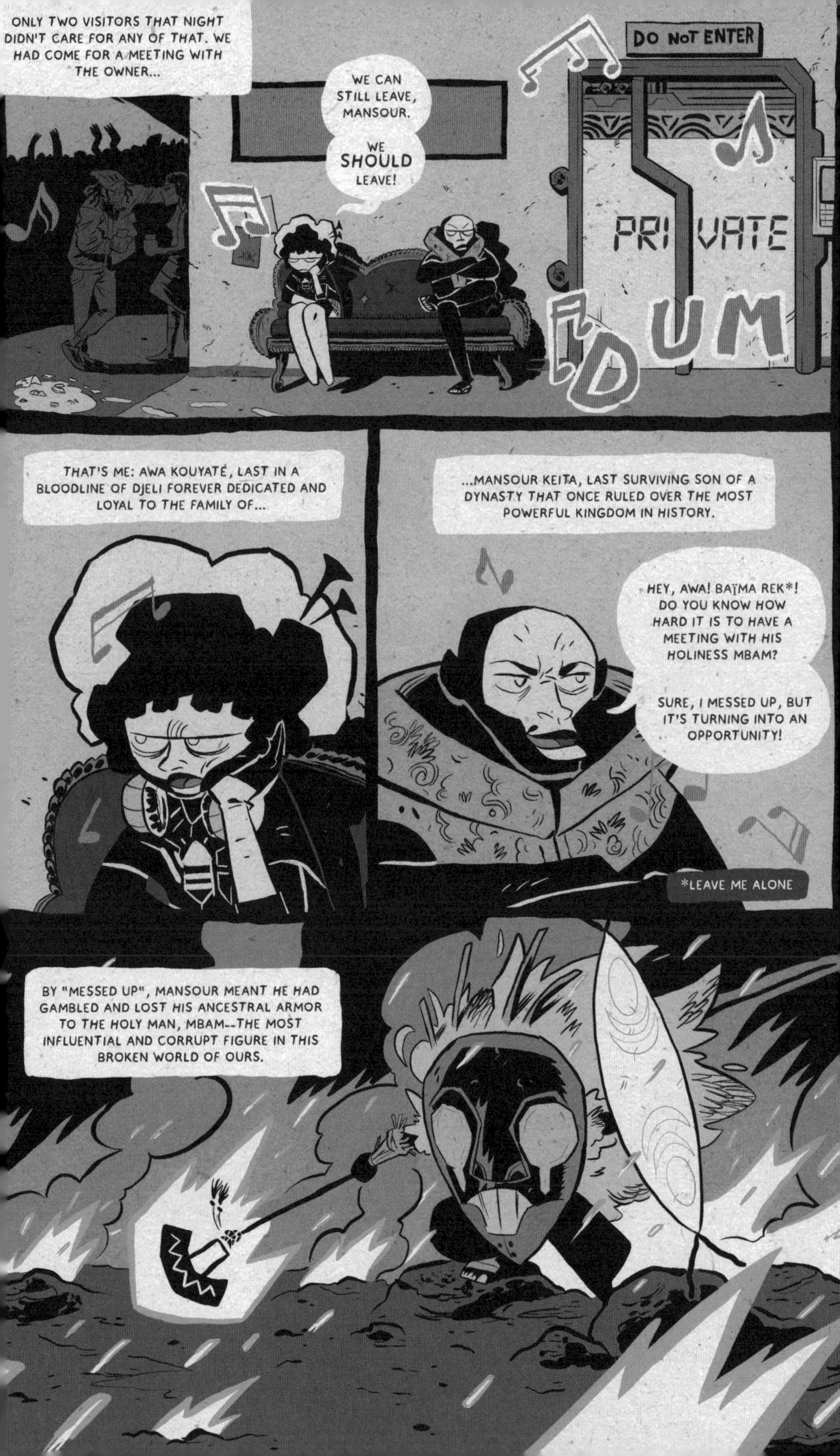
ONLY TWO VISITORS THAT NIGHT DIDN'T CARE FOR ANY OF THAT. WE HAD COME FOR A MEETING WITH THE OWNER...
DO NOT ENTER
WE CAN STILL LEAVE, MANSOUR.
WE SHOULD LEAVE!
PRIVATE
DUM
THAT'S ME: AWA KOUYATÉ, LAST IN A BLOODLINE OF DJELI FOREVER DEDICATED AND LOYAL TO THE FAMILY OF...
...MANSOUR KEITA, LAST SURVIVING SON OF A DYNASTY THAT ONCE RULED OVER THE MOST POWERFUL KINGDOM IN HISTORY.
HEY, AWA! BAÏMA REK*! DO YOU KNOW HOW HARD IT IS TO HAVE A MEETING WITH HIS HOLINESS MBAM?
SURE, I MESSED UP, BUT IT'S TURNING INTO AN OPPORTUNITY!
*LEAVE ME ALONE
BY "MESSED UP", MANSOUR MEANT HE HAD GAMBLED AND LOST HIS ANCESTRAL ARMOR TO THE HOLY MAN, MBAM--THE MOST INFLUENTIAL AND CORRUPT FIGURE IN THIS BROKEN WORLD OF OURS.

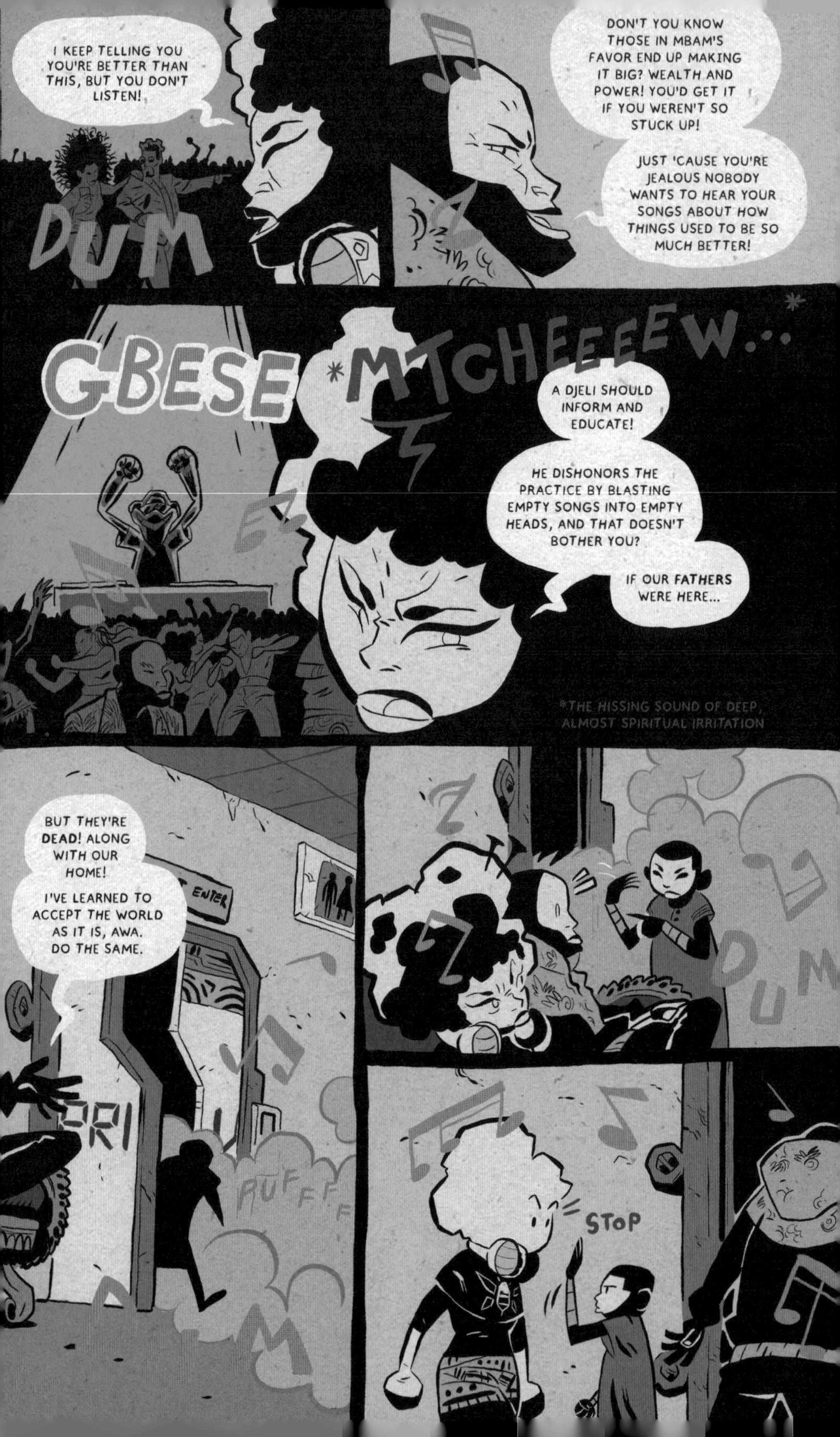
I KEEP TELLING YOU YOU'RE BETTER THAN THIS, BUT YOU DON'T LISTEN!
DUM
DON'T YOU KNOW THOSE IN MBAM'S FAVOR END UP MAKING IT BIG? WEALTH AND POWER! YOU'D GET IT IF YOU WEREN'T SO STUCK UP!
JUST 'CAUSE YOU'RE JEALOUS NOBODY WANTS TO HEAR YOUR SONGS ABOUT HOW THINGS USED TO BE SO MUCH BETTER!
GBESE
MTCHEEEEW...
A DJELI SHOULD INFORM AND EDUCATE!
HE DISHONORS THE PRACTICE BY BLASTING EMPTY SONGS INTO EMPTY HEADS, AND THAT DOESN'T BOTHER YOU?
IF OUR FATHERS WERE HERE...
*THE HISSING SOUND OF DEEP, ALMOST SPIRITUAL IRRITATION
BUT THEY'RE DEAD! ALONG WITH OUR HOME!
I'VE LEARNED TO ACCEPT THE WORLD AS IT IS, AWA. DO THE SAME.
ENTER
PUFFFF
DUM
STOP

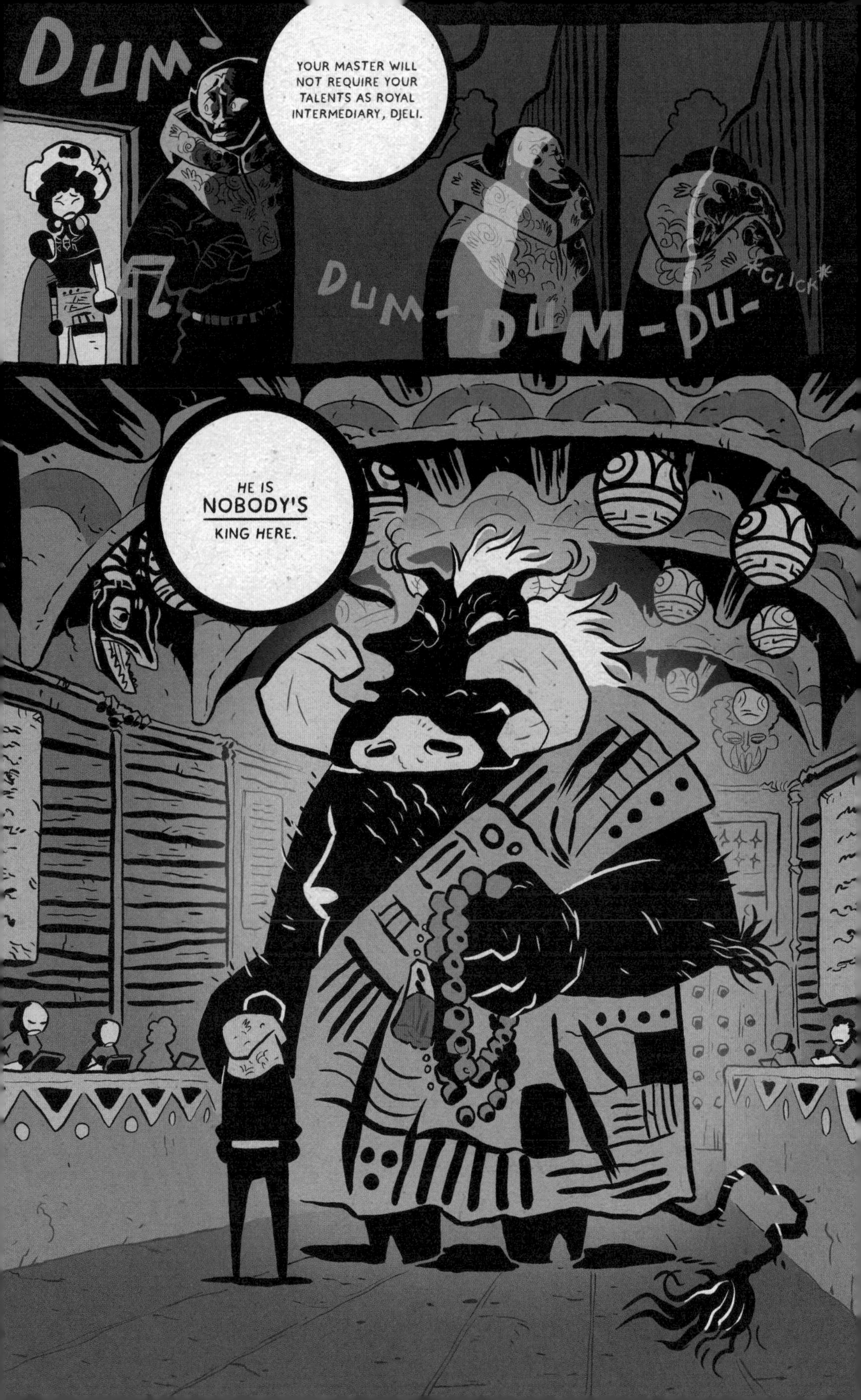
DUM-
YOUR MASTER WILL NOT REQUIRE YOUR TALENTS AS ROYAL INTERMEDIARY, DJELI.
DUM-DUM-DU-
CLICK
HE IS NOBODY'S KING HERE.

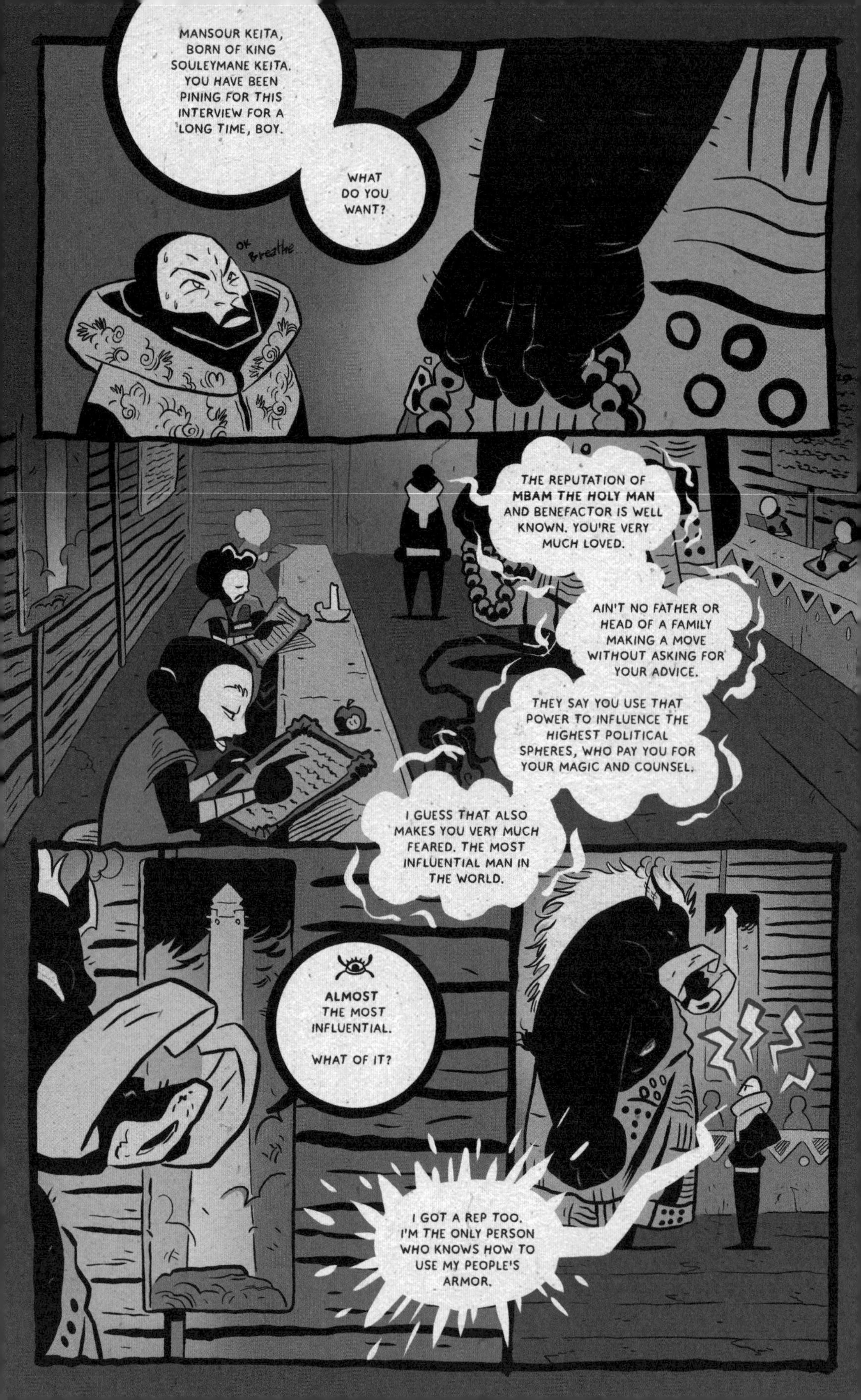
MANSOUR KEITA, BORN OF KING SOULEYMANE KEITA. YOU HAVE BEEN PINING FOR THIS INTERVIEW FOR A LONG TIME, BOY.
WHAT DO YOU WANT?
OK Breathe
THE REPUTATION OF MBAM THE HOLY MAN AND BENEFACTOR IS WELL KNOWN. YOU'RE VERY MUCH LOVED.
AIN'T NO FATHER OR HEAD OF A FAMILY MAKING A MOVE WITHOUT ASKING FOR YOUR ADVICE.
THEY SAY YOU USE THAT POWER TO INFLUENCE THE HIGHEST POLITICAL SPHERES, WHO PAY YOU FOR YOUR MAGIC AND COUNSEL.
I GUESS THAT ALSO MAKES YOU VERY MUCH FEARED. THE MOST INFLUENTIAL MAN IN THE WORLD.
ALMOST THE MOST INFLUENTIAL.
WHAT OF IT?
I GOT A REP TOO. I'M THE ONLY PERSON WHO KNOWS HOW TO USE MY PEOPLE'S ARMOR.

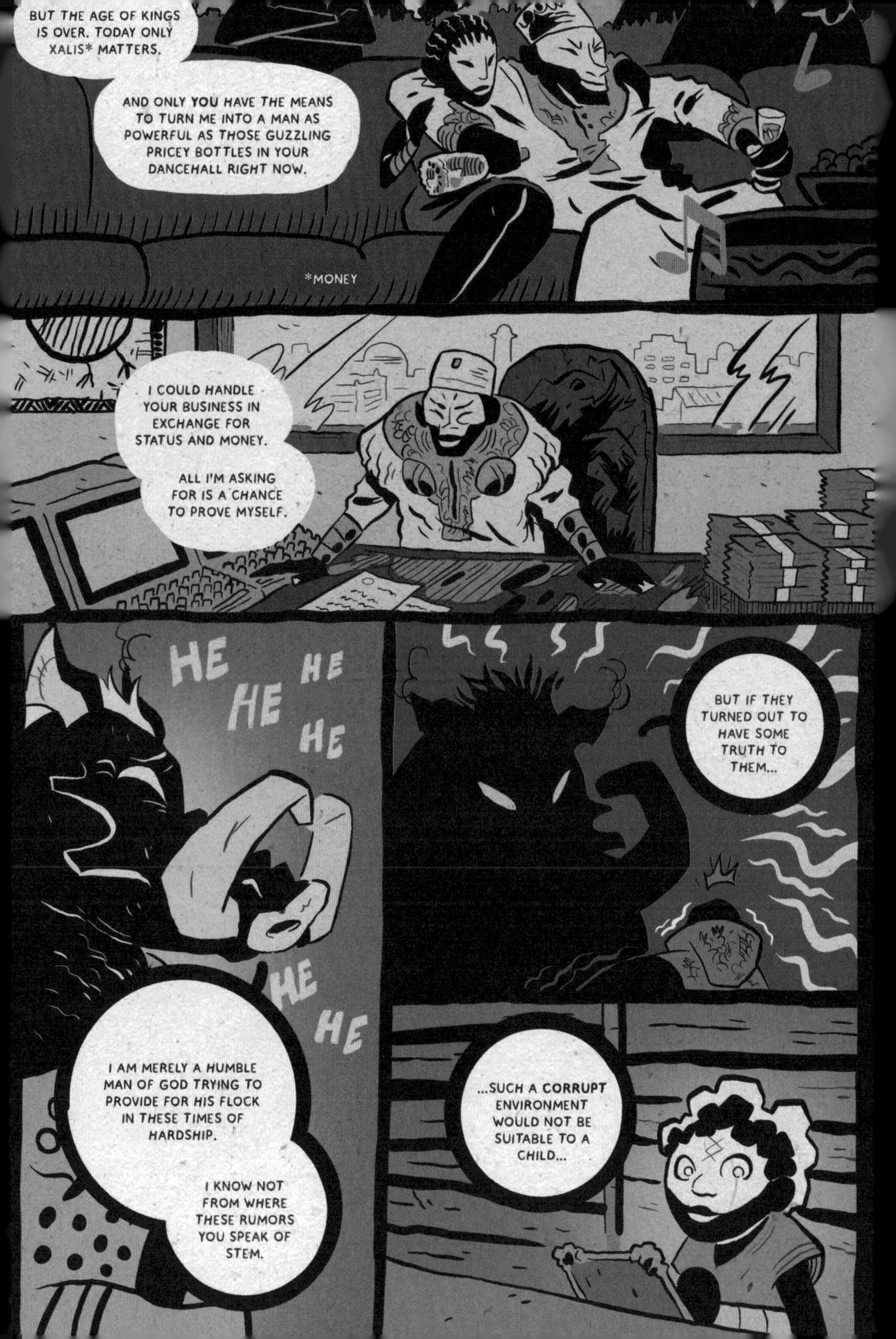
BUT THE AGE OF KINGS IS OVER. TODAY ONLY XALIS* MATTERS.
AND ONLY YOU HAVE THE MEANS TO TURN ME INTO A MAN AS POWERFUL AS THOSE GUZZLING PRICEY BOTTLES IN YOUR DANCEHALL RIGHT NOW.
*MONEY
I COULD HANDLE YOUR BUSINESS IN EXCHANGE FOR STATUS AND MONEY.
ALL I'M ASKING FOR IS A CHANCE TO PROVE MYSELF.
HE HE HE HE
HE HE
I AM MERELY A HUMBLE MAN OF GOD TRYING TO PROVIDE FOR HIS FLOCK IN THESE TIMES OF HARDSHIP.
I KNOW NOT FROM WHERE THESE RUMORS YOU SPEAK OF STEM.
BUT IF THEY TURNED OUT TO HAVE SOME TRUTH TO THEM...
...SUCH A CORRUPT ENVIRONMENT WOULD NOT BE SUITABLE TO A CHILD...

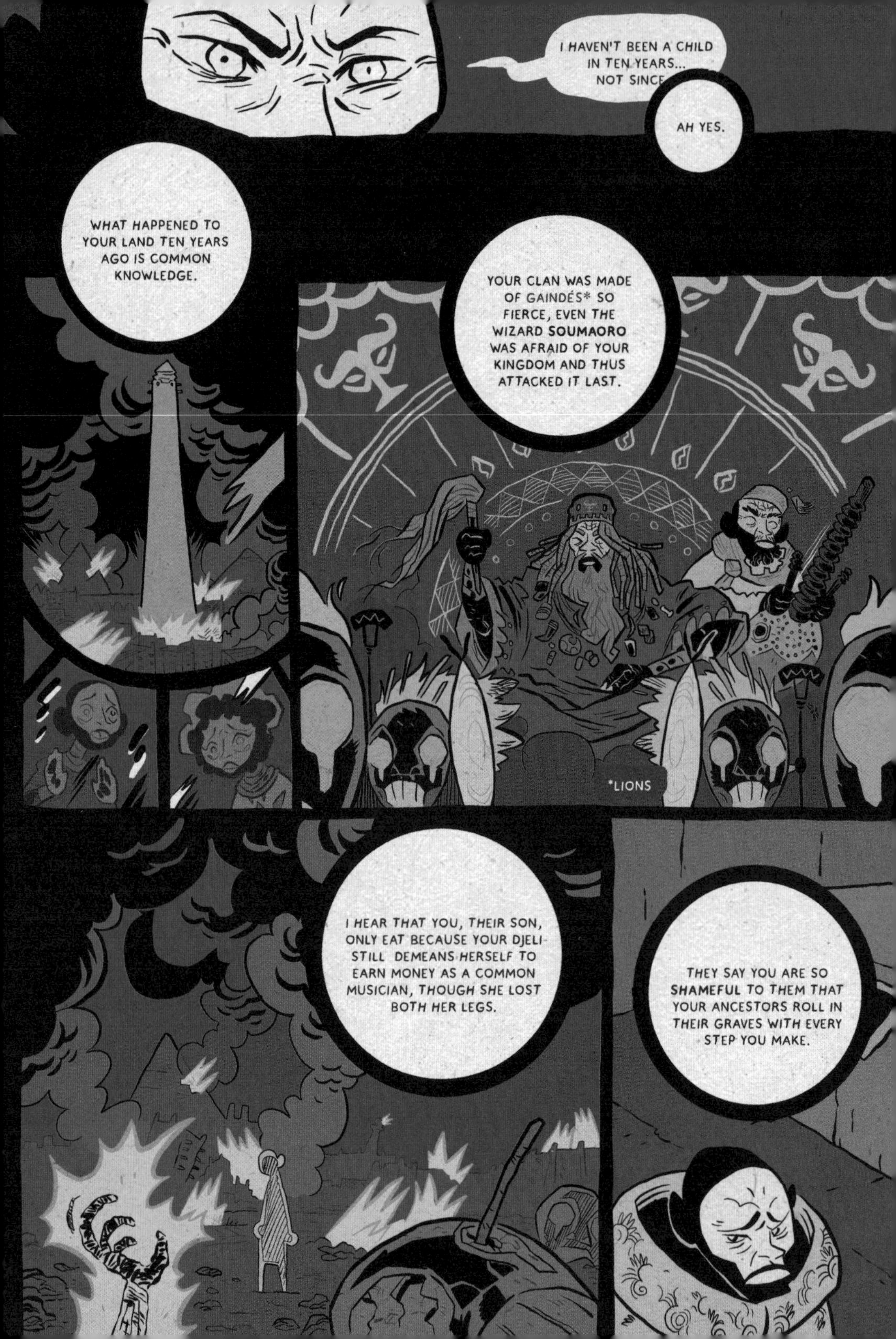
I HAVEN'T BEEN A CHILD IN TEN YEARS... NOT SINCE
AH YES.
WHAT HAPPENED TO YOUR LAND TEN YEARS AGO IS COMMON KNOWLEDGE.
YOUR CLAN WAS MADE OF GAINDÉS* SO FIERCE, EVEN THE WIZARD SOUMAORO WAS AFRAID OF YOUR KINGDOM AND THUS ATTACKED IT LAST.
*LIONS
I HEAR THAT YOU, THEIR SON, ONLY EAT BECAUSE YOUR DJELI STILL DEMEANS HERSELF TO EARN MONEY AS A COMMON MUSICIAN, THOUGH SHE LOST BOTH HER LEGS.
THEY SAY YOU ARE SO SHAMEFUL TO THEM THAT YOUR ANCESTORS ROLL IN THEIR GRAVES WITH EVERY STEP YOU MAKE.

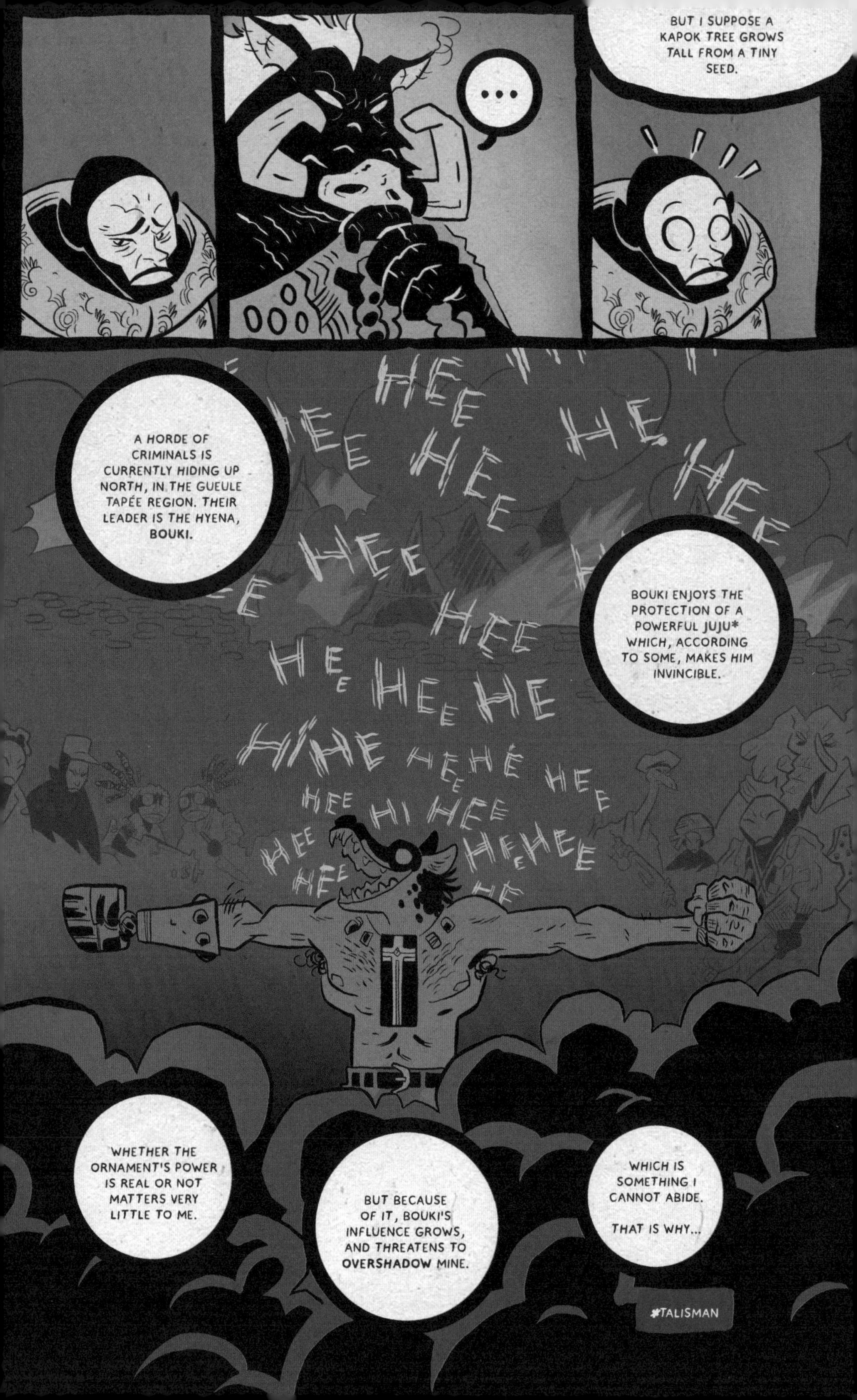
...
BUT I SUPPOSE A KAPOK TREE GROWS TALL FROM A TINY SEED.
A HORDE OF CRIMINALS IS CURRENTLY HIDING UP NORTH, IN THE GUEULE TAPÉE REGION. THEIR LEADER IS THE HYENA, BOUKI.
HEE HEE HEE HEE HEE HEE HEE HEE HE HEE HE HIHE HEHÉ HEE HEE HI HEE HEE HEHEE
BOUKI ENJOYS THE PROTECTION OF A POWERFUL JUJU* WHICH, ACCORDING TO SOME, MAKES HIM INVINCIBLE.
WHETHER THE ORNAMENT'S POWER IS REAL OR NOT MATTERS VERY LITTLE TO ME.
BUT BECAUSE OF IT, BOUKI'S INFLUENCE GROWS, AND THREATENS TO OVERSHADOW MINE.
WHICH IS SOMETHING I CANNOT ABIDE.
THAT IS WHY...
*TALISMAN

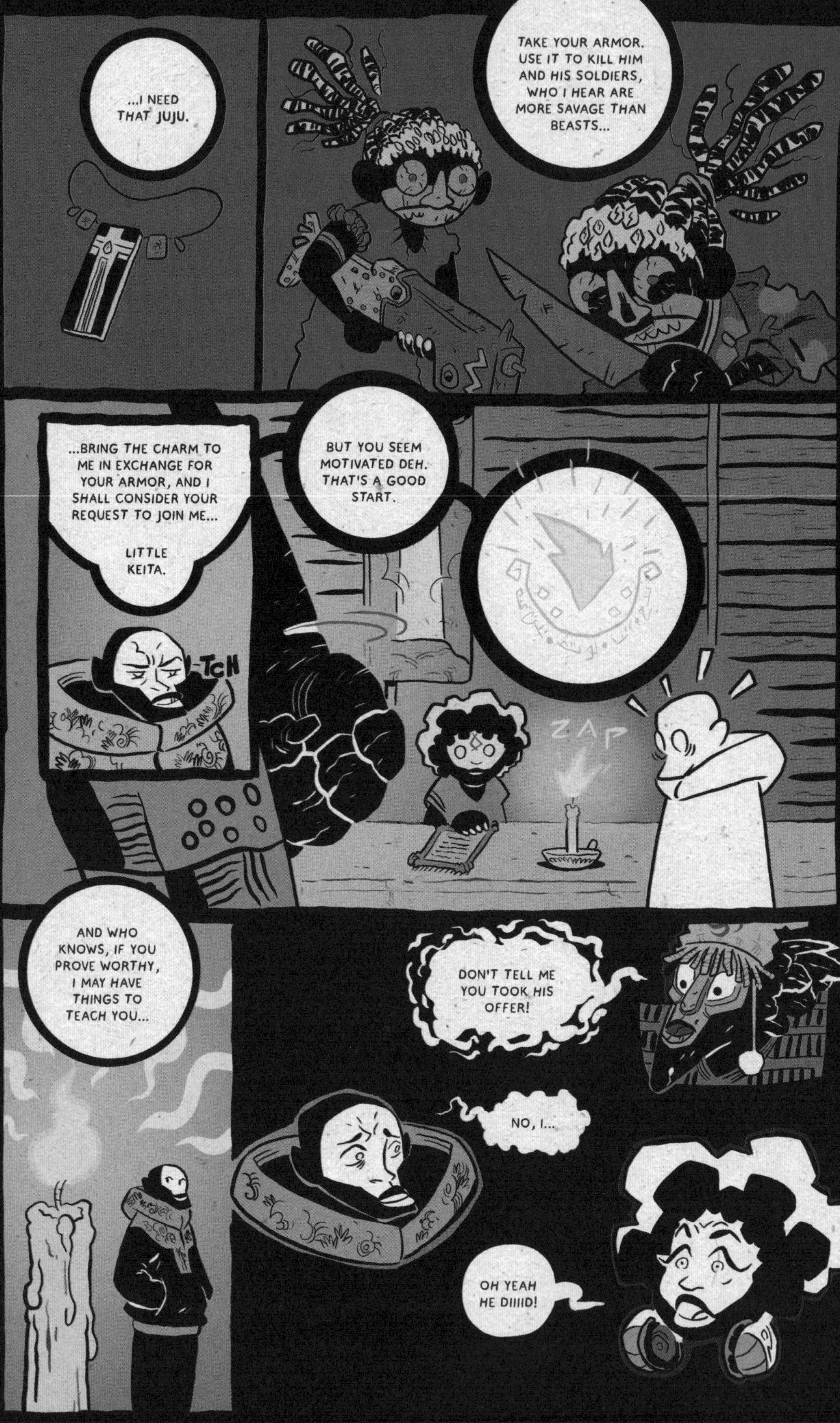
...I NEED THAT JUJU.
TAKE YOUR ARMOR. USE IT TO KILL HIM AND HIS SOLDIERS, WHO I HEAR ARE MORE SAVAGE THAN BEASTS...
...BRING THE CHARM TO ME IN EXCHANGE FOR YOUR ARMOR, AND I SHALL CONSIDER YOUR REQUEST TO JOIN ME...
LITTLE KEITA.
TCH
BUT YOU SEEM MOTIVATED DEH. THAT'S A GOOD START.
ZAP
AND WHO KNOWS, IF YOU PROVE WORTHY, I MAY HAVE THINGS TO TEACH YOU...
DON'T TELL ME YOU TOOK HIS OFFER!
NO, I...
OH YEAH HE DIIIID!

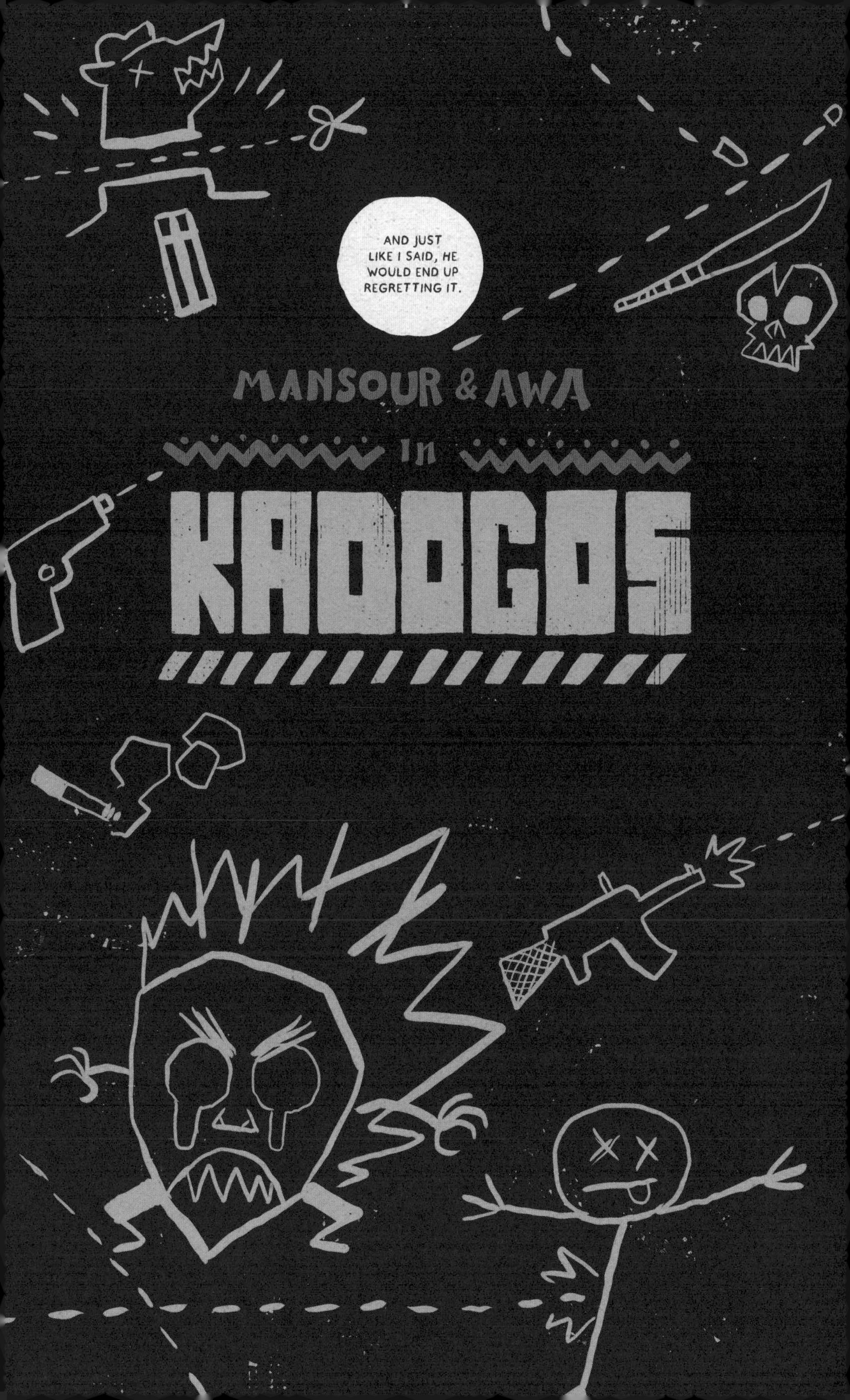
AND JUST LIKE I SAID, HE WOULD END UP REGRETTING IT.
MANSOUR & AWA
in
KADOGOS

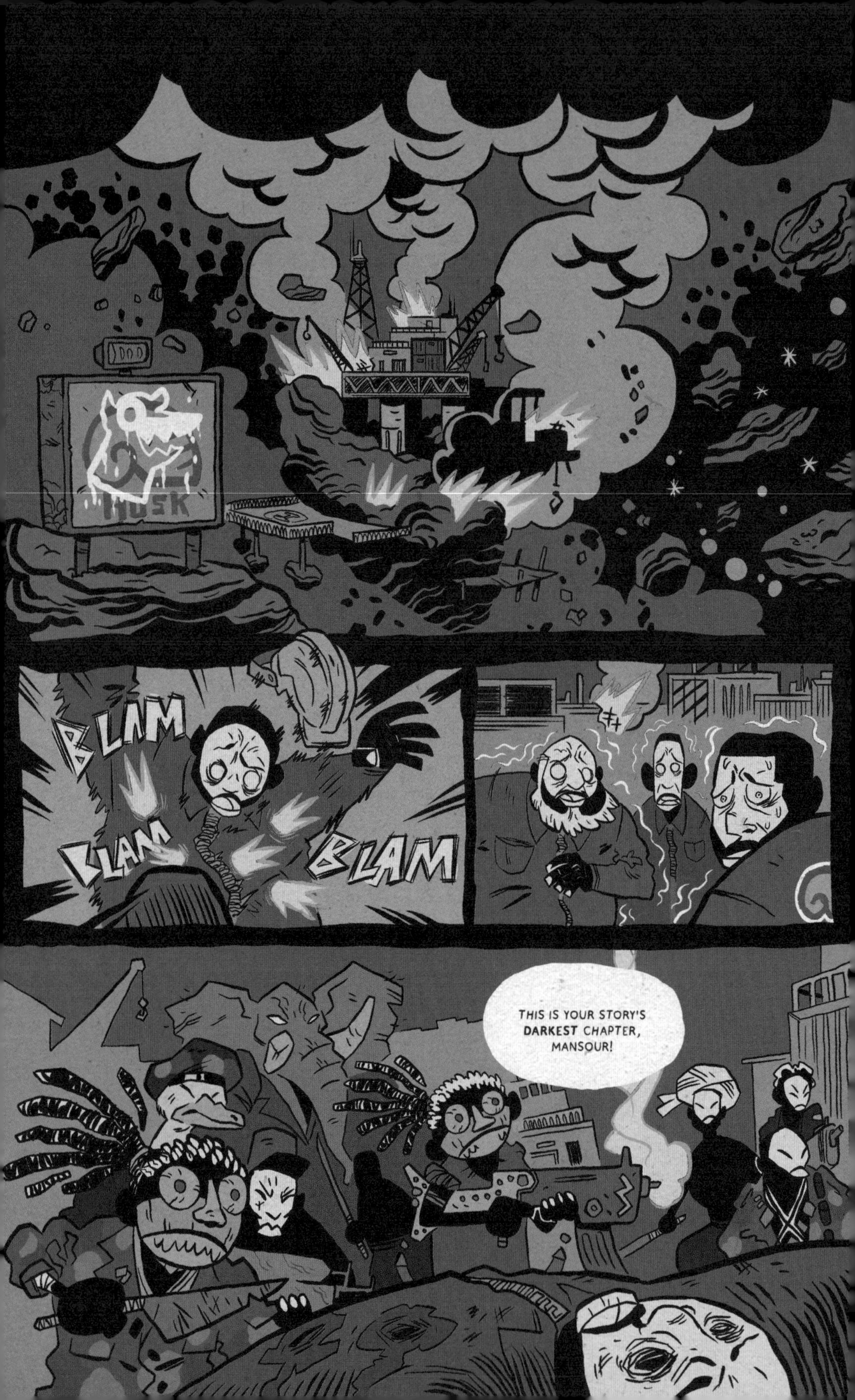
BLAM
BLAM
BLAM
THIS IS YOUR STORY'S DARKEST CHAPTER, MANSOUR!

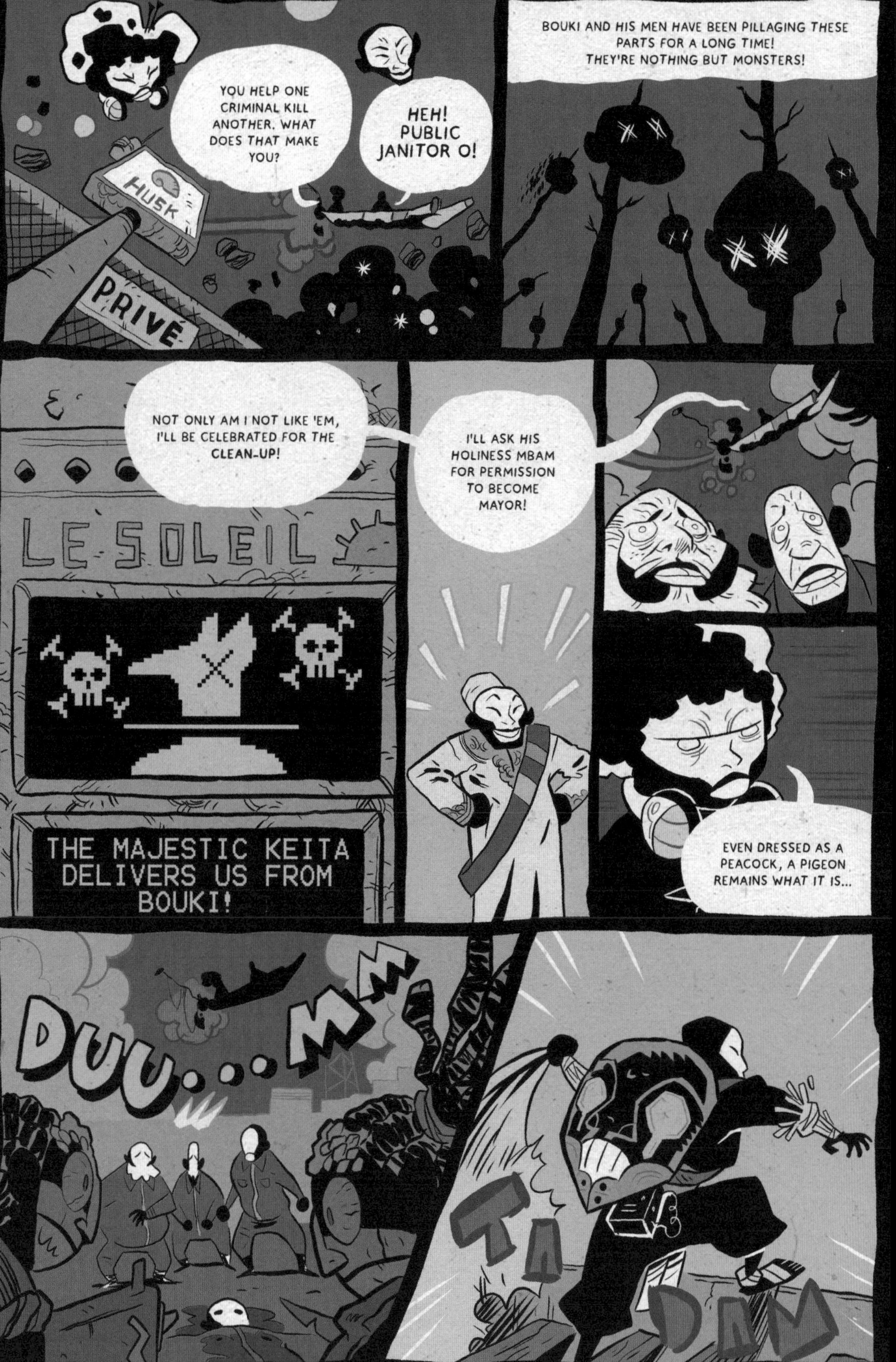

HUSK
PRIVÉ
YOU HELP ONE CRIMINAL KILL ANOTHER. WHAT DOES THAT MAKE YOU?
HEH! PUBLIC JANITOR O!
BOUKI AND HIS MEN HAVE BEEN PILLAGING THESE PARTS FOR A LONG TIME! THEY'RE NOTHING BUT MONSTERS!
NOT ONLY AM I NOT LIKE 'EM, I'LL BE CELEBRATED FOR THE CLEAN-UP!
I'LL ASK HIS HOLINESS MBAM FOR PERMISSION TO BECOME MAYOR!
LE SOLEIL
THE MAJESTIC KEITA DELIVERS US FROM BOUKI!
EVEN DRESSED AS A PEACOCK, A PIGEON REMAINS WHAT IT IS...
DUU...MM
TIDAM

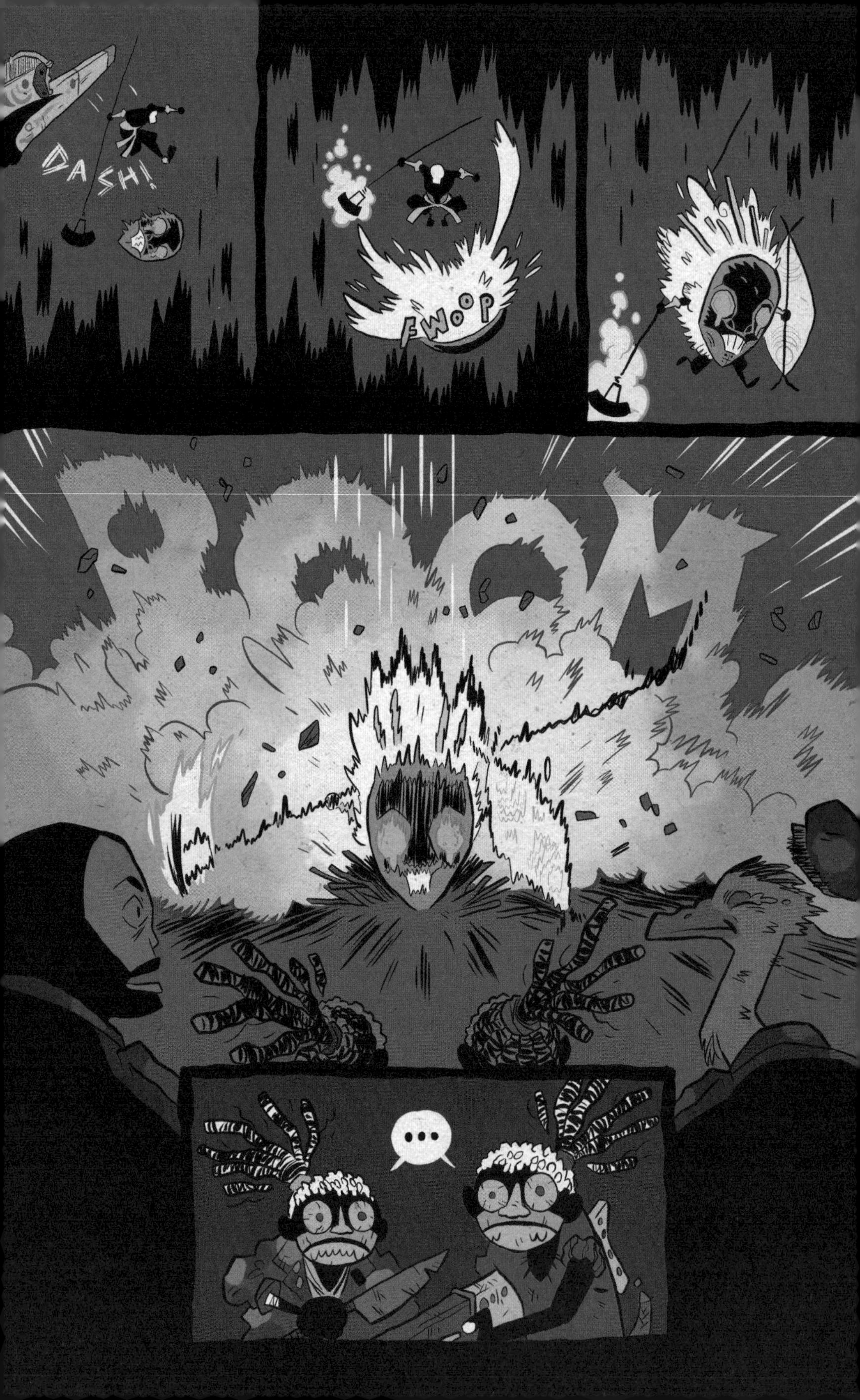
DASH!
FWOOP
BOOM
...

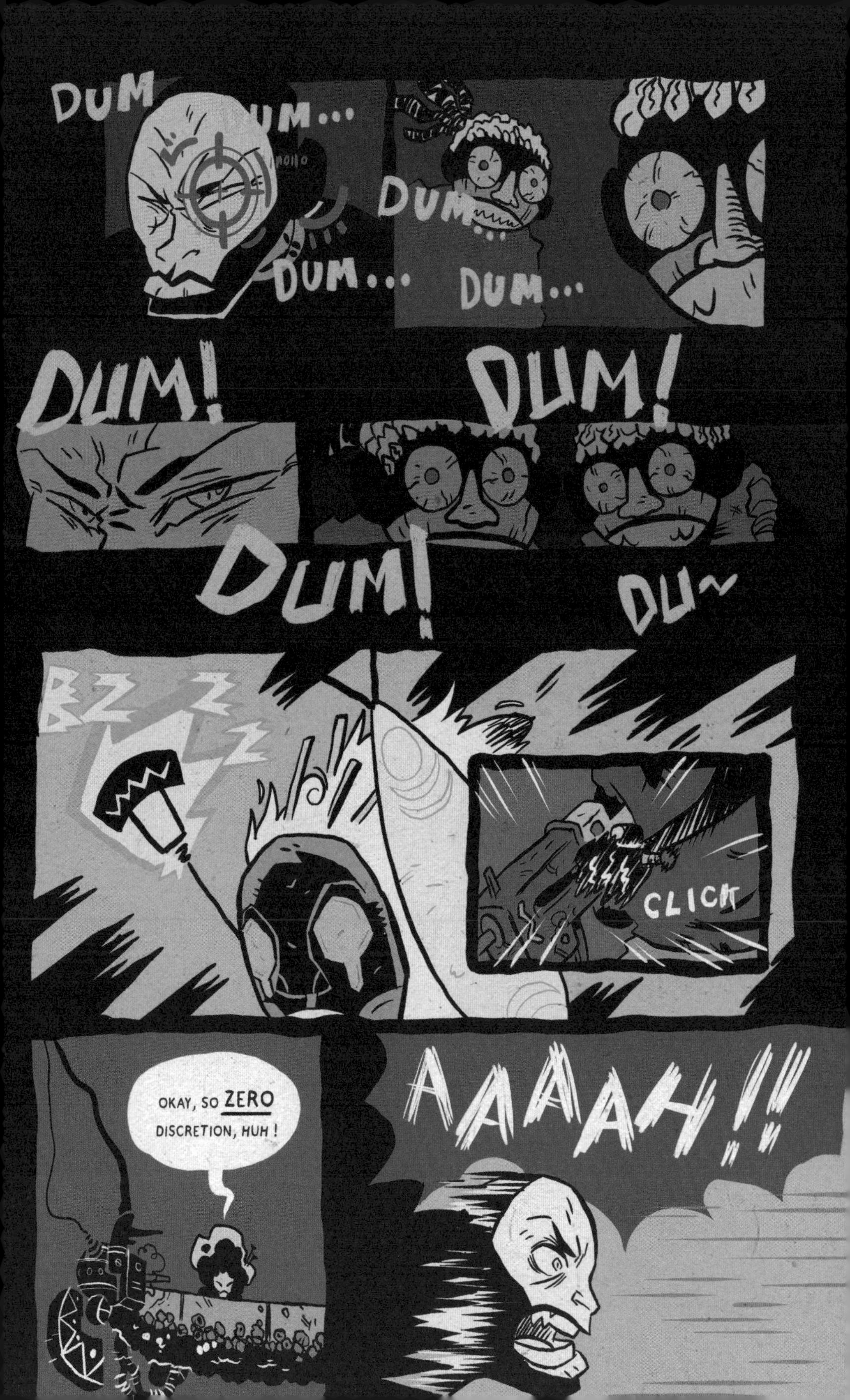
DUM
DUM...
DUM...
DUM...
DUM...
DUM!
DUM!
DUM!
DU~
BZZZZ
CLICK
OKAY, SO ZERO DISCRETION, HUH !
AAAAH!!

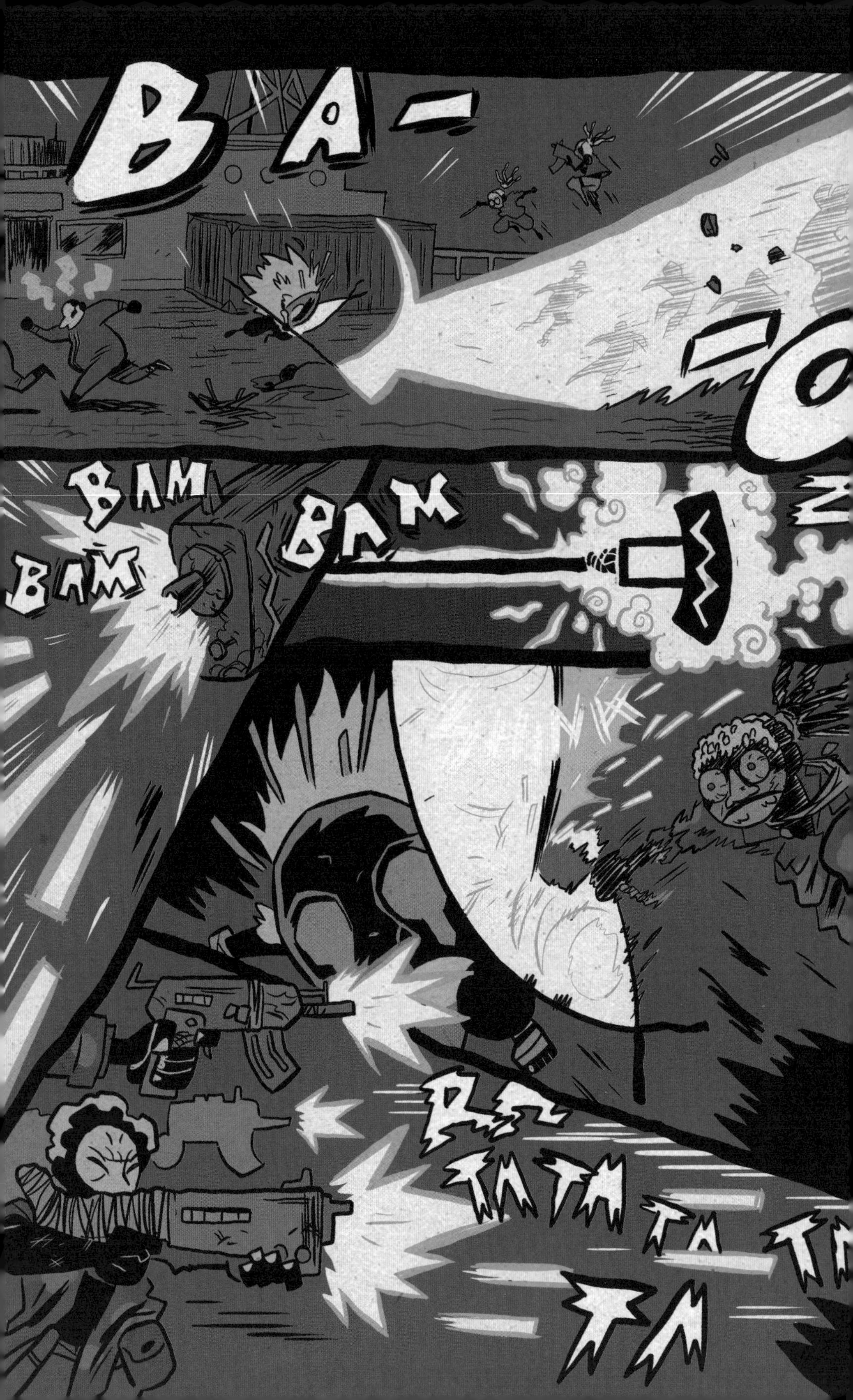
BA-
-OOM
BAM
BAM
BAM
BRR
TATATA TA TA
TA

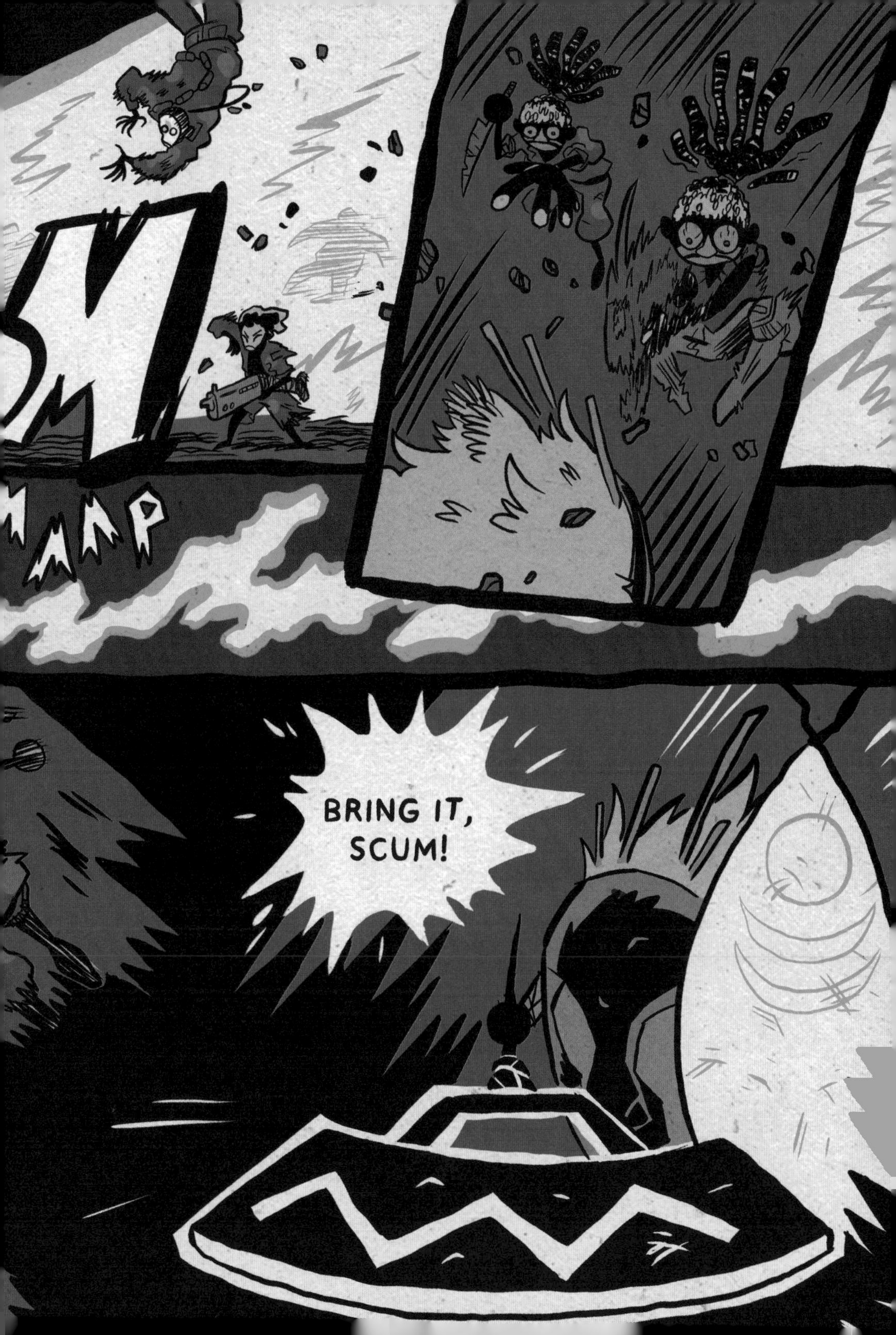
BRING IT, SCUM!

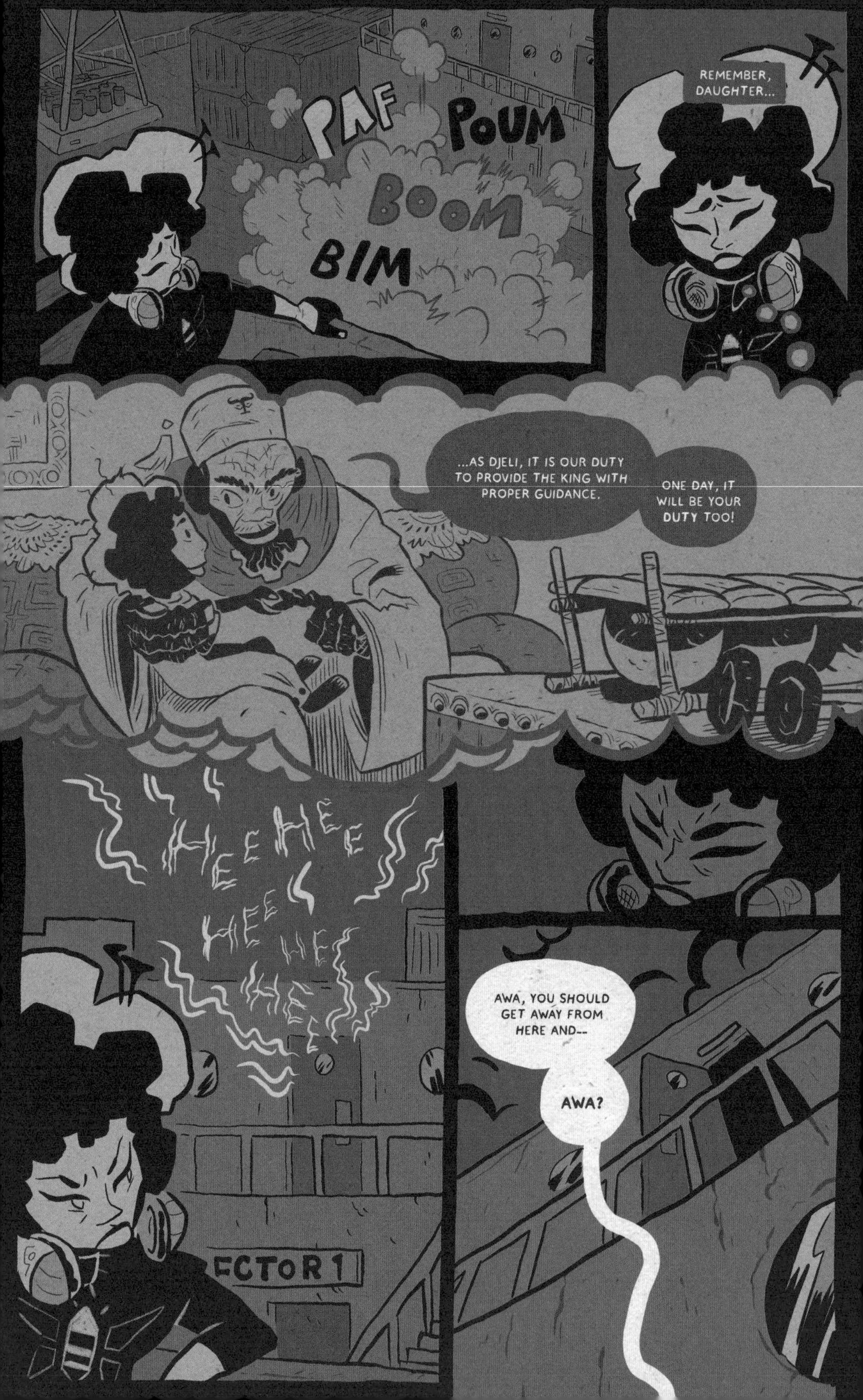
PAF
POUM
BOOM
BIM
REMEMBER, DAUGHTER...
...AS DJELI, IT IS OUR DUTY TO PROVIDE THE KING WITH PROPER GUIDANCE.
ONE DAY, IT WILL BE YOUR DUTY TOO!
HEEHEE HEE HEE HEE HEE HEE
CTOR 1
AWA, YOU SHOULD GET AWAY FROM HERE AND--
AWA?

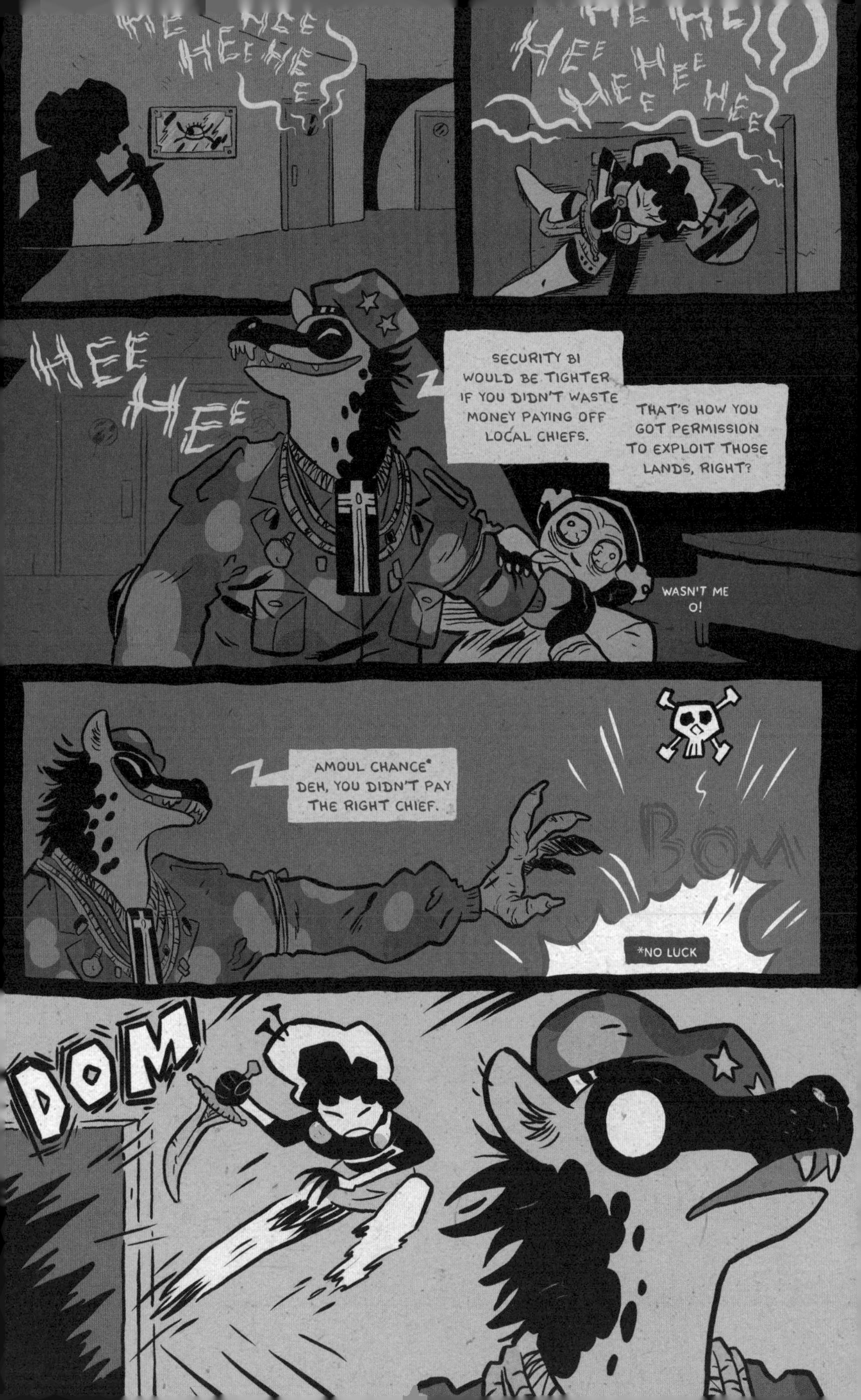
HEE HEE
HEE HEE HEE HEE
HEE HEE
SECURITY BI WOULD BE TIGHTER IF YOU DIDN'T WASTE MONEY PAYING OFF LOCAL CHIEFS.
THAT'S HOW YOU GOT PERMISSION TO EXPLOIT THOSE LANDS, RIGHT?
WASN'T ME O!
AMOUL CHANCE* DEH, YOU DIDN'T PAY THE RIGHT CHIEF.
BOM
*NO LUCK
DOM

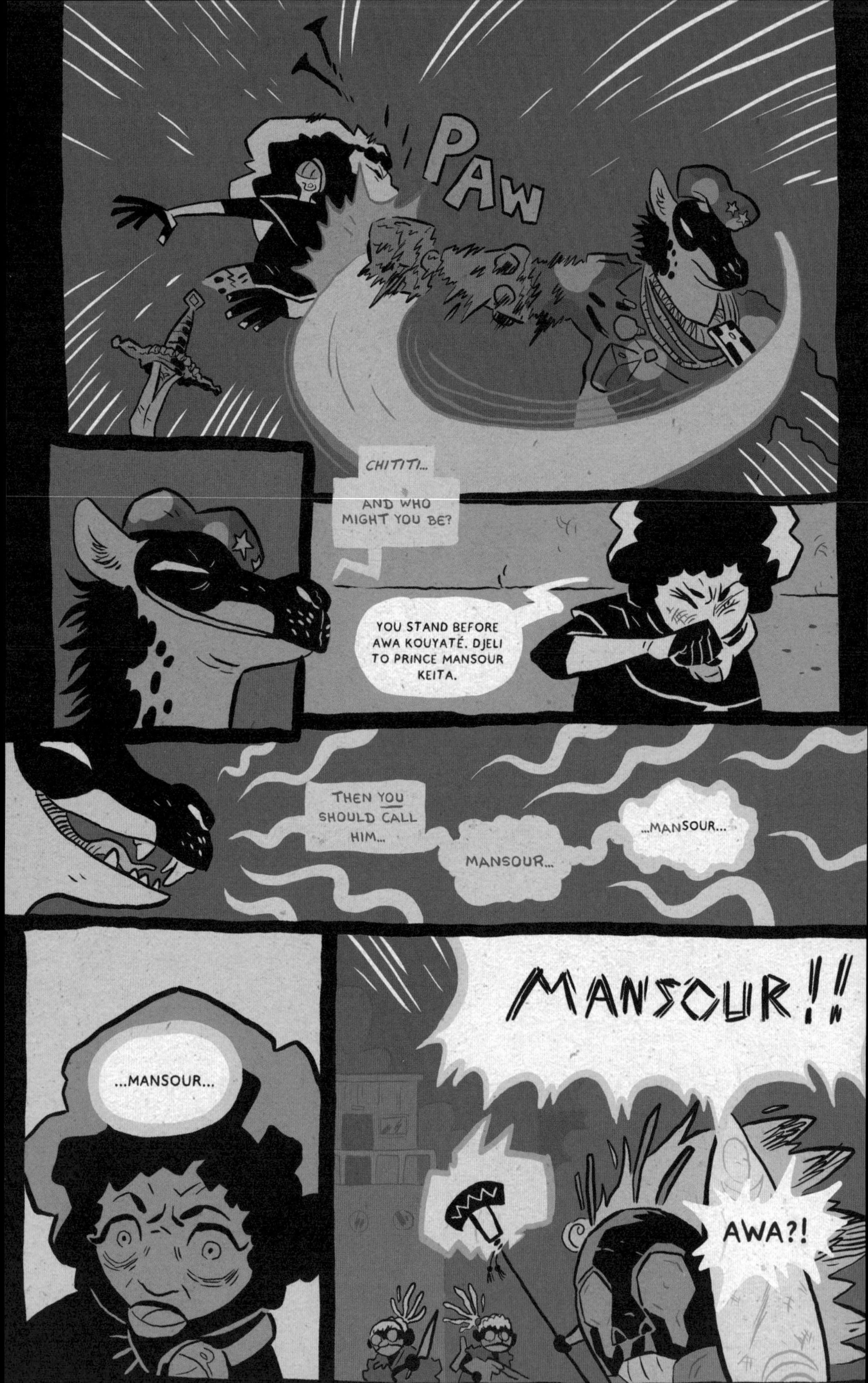
PAW
CHITITI...
AND WHO MIGHT YOU BE?
YOU STAND BEFORE AWA KOUYATÉ. DJELI TO PRINCE MANSOUR KEITA.
THEN YOU SHOULD CALL HIM...
MANSOUR...
...MANSOUR...
...MANSOUR...
MANSOUR!!
AWA?!

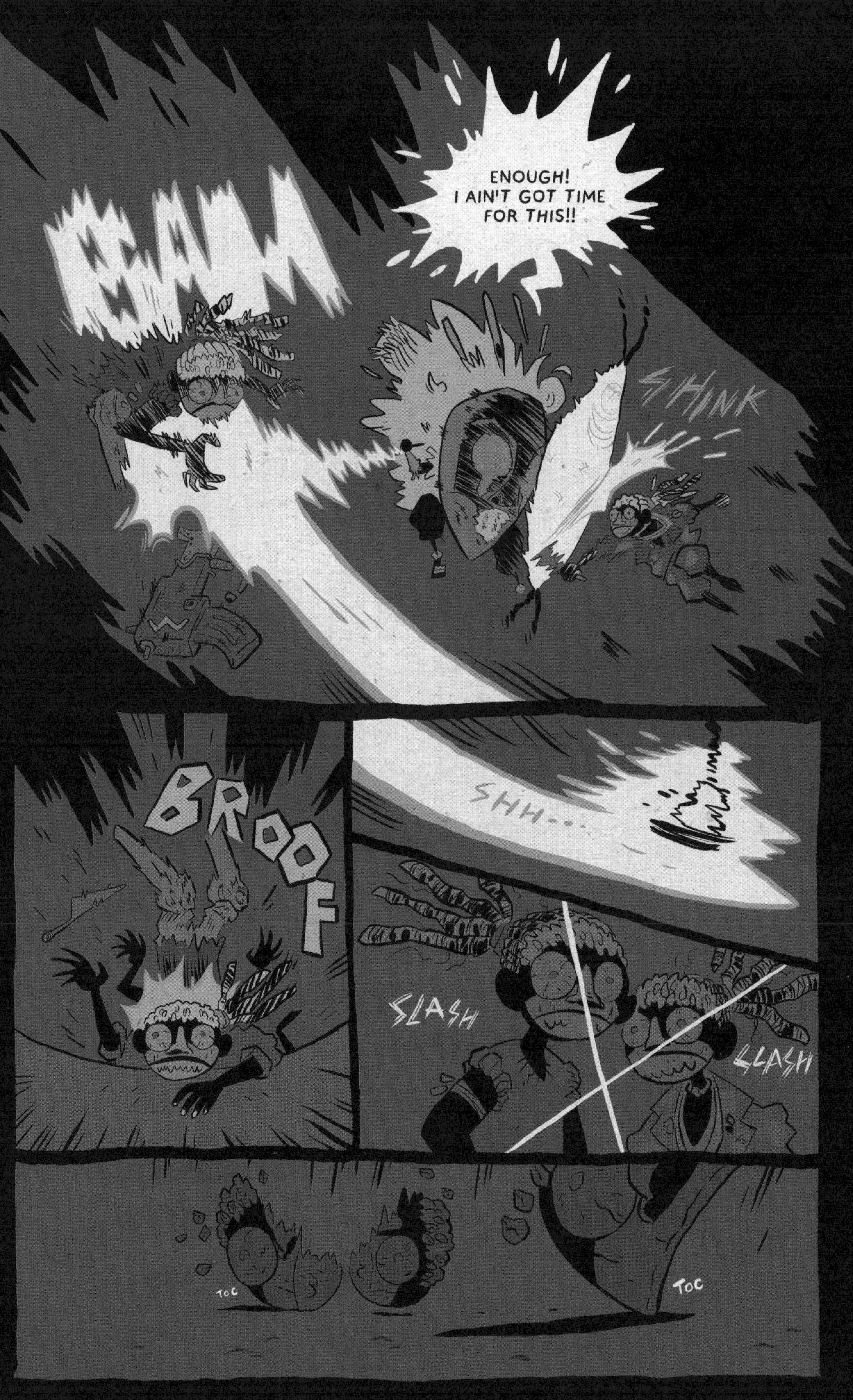
BAM
ENOUGH! I AIN'T GOT TIME FOR THIS!!
SHINK
BROOF
SHH...
SLASH
SLASH
TOC
TOC

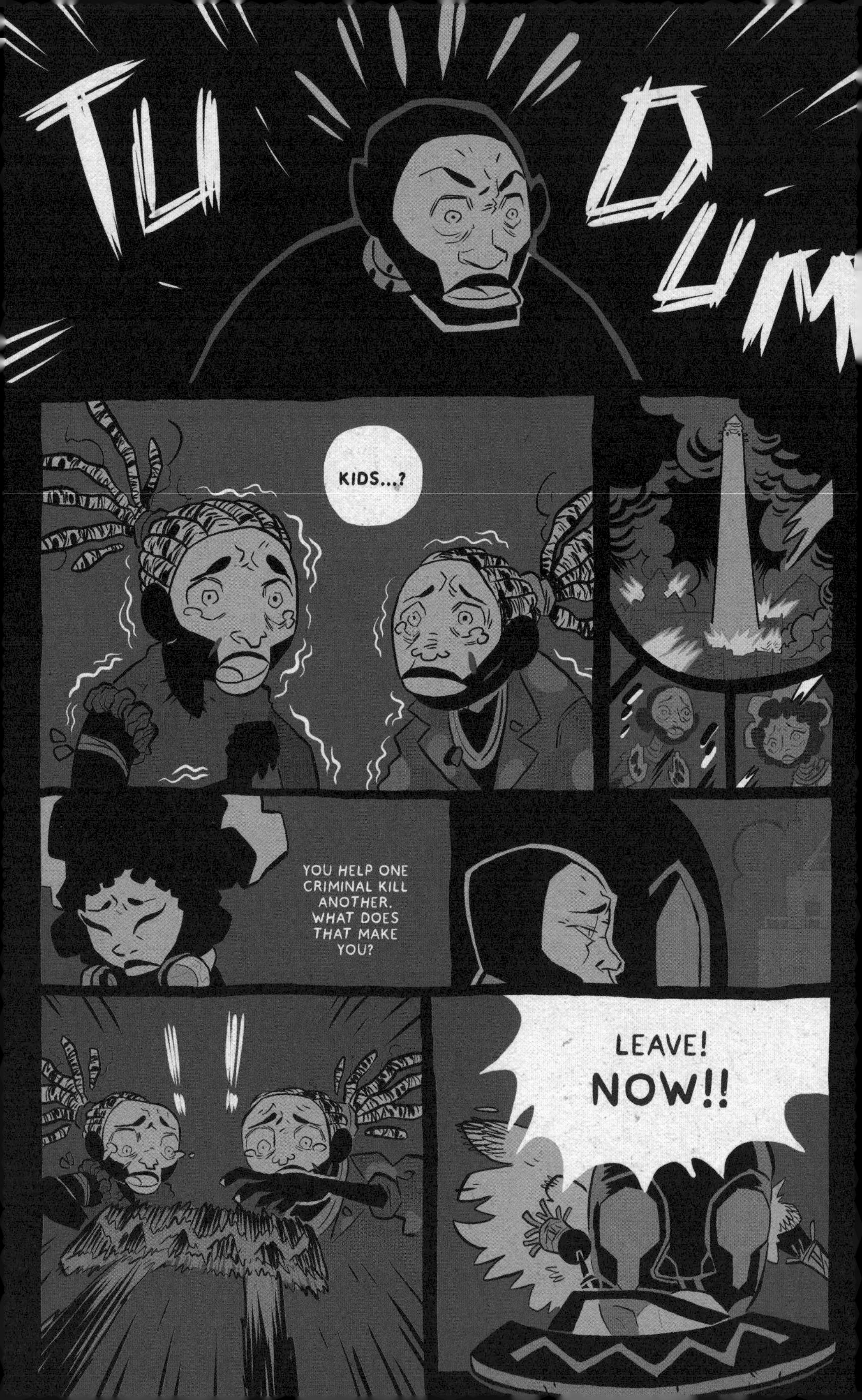
TU DUM
KIDS...?
YOU HELP ONE CRIMINAL KILL ANOTHER. WHAT DOES THAT MAKE YOU?
LEAVE! NOW!!

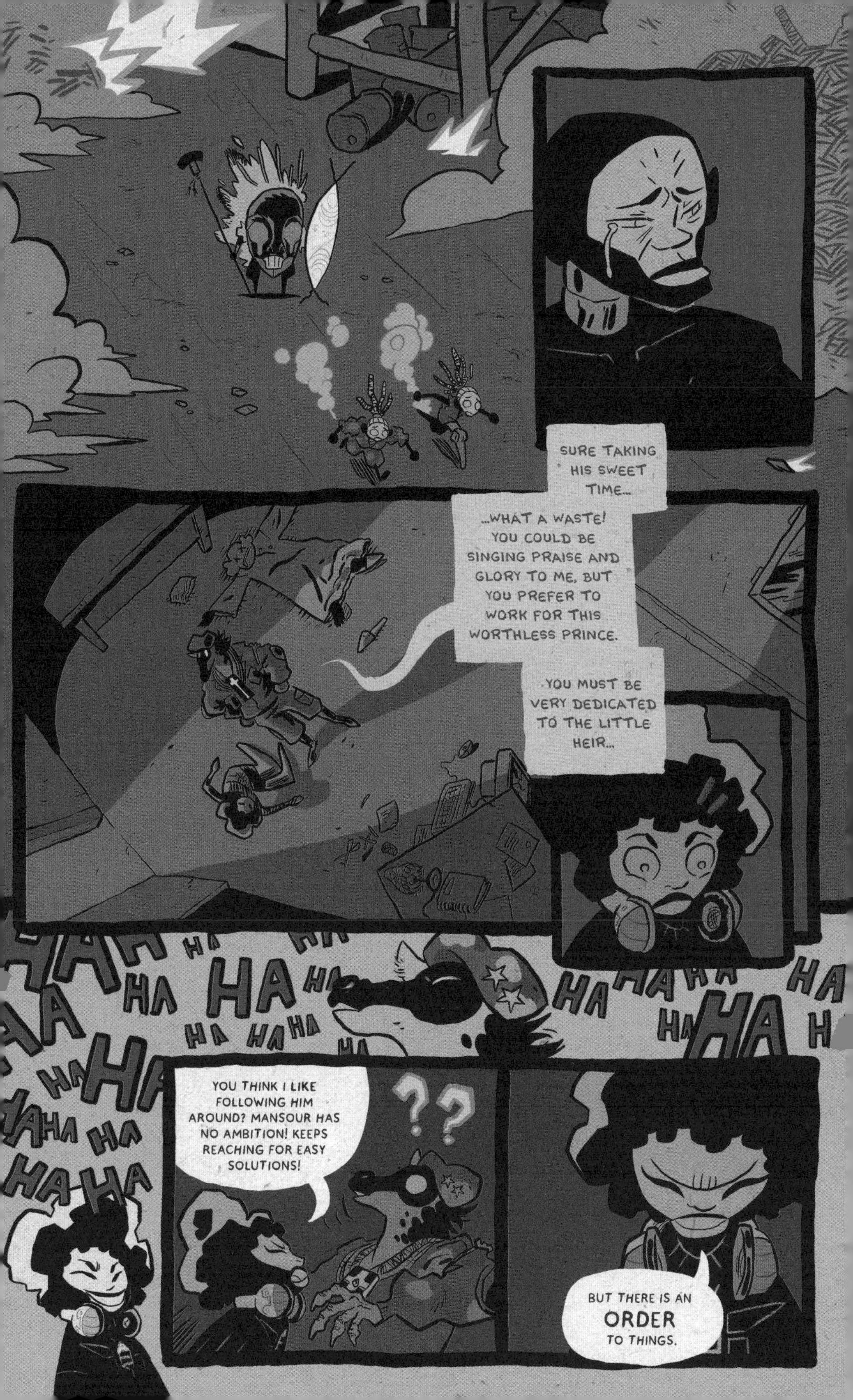
SURE TAKING HIS SWEET TIME...
...WHAT A WASTE! YOU COULD BE SINGING PRAISE AND GLORY TO ME, BUT YOU PREFER TO WORK FOR THIS WORTHLESS PRINCE.
YOU MUST BE VERY DEDICATED TO THE LITTLE HEIR...
HA HA HA HA HA HA HA HA HA HA HA HA HA HA HA HA HA HA HA HA
YOU THINK I LIKE FOLLOWING HIM AROUND? MANSOUR HAS NO AMBITION! KEEPS REACHING FOR EASY SOLUTIONS!
??
BUT THERE IS AN ORDER TO THINGS.

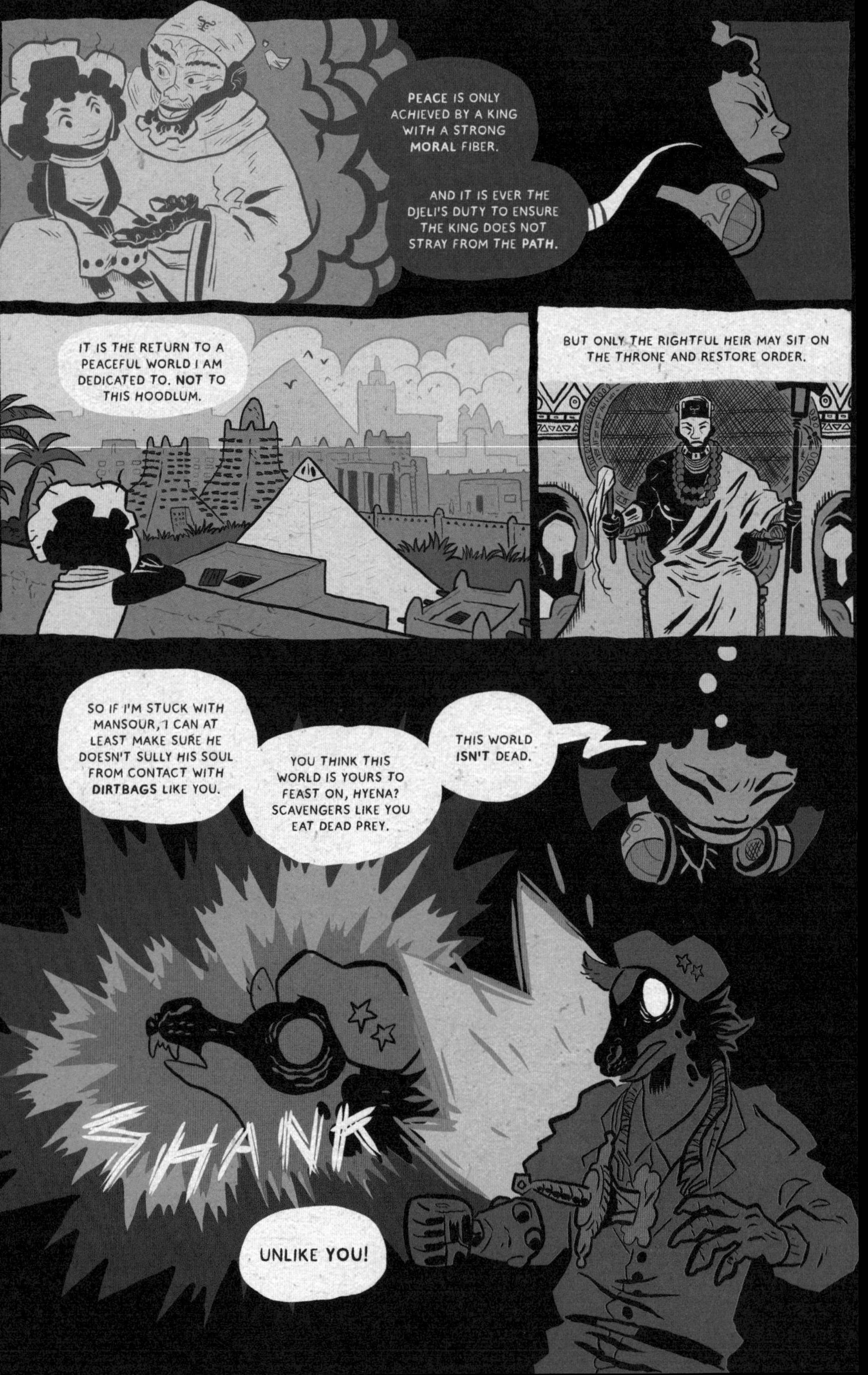
PEACE IS ONLY ACHIEVED BY A KING WITH A STRONG MORAL FIBER.
AND IT IS EVER THE DJELI'S DUTY TO ENSURE THE KING DOES NOT STRAY FROM THE PATH.
IT IS THE RETURN TO A PEACEFUL WORLD I AM DEDICATED TO. NOT TO THIS HOODLUM.
BUT ONLY THE RIGHTFUL HEIR MAY SIT ON THE THRONE AND RESTORE ORDER.
SO IF I'M STUCK WITH MANSOUR, I CAN AT LEAST MAKE SURE HE DOESN'T SULLY HIS SOUL FROM CONTACT WITH DIRTBAGS LIKE YOU.
YOU THINK THIS WORLD IS YOURS TO FEAST ON, HYENA? SCAVENGERS LIKE YOU EAT DEAD PREY.
THIS WORLD ISN'T DEAD.
SHANK
UNLIKE YOU!

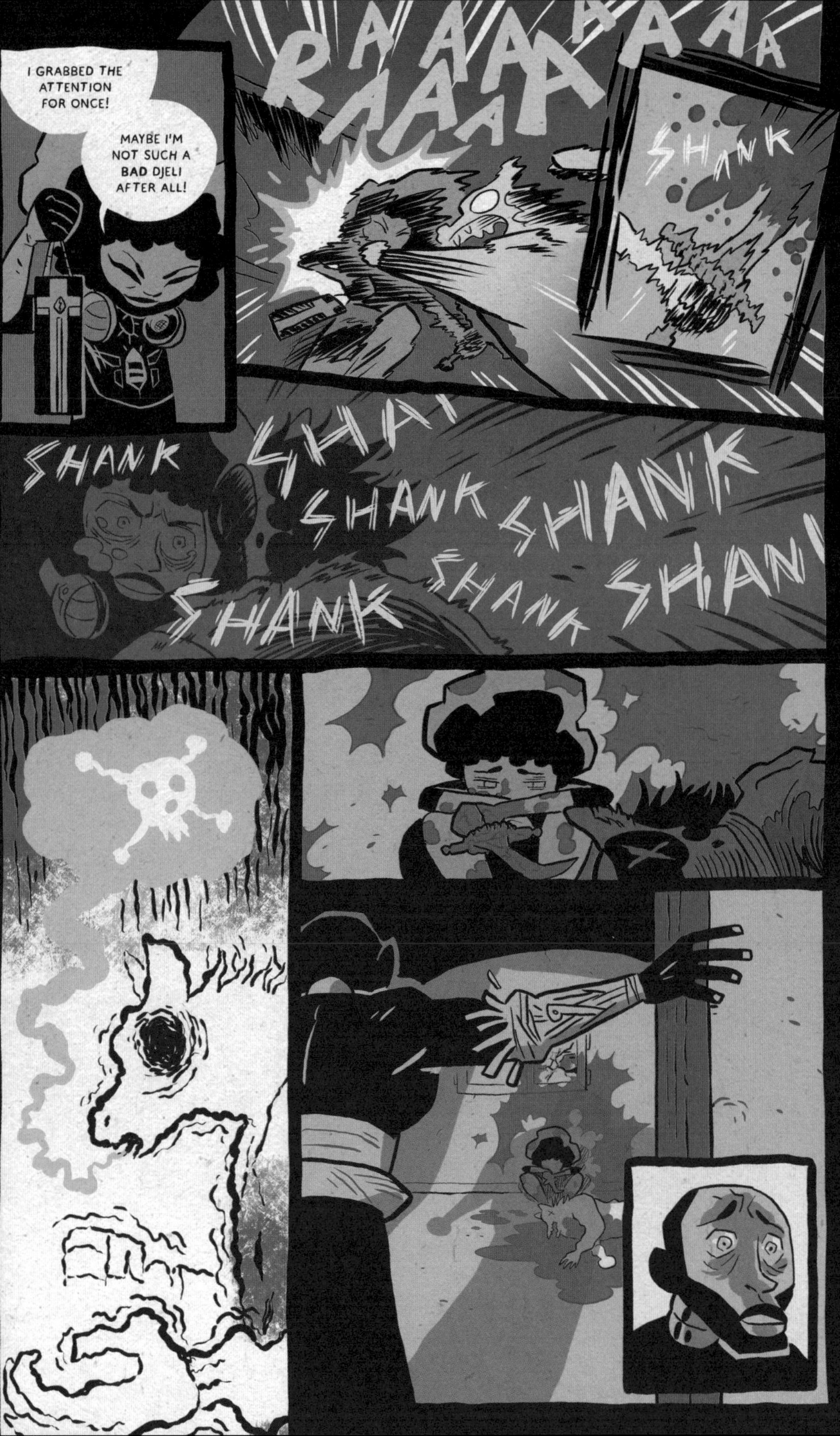
I GRABBED THE ATTENTION FOR ONCE!
MAYBE I'M NOT SUCH A BAD DJELI AFTER ALL!
RAAAAAAAAAAAA
SHANK
SHANK
SHANK
SHANK
SHANK
SHANK

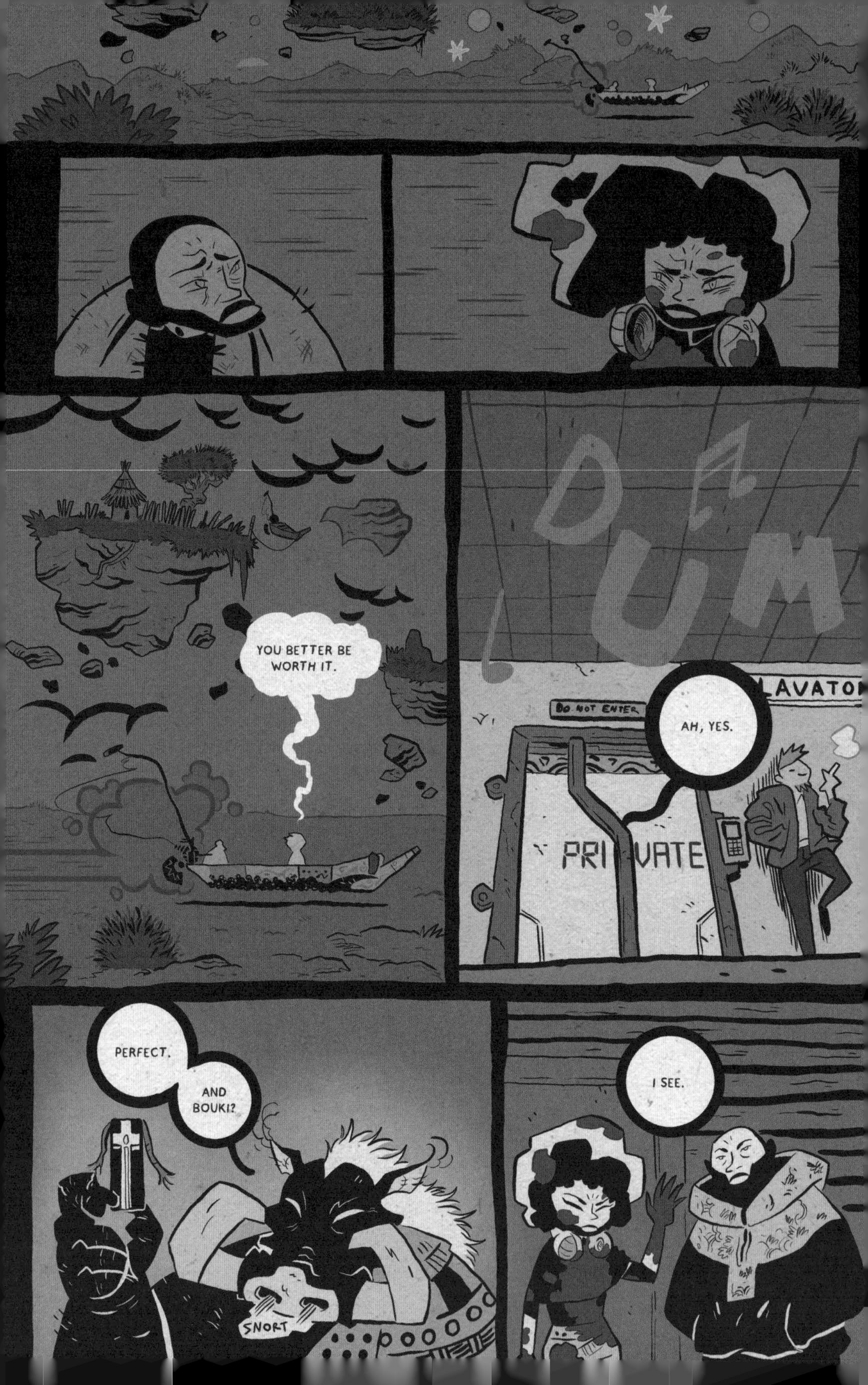
YOU BETTER BE WORTH IT.
DUM
DO NOT ENTER
AH, YES.
PERFECT.
AND BOUKI?
SNORT
I SEE.

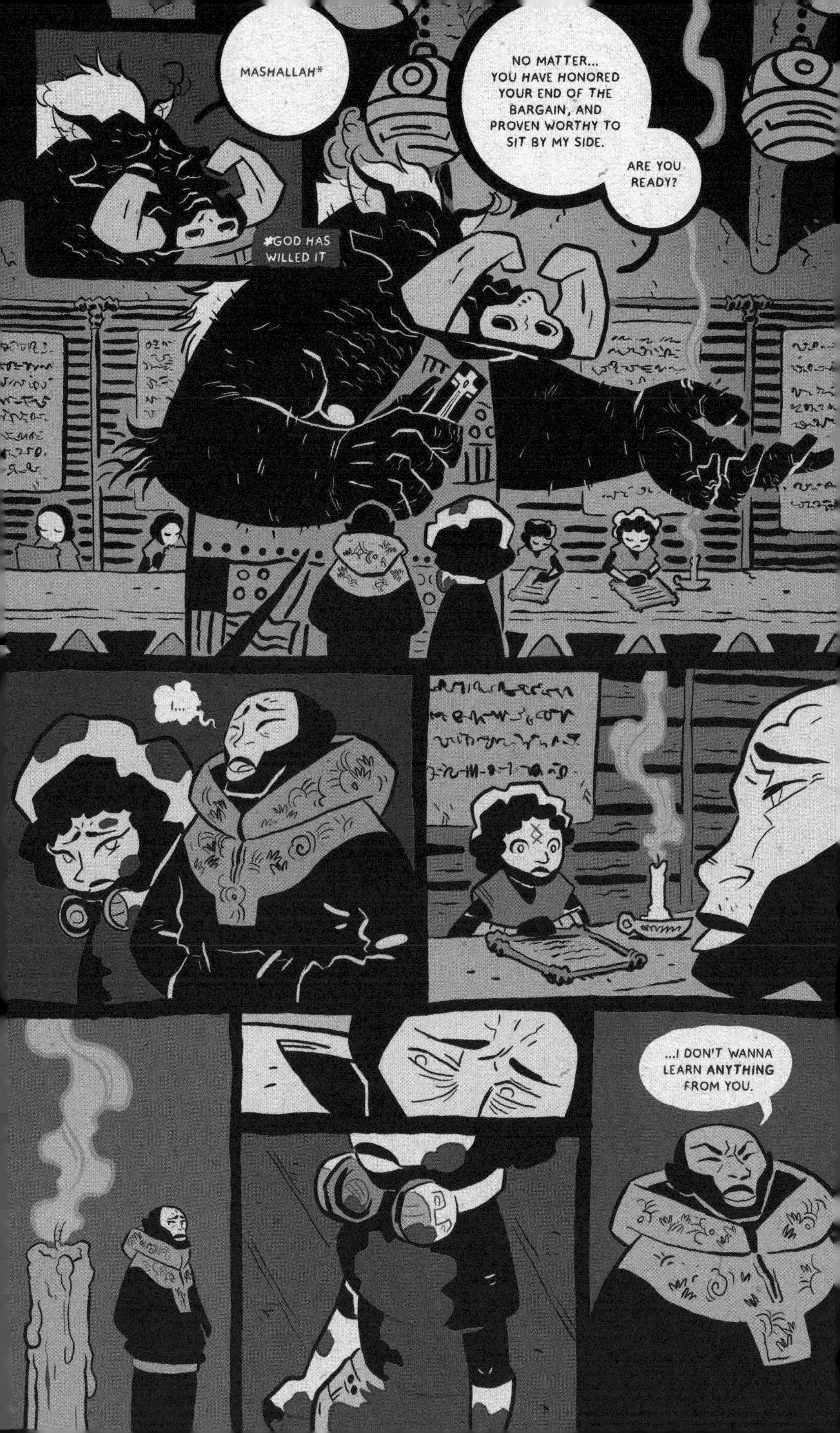
MASHALLAH*
*GOD HAS WILLED IT
NO MATTER... YOU HAVE HONORED YOUR END OF THE BARGAIN, AND PROVEN WORTHY TO SIT BY MY SIDE.
ARE YOU READY?
I...
...I DON'T WANNA LEARN ANYTHING FROM YOU.

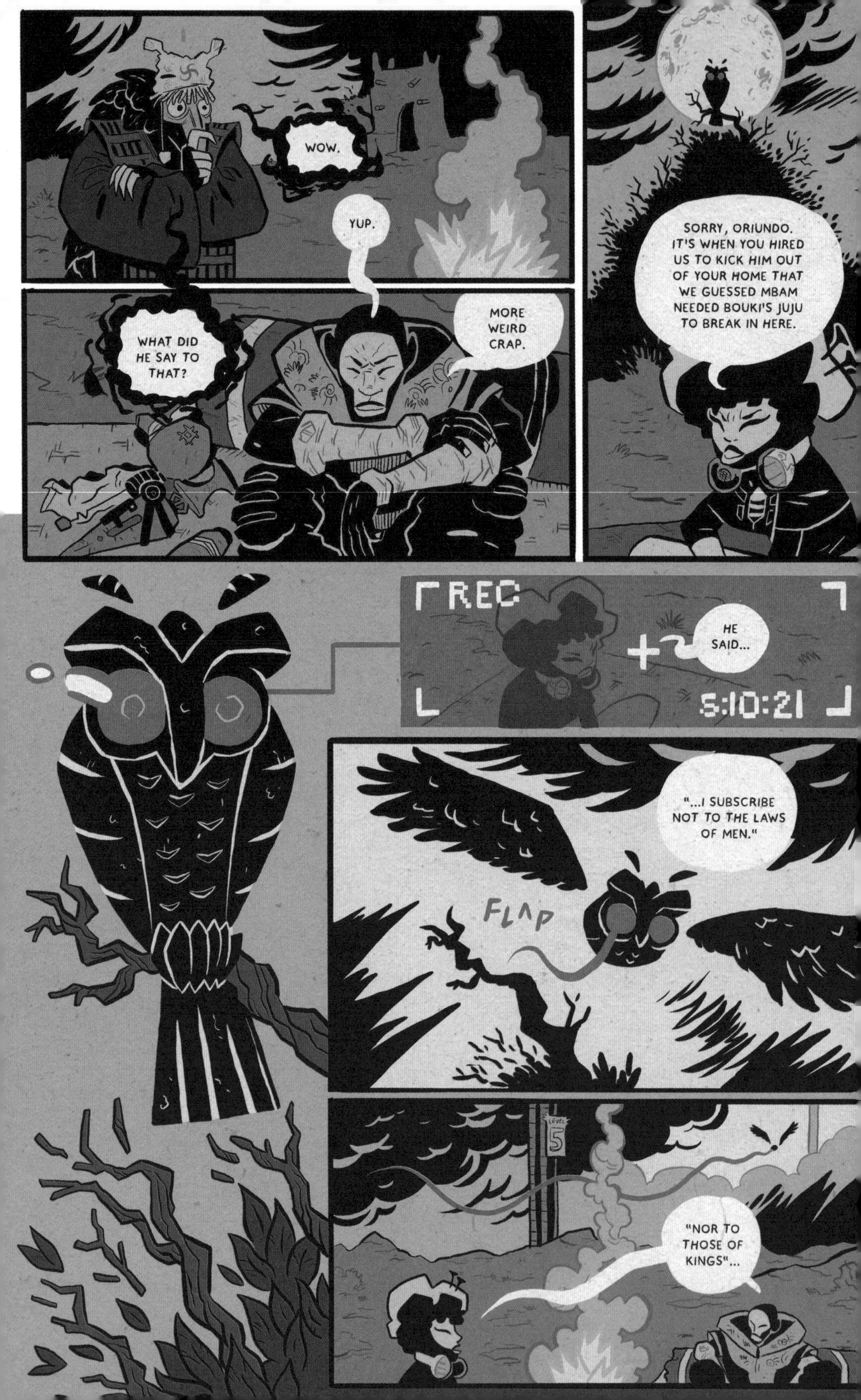
WOW.
YUP.
WHAT DID HE SAY TO THAT?
MORE WEIRD CRAP.
SORRY, ORIUNDO. IT'S WHEN YOU HIRED US TO KICK HIM OUT OF YOUR HOME THAT WE GUESSED MBAM NEEDED BOUKI'S JUJU TO BREAK IN HERE.
REC
HE SAID...
5:10:21
"...I SUBSCRIBE NOT TO THE LAWS OF MEN."
FLAP
LEVEL 5
"NOR TO THOSE OF KINGS"...

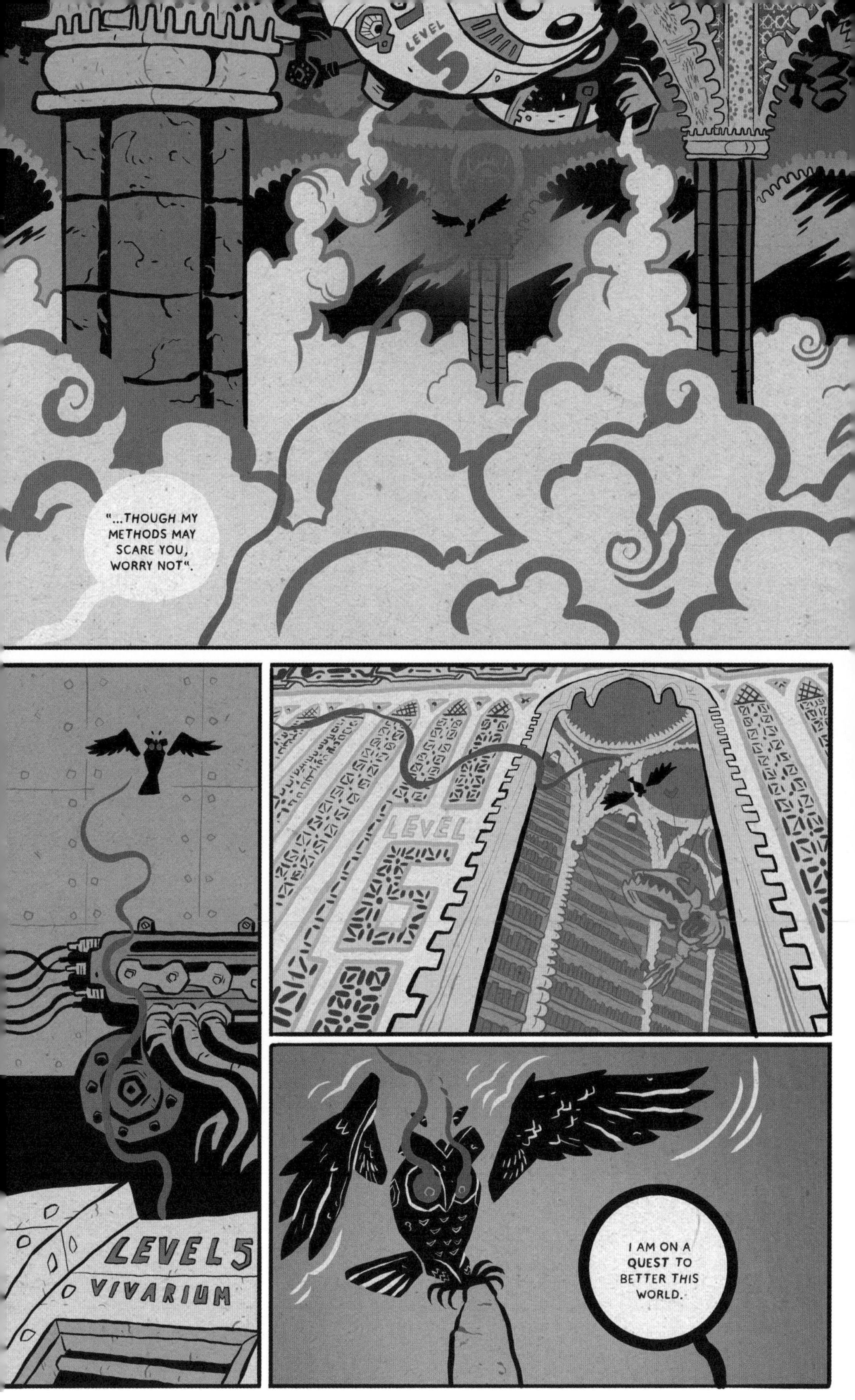
LEVEL 5
"...THOUGH MY METHODS MAY SCARE YOU, WORRY NOT".
LEVEL 5
VIVARIUM
LEVEL 5
I AM ON A **QUEST** TO BETTER THIS WORLD.

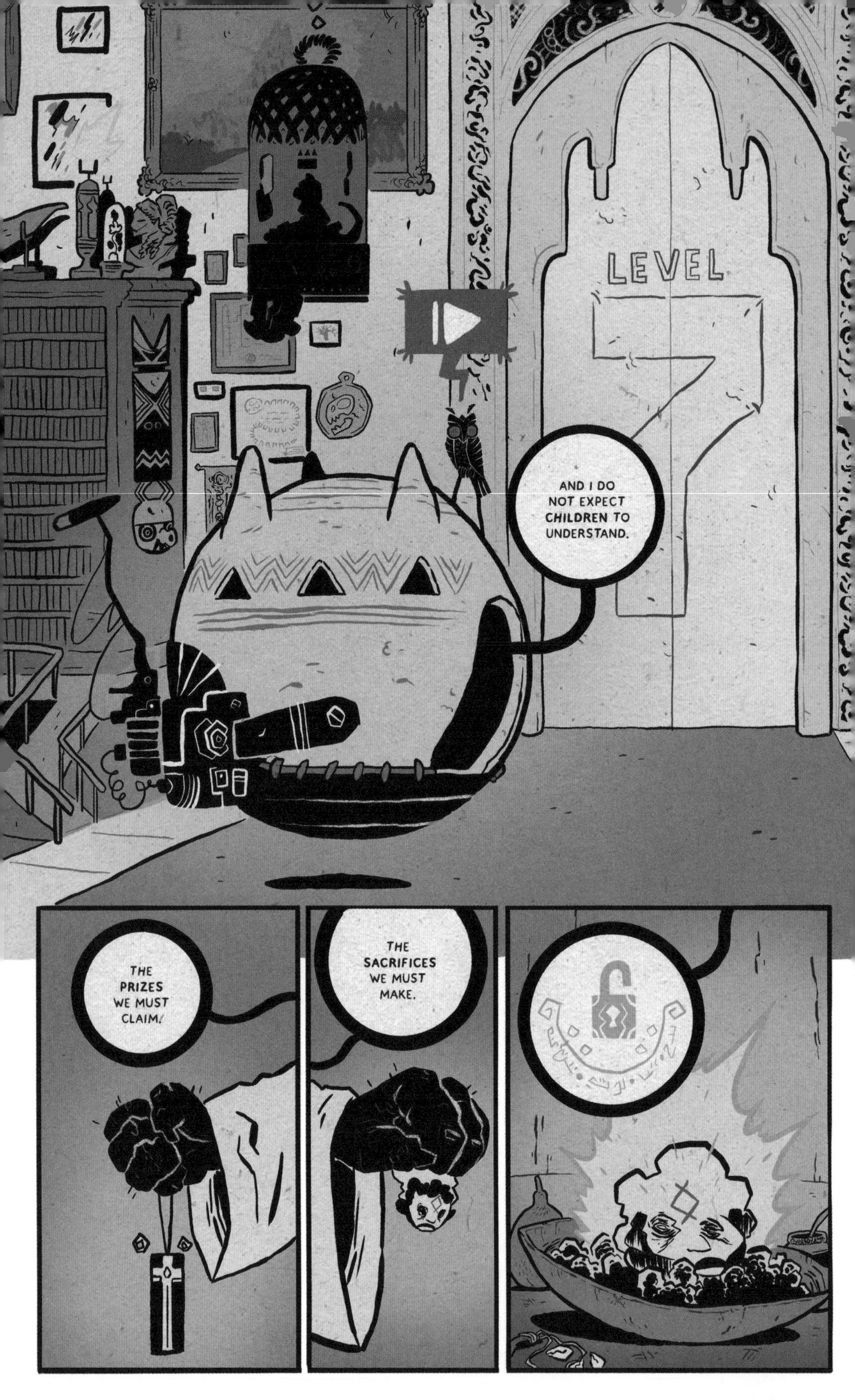
LEVEL 7
AND I DO NOT EXPECT CHILDREN TO UNDERSTAND.
THE PRIZES WE MUST CLAIM.
THE SACRIFICES WE MUST MAKE.

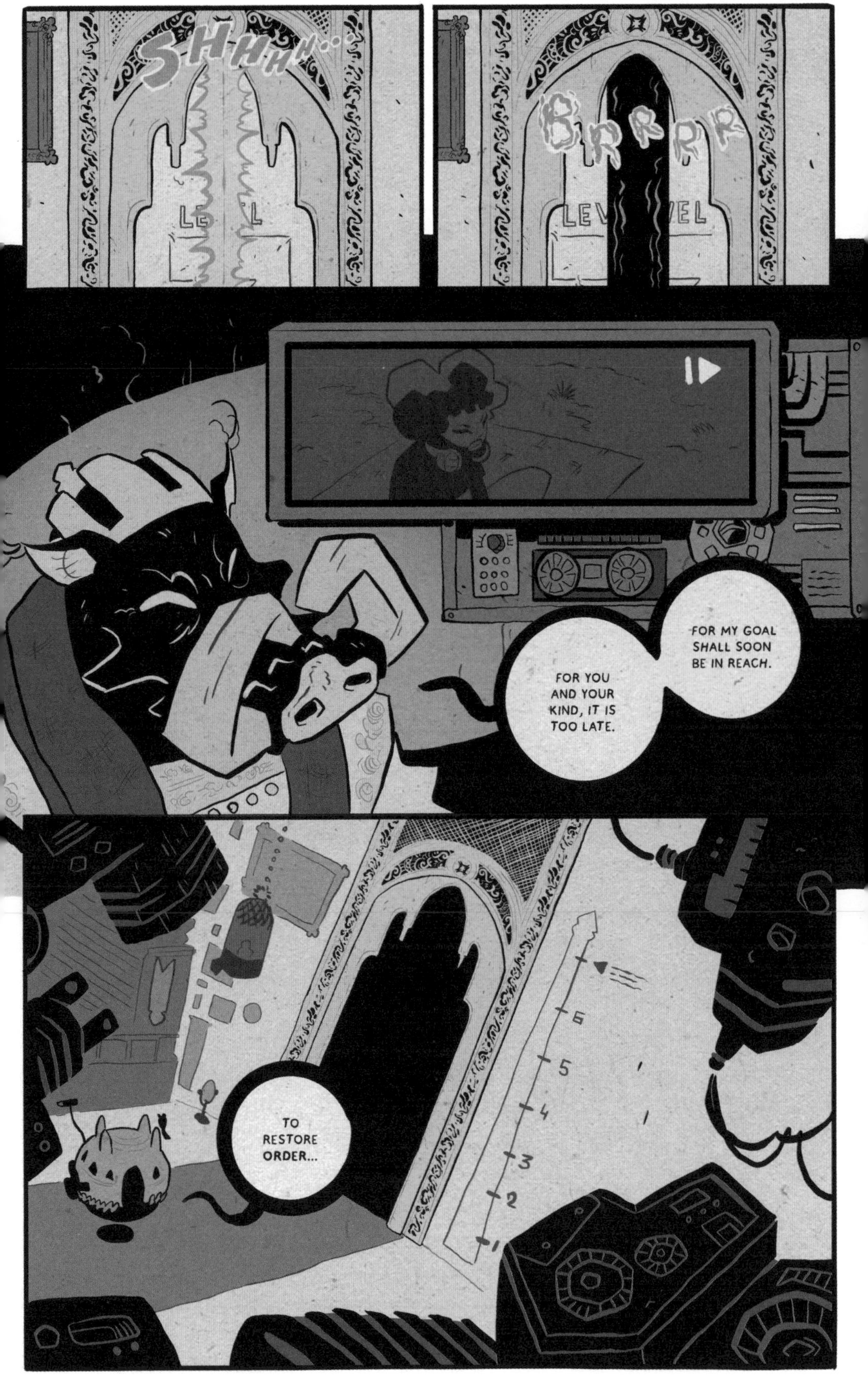
SHHHH...
LE L
BRRRR
LEV VEL
FOR YOU AND YOUR KIND, IT IS TOO LATE.
FOR MY GOAL SHALL SOON BE IN REACH.
TO RESTORE ORDER...
6
5
4
3
2
1

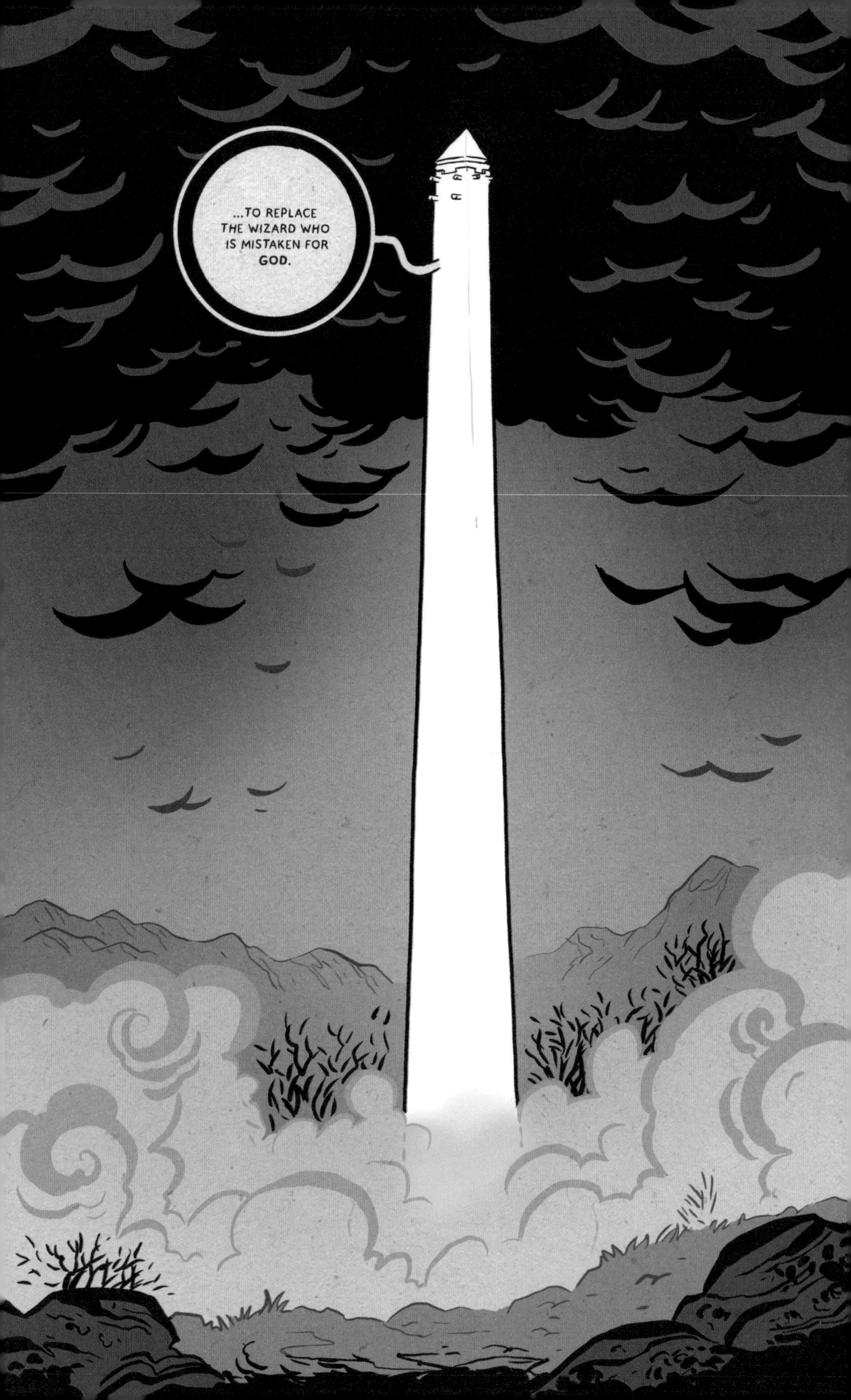
...TO REPLACE THE WIZARD WHO IS MISTAKEN FOR GOD.

II

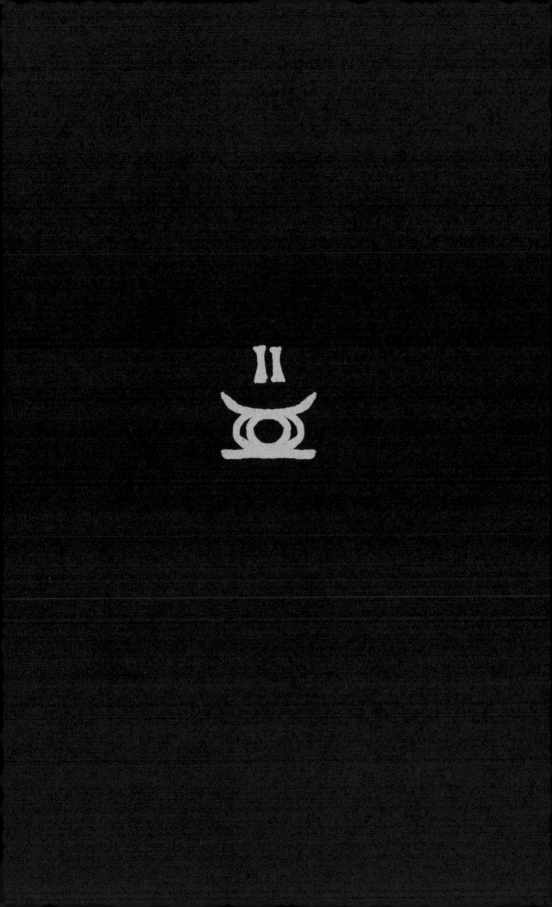

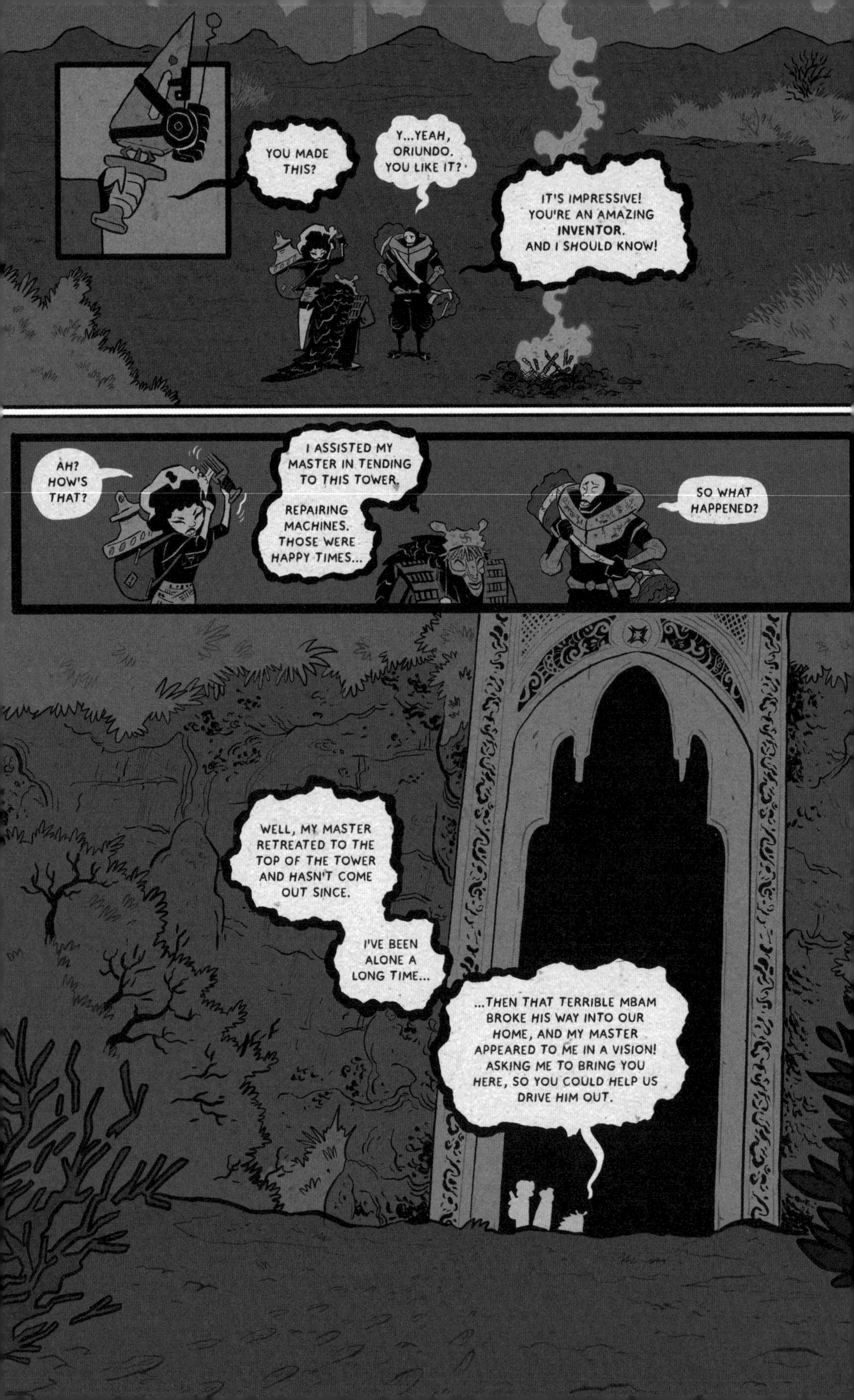
YOU MADE THIS?
Y...YEAH, ORIUNDO. YOU LIKE IT?
IT'S IMPRESSIVE! YOU'RE AN AMAZING **INVENTOR**. AND I SHOULD KNOW!
AH? HOW'S THAT?
I ASSISTED MY MASTER IN TENDING TO THIS TOWER.
REPAIRING MACHINES. THOSE WERE HAPPY TIMES...
SO WHAT HAPPENED?
WELL, MY MASTER RETREATED TO THE TOP OF THE TOWER AND HASN'T COME OUT SINCE.
I'VE BEEN ALONE A LONG TIME...
...THEN THAT TERRIBLE MBAM BROKE HIS WAY INTO OUR HOME, AND MY MASTER APPEARED TO ME IN A VISION! ASKING ME TO BRING YOU HERE, SO YOU COULD HELP US DRIVE HIM OUT.

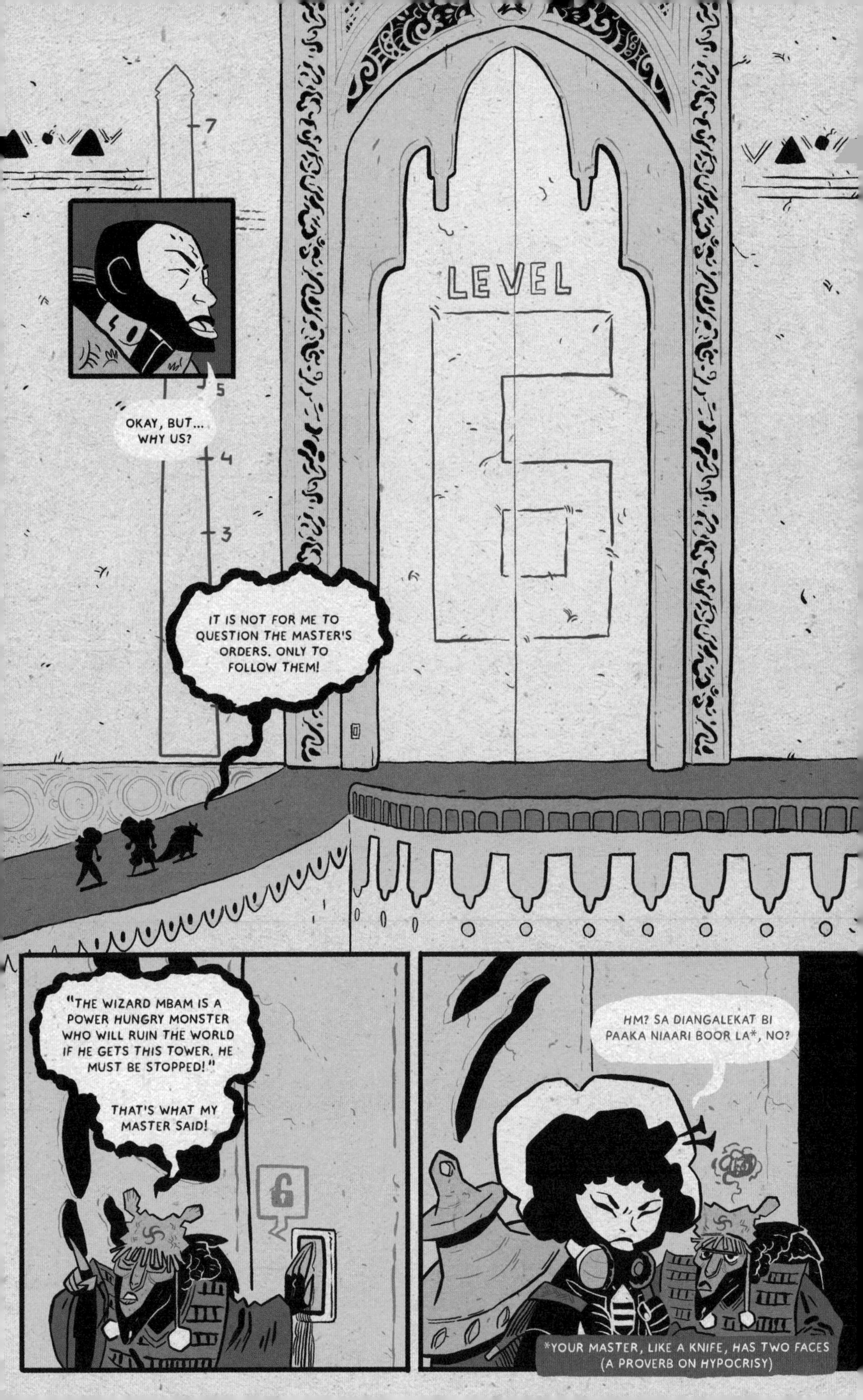
LEVEL
OKAY, BUT... WHY US?
IT IS NOT FOR ME TO QUESTION THE MASTER'S ORDERS. ONLY TO FOLLOW THEM!
"THE WIZARD MBAM IS A POWER HUNGRY MONSTER WHO WILL RUIN THE WORLD IF HE GETS THIS TOWER. HE MUST BE STOPPED!"
THAT'S WHAT MY MASTER SAID!
HM? SA DIANGALEKAT BI PAAKA NIAARI BOOR LA*, NO?
*YOUR MASTER, LIKE A KNIFE, HAS TWO FACES (A PROVERB ON HYPOCRISY)

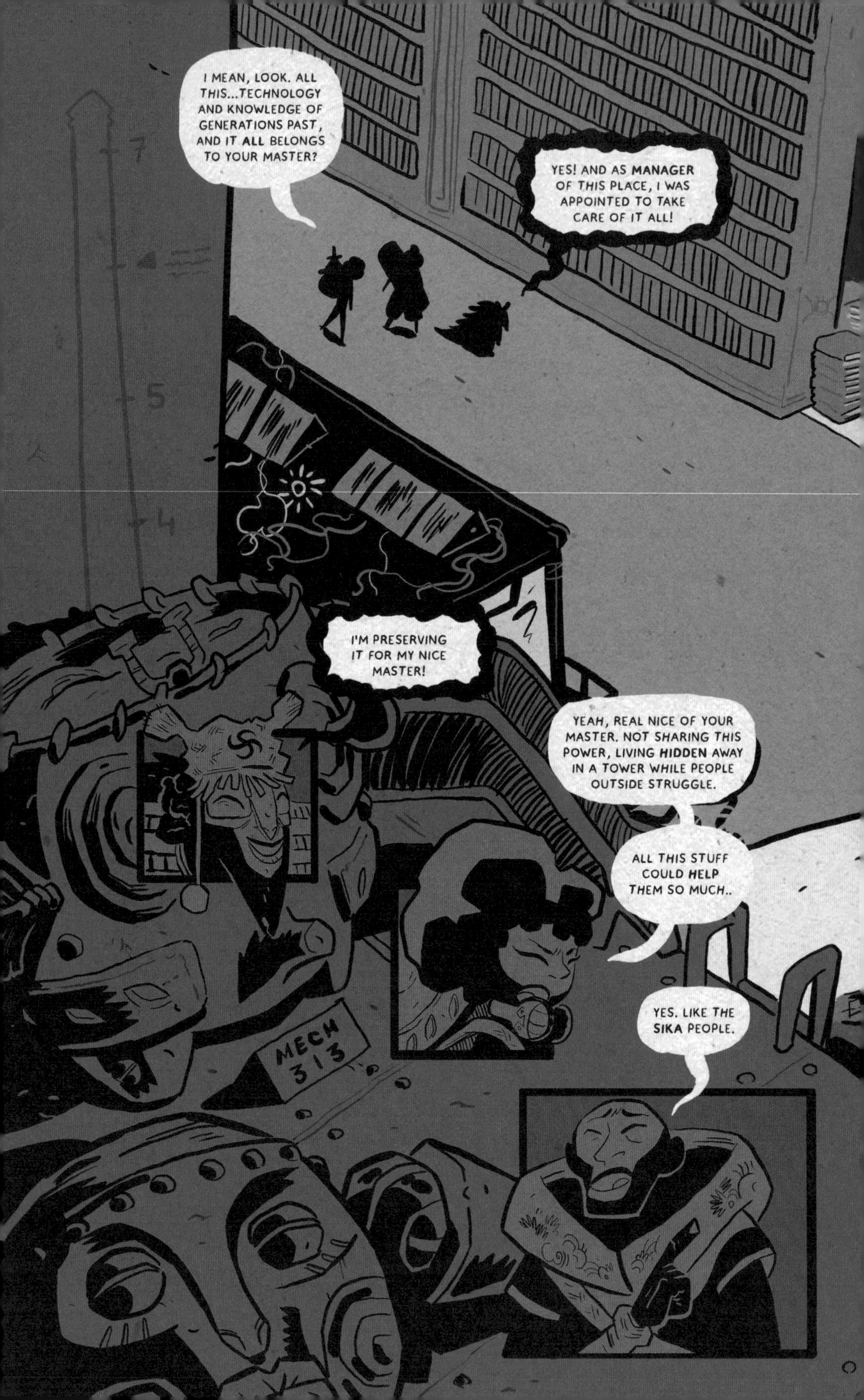
I MEAN, LOOK. ALL THIS...TECHNOLOGY AND KNOWLEDGE OF GENERATIONS PAST, AND IT ALL BELONGS TO YOUR MASTER?
YES! AND AS MANAGER OF THIS PLACE, I WAS APPOINTED TO TAKE CARE OF IT ALL!
I'M PRESERVING IT FOR MY NICE MASTER!
YEAH, REAL NICE OF YOUR MASTER. NOT SHARING THIS POWER, LIVING HIDDEN AWAY IN A TOWER WHILE PEOPLE OUTSIDE STRUGGLE.
ALL THIS STUFF COULD HELP THEM SO MUCH..
YES. LIKE THE SIKA PEOPLE.
MECH 313

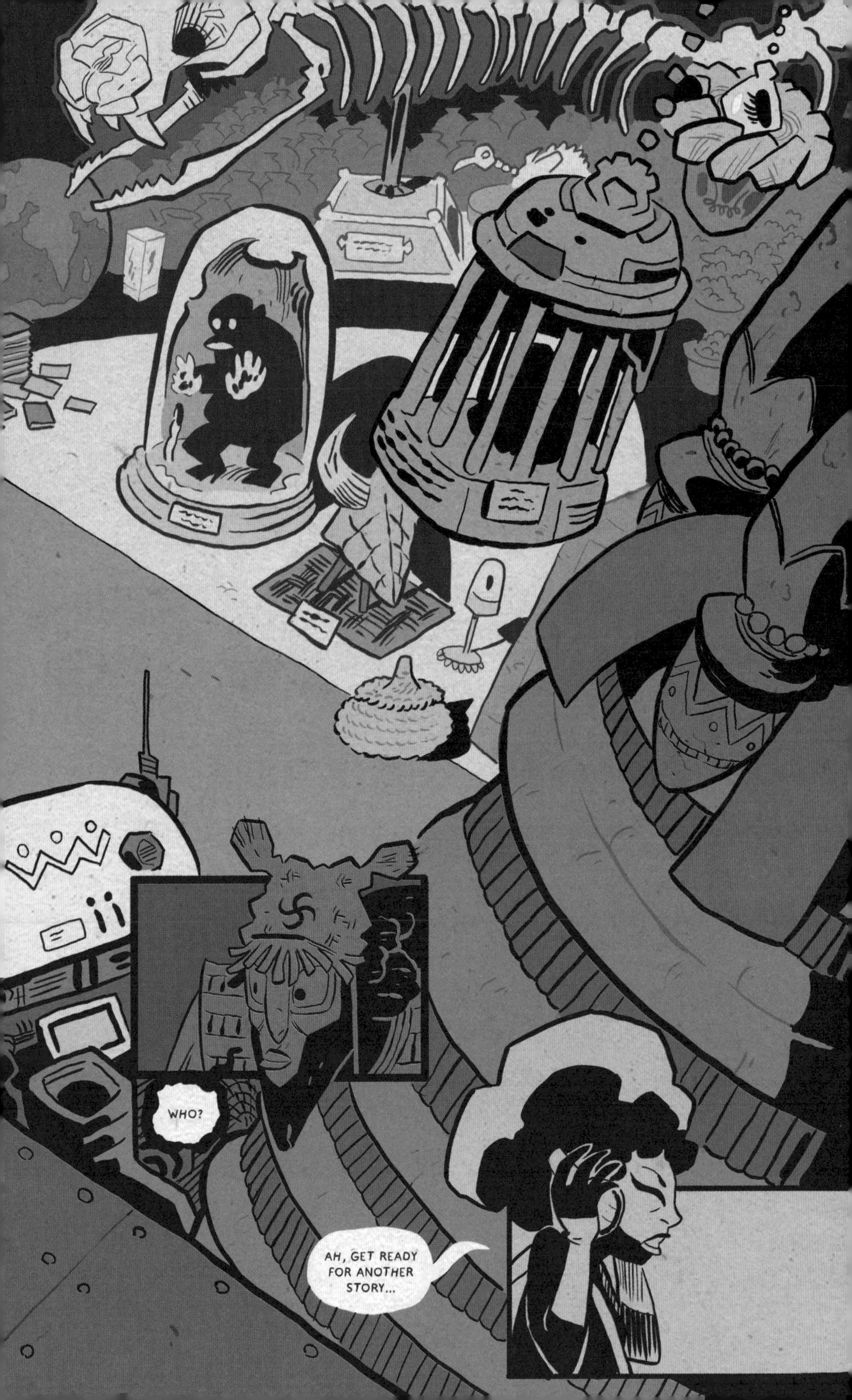
WHO?
AH, GET READY FOR ANOTHER STORY...

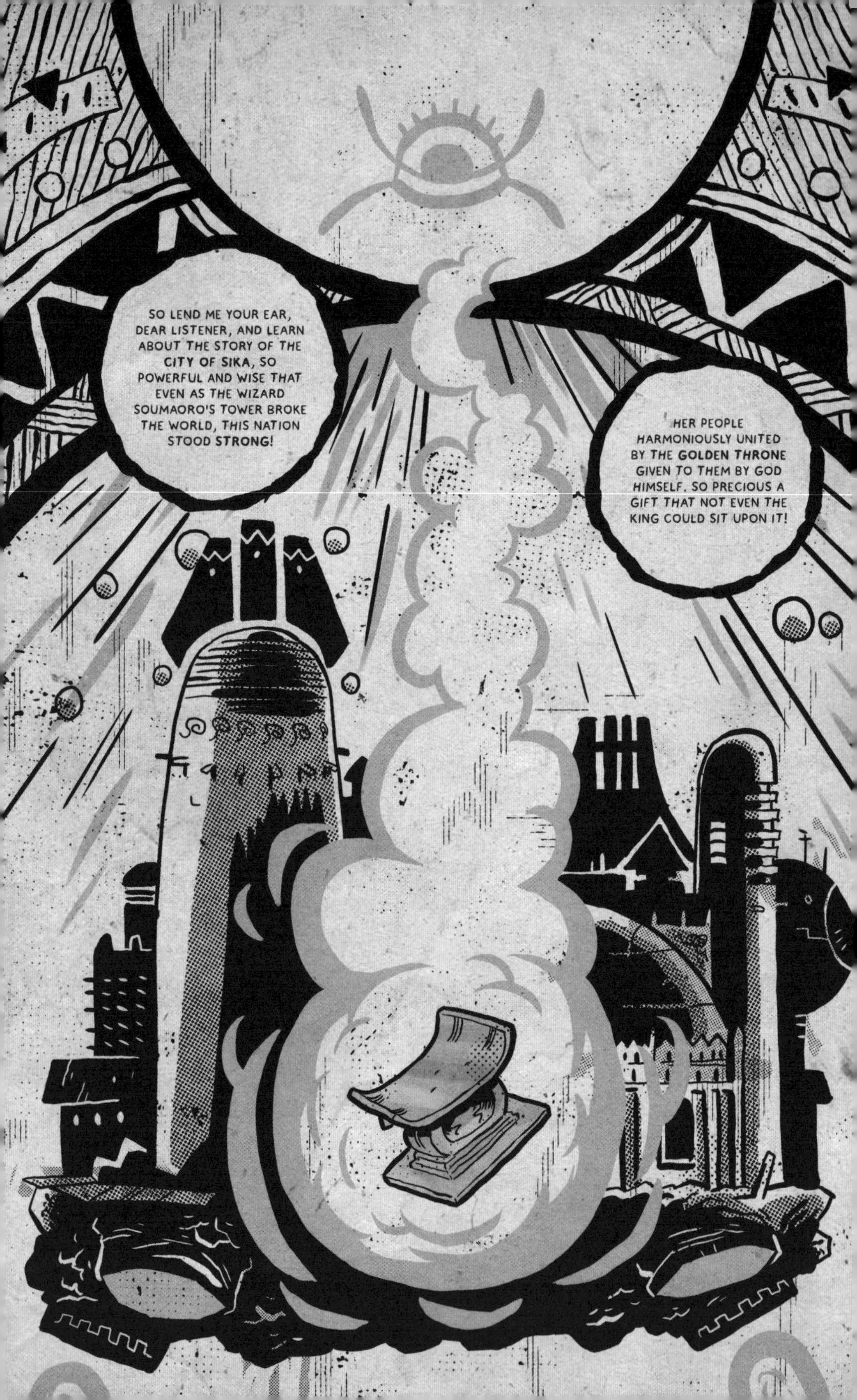
SO LEND ME YOUR EAR, DEAR LISTENER, AND LEARN ABOUT THE STORY OF THE **CITY OF SIKA**, SO POWERFUL AND WISE THAT EVEN AS THE WIZARD SOUMAORO'S TOWER BROKE THE WORLD, THIS NATION STOOD **STRONG**!
HER PEOPLE HARMONIOUSLY UNITED BY THE **GOLDEN THRONE** GIVEN TO THEM BY GOD HIMSELF. SO PRECIOUS A GIFT THAT NOT EVEN THE KING COULD SIT UPON IT!

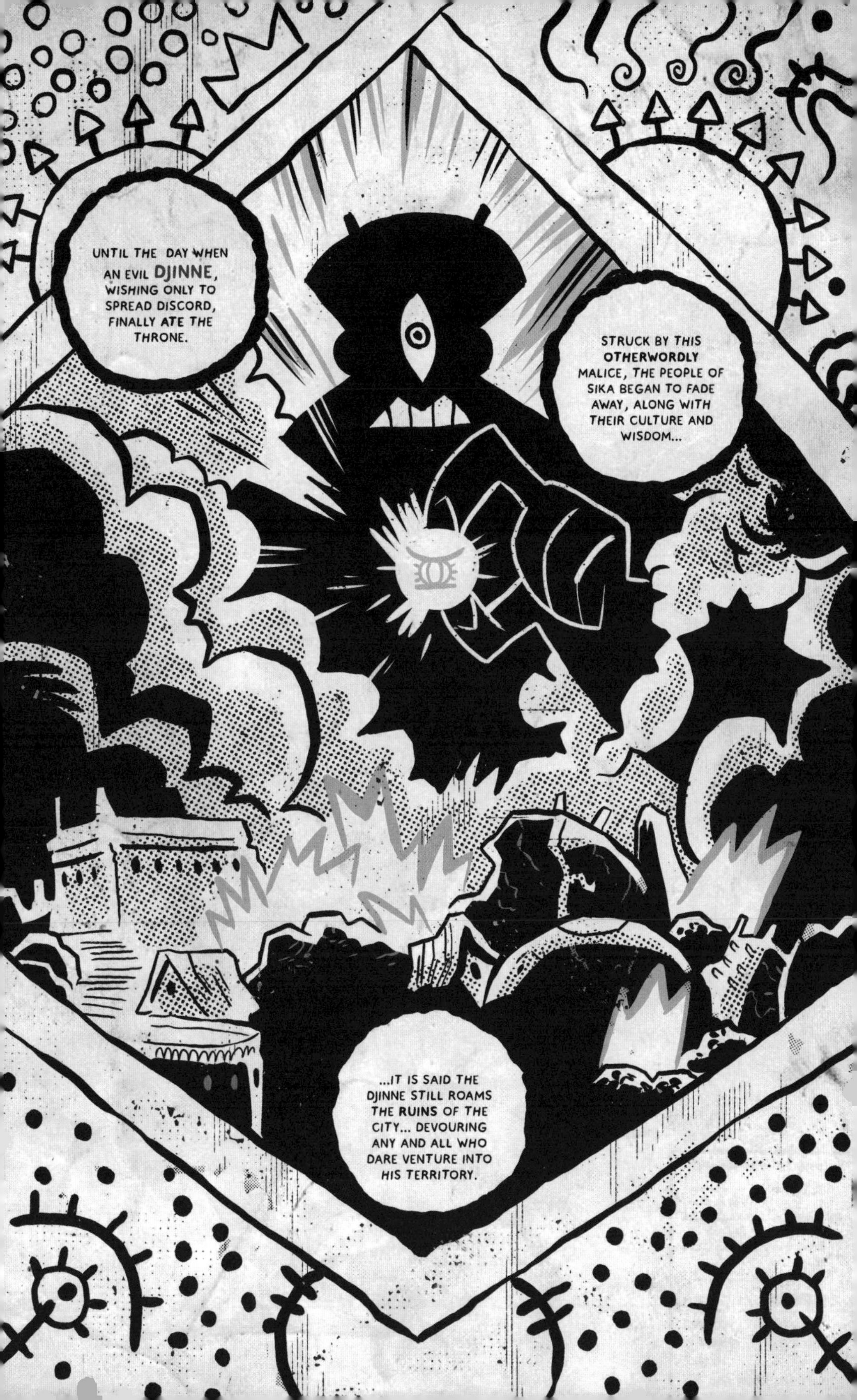
UNTIL THE DAY WHEN AN EVIL DJINNE, WISHING ONLY TO SPREAD DISCORD, FINALLY ATE THE THRONE.
STRUCK BY THIS OTHERWORDLY MALICE, THE PEOPLE OF SIKA BEGAN TO FADE AWAY, ALONG WITH THEIR CULTURE AND WISDOM...
...IT IS SAID THE DJINNE STILL ROAMS THE RUINS OF THE CITY... DEVOURING ANY AND ALL WHO DARE VENTURE INTO HIS TERRITORY.

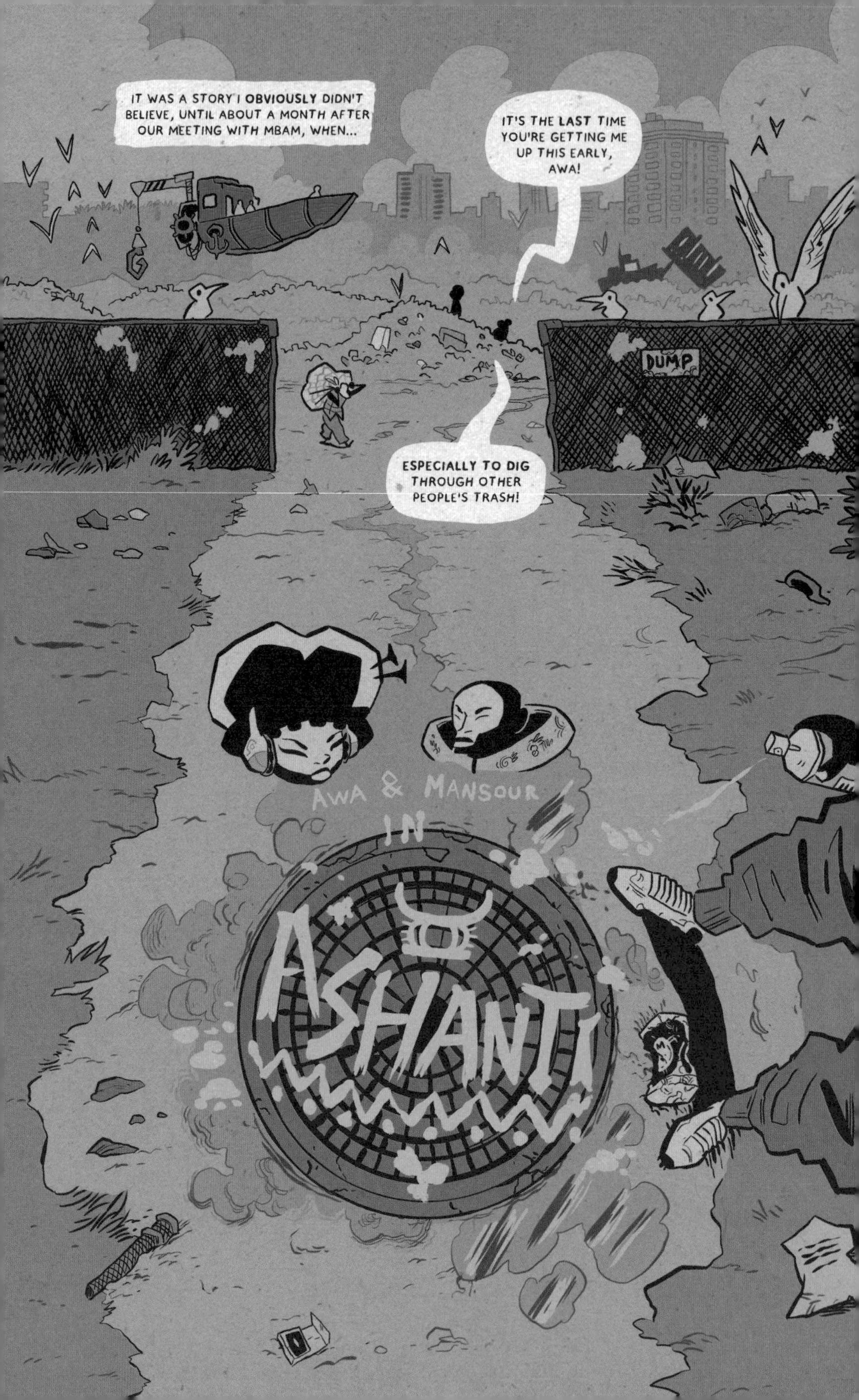
IT WAS A STORY I OBVIOUSLY DIDN'T BELIEVE, UNTIL ABOUT A MONTH AFTER OUR MEETING WITH MBAM, WHEN...
IT'S THE LAST TIME YOU'RE GETTING ME UP THIS EARLY, AWA!
DUMP
ESPECIALLY TO DIG THROUGH OTHER PEOPLE'S TRASH!
AWA & MANSOUR IN
ASHANTI

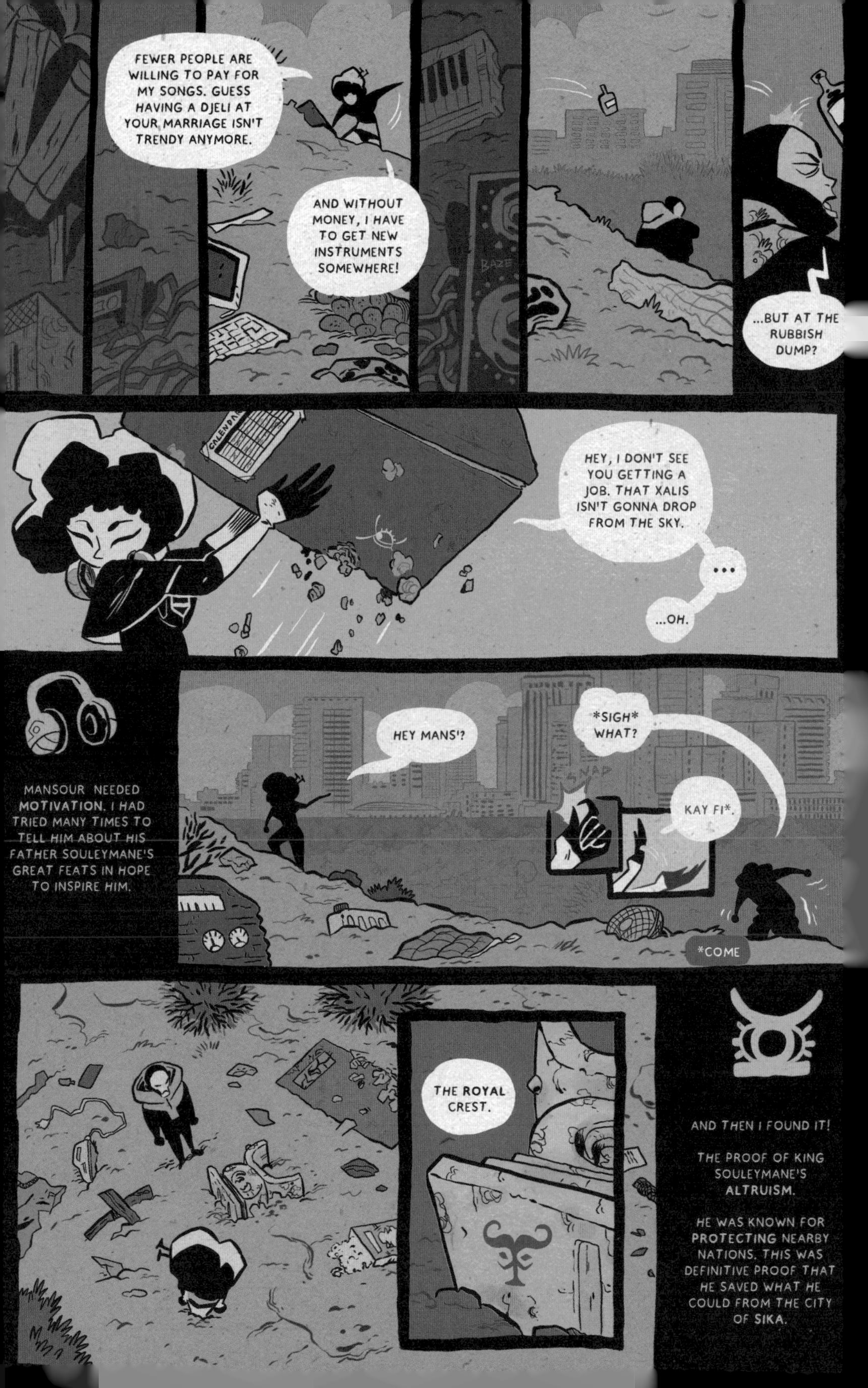
FEWER PEOPLE ARE WILLING TO PAY FOR MY SONGS. GUESS HAVING A DJELI AT YOUR MARRIAGE ISN'T TRENDY ANYMORE.
AND WITHOUT MONEY, I HAVE TO GET NEW INSTRUMENTS SOMEWHERE!
...BUT AT THE RUBBISH DUMP?
HEY, I DON'T SEE YOU GETTING A JOB. THAT XALIS ISN'T GONNA DROP FROM THE SKY.
...
...OH.
MANSOUR NEEDED MOTIVATION. I HAD TRIED MANY TIMES TO TELL HIM ABOUT HIS FATHER SOULEYMANE'S GREAT FEATS IN HOPE TO INSPIRE HIM.
HEY MANS'?
SIGH WHAT?
SNAP
KAY FI*.
*COME
THE ROYAL CREST.
AND THEN I FOUND IT!
THE PROOF OF KING SOULEYMANE'S ALTRUISM.
HE WAS KNOWN FOR PROTECTING NEARBY NATIONS. THIS WAS DEFINITIVE PROOF THAT HE SAVED WHAT HE COULD FROM THE CITY OF SIKA.

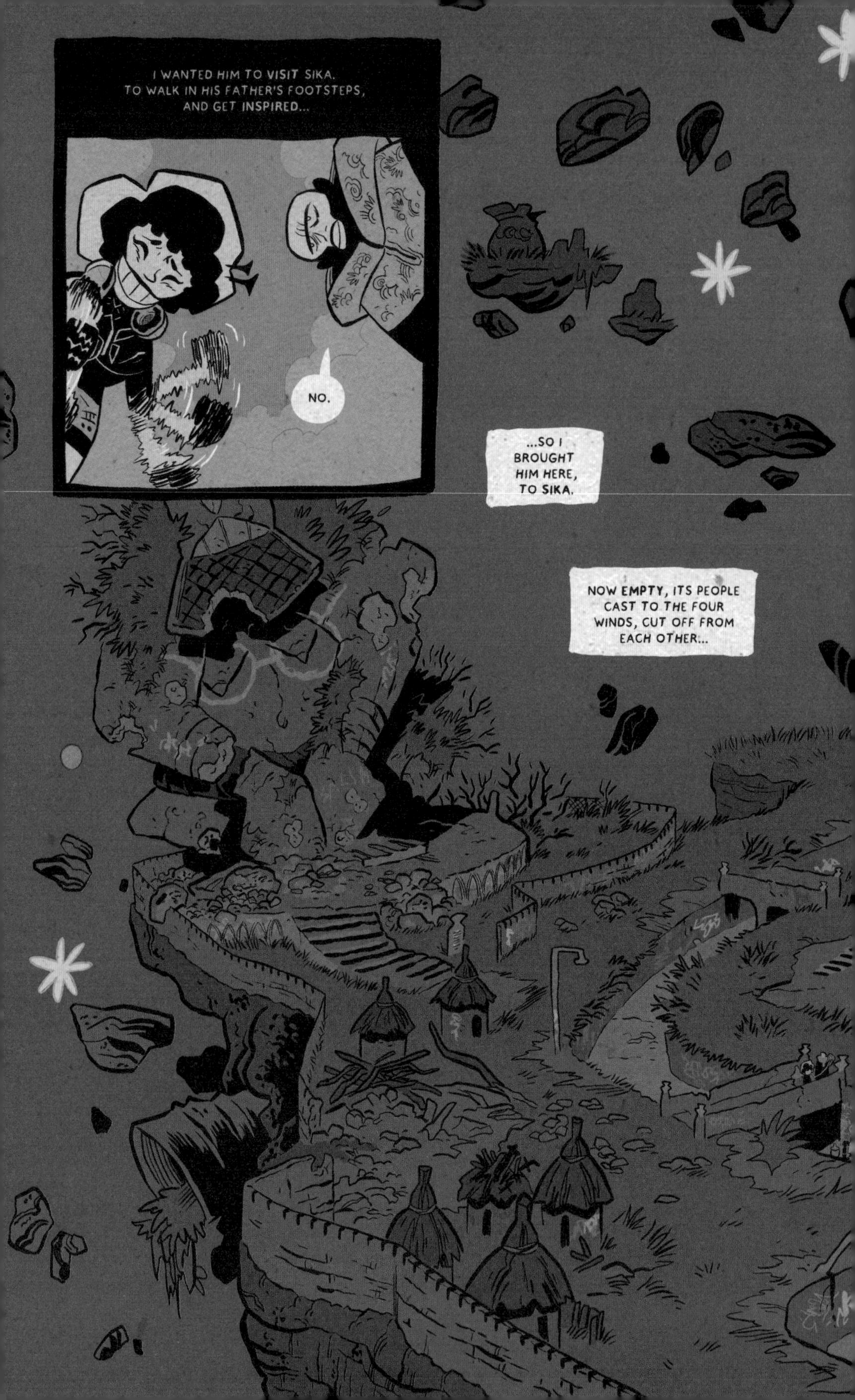
I WANTED HIM TO VISIT SIKA. TO WALK IN HIS FATHER'S FOOTSTEPS, AND GET INSPIRED...
NO.
...SO I BROUGHT HIM HERE, TO SIKA.
NOW EMPTY, ITS PEOPLE CAST TO THE FOUR WINDS, CUT OFF FROM EACH OTHER...

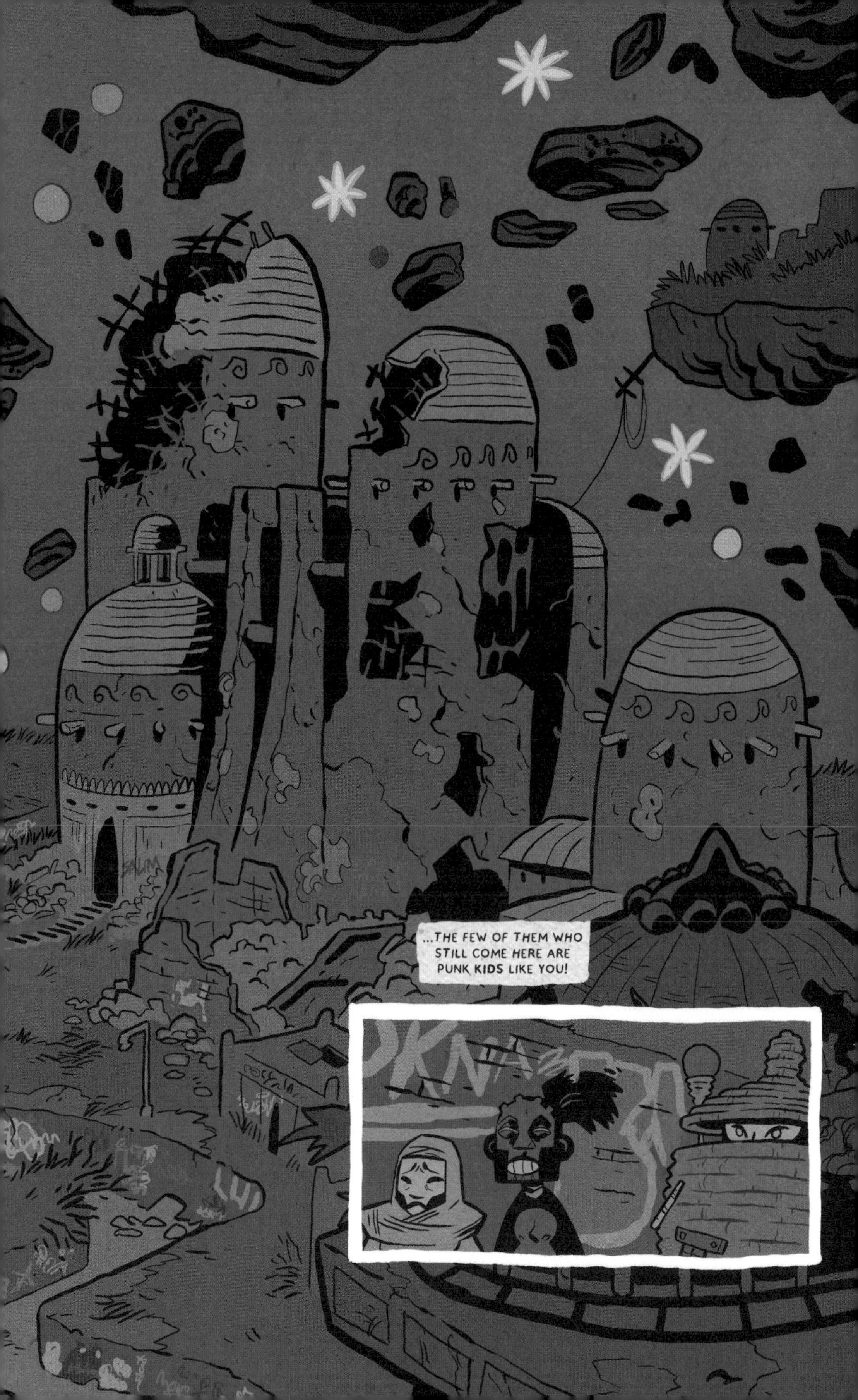
...THE FEW OF THEM WHO STILL COME HERE ARE PUNK KIDS LIKE YOU!

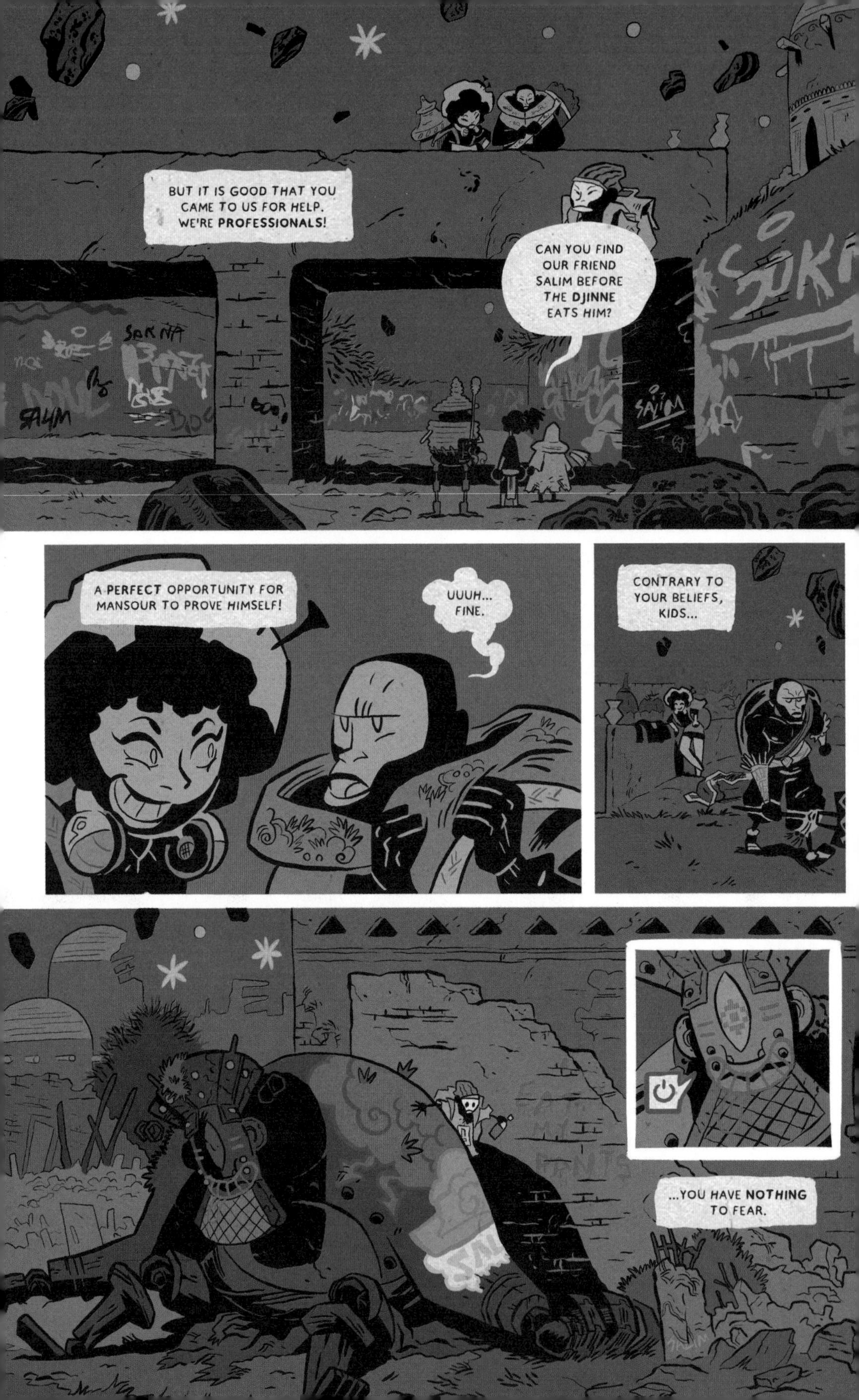
BUT IT IS GOOD THAT YOU CAME TO US FOR HELP. WE'RE **PROFESSIONALS!**
CAN YOU FIND OUR FRIEND SALIM BEFORE **THE DJINNE** EATS HIM?
A **PERFECT** OPPORTUNITY FOR MANSOUR TO PROVE HIMSELF!
UUUH... FINE.
CONTRARY TO YOUR BELIEFS, KIDS...
...YOU HAVE **NOTHING** TO FEAR.

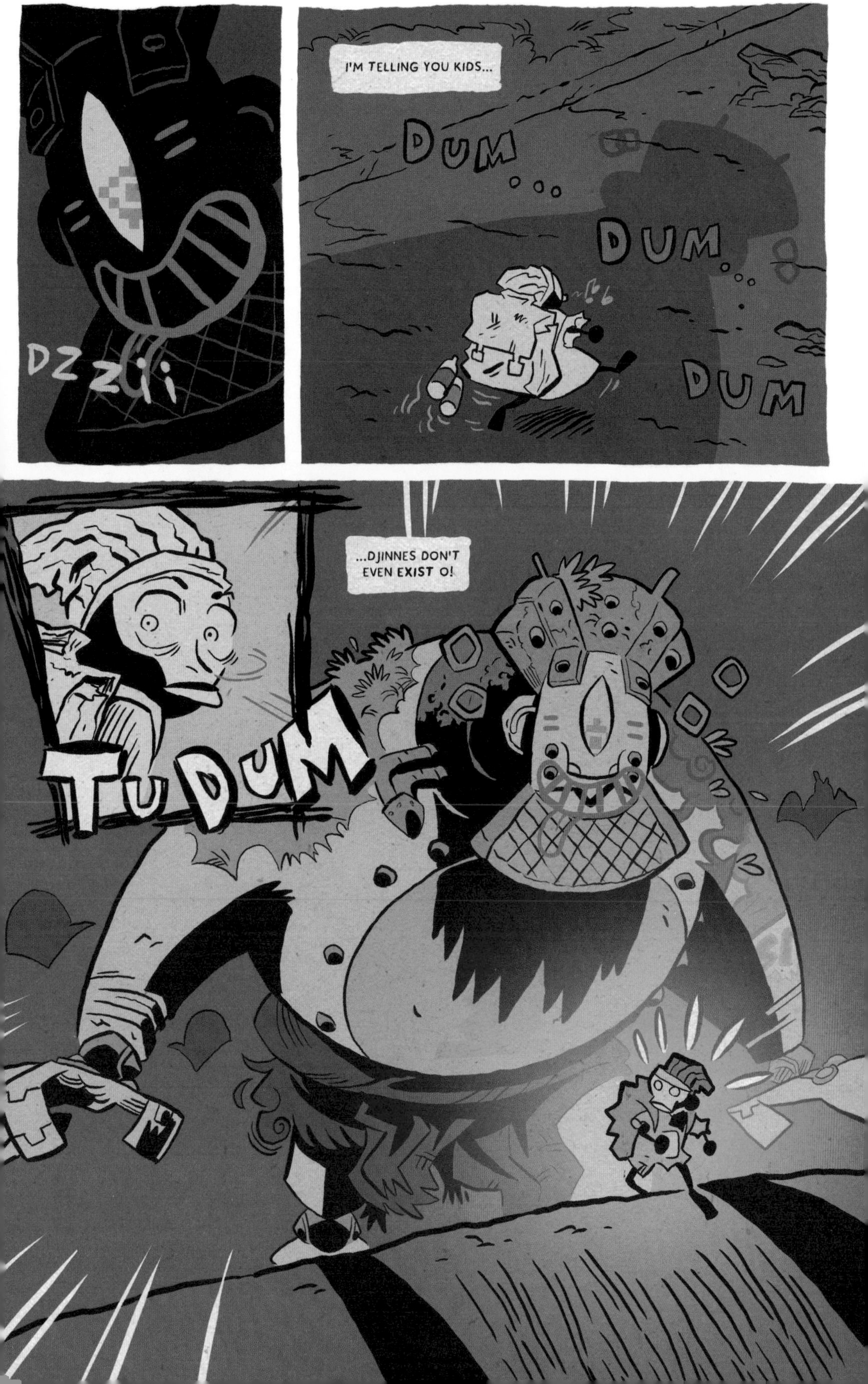

DZZiii
I'M TELLING YOU KIDS...
DUM
DUM
DUM
...DJINNES DON'T EVEN EXIST O!
TUDUM

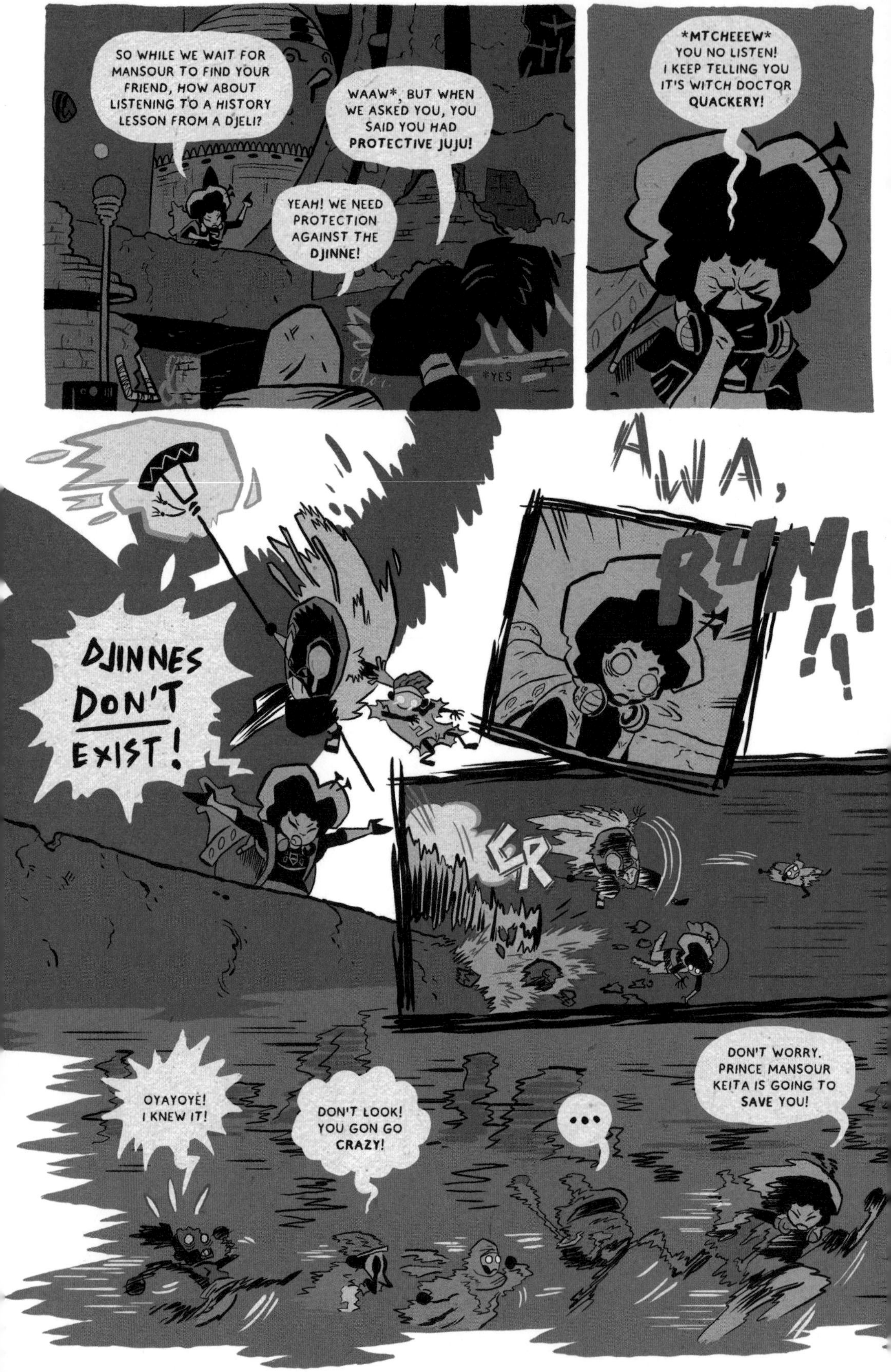

SO WHILE WE WAIT FOR MANSOUR TO FIND YOUR FRIEND, HOW ABOUT LISTENING TO A HISTORY LESSON FROM A DJELI?
WAAW*, BUT WHEN WE ASKED YOU, YOU SAID YOU HAD PROTECTIVE JUJU!
YEAH! WE NEED PROTECTION AGAINST THE DJINNE!
*YES
MTCHEEEW YOU NO LISTEN! I KEEP TELLING YOU IT'S WITCH DOCTOR QUACKERY!
DJINNES DON'T EXIST!
AWA, RUN!!!
CR
OYAYOYE! I KNEW IT!
DON'T LOOK! YOU GON GO CRAZY!
...
DON'T WORRY. PRINCE MANSOUR KEITA IS GOING TO SAVE YOU!

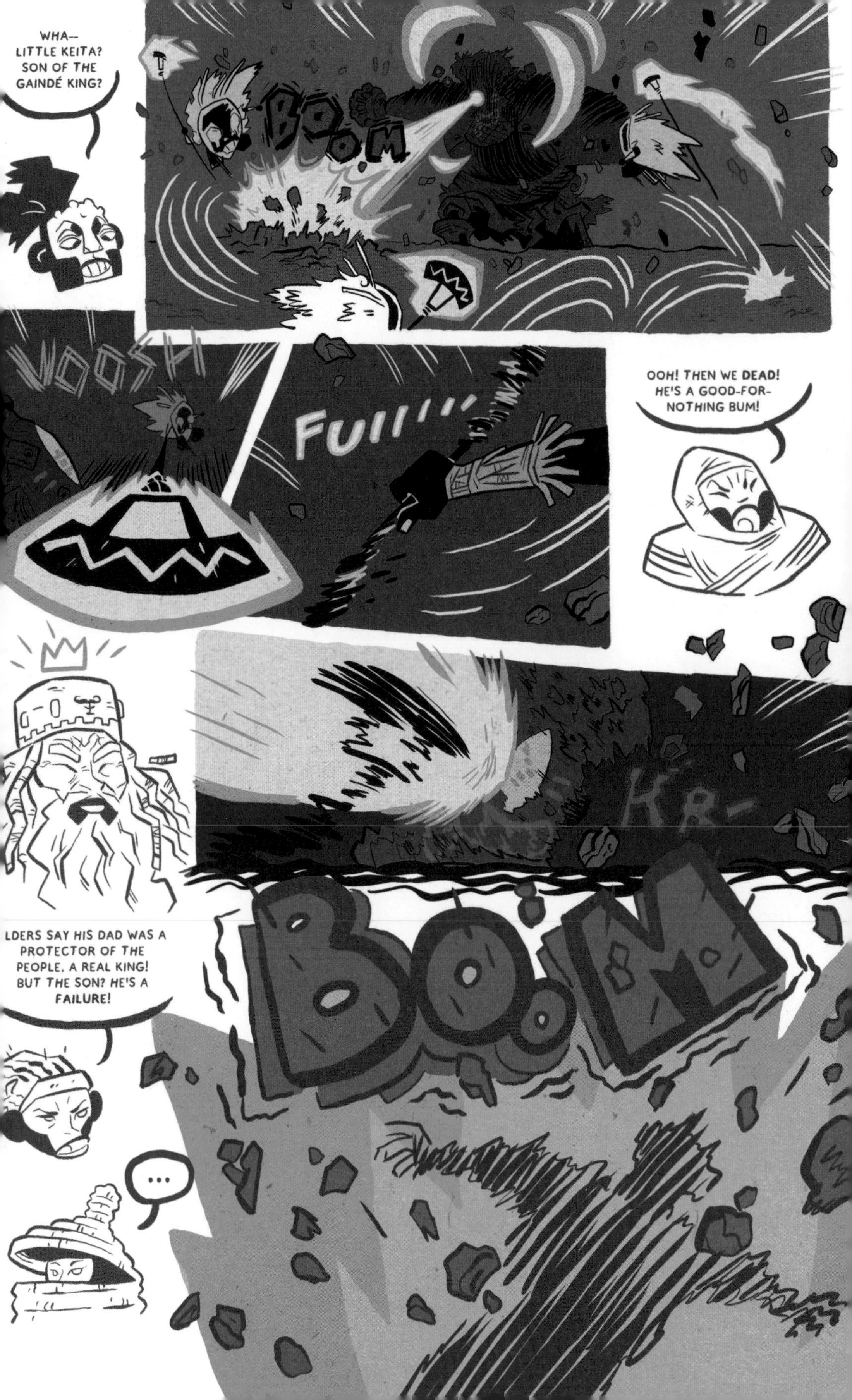
WHA-- LITTLE KEITA? SON OF THE GAINDÉ KING?
BOOM
WOOSH
FUII''
OOH! THEN WE **DEAD**! HE'S A GOOD-FOR-NOTHING BUM!
KR-
LDERS SAY HIS DAD WAS A PROTECTOR OF THE PEOPLE. A REAL KING! BUT THE SON? HE'S A **FAILURE**!
BOOM
...

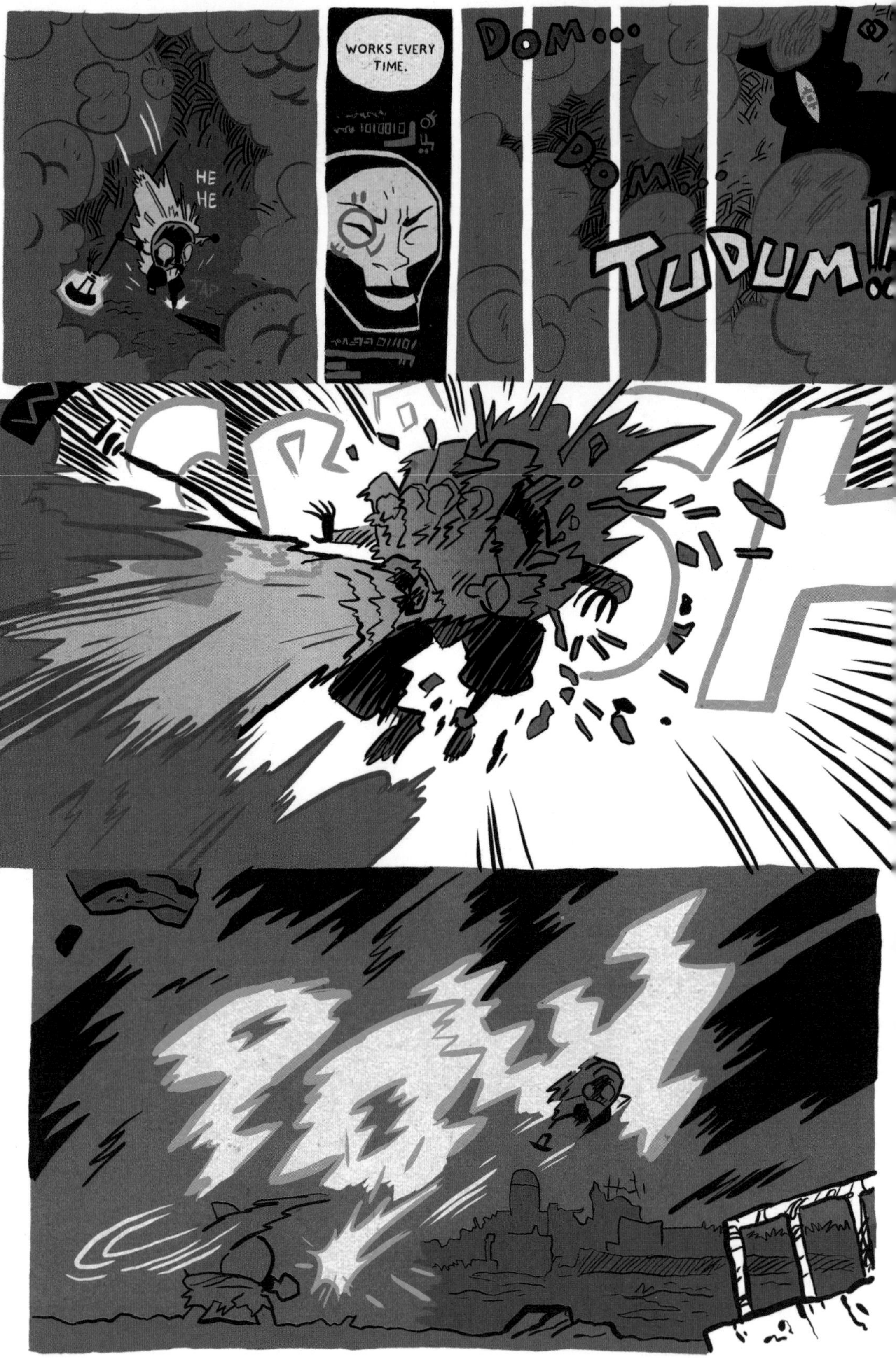

HE HE
TAP
WORKS EVERY TIME.
DOM...
DOM...
TUDUM!!

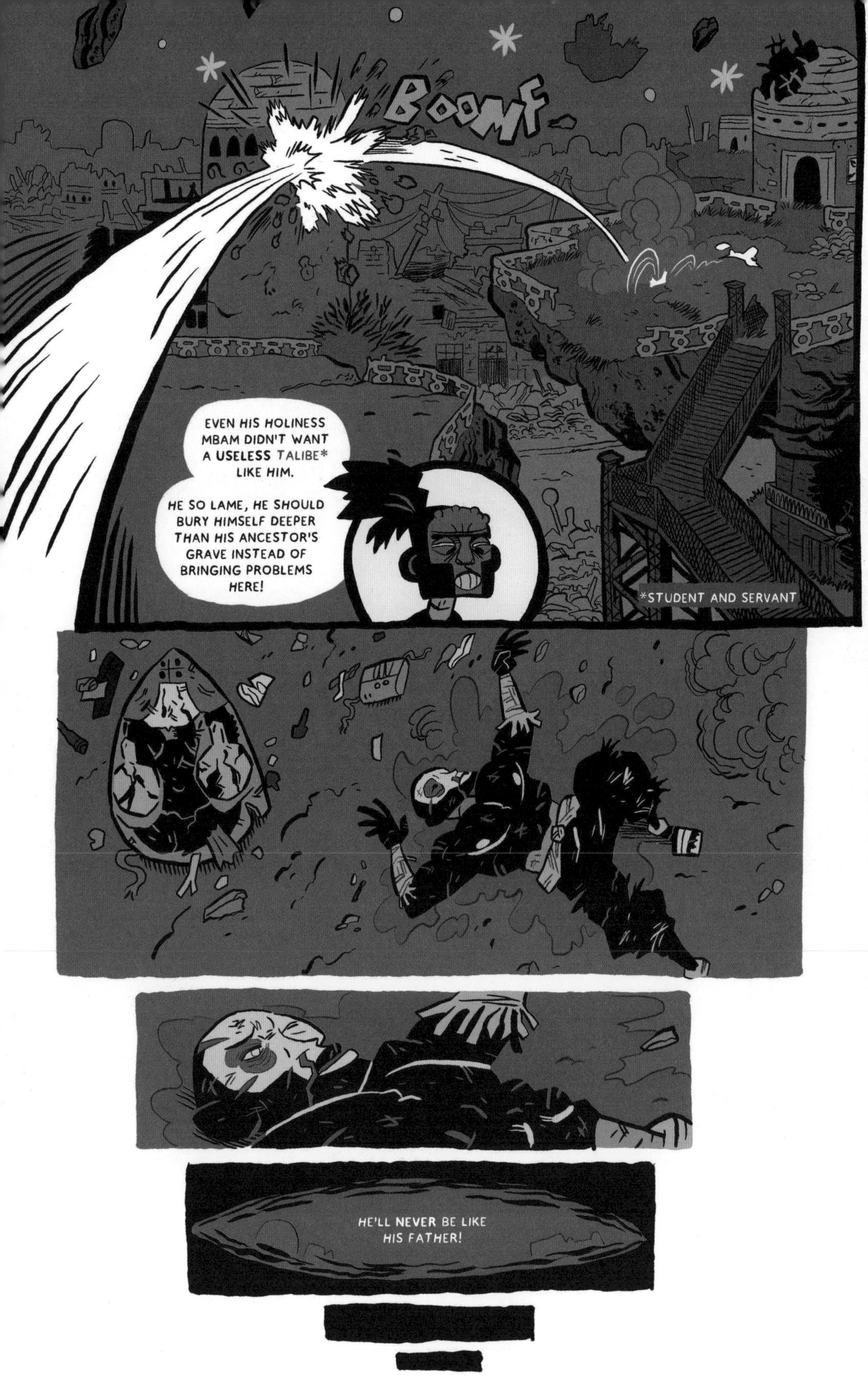
BOOMF
EVEN HIS HOLINESS MBAM DIDN'T WANT A USELESS TALIBE* LIKE HIM.
HE SO LAME, HE SHOULD BURY HIMSELF DEEPER THAN HIS ANCESTOR'S GRAVE INSTEAD OF BRINGING PROBLEMS HERE!
*STUDENT AND SERVANT
HE'LL NEVER BE LIKE HIS FATHER!

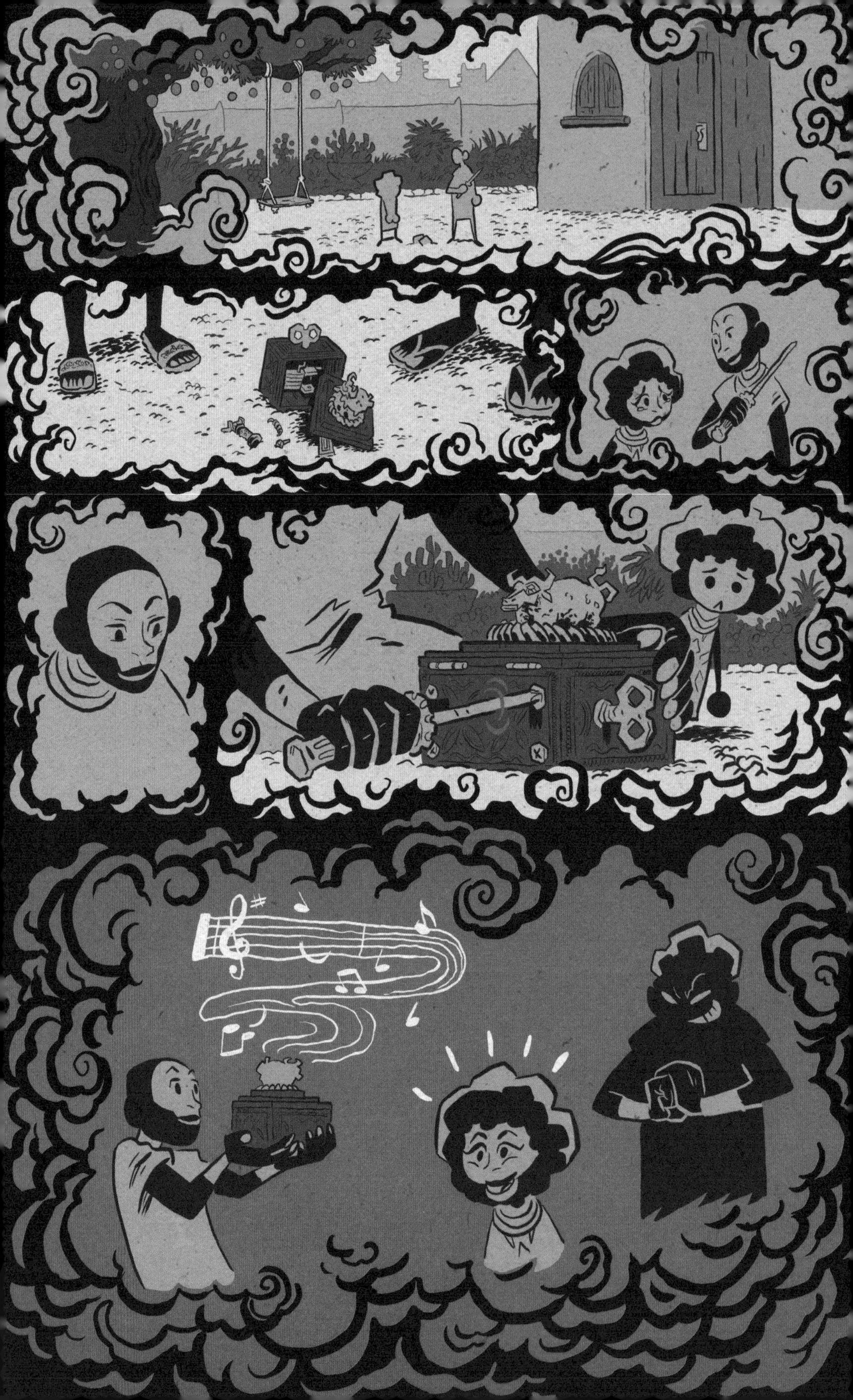

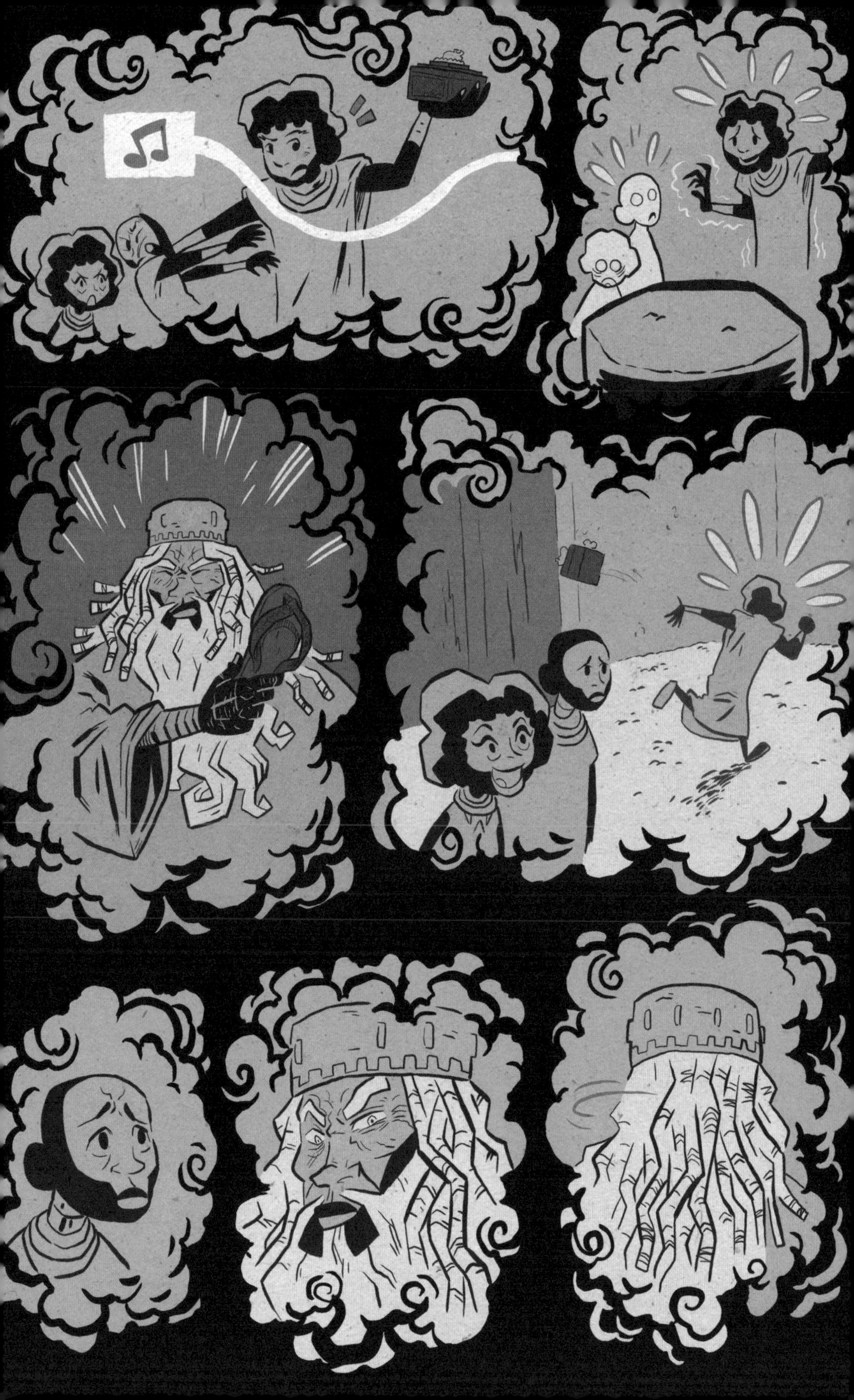

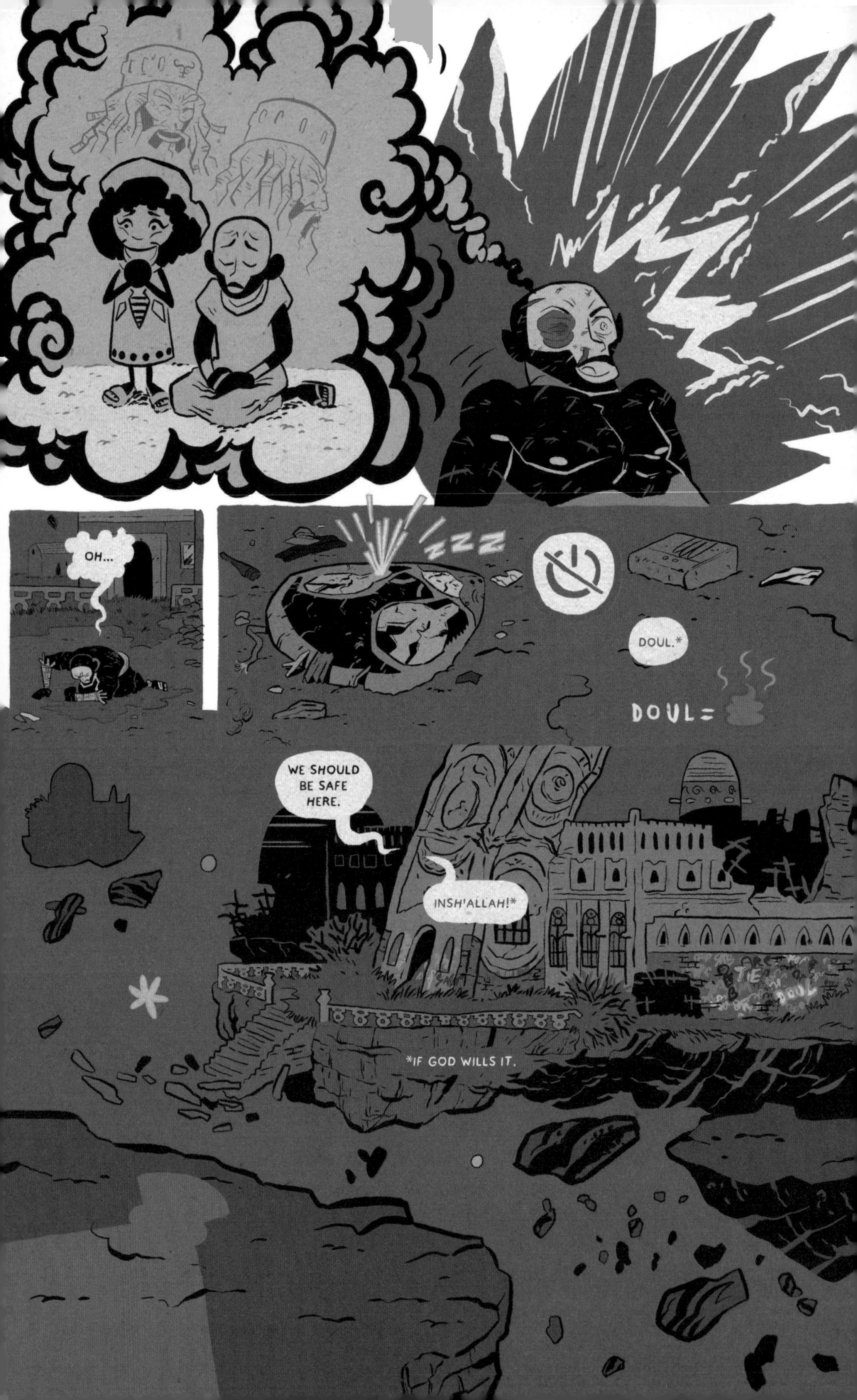
OH...
DOUL.*
DOUL=
WE SHOULD BE SAFE HERE.
INSH'ALLAH!*
*IF GOD WILLS IT.

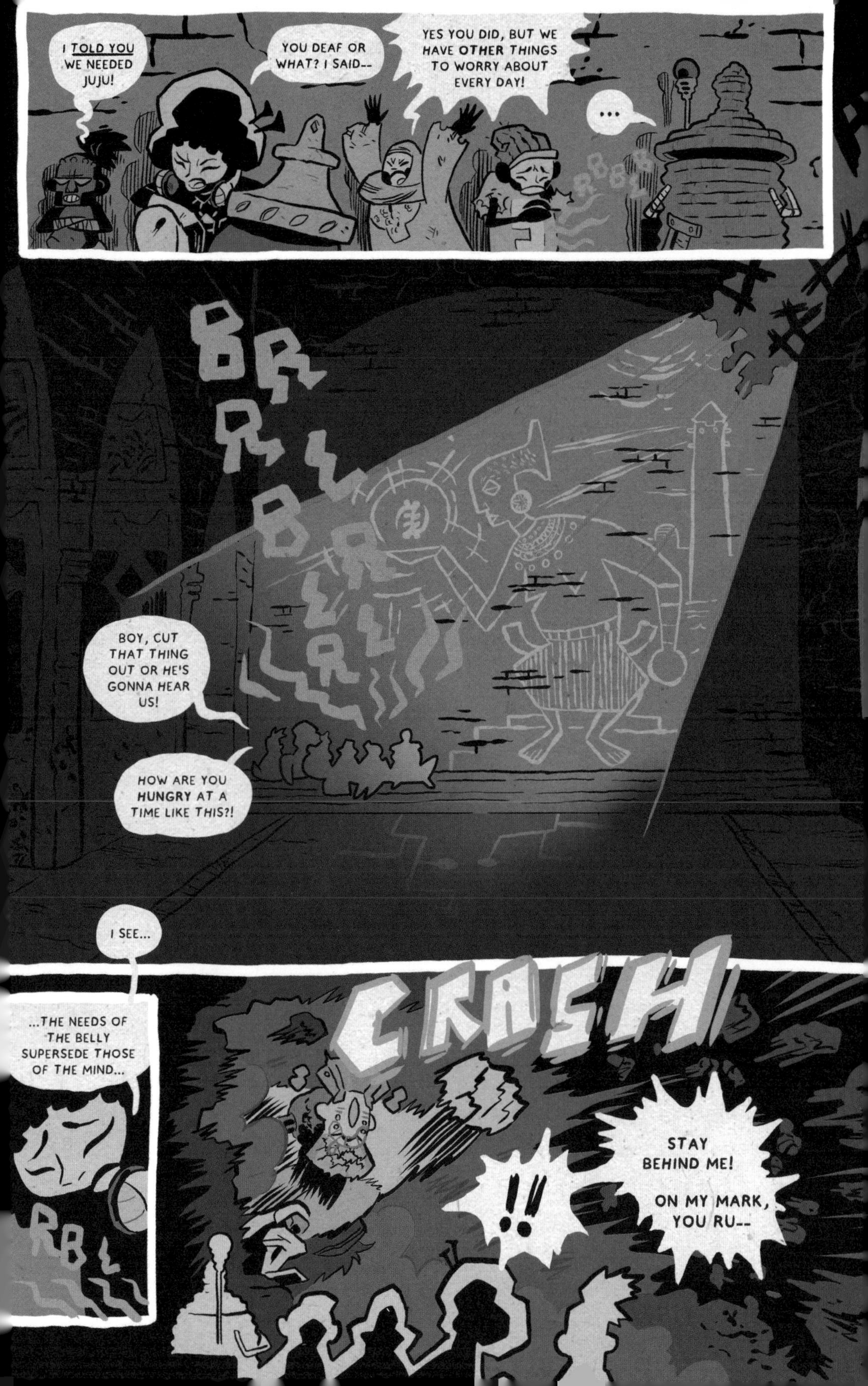

I TOLD YOU WE NEEDED JUJU!
YOU DEAF OR WHAT? I SAID--
YES YOU DID, BUT WE HAVE OTHER THINGS TO WORRY ABOUT EVERY DAY!
...
RBBBL
BRRLBRRLLR
BOY, CUT THAT THING OUT OR HE'S GONNA HEAR US!
HOW ARE YOU HUNGRY AT A TIME LIKE THIS?!
I SEE...
...THE NEEDS OF THE BELLY SUPERSEDE THOSE OF THE MIND...
CRASH
RBL
!!
STAY BEHIND ME!
ON MY MARK, YOU RU--

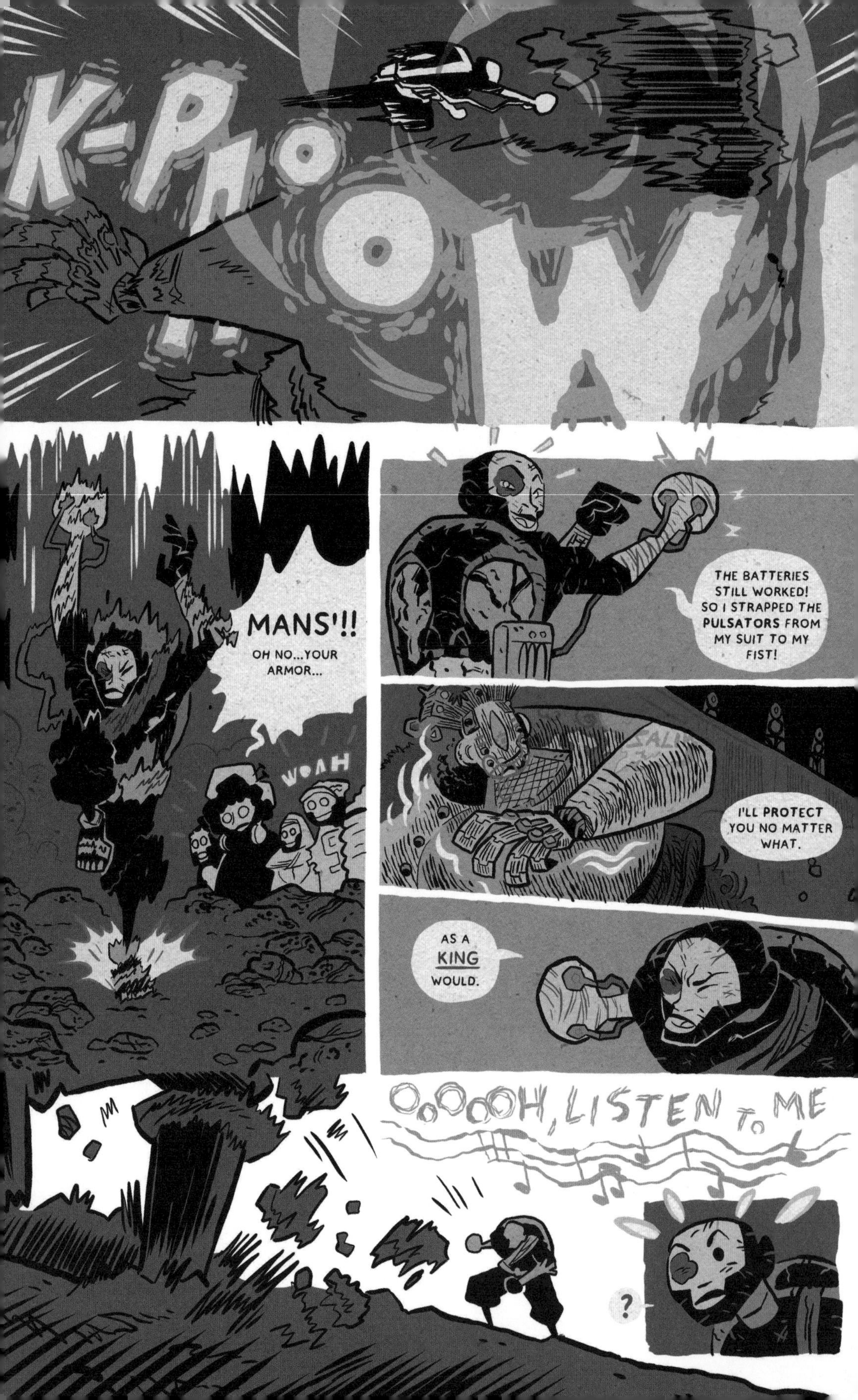
K-PHOOW
MANS'!!
OH NO...YOUR ARMOR...
WOAH
THE BATTERIES STILL WORKED! SO I STRAPPED THE PULSATORS FROM MY SUIT TO MY FIST!
I'LL PROTECT YOU NO MATTER WHAT.
AS A KING WOULD.
OoOOOOH, LISTEN TO ME
?

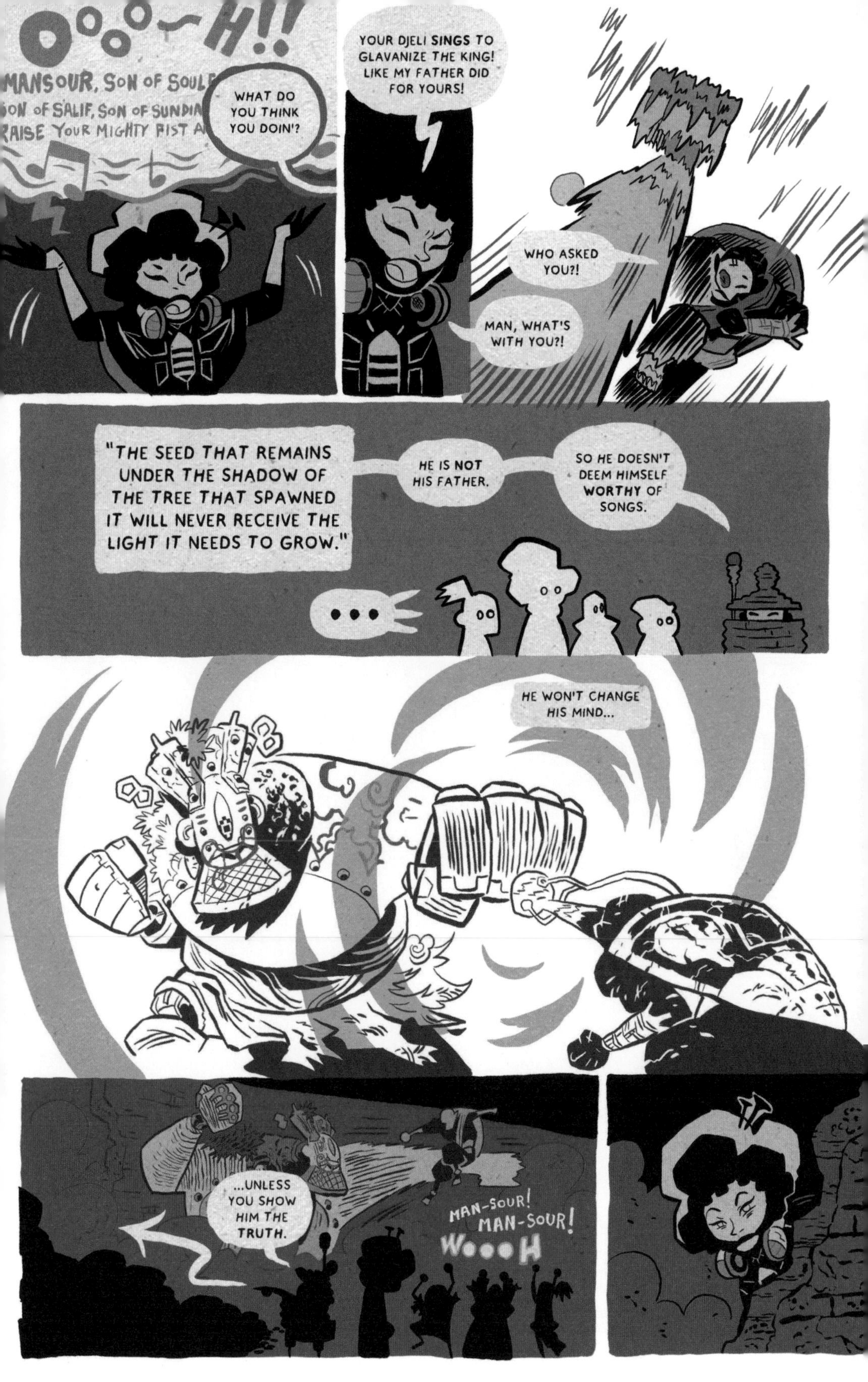
Oooo~H!!
MANSOUR, SON OF SOUL
SON OF SALIF, SON OF SUNDIA
RAISE YOUR MIGHTY FIST A
WHAT DO YOU THINK YOU DOIN'?
YOUR DJELI SINGS TO GLAVANIZE THE KING! LIKE MY FATHER DID FOR YOURS!
WHO ASKED YOU?!
MAN, WHAT'S WITH YOU?!
"THE SEED THAT REMAINS UNDER THE SHADOW OF THE TREE THAT SPAWNED IT WILL NEVER RECEIVE THE LIGHT IT NEEDS TO GROW."
HE IS NOT HIS FATHER.
SO HE DOESN'T DEEM HIMSELF WORTHY OF SONGS.
...
HE WON'T CHANGE HIS MIND...
...UNLESS YOU SHOW HIM THE TRUTH.
MAN-SOUR!
MAN-SOUR!
WoooH

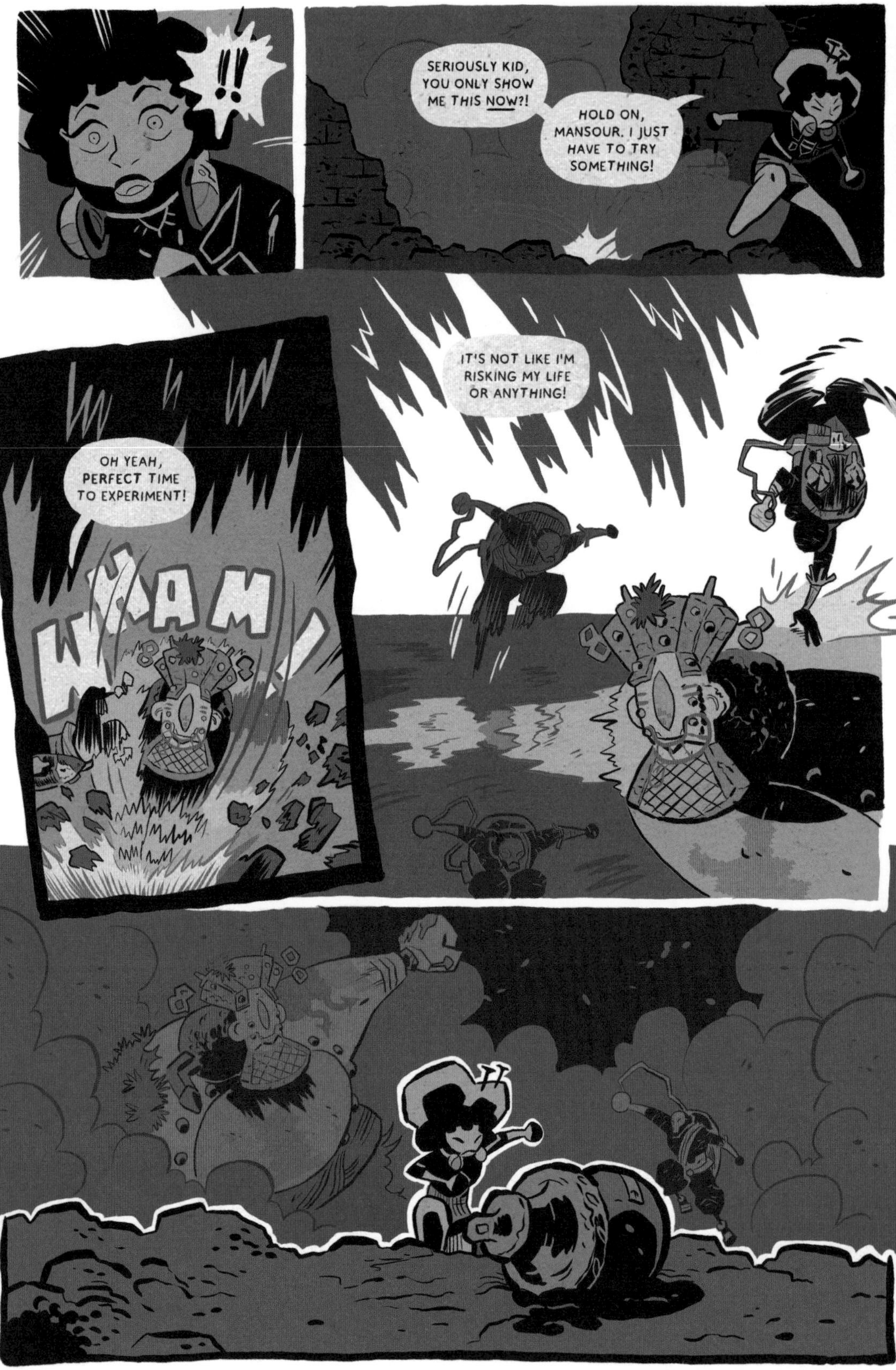
!!
SERIOUSLY KID, YOU ONLY SHOW ME THIS NOW?!
HOLD ON, MANSOUR. I JUST HAVE TO TRY SOMETHING!
IT'S NOT LIKE I'M RISKING MY LIFE OR ANYTHING!
OH YEAH, PERFECT TIME TO EXPERIMENT!
WHAM!

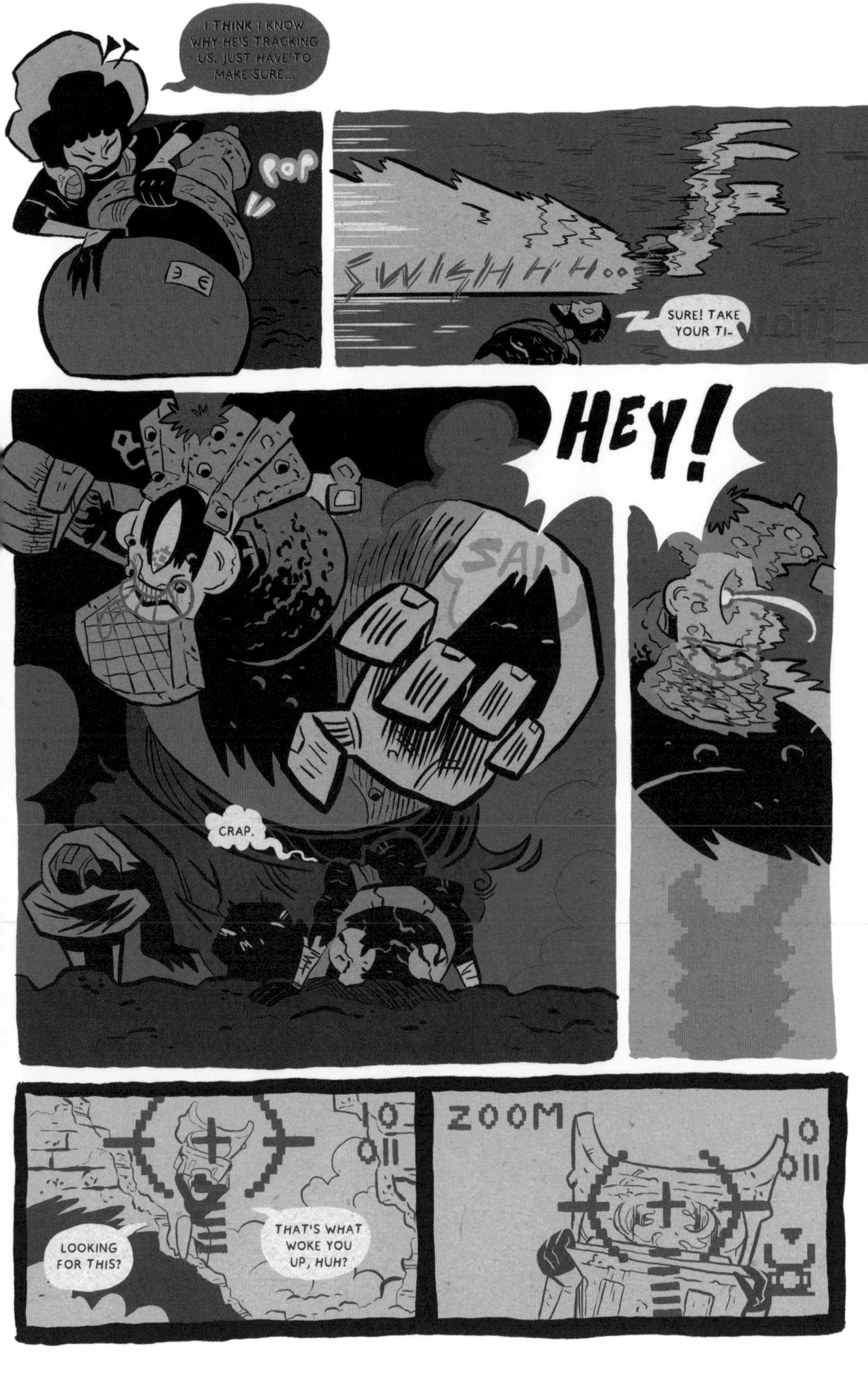
I THINK I KNOW WHY HE'S TRACKING US. JUST HAVE TO MAKE SURE...
POP
SWISHHH...
SURE! TAKE YOUR TI-
HEY!
CRAP.
LOOKING FOR THIS?
THAT'S WHAT WOKE YOU UP, HUH?
ZOOM

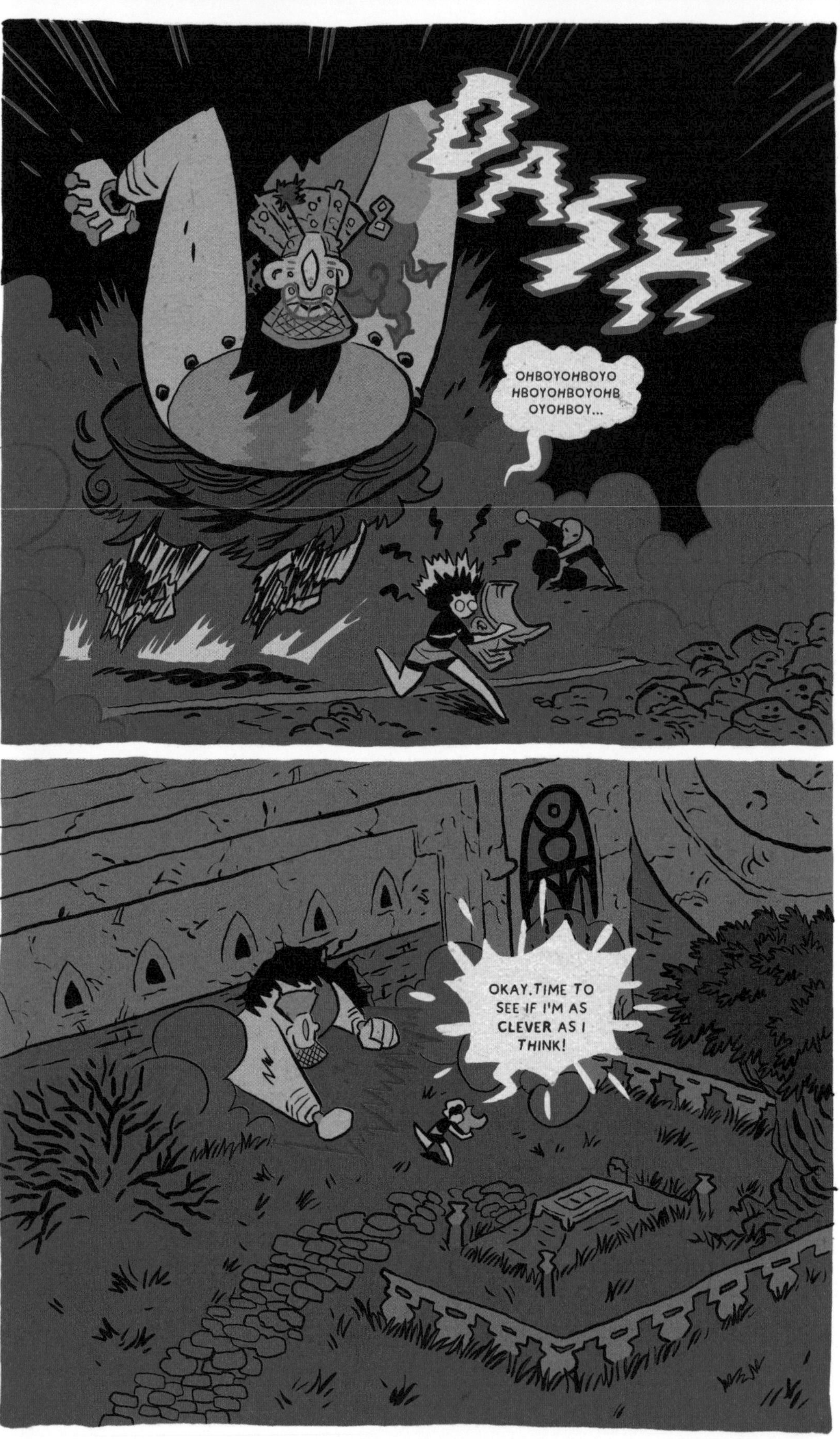
DASH
OHBOYOHBOYO
HBOYOHBOYOHB
OYOHBOY...
OKAY. TIME TO
SEE IF I'M AS
CLEVER AS I
THINK!

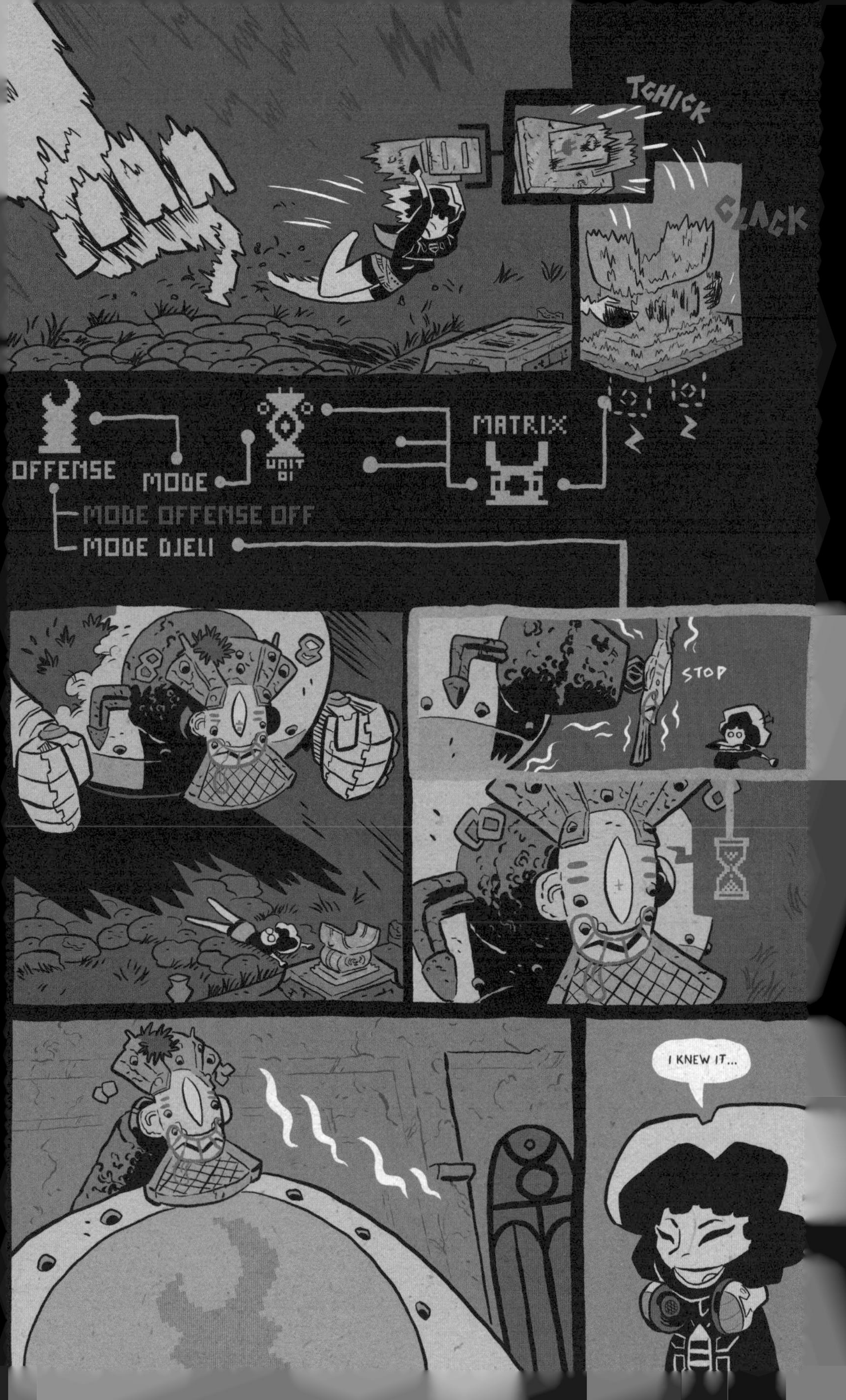
TCHICK
CLACK
OFFENSE
MODE
UNIT 01
MATRIX
MODE OFFENSE OFF
MODE DJELI
STOP
I KNEW IT...

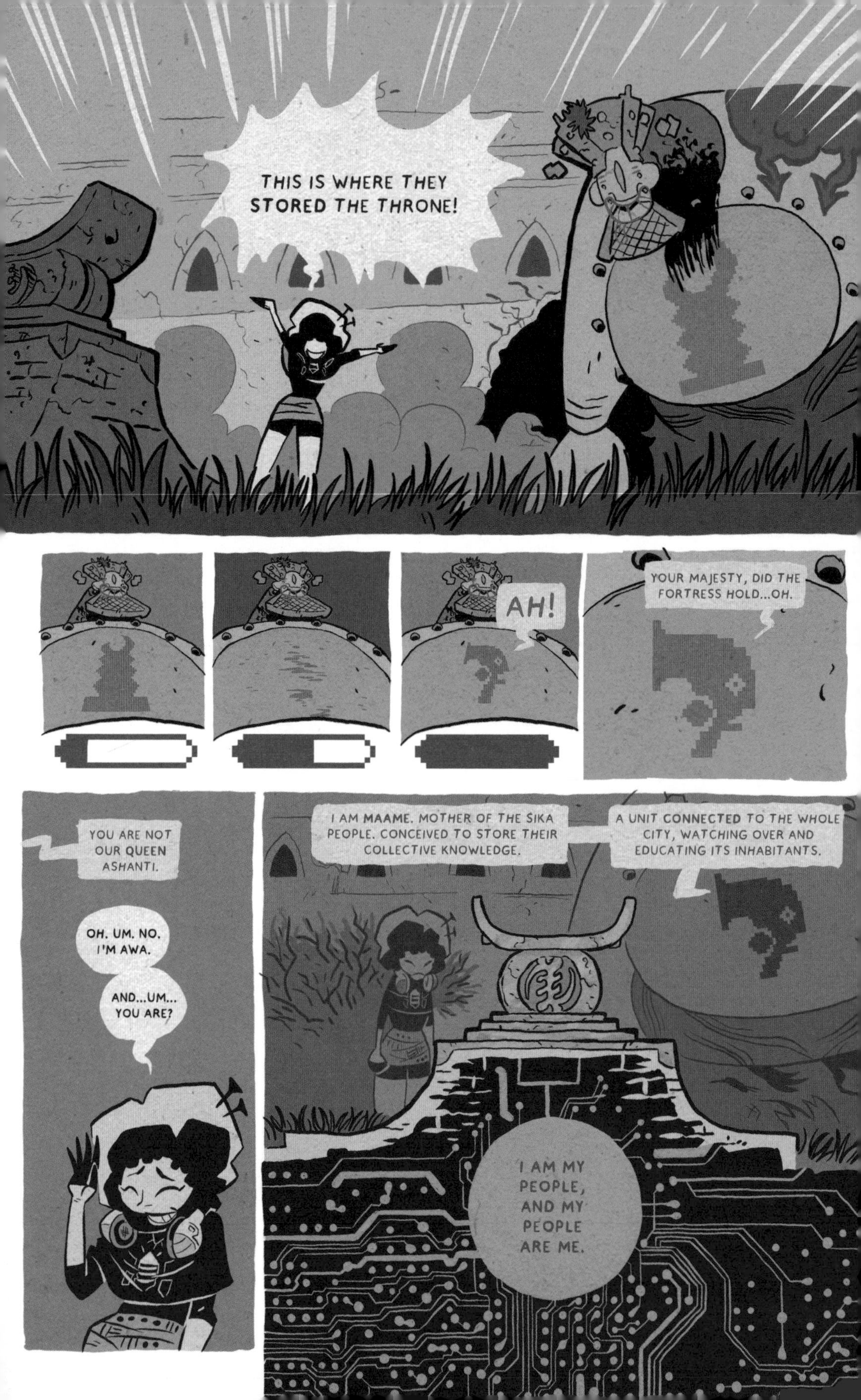
THIS IS WHERE THEY STORED THE THRONE!
AH!
YOUR MAJESTY, DID THE FORTRESS HOLD...OH.
YOU ARE NOT OUR QUEEN ASHANTI.
OH. UM. NO. I'M AWA.
AND...UM... YOU ARE?
I AM MAAME. MOTHER OF THE SIKA PEOPLE. CONCEIVED TO STORE THEIR COLLECTIVE KNOWLEDGE.
A UNIT CONNECTED TO THE WHOLE CITY, WATCHING OVER AND EDUCATING ITS INHABITANTS.
I AM MY PEOPLE, AND MY PEOPLE ARE ME.

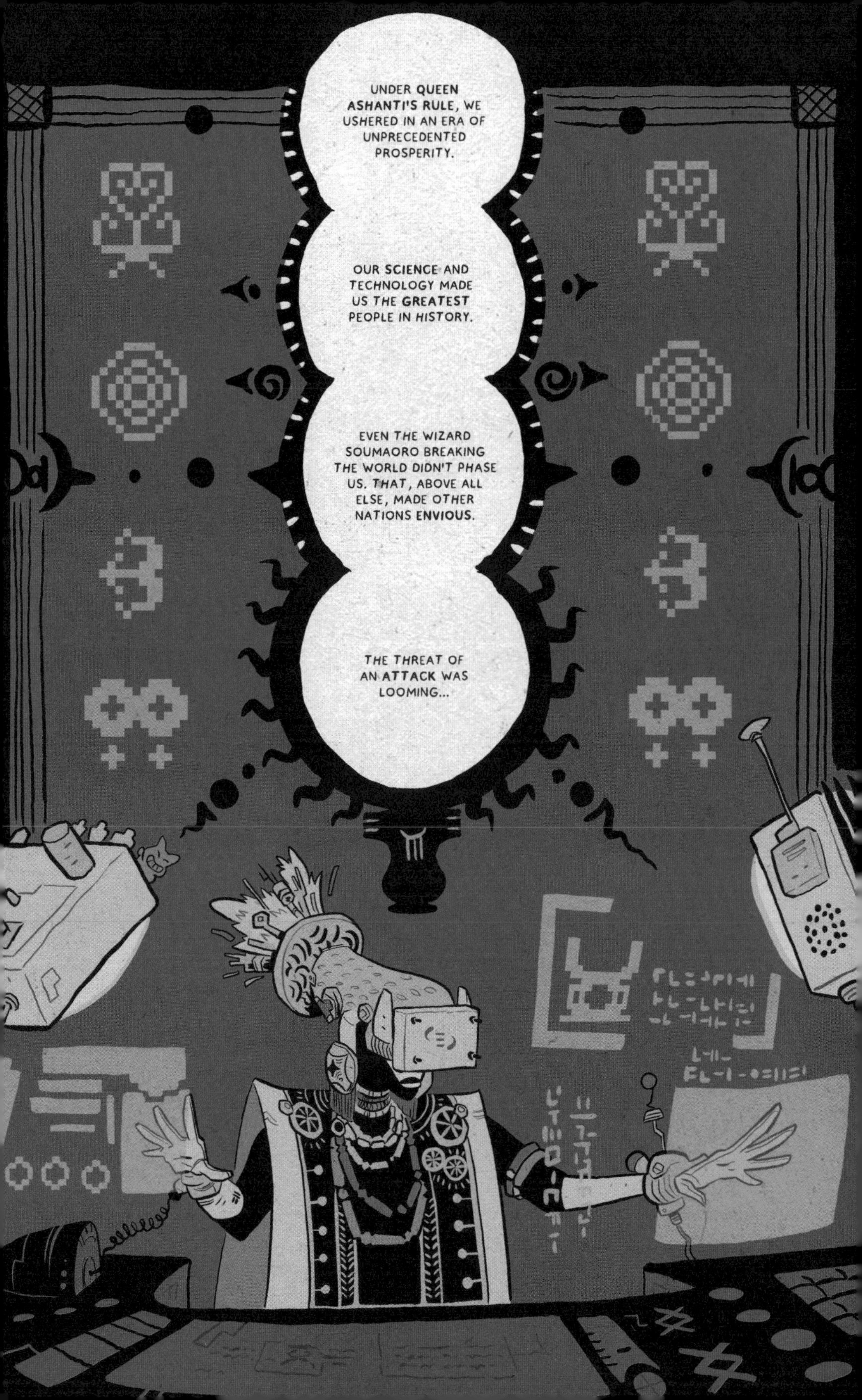
UNDER QUEEN ASHANTI'S RULE, WE USHERED IN AN ERA OF UNPRECEDENTED PROSPERITY.
OUR SCIENCE AND TECHNOLOGY MADE US THE GREATEST PEOPLE IN HISTORY.
EVEN THE WIZARD SOUMAORO BREAKING THE WORLD DIDN'T PHASE US. THAT, ABOVE ALL ELSE, MADE OTHER NATIONS ENVIOUS.
THE THREAT OF AN ATTACK WAS LOOMING...

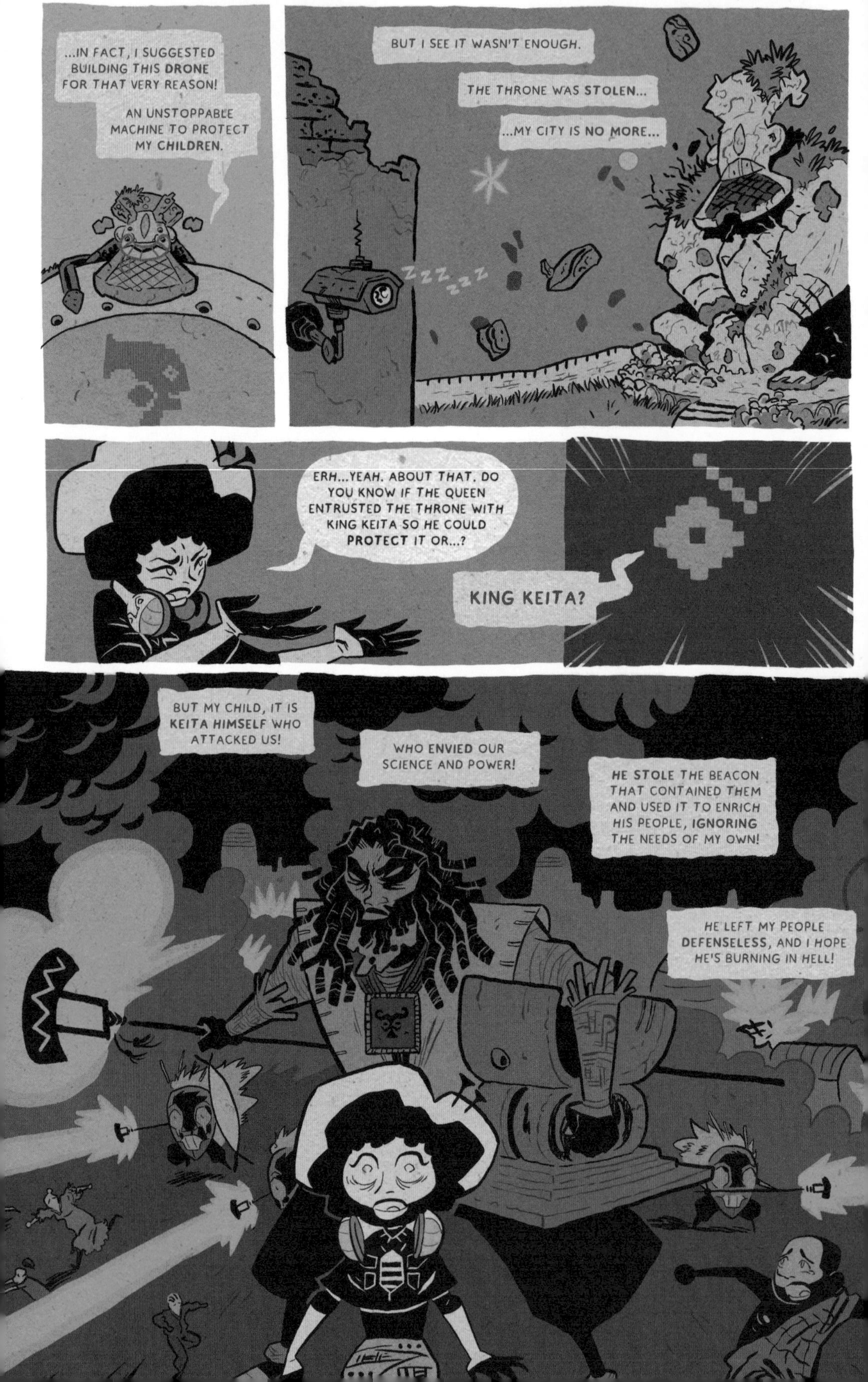
...IN FACT, I SUGGESTED BUILDING THIS DRONE FOR THAT VERY REASON!
AN UNSTOPPABLE MACHINE TO PROTECT MY CHILDREN.
BUT I SEE IT WASN'T ENOUGH.
THE THRONE WAS STOLEN...
...MY CITY IS NO MORE...
ZZZ ZZZ
ERH...YEAH. ABOUT THAT. DO YOU KNOW IF THE QUEEN ENTRUSTED THE THRONE WITH KING KEITA SO HE COULD PROTECT IT OR...?
KING KEITA?
BUT MY CHILD, IT IS KEITA HIMSELF WHO ATTACKED US!
WHO ENVIED OUR SCIENCE AND POWER!
HE STOLE THE BEACON THAT CONTAINED THEM AND USED IT TO ENRICH HIS PEOPLE, IGNORING THE NEEDS OF MY OWN!
HE LEFT MY PEOPLE DEFENSELESS, AND I HOPE HE'S BURNING IN HELL!

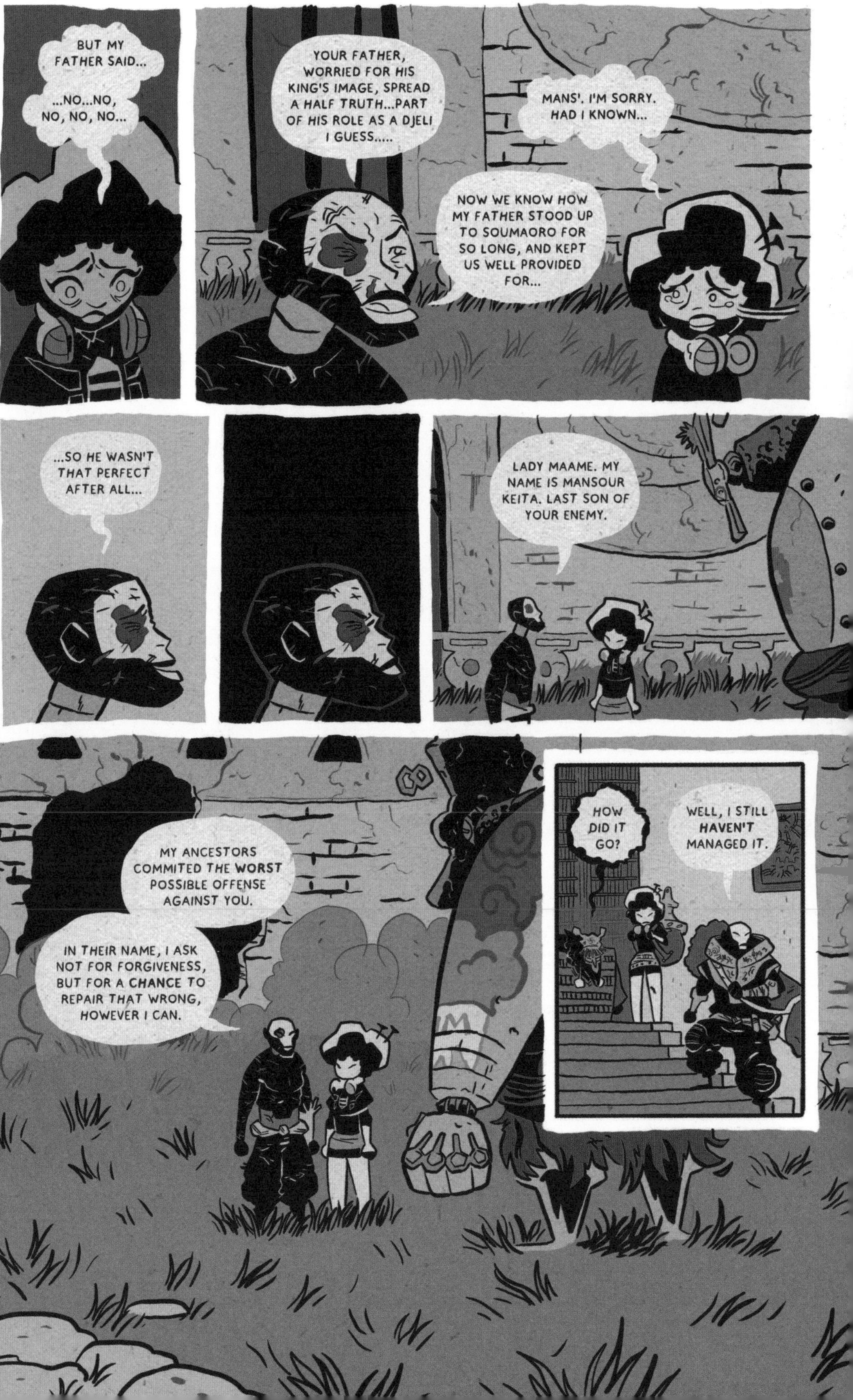
BUT MY FATHER SAID...
...NO...NO, NO, NO, NO...
YOUR FATHER, WORRIED FOR HIS KING'S IMAGE, SPREAD A HALF TRUTH...PART OF HIS ROLE AS A DJELI I GUESS.....
MANS'. I'M SORRY. HAD I KNOWN...
NOW WE KNOW HOW MY FATHER STOOD UP TO SOUMAORO FOR SO LONG, AND KEPT US WELL PROVIDED FOR...
...SO HE WASN'T THAT PERFECT AFTER ALL...
LADY MAAME. MY NAME IS MANSOUR KEITA. LAST SON OF YOUR ENEMY.
MY ANCESTORS COMMITED THE WORST POSSIBLE OFFENSE AGAINST YOU.
IN THEIR NAME, I ASK NOT FOR FORGIVENESS, BUT FOR A CHANCE TO REPAIR THAT WRONG, HOWEVER I CAN.
HOW DID IT GO?
WELL, I STILL HAVEN'T MANAGED IT.

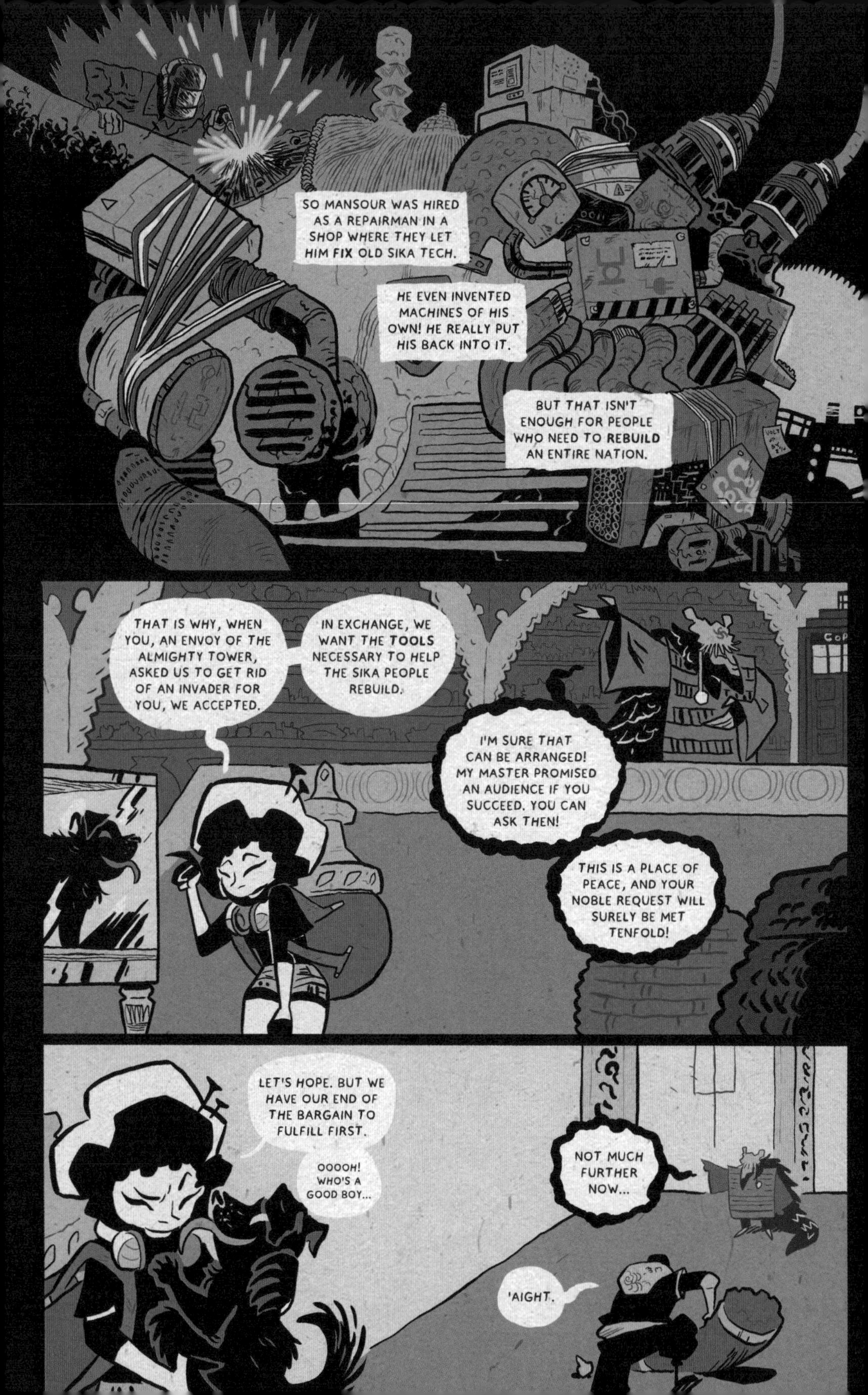
SO MANSOUR WAS HIRED AS A REPAIRMAN IN A SHOP WHERE THEY LET HIM FIX OLD SIKA TECH.
HE EVEN INVENTED MACHINES OF HIS OWN! HE REALLY PUT HIS BACK INTO IT.
BUT THAT ISN'T ENOUGH FOR PEOPLE WHO NEED TO REBUILD AN ENTIRE NATION.
THAT IS WHY, WHEN YOU, AN ENVOY OF THE ALMIGHTY TOWER, ASKED US TO GET RID OF AN INVADER FOR YOU, WE ACCEPTED.
IN EXCHANGE, WE WANT THE TOOLS NECESSARY TO HELP THE SIKA PEOPLE REBUILD.
I'M SURE THAT CAN BE ARRANGED! MY MASTER PROMISED AN AUDIENCE IF YOU SUCCEED. YOU CAN ASK THEN!
THIS IS A PLACE OF PEACE, AND YOUR NOBLE REQUEST WILL SURELY BE MET TENFOLD!
LET'S HOPE. BUT WE HAVE OUR END OF THE BARGAIN TO FULFILL FIRST.
OOOOH! WHO'S A GOOD BOY...
NOT MUCH FURTHER NOW...
'AIGHT.

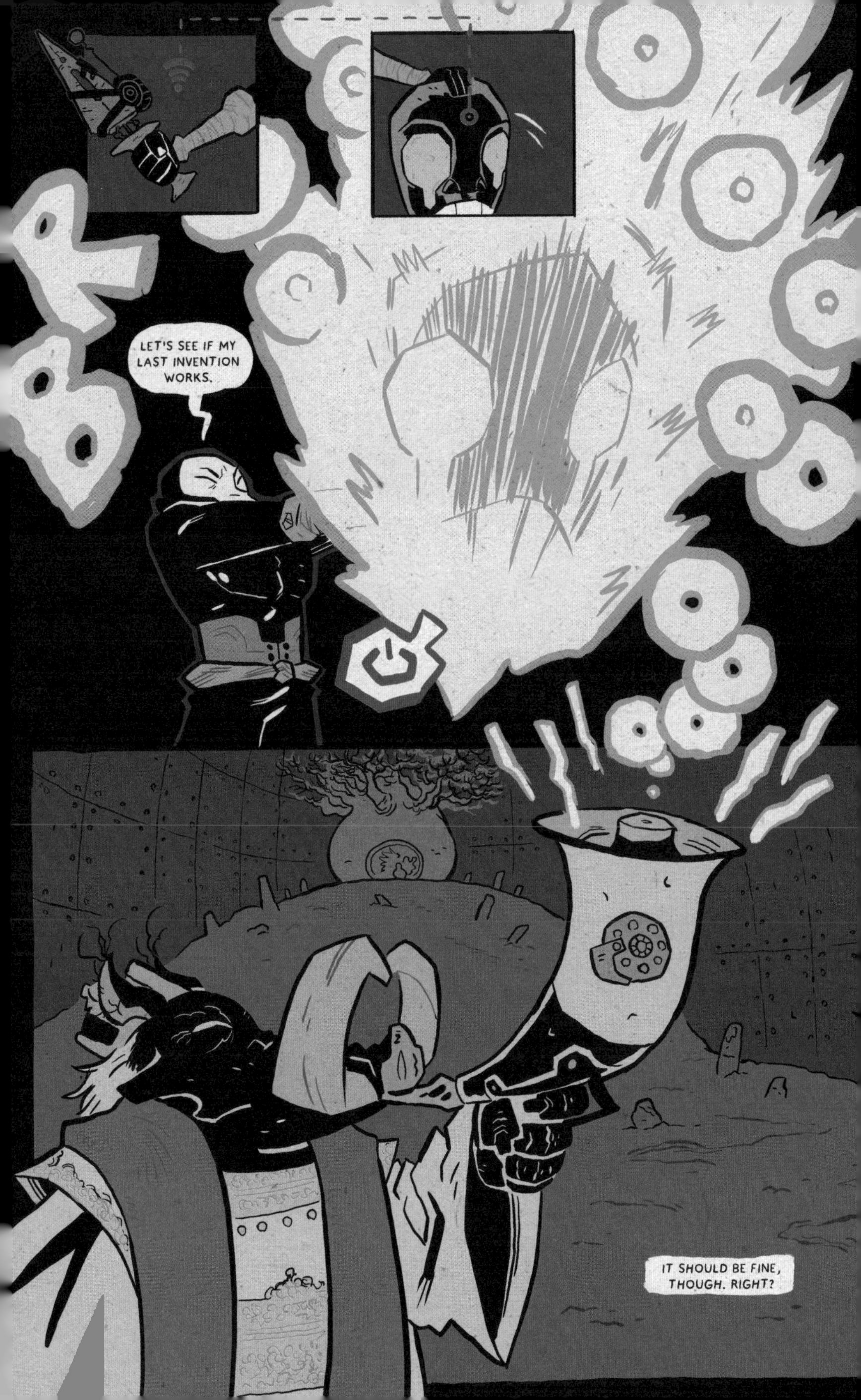
LET'S SEE IF MY LAST INVENTION WORKS.
IT SHOULD BE FINE, THOUGH. RIGHT?

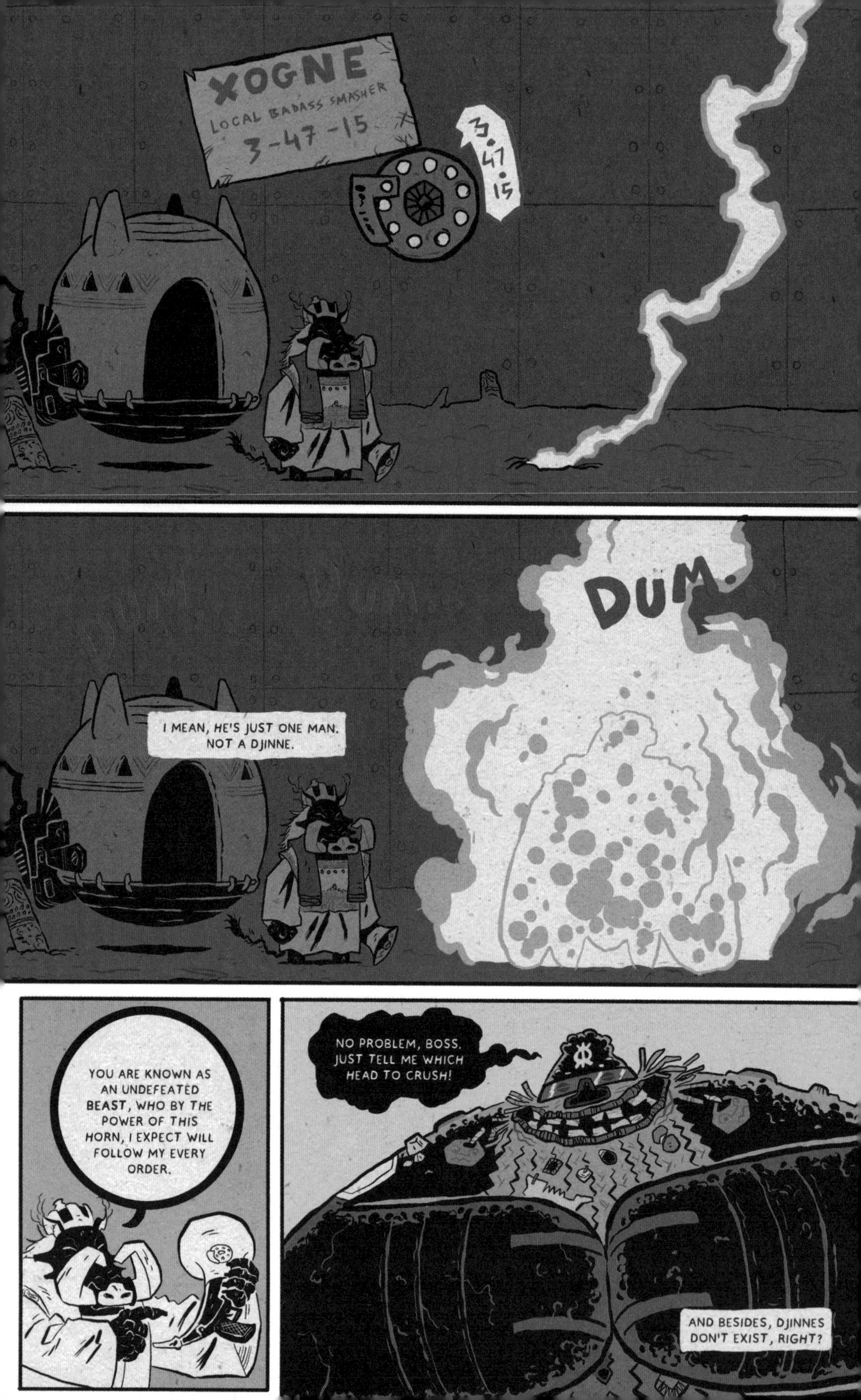
XOGNE
LOCAL BADASS SMASHER
3-47-15
3.47.15
DUM
I MEAN, HE'S JUST ONE MAN. NOT A DJINNE.
YOU ARE KNOWN AS AN UNDEFEATED BEAST, WHO BY THE POWER OF THIS HORN, I EXPECT WILL FOLLOW MY EVERY ORDER.
NO PROBLEM, BOSS. JUST TELL ME WHICH HEAD TO CRUSH!
AND BESIDES, DJINNES DON'T EXIST, RIGHT?

III

AND NOW FOR A LITTLE INTERLUDE...

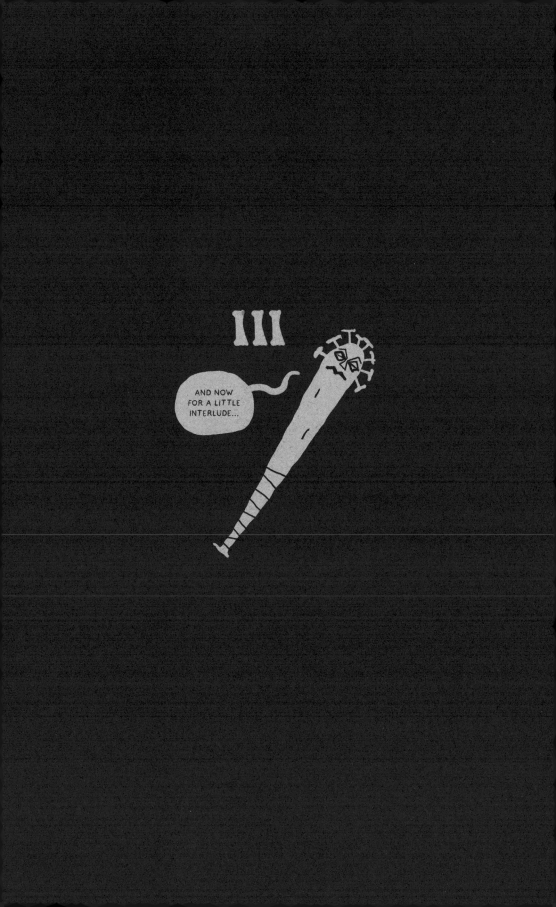

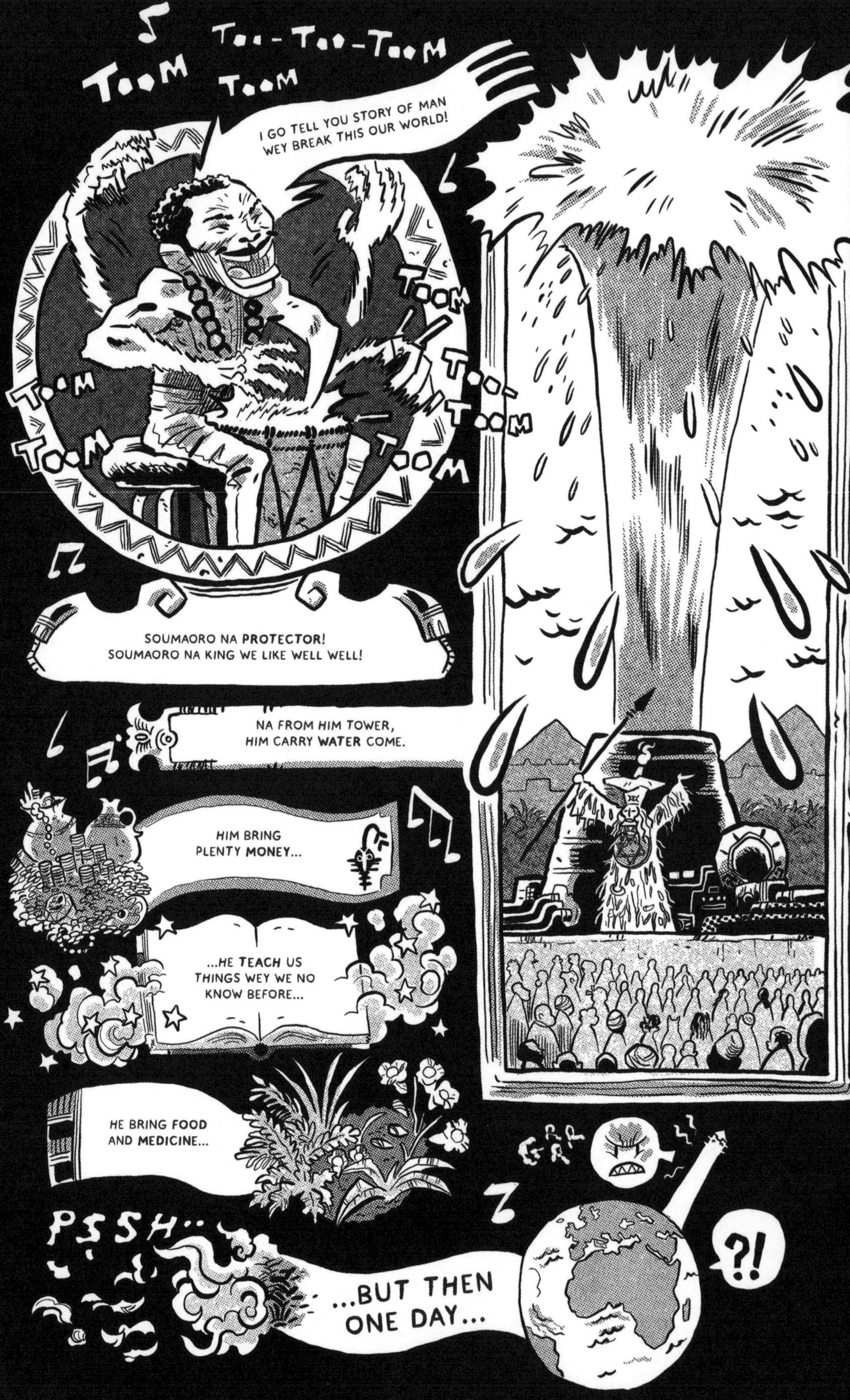

TOOM TOO-TOO-TOOM TOOM
I GO TELL YOU STORY OF MAN WEY BREAK THIS OUR WORLD!
TOOM
TOO-TOOM
TOOM
TOOM TOOM
SOUMAORO NA **PROTECTOR**! SOUMAORO NA KING WE LIKE WELL WELL!
NA FROM HIM TOWER, HIM CARRY **WATER** COME.
HIM BRING PLENTY **MONEY**...
...HE **TEACH** US THINGS WEY WE NO KNOW BEFORE...
HE BRING **FOOD** AND **MEDICINE**...
GRR
?!
PSSH..
...BUT THEN ONE DAY...

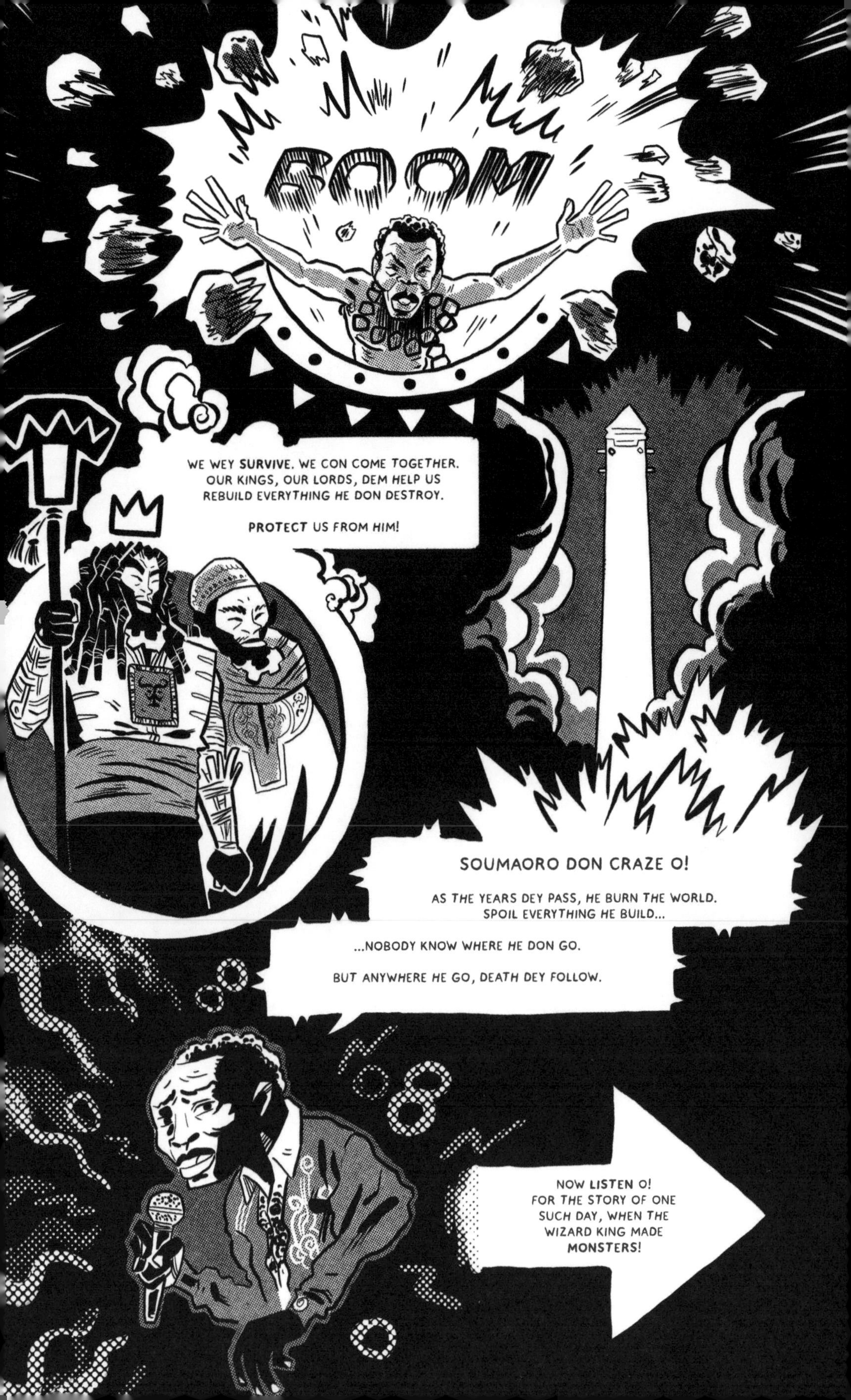
BOOM
WE WEY SURVIVE. WE CON COME TOGETHER. OUR KINGS, OUR LORDS, DEM HELP US REBUILD EVERYTHING HE DON DESTROY.
PROTECT US FROM HIM!
SOUMAORO DON CRAZE O!
AS THE YEARS DEY PASS, HE BURN THE WORLD. SPOIL EVERYTHING HE BUILD...
...NOBODY KNOW WHERE HE DON GO.
BUT ANYWHERE HE GO, DEATH DEY FOLLOW.
NOW LISTEN O! FOR THE STORY OF ONE SUCH DAY, WHEN THE WIZARD KING MADE MONSTERS!

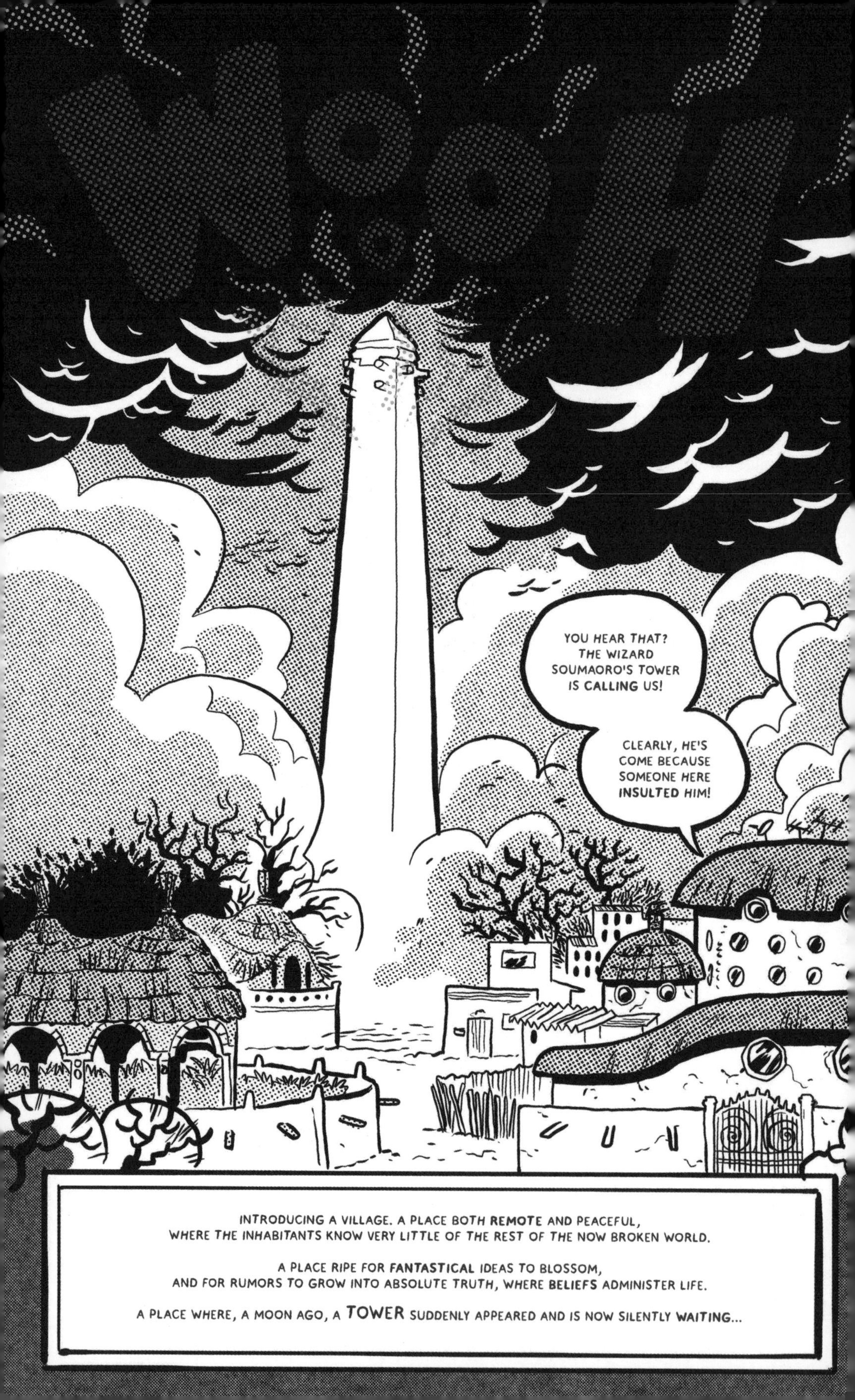

YOU HEAR THAT? THE WIZARD SOUMAORO'S TOWER IS CALLING US!
CLEARLY, HE'S COME BECAUSE SOMEONE HERE INSULTED HIM!
INTRODUCING A VILLAGE. A PLACE BOTH REMOTE AND PEACEFUL, WHERE THE INHABITANTS KNOW VERY LITTLE OF THE REST OF THE NOW BROKEN WORLD.
A PLACE RIPE FOR FANTASTICAL IDEAS TO BLOSSOM, AND FOR RUMORS TO GROW INTO ABSOLUTE TRUTH, WHERE BELIEFS ADMINISTER LIFE.
A PLACE WHERE, A MOON AGO, A TOWER SUDDENLY APPEARED AND IS NOW SILENTLY WAITING...

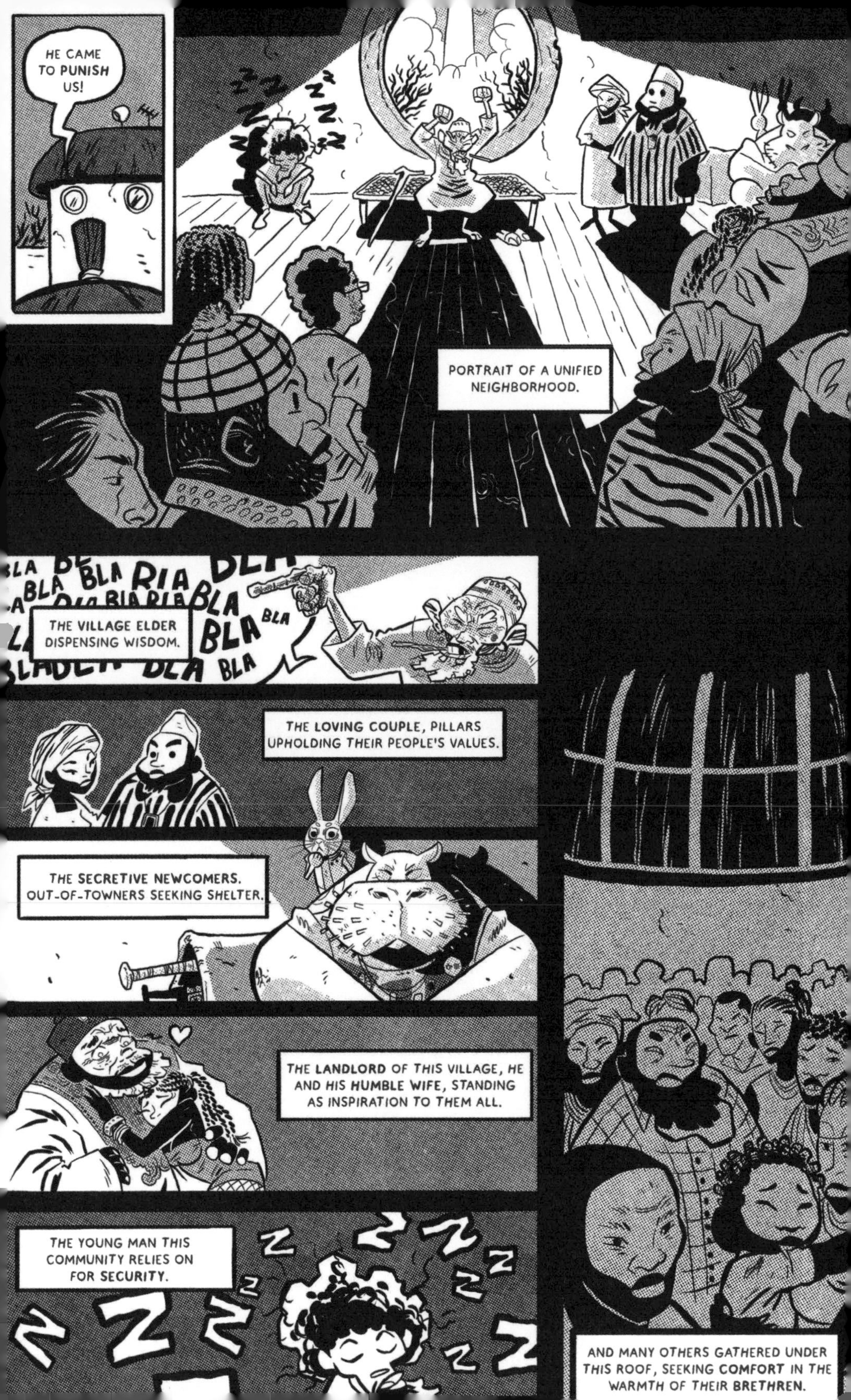
HE CAME TO PUNISH US!
PORTRAIT OF A UNIFIED NEIGHBORHOOD.
BLA BLA BLA BLA BLA BLA BLA BLA
THE VILLAGE ELDER DISPENSING WISDOM.
THE LOVING COUPLE, PILLARS UPHOLDING THEIR PEOPLE'S VALUES.
THE SECRETIVE NEWCOMERS. OUT-OF-TOWNERS SEEKING SHELTER.
THE LANDLORD OF THIS VILLAGE, HE AND HIS HUMBLE WIFE, STANDING AS INSPIRATION TO THEM ALL.
THE YOUNG MAN THIS COMMUNITY RELIES ON FOR SECURITY.
AND MANY OTHERS GATHERED UNDER THIS ROOF, SEEKING COMFORT IN THE WARMTH OF THEIR BRETHREN.

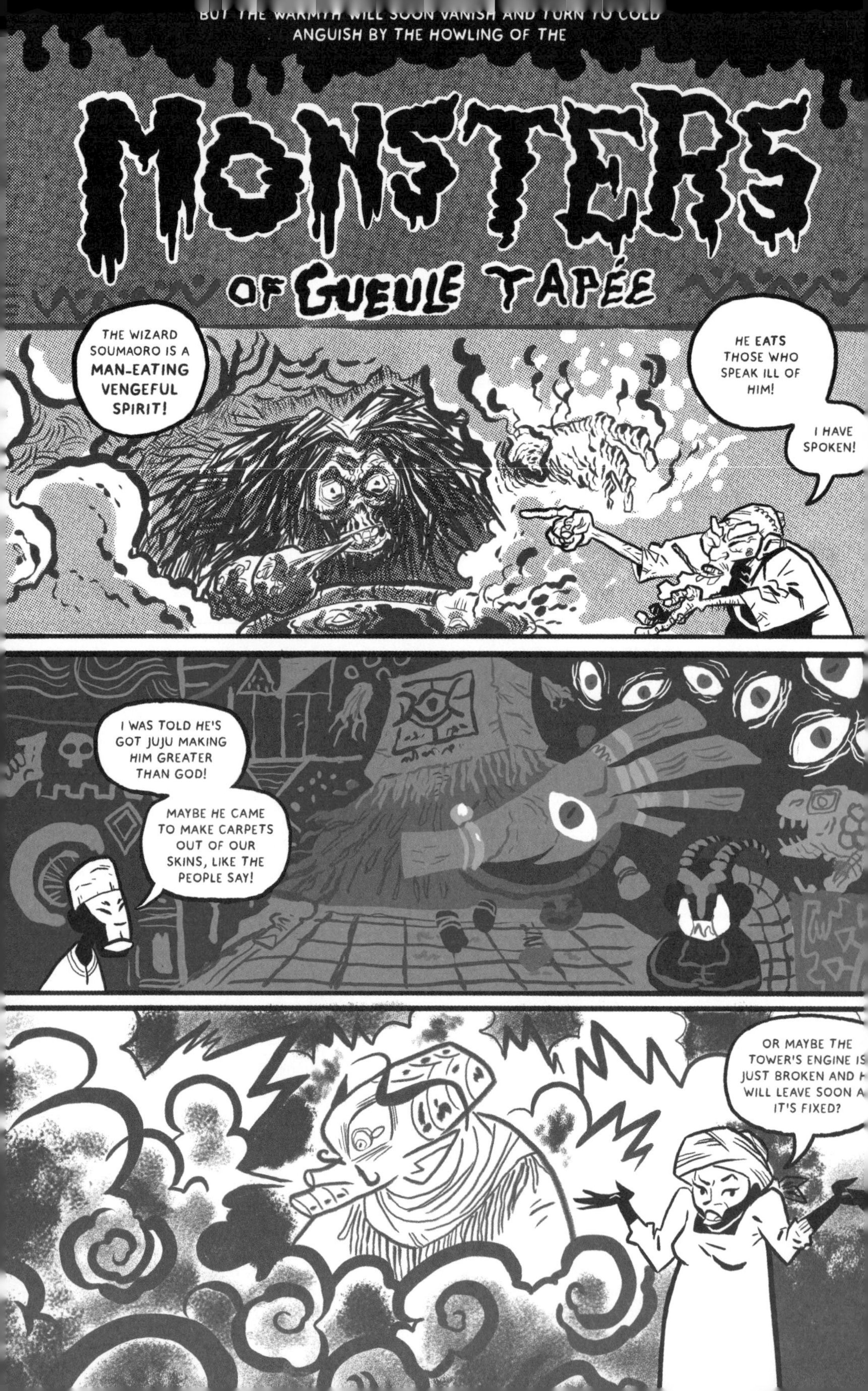
BUT THE WARMTH WILL SOON VANISH AND TURN TO COLD
ANGUISH BY THE HOWLING OF THE
MONSTERS OF GUEULE TAPÉE
THE WIZARD SOUMAORO IS A MAN-EATING VENGEFUL SPIRIT!
HE EATS THOSE WHO SPEAK ILL OF HIM!
I HAVE SPOKEN!
I WAS TOLD HE'S GOT JUJU MAKING HIM GREATER THAN GOD!
MAYBE HE CAME TO MAKE CARPETS OUT OF OUR SKINS, LIKE THE PEOPLE SAY!
OR MAYBE THE TOWER'S ENGINE IS JUST BROKEN AND H WILL LEAVE SOON A IT'S FIXED?

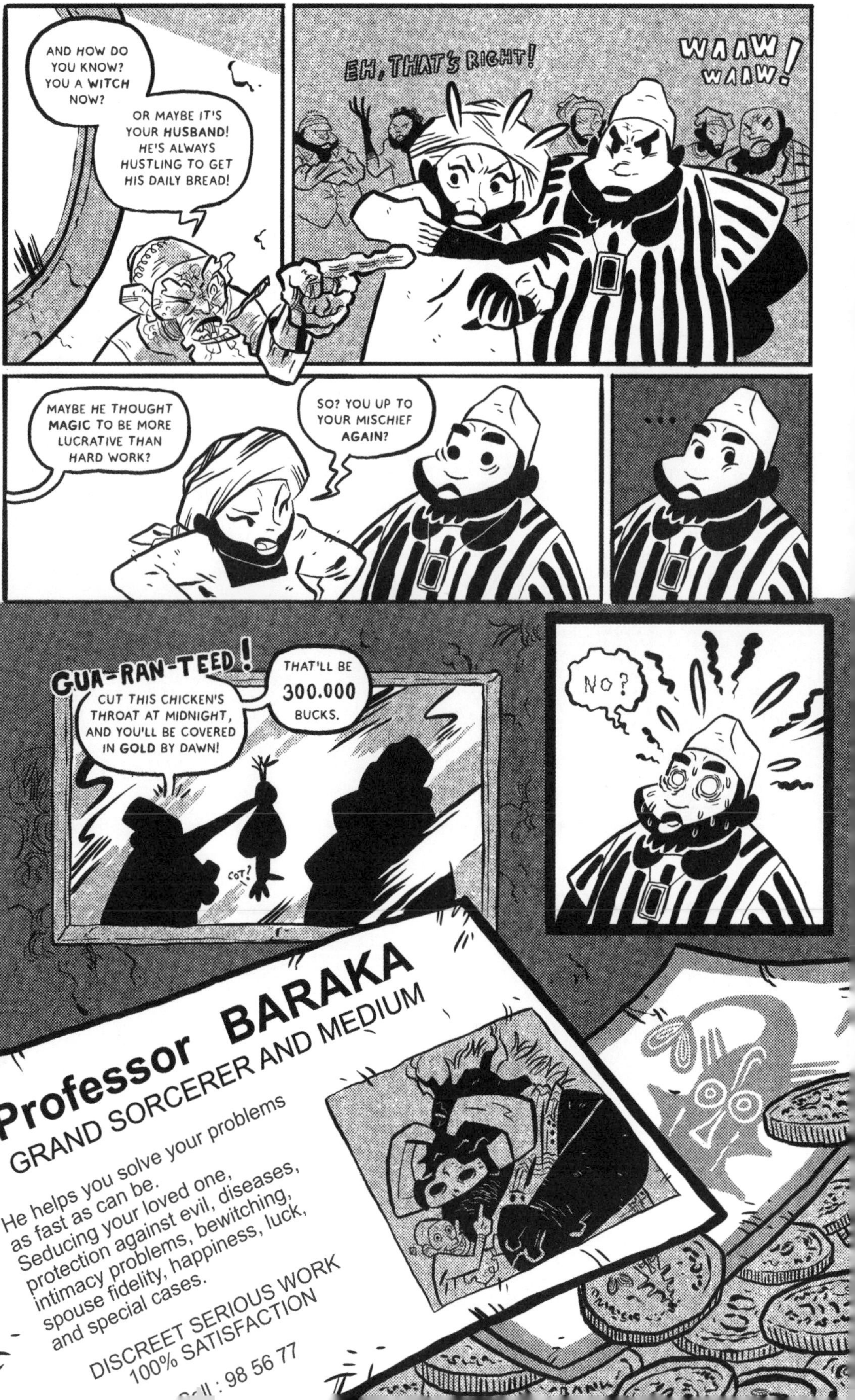
AND HOW DO YOU KNOW? YOU A WITCH NOW?
OR MAYBE IT'S YOUR HUSBAND! HE'S ALWAYS HUSTLING TO GET HIS DAILY BREAD!
EH, THAT'S RIGHT!
WAAW WAAW!
MAYBE HE THOUGHT MAGIC TO BE MORE LUCRATIVE THAN HARD WORK?
SO? YOU UP TO YOUR MISCHIEF AGAIN?
...
GUA-RAN-TEED!
CUT THIS CHICKEN'S THROAT AT MIDNIGHT, AND YOU'LL BE COVERED IN GOLD BY DAWN!
THAT'LL BE 300.000 BUCKS.
COT?
NO?
Professor BARAKA
GRAND SORCERER AND MEDIUM
He helps you solve your problems as fast as can be.
Seducing your loved one, protection against evil, diseases, intimacy problems, bewitching, spouse fidelity, happiness, luck, and special cases.
DISCREET SERIOUS WORK
100% SATISFACTION
ll : 98 56 77

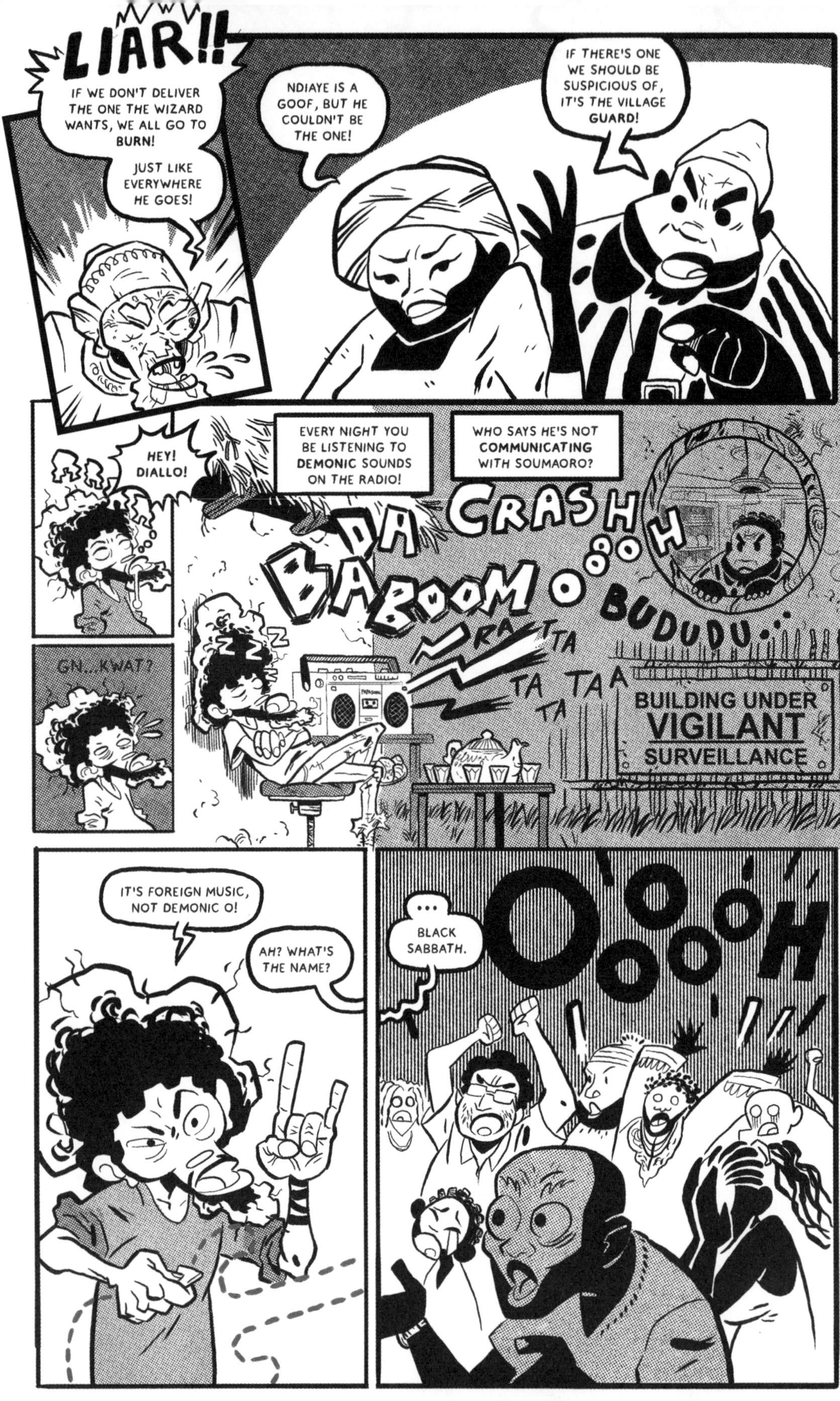
LIAR!!
IF WE DON'T DELIVER THE ONE THE WIZARD WANTS, WE ALL GO TO BURN!
JUST LIKE EVERYWHERE HE GOES!
NDIAYE IS A GOOF, BUT HE COULDN'T BE THE ONE!
IF THERE'S ONE WE SHOULD BE SUSPICIOUS OF, IT'S THE VILLAGE GUARD!
HEY! DIALLO!
EVERY NIGHT YOU BE LISTENING TO DEMONIC SOUNDS ON THE RADIO!
WHO SAYS HE'S NOT COMMUNICATING WITH SOUMAORO?
CRASH
DA BABOOM
OOOOH
BUDUDU...
RATTA TA TA TAA
BUILDING UNDER VIGILANT SURVEILLANCE
GN...KWAT?
IT'S FOREIGN MUSIC, NOT DEMONIC O!
AH? WHAT'S THE NAME?
...
BLACK SABBATH.
OOOOOOH

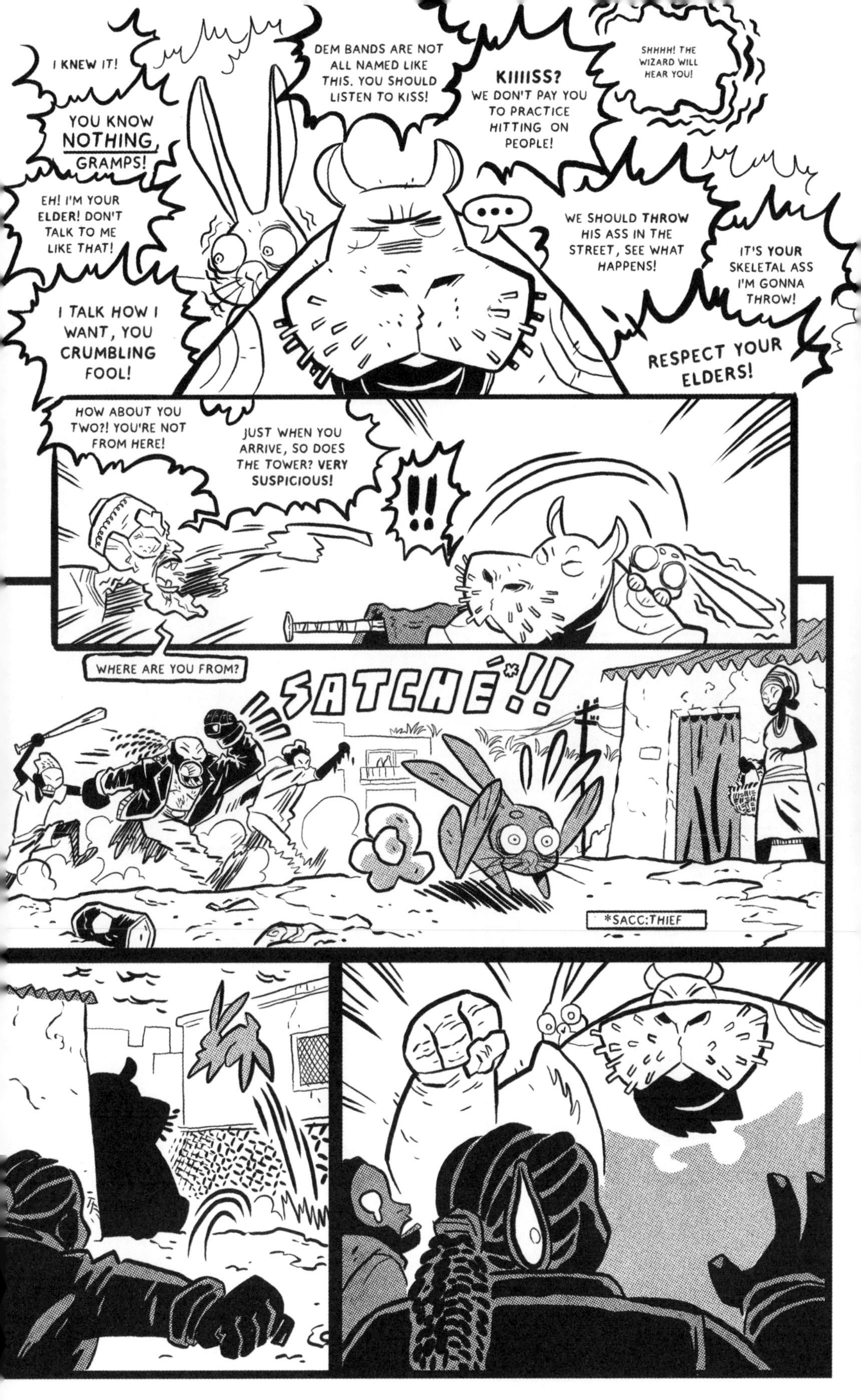

I KNEW IT!
YOU KNOW NOTHING, GRAMPS!
EH! I'M YOUR ELDER! DON'T TALK TO ME LIKE THAT!
I TALK HOW I WANT, YOU CRUMBLING FOOL!
DEM BANDS ARE NOT ALL NAMED LIKE THIS. YOU SHOULD LISTEN TO KISS!
KIIIISS? WE DON'T PAY YOU TO PRACTICE HITTING ON PEOPLE!
SHHHH! THE WIZARD WILL HEAR YOU!
...
WE SHOULD THROW HIS ASS IN THE STREET, SEE WHAT HAPPENS!
IT'S YOUR SKELETAL ASS I'M GONNA THROW!
RESPECT YOUR ELDERS!
HOW ABOUT YOU TWO?! YOU'RE NOT FROM HERE!
JUST WHEN YOU ARRIVE, SO DOES THE TOWER? VERY SUSPICIOUS!
!!
WHERE ARE YOU FROM?
SATCHÉ*!!
*SACC:THIEF

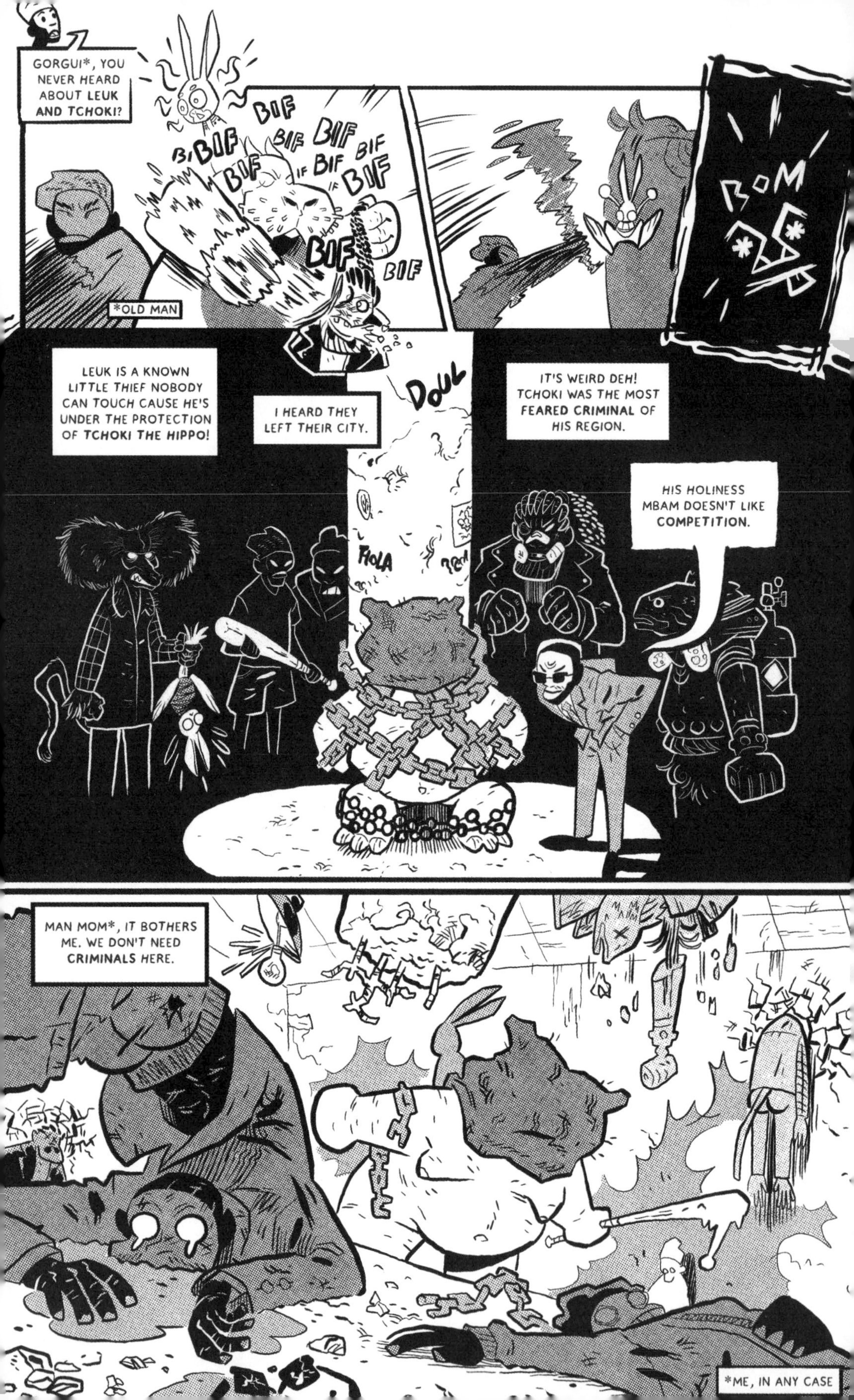
GORGUI*, YOU NEVER HEARD ABOUT LEUK AND TCHOKI?
BIF BIF BI BIF BIF BIF BIF BIF IF BIF BIF IF BIF BIF BIF
*OLD MAN
BOM
LEUK IS A KNOWN LITTLE THIEF NOBODY CAN TOUCH CAUSE HE'S UNDER THE PROTECTION OF TCHOKI THE HIPPO!
I HEARD THEY LEFT THEIR CITY.
DOUL
IT'S WEIRD DEH! TCHOKI WAS THE MOST FEARED CRIMINAL OF HIS REGION.
HIS HOLINESS MBAM DOESN'T LIKE COMPETITION.
MAN MOM*, IT BOTHERS ME. WE DON'T NEED CRIMINALS HERE.
*ME, IN ANY CASE

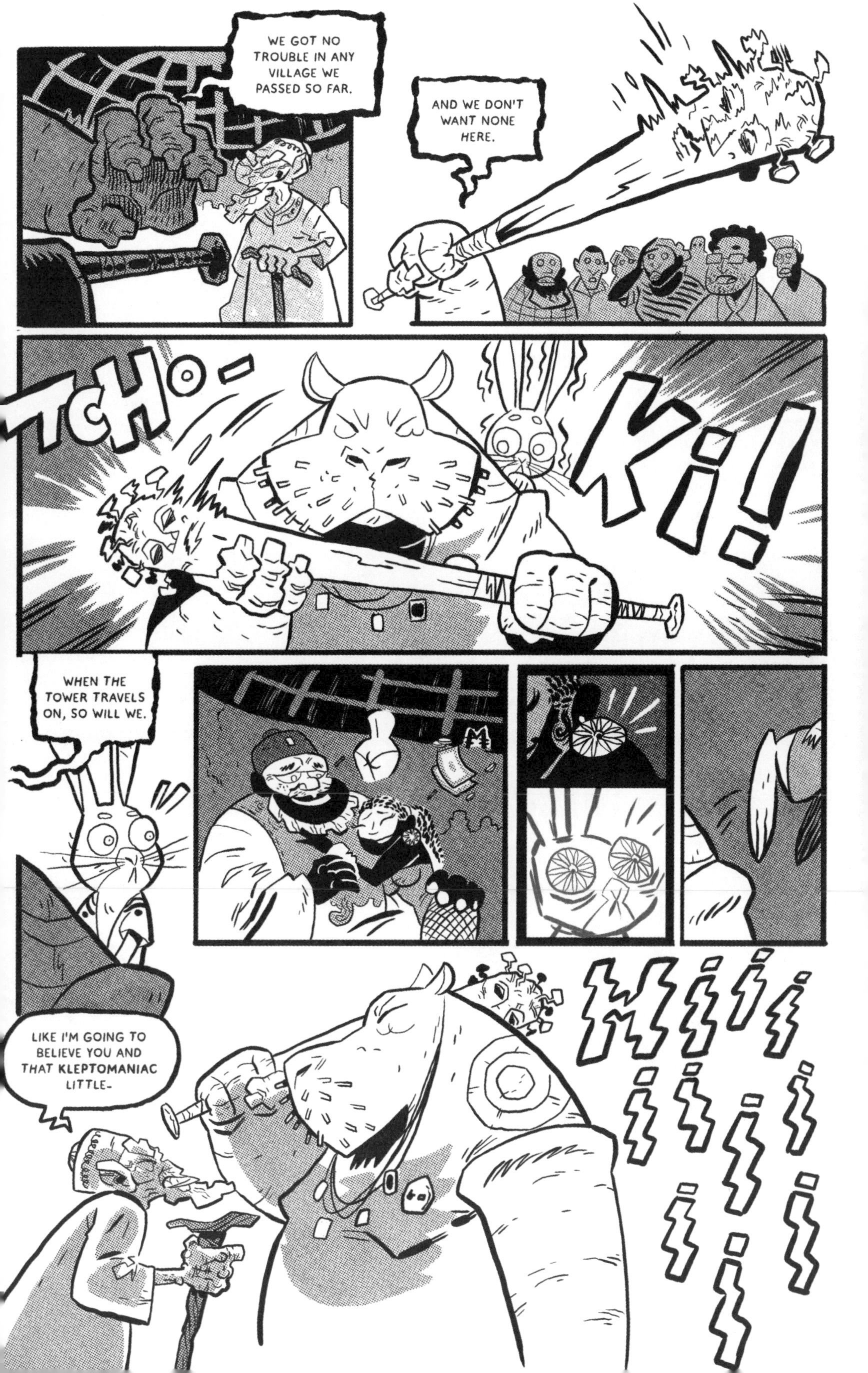
WE GOT NO TROUBLE IN ANY VILLAGE WE PASSED SO FAR.
AND WE DON'T WANT NONE HERE.
TCHO-
KI!!
WHEN THE TOWER TRAVELS ON, SO WILL WE.
LIKE I'M GOING TO BELIEVE YOU AND THAT KLEPTOMANIAC LITTLE-
Hiiiiiiiiiiii

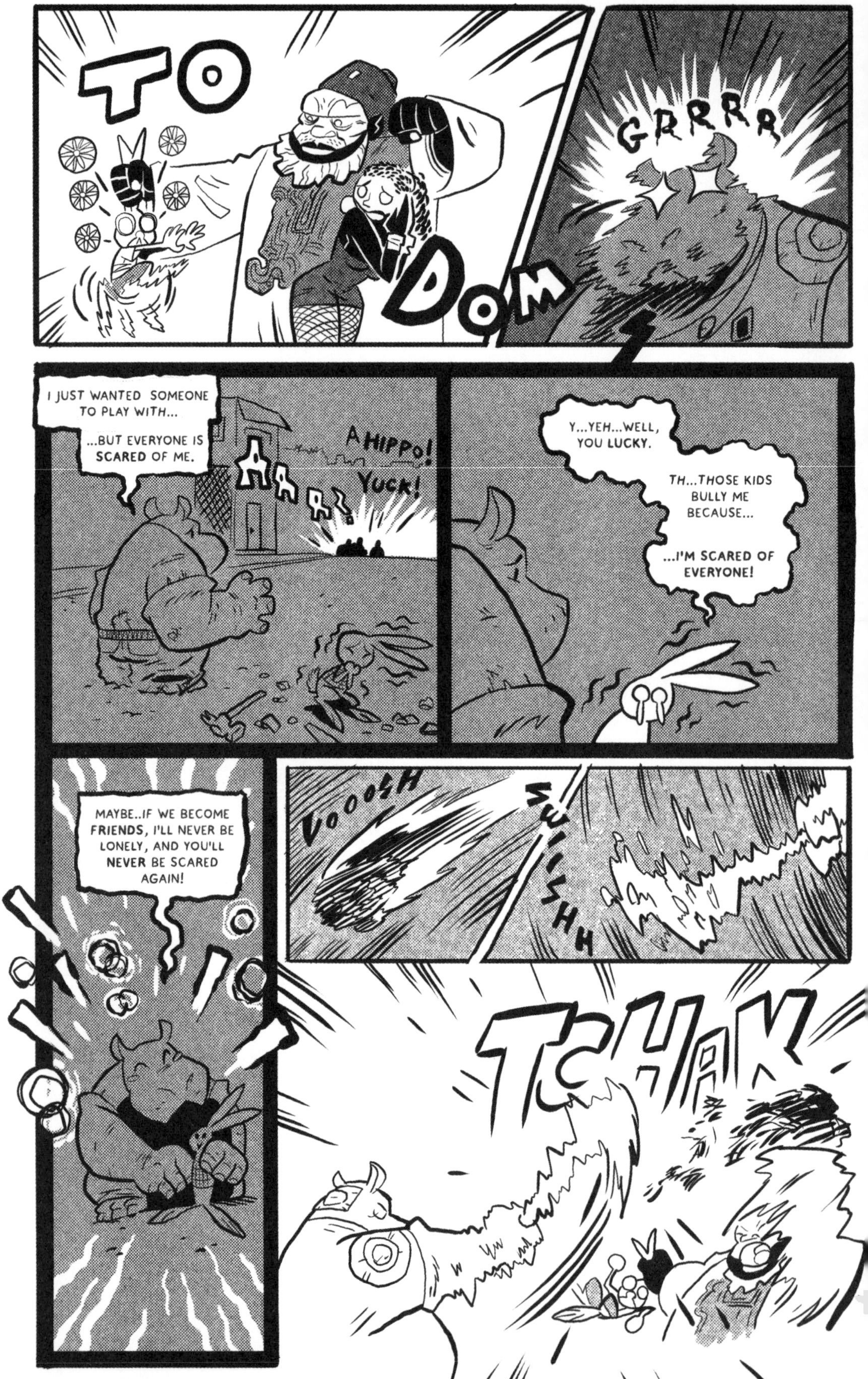
TO
DOM
GRRRR
I JUST WANTED SOMEONE TO PLAY WITH...
...BUT EVERYONE IS SCARED OF ME.
A HIPPO!
AAAA
YUCK!
Y...YEH...WELL, YOU LUCKY.
TH...THOSE KIDS BULLY ME BECAUSE...
...I'M SCARED OF EVERYONE!
MAYBE..IF WE BECOME FRIENDS, I'LL NEVER BE LONELY, AND YOU'LL NEVER BE SCARED AGAIN!
VOOOSH
SWISHH
TCHAK

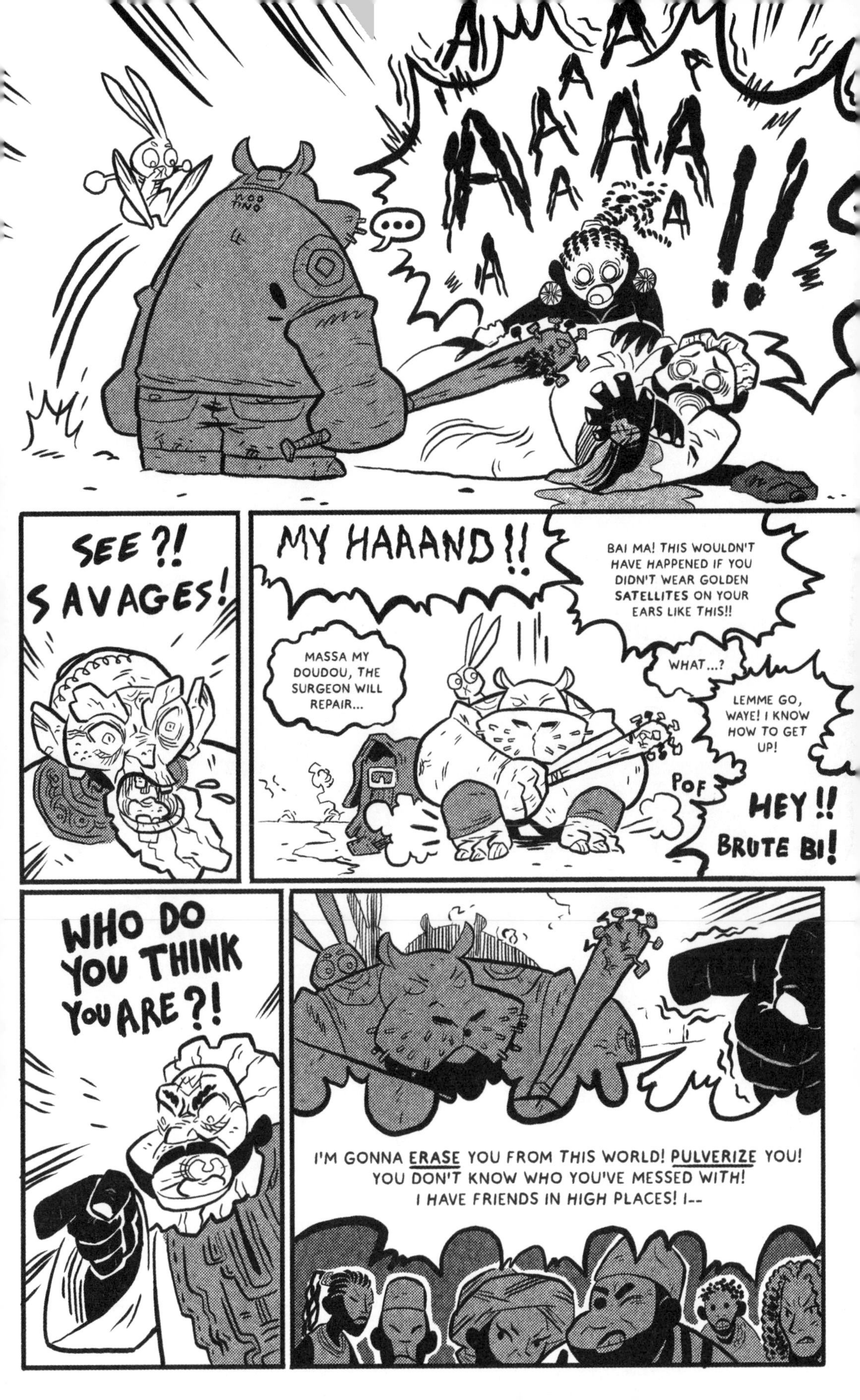
AAAAAAAAAA!!
...
SEE?! SAVAGES!
MY HAAAND!!
BAI MA! THIS WOULDN'T HAVE HAPPENED IF YOU DIDN'T WEAR GOLDEN SATELLITES ON YOUR EARS LIKE THIS!!
MASSA MY DOUDOU, THE SURGEON WILL REPAIR...
WHAT...?
LEMME GO, WAYE! I KNOW HOW TO GET UP!
POF
HEY!! BRUTE BI!
WHO DO YOU THINK YOU ARE?!
I'M GONNA ERASE YOU FROM THIS WORLD! PULVERIZE YOU! YOU DON'T KNOW WHO YOU'VE MESSED WITH! I HAVE FRIENDS IN HIGH PLACES! I--

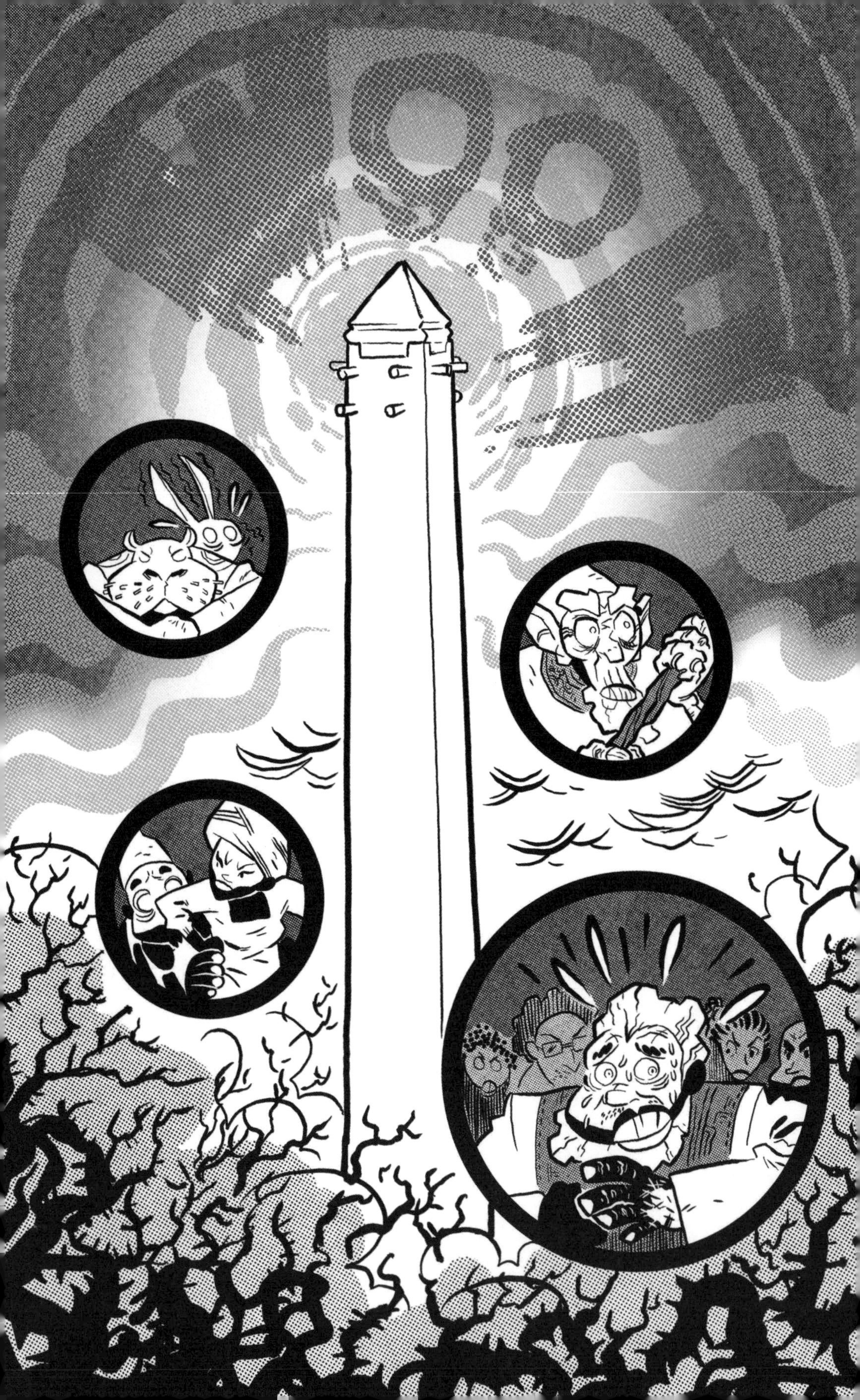

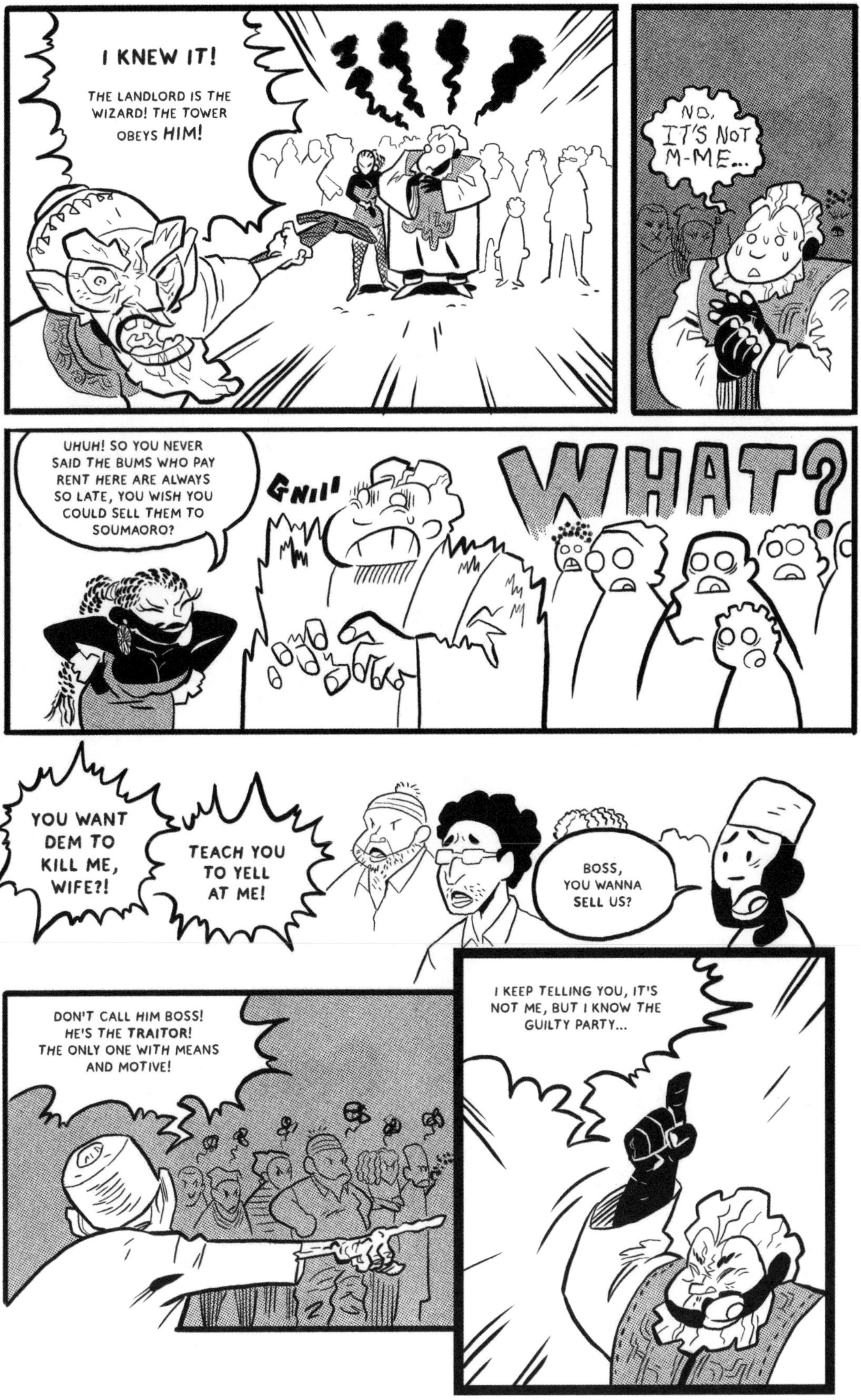
I KNEW IT!
THE LANDLORD IS THE WIZARD! THE TOWER OBEYS HIM!
NO, IT'S NOT M-ME...
UHUH! SO YOU NEVER SAID THE BUMS WHO PAY RENT HERE ARE ALWAYS SO LATE, YOU WISH YOU COULD SELL THEM TO SOUMAORO?
GNIII
WHAT?
YOU WANT DEM TO KILL ME, WIFE?!
TEACH YOU TO YELL AT ME!
BOSS, YOU WANNA SELL US?
DON'T CALL HIM BOSS! HE'S THE TRAITOR! THE ONLY ONE WITH MEANS AND MOTIVE!
I KEEP TELLING YOU, IT'S NOT ME, BUT I KNOW THE GUILTY PARTY...

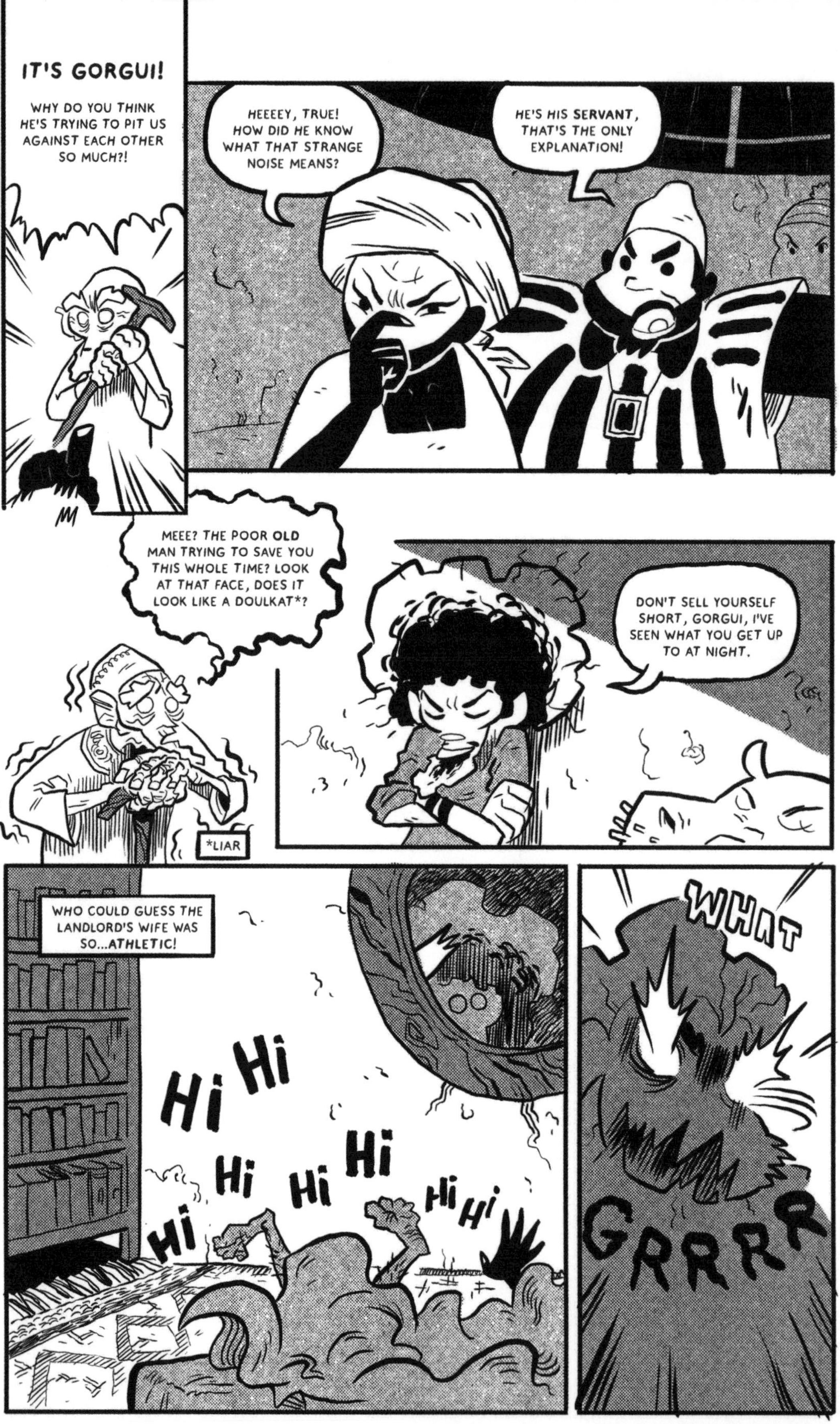
IT'S GORGUI!
WHY DO YOU THINK HE'S TRYING TO PIT US AGAINST EACH OTHER SO MUCH?!
HEEEEY, TRUE! HOW DID HE KNOW WHAT THAT STRANGE NOISE MEANS?
HE'S HIS SERVANT, THAT'S THE ONLY EXPLANATION!
MEEE? THE POOR OLD MAN TRYING TO SAVE YOU THIS WHOLE TIME? LOOK AT THAT FACE, DOES IT LOOK LIKE A DOULKAT*?
*LIAR
DON'T SELL YOURSELF SHORT, GORGUI, I'VE SEEN WHAT YOU GET UP TO AT NIGHT.
WHO COULD GUESS THE LANDLORD'S WIFE WAS SO...ATHLETIC!
Hi Hi
Hi Hi Hi Hi Hi Hi Hi
WHAT
GRRRRR

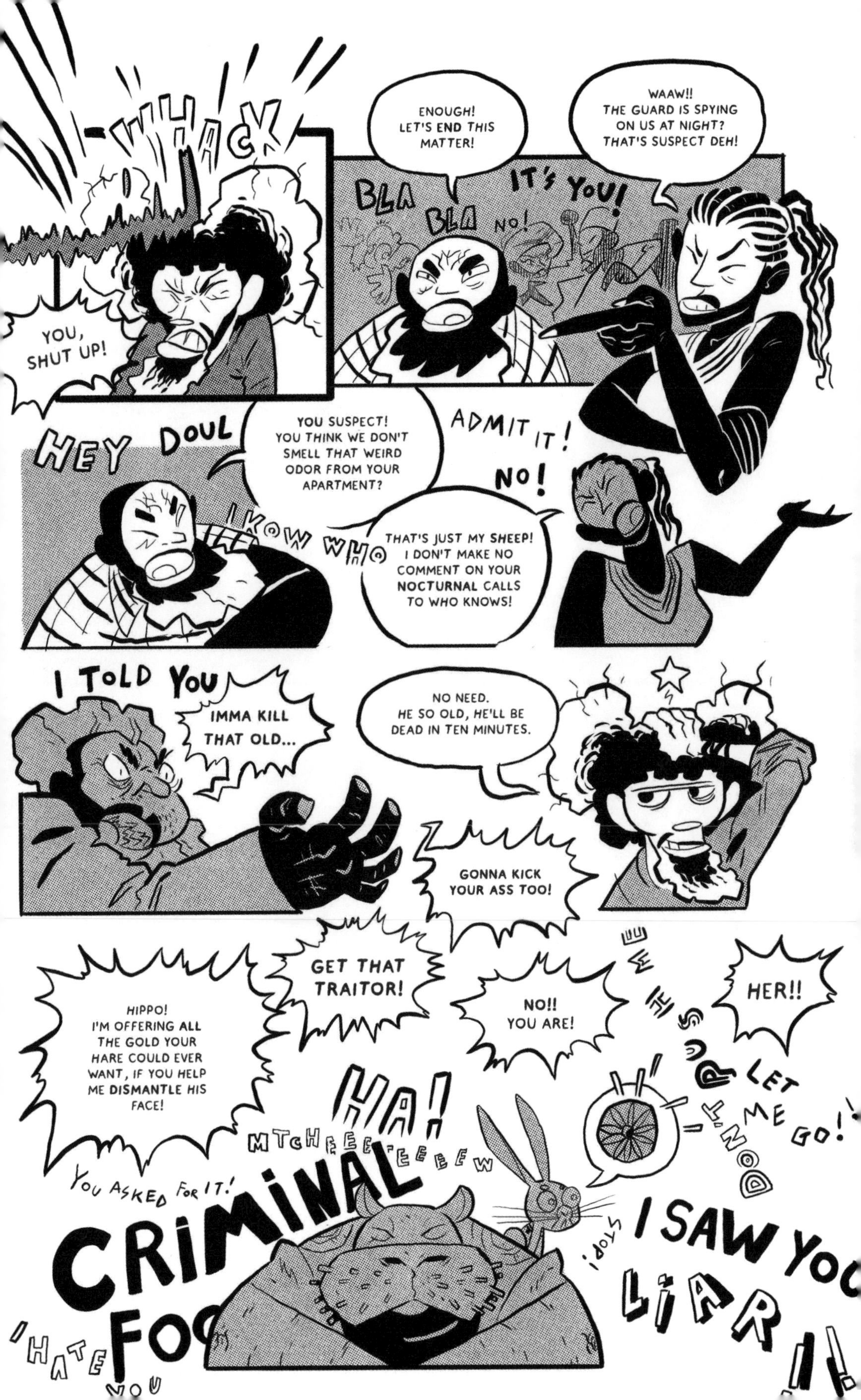
WHACK
YOU, SHUT UP!
ENOUGH! LET'S END THIS MATTER!
WAAW!! THE GUARD IS SPYING ON US AT NIGHT? THAT'S SUSPECT DEH!
BLA BLA
NO!
IT'S YOU!
HEY DOUL
YOU SUSPECT! YOU THINK WE DON'T SMELL THAT WEIRD ODOR FROM YOUR APARTMENT?
ADMIT IT!
NO!
IKOW WHO
THAT'S JUST MY SHEEP! I DON'T MAKE NO COMMENT ON YOUR NOCTURNAL CALLS TO WHO KNOWS!
I TOLD YOU
IMMA KILL THAT OLD...
NO NEED. HE SO OLD, HE'LL BE DEAD IN TEN MINUTES.
GONNA KICK YOUR ASS TOO!
HIPPO! I'M OFFERING ALL THE GOLD YOUR HARE COULD EVER WANT, IF YOU HELP ME DISMANTLE HIS FACE!
GET THAT TRAITOR!
NO!! YOU ARE!
HER!!
HA!
MTCHEEEEEEEEEW
LET ME GO!!
YOU ASKED FOR IT!
CRIMINAL
STOP!
I SAW YOU
LIAR!!
I HATE YOU

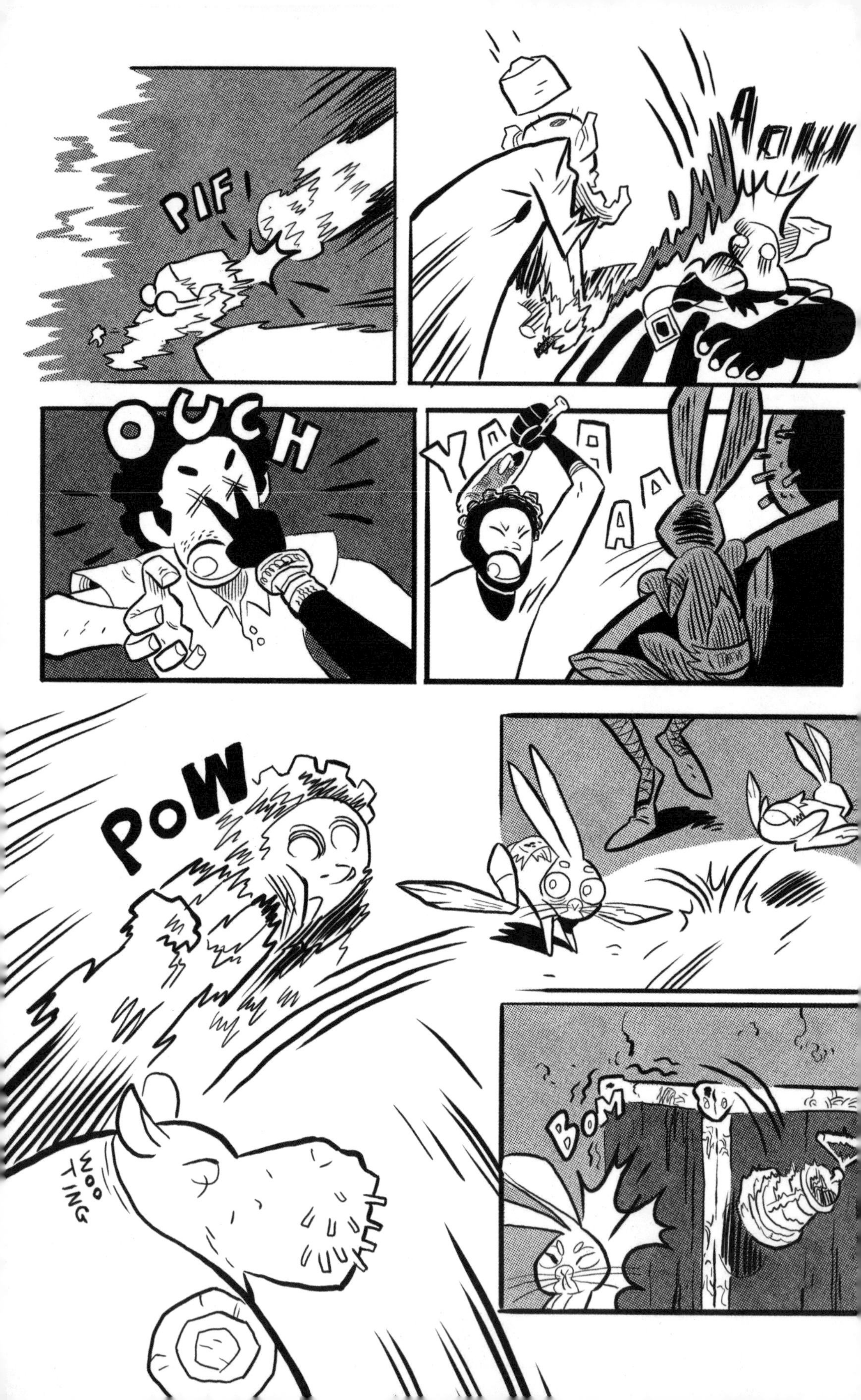
PIF
AOHH
OUCH
YAAAAA
POW
WOO TING
BOM

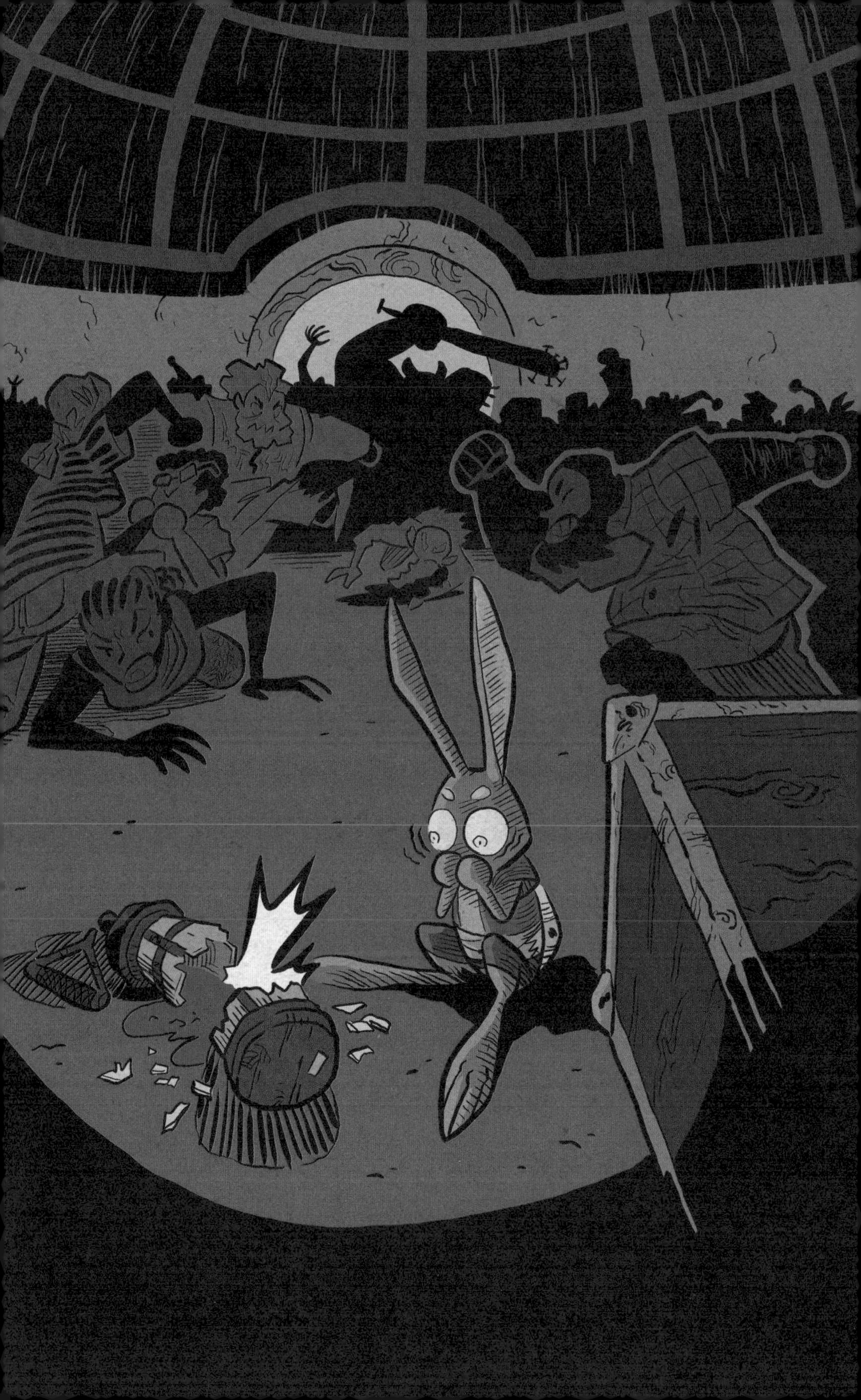

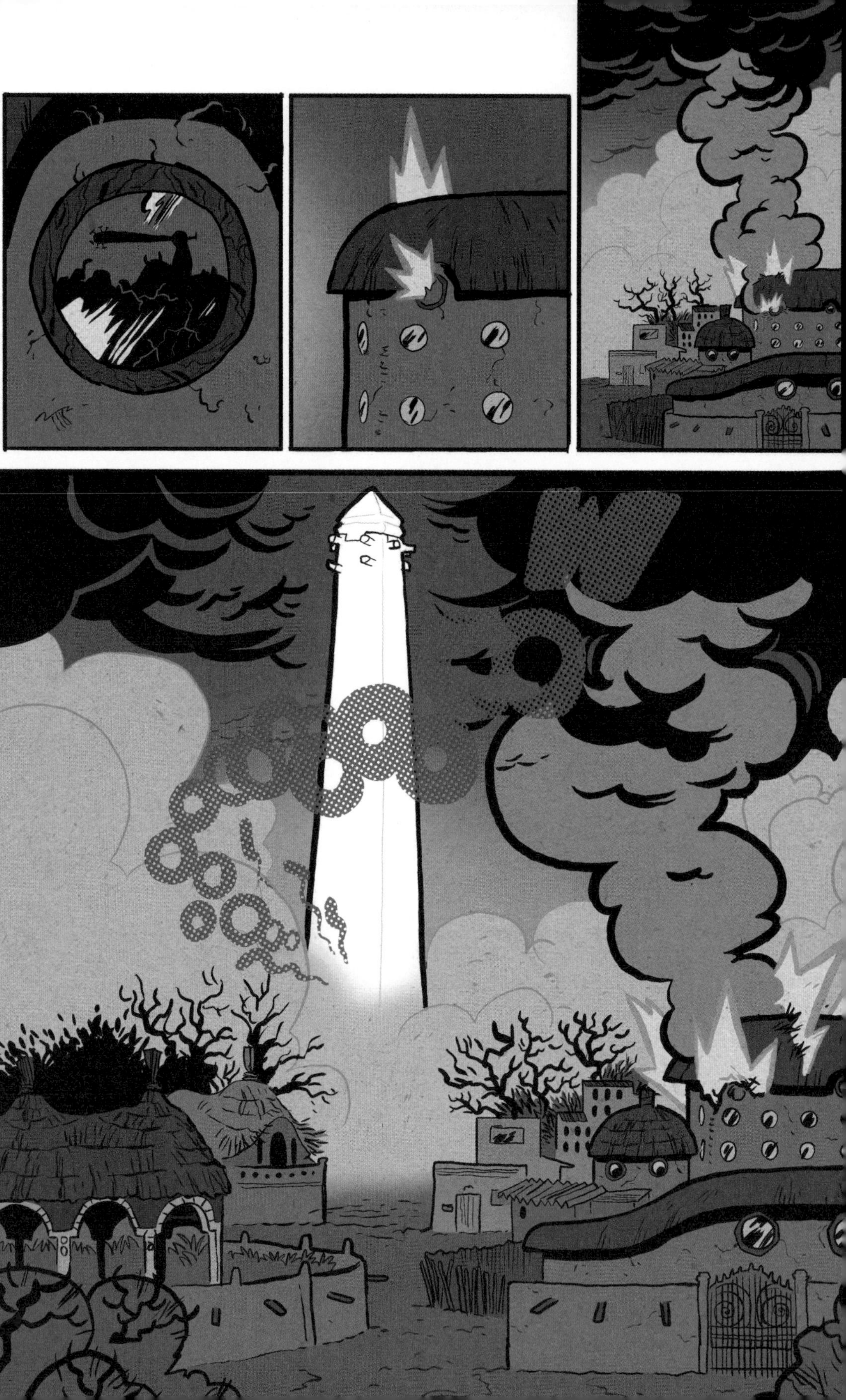

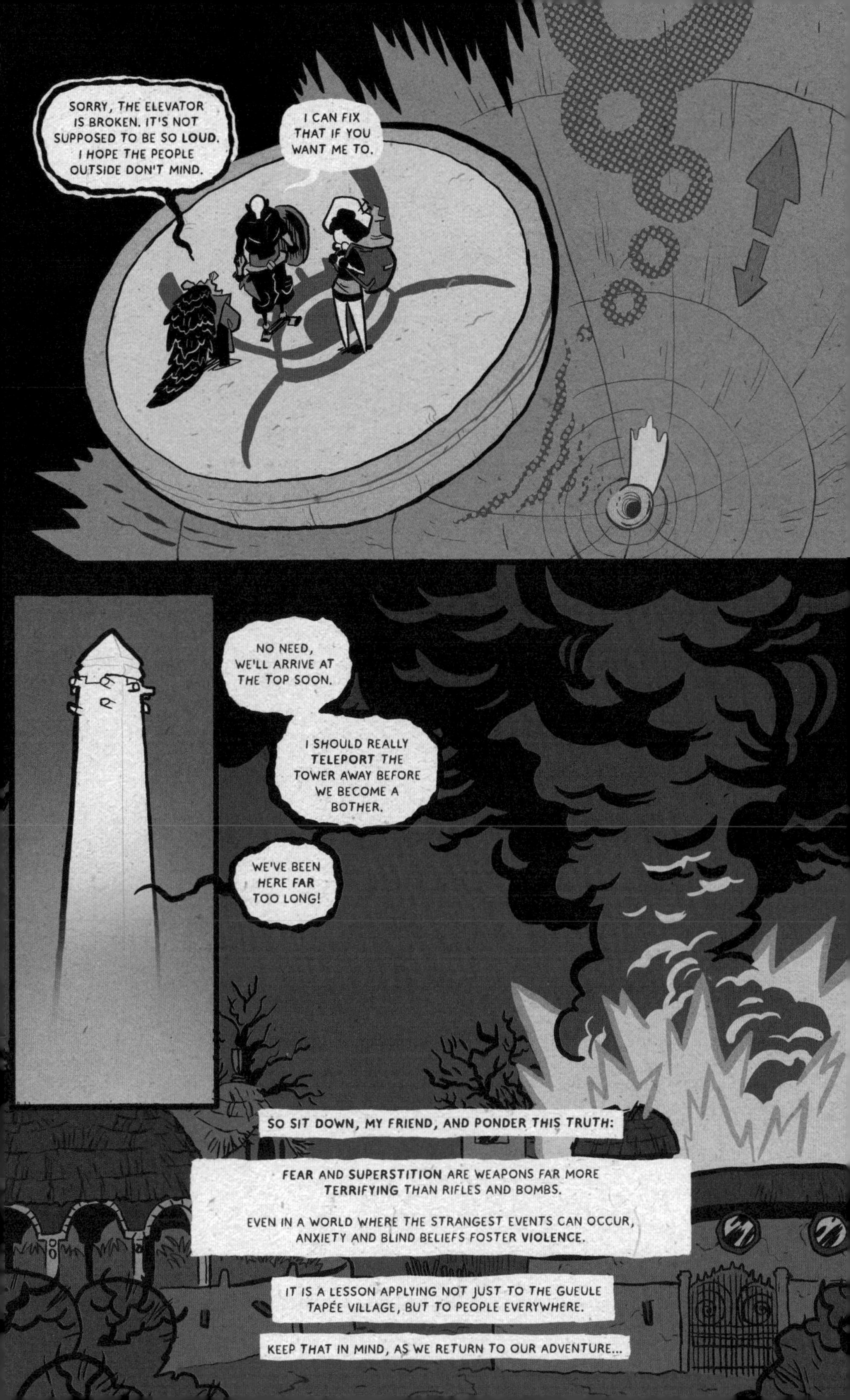
SORRY, THE ELEVATOR IS BROKEN. IT'S NOT SUPPOSED TO BE SO LOUD. I HOPE THE PEOPLE OUTSIDE DON'T MIND.
I CAN FIX THAT IF YOU WANT ME TO.
NO NEED, WE'LL ARRIVE AT THE TOP SOON.
I SHOULD REALLY TELEPORT THE TOWER AWAY BEFORE WE BECOME A BOTHER.
WE'VE BEEN HERE FAR TOO LONG!
SO SIT DOWN, MY FRIEND, AND PONDER THIS TRUTH:
FEAR AND SUPERSTITION ARE WEAPONS FAR MORE TERRIFYING THAN RIFLES AND BOMBS.
EVEN IN A WORLD WHERE THE STRANGEST EVENTS CAN OCCUR, ANXIETY AND BLIND BELIEFS FOSTER VIOLENCE.
IT IS A LESSON APPLYING NOT JUST TO THE GUEULE TAPÉE VILLAGE, BUT TO PEOPLE EVERYWHERE.
KEEP THAT IN MIND, AS WE RETURN TO OUR ADVENTURE...

IV

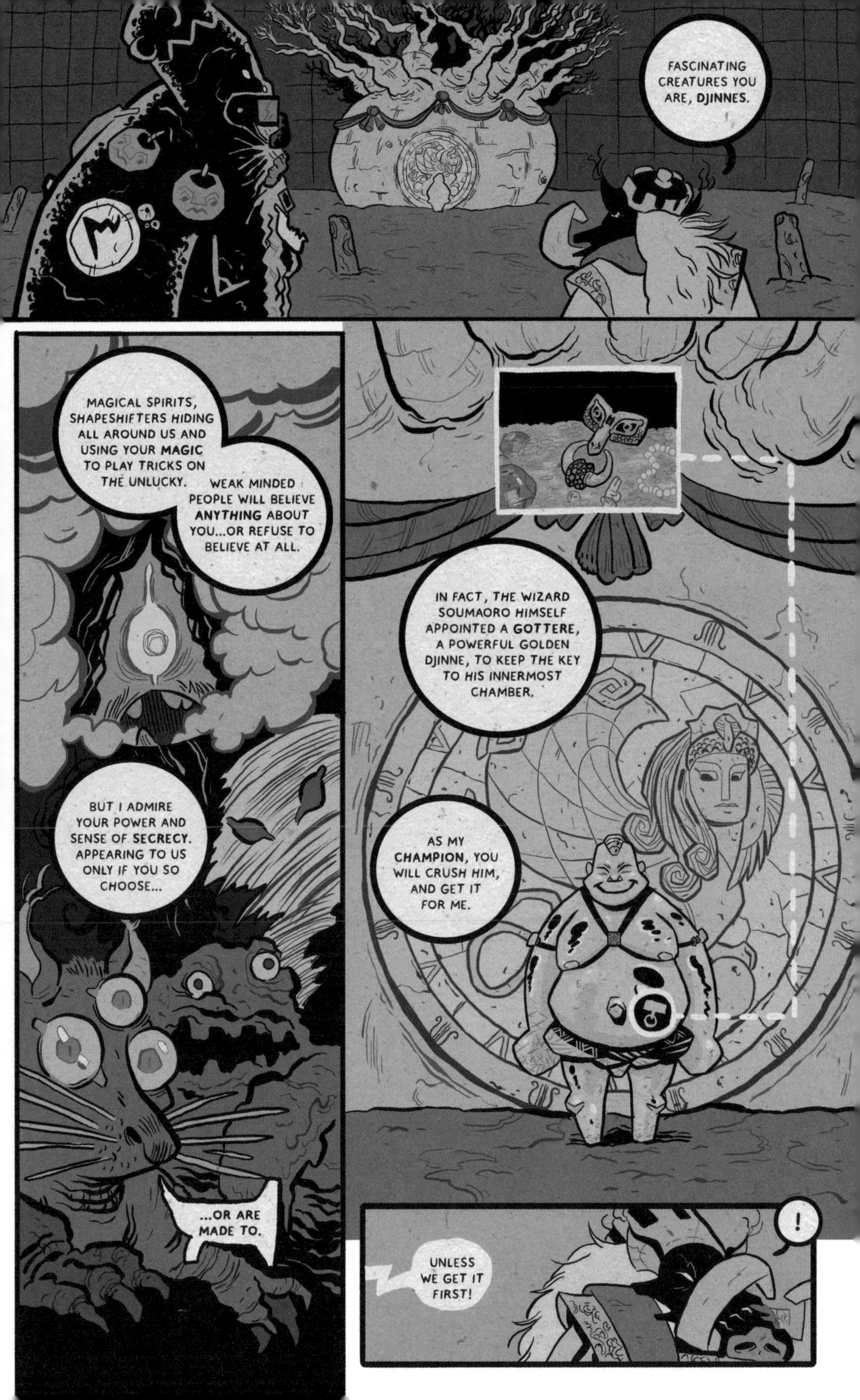
FASCINATING CREATURES YOU ARE, DJINNES.
MAGICAL SPIRITS, SHAPESHIFTERS HIDING ALL AROUND US AND USING YOUR MAGIC TO PLAY TRICKS ON THE UNLUCKY.
WEAK MINDED PEOPLE WILL BELIEVE ANYTHING ABOUT YOU...OR REFUSE TO BELIEVE AT ALL.
BUT I ADMIRE YOUR POWER AND SENSE OF SECRECY. APPEARING TO US ONLY IF YOU SO CHOOSE...
...OR ARE MADE TO.
IN FACT, THE WIZARD SOUMAORO HIMSELF APPOINTED A GOTTERE, A POWERFUL GOLDEN DJINNE, TO KEEP THE KEY TO HIS INNERMOST CHAMBER.
AS MY CHAMPION, YOU WILL CRUSH HIM, AND GET IT FOR ME.
UNLESS WE GET IT FIRST!
!

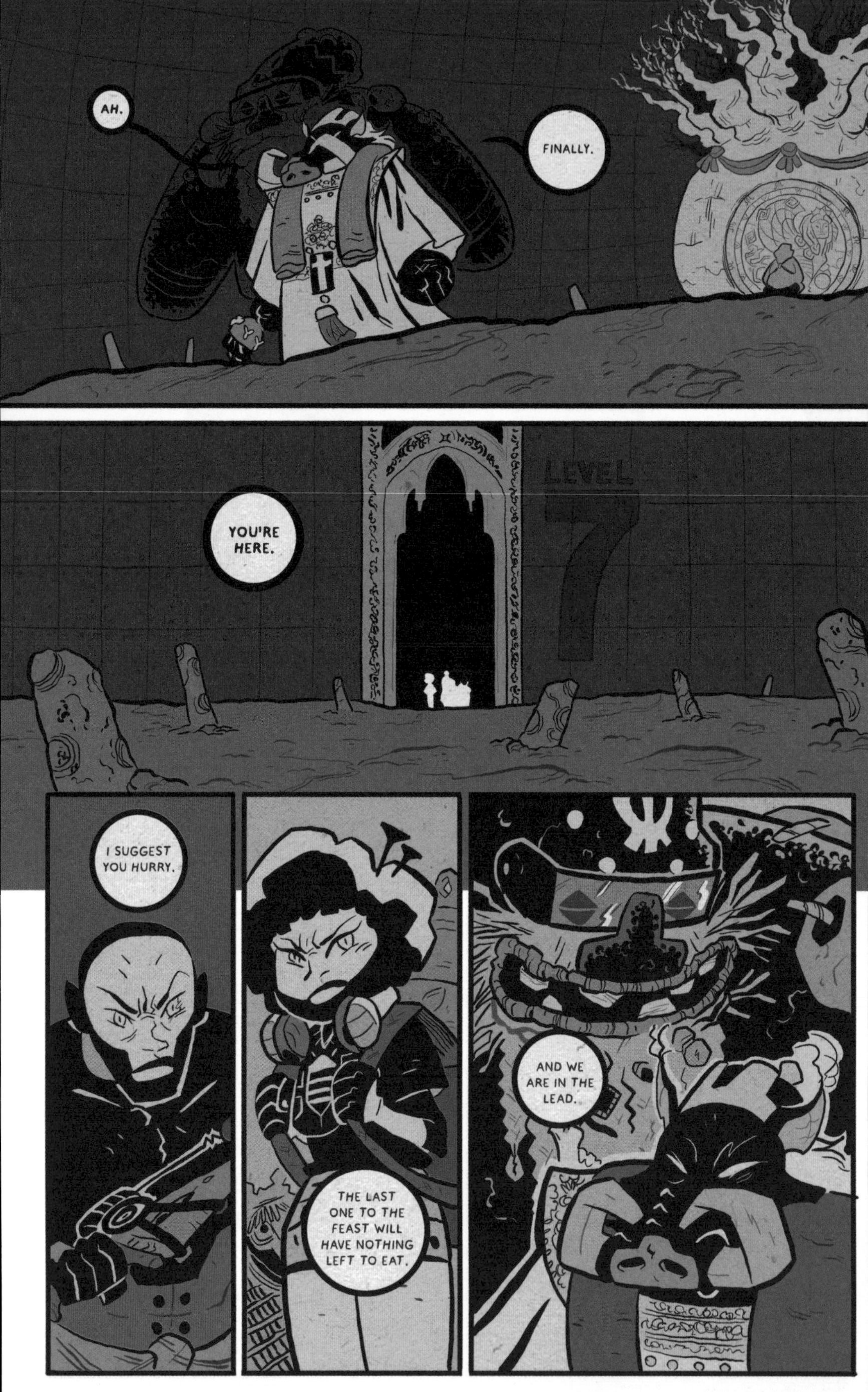
AH.
FINALLY.
YOU'RE HERE.
LEVEL 7
I SUGGEST YOU HURRY.
THE LAST ONE TO THE FEAST WILL HAVE NOTHING LEFT TO EAT.
AND WE ARE IN THE LEAD.

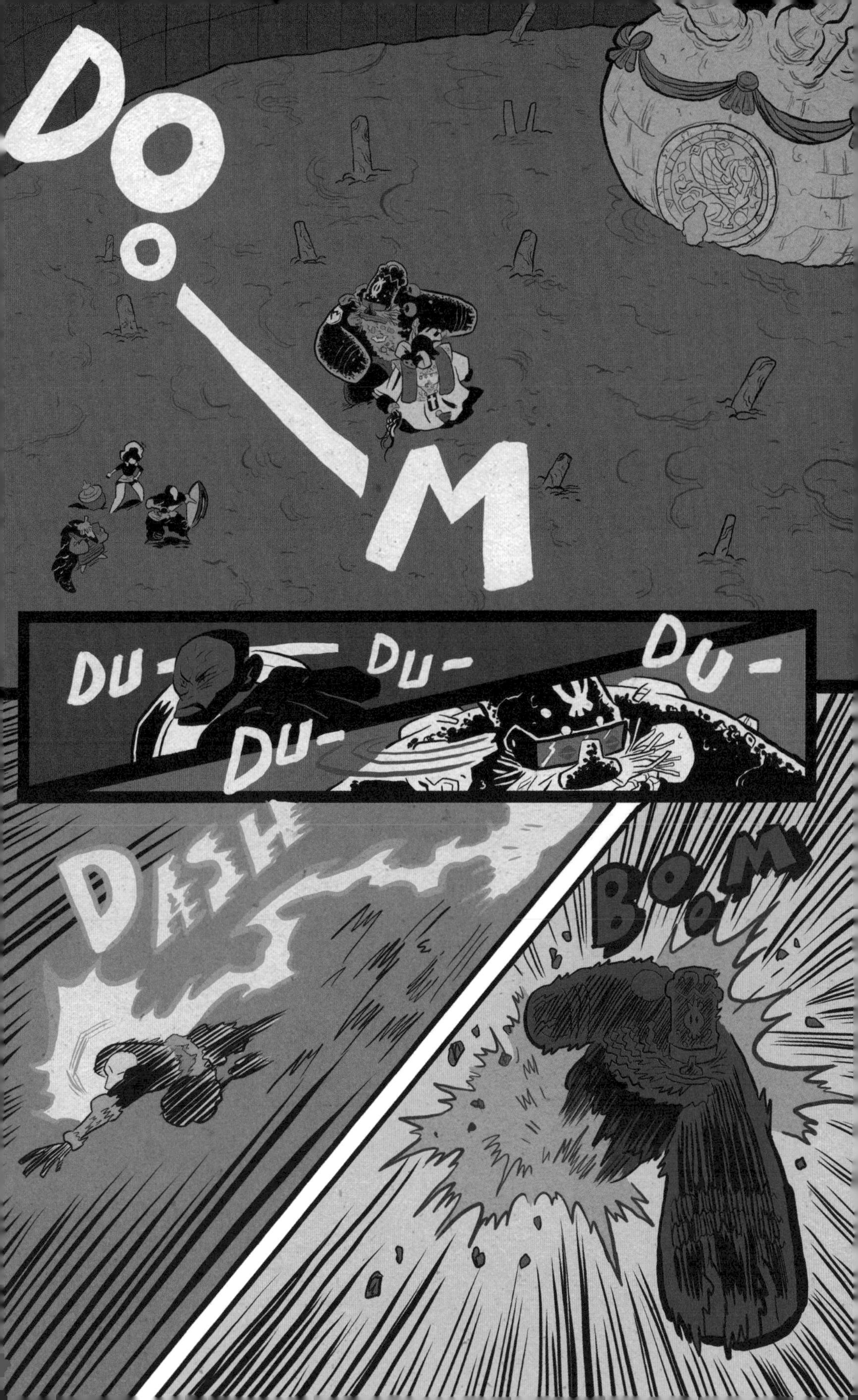
DOOOOM
DU- DU- DU- DU-
DASH
BOOOM

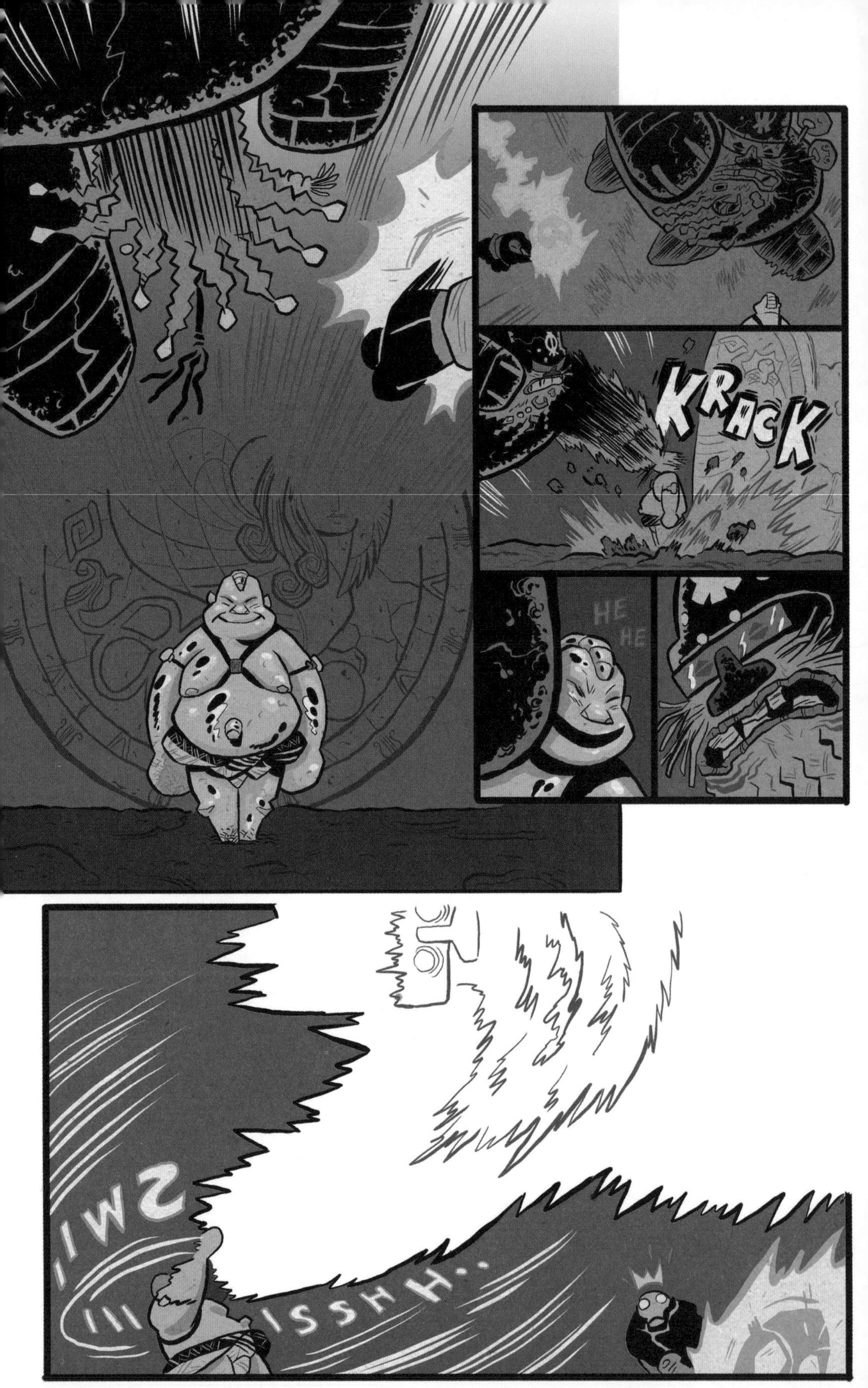
KRACK
HE HE
SWIIIIIISSHH..

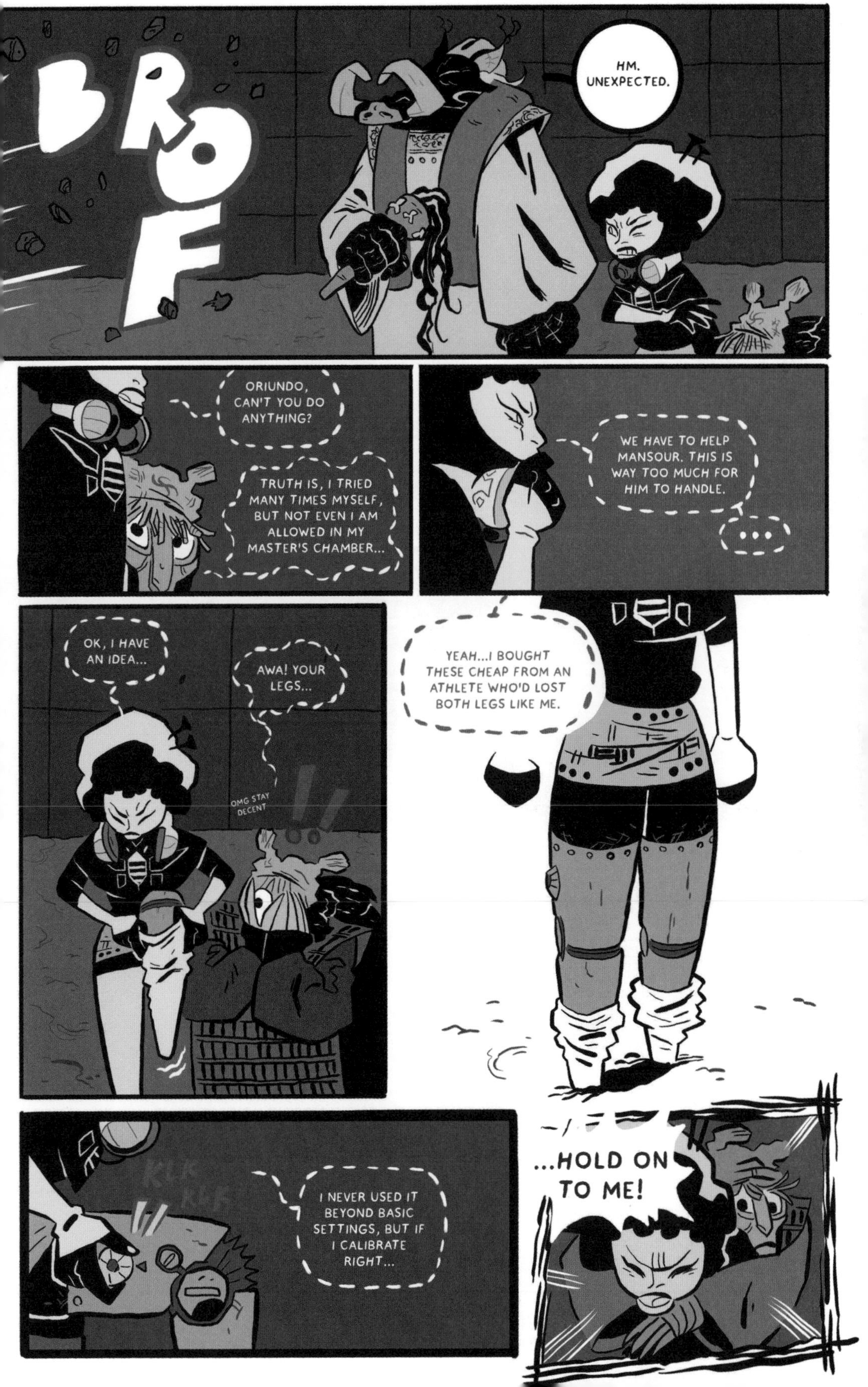
BROF
HM. UNEXPECTED.
ORIUNDO, CAN'T YOU DO ANYTHING?
TRUTH IS, I TRIED MANY TIMES MYSELF, BUT NOT EVEN I AM ALLOWED IN MY MASTER'S CHAMBER...
WE HAVE TO HELP MANSOUR. THIS IS WAY TOO MUCH FOR HIM TO HANDLE.
...
OK, I HAVE AN IDEA...
AWA! YOUR LEGS...
OMG STAY DECENT
YEAH...I BOUGHT THESE CHEAP FROM AN ATHLETE WHO'D LOST BOTH LEGS LIKE ME.
I NEVER USED IT BEYOND BASIC SETTINGS, BUT IF I CALIBRATE RIGHT...
...HOLD ON TO ME!

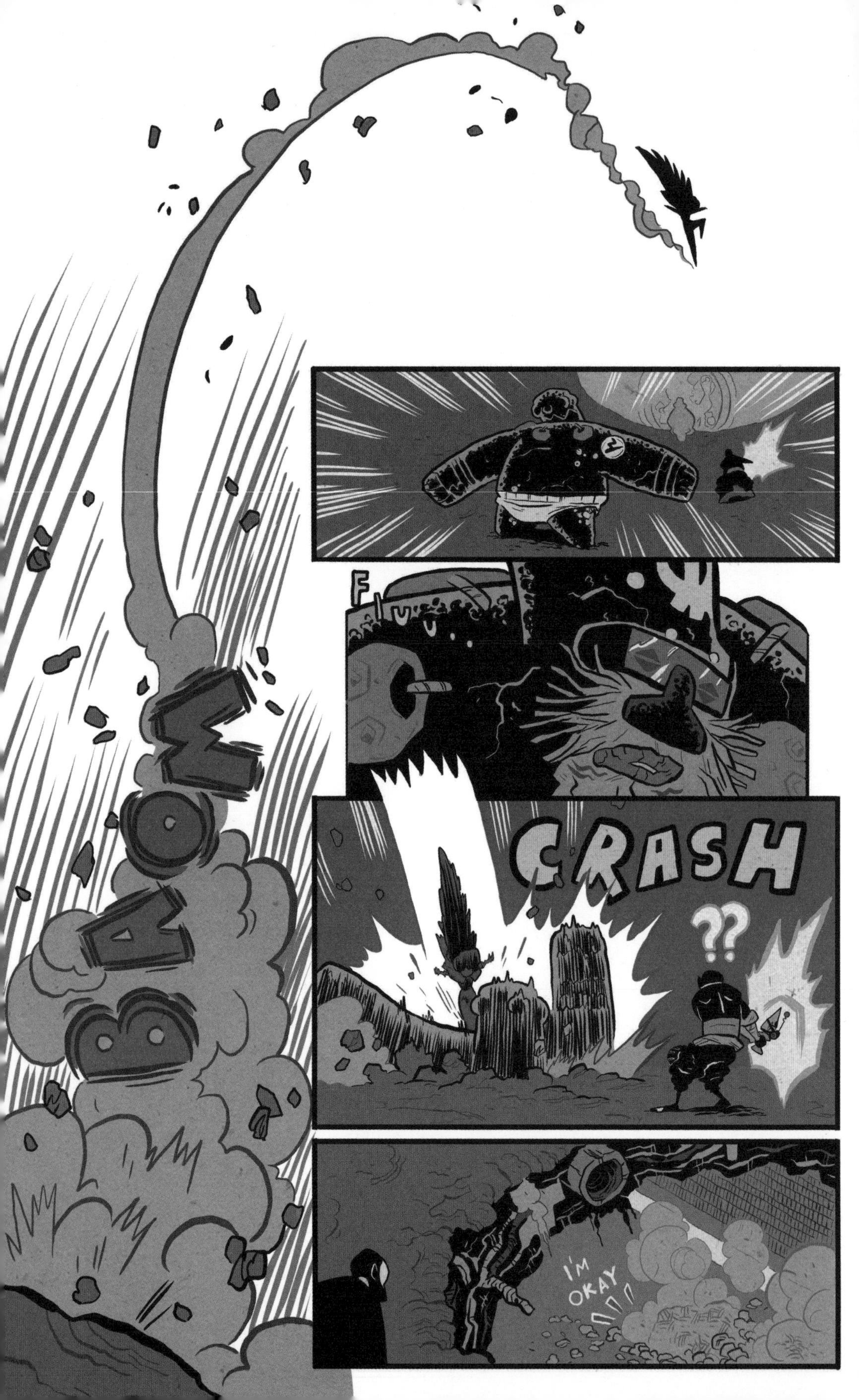
BAOOM
FIUU
CRASH
??
I'M OKAY

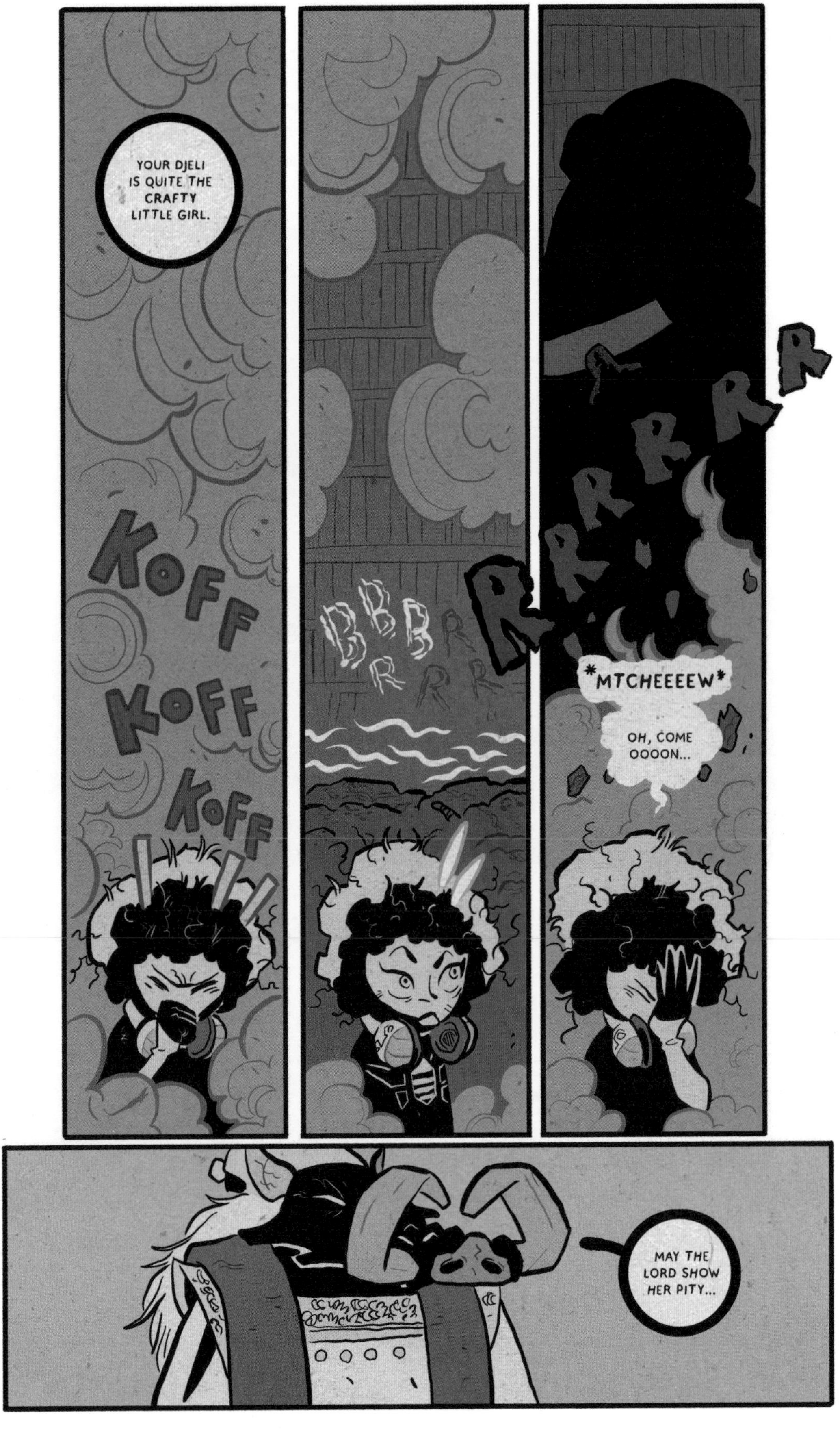
YOUR DJELI IS QUITE THE CRAFTY LITTLE GIRL.
KOFF KOFF KOFF
BBBRRRR
RRRRRRRRR
MTCHEEEEW
OH, COME OOOON...
MAY THE LORD SHOW HER PITY...

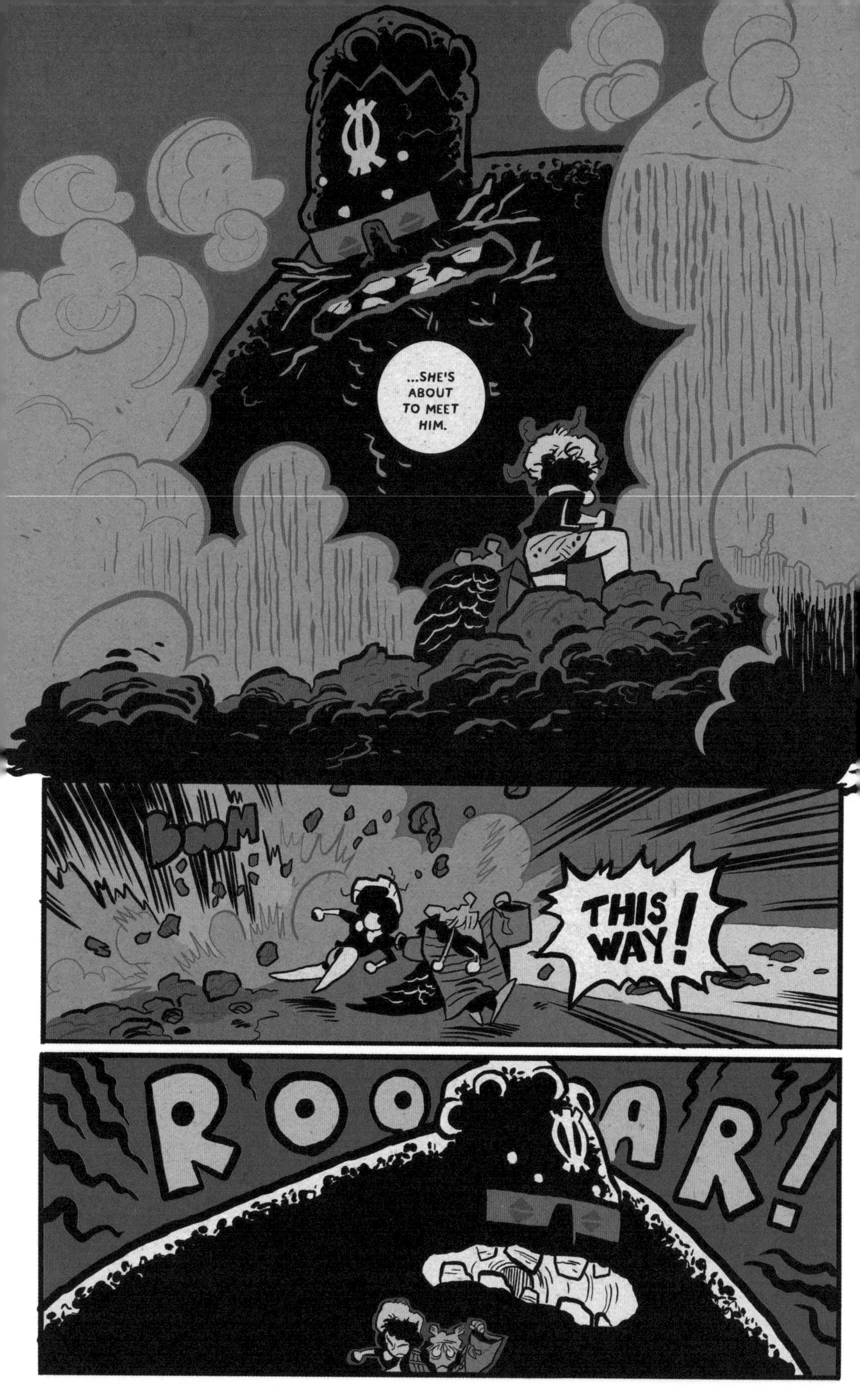
...SHE'S ABOUT TO MEET HIM.
BOOM
THIS WAY!
ROOAR!

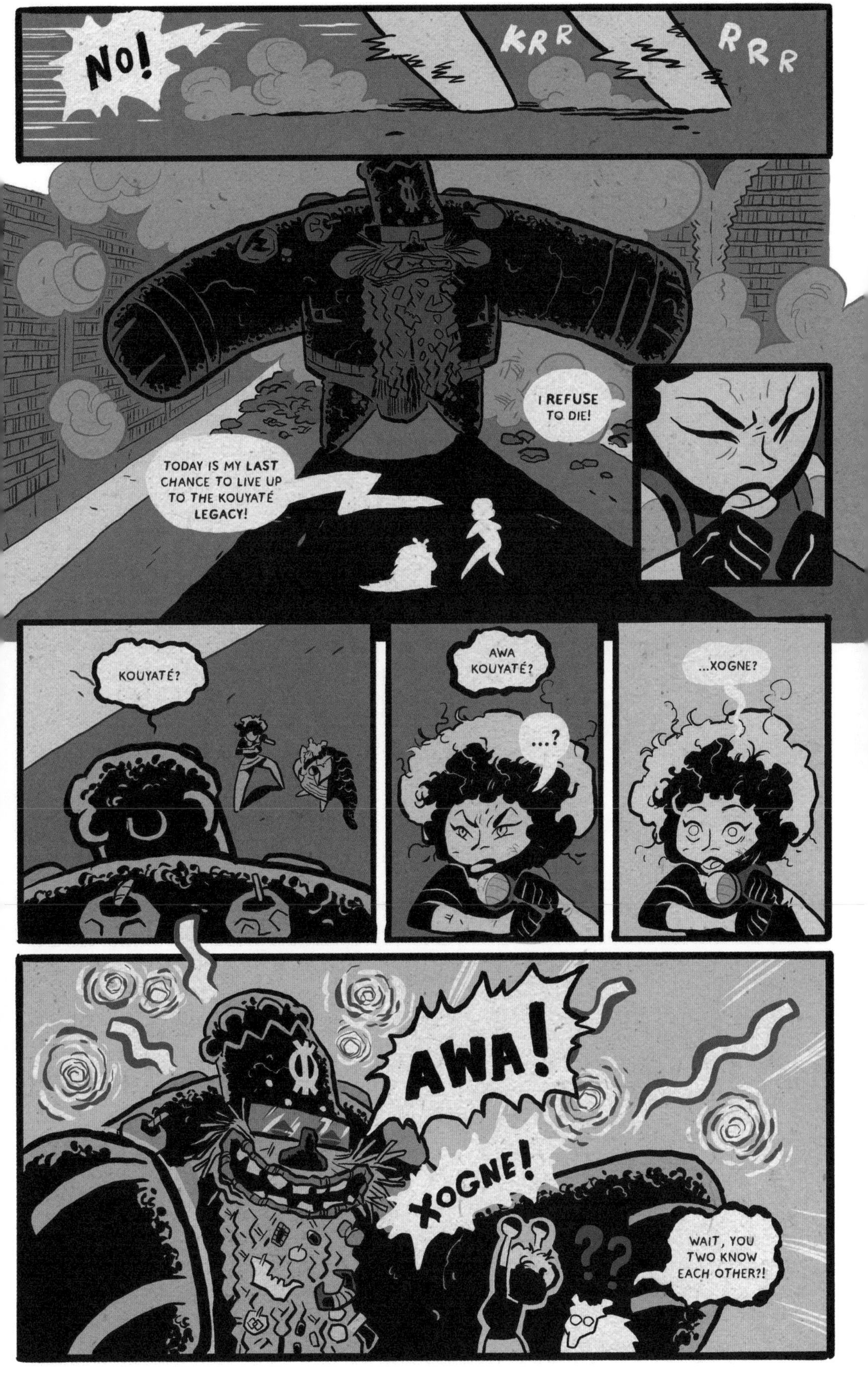
No!
KRRR
RRRR
I REFUSE TO DIE!
TODAY IS MY LAST CHANCE TO LIVE UP TO THE KOUYATÉ LEGACY!
KOUYATÉ?
AWA KOUYATÉ?
...?
...XOGNE?
AWA!
XOGNE!
??
WAIT, YOU TWO KNOW EACH OTHER?!

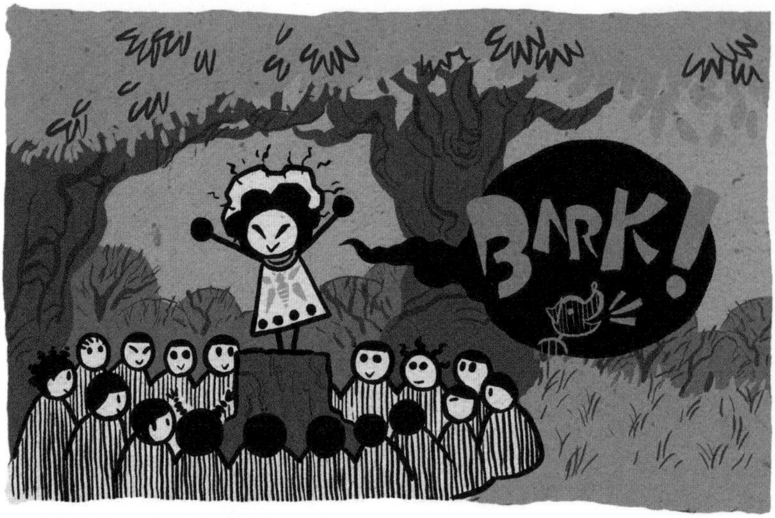
BARK!

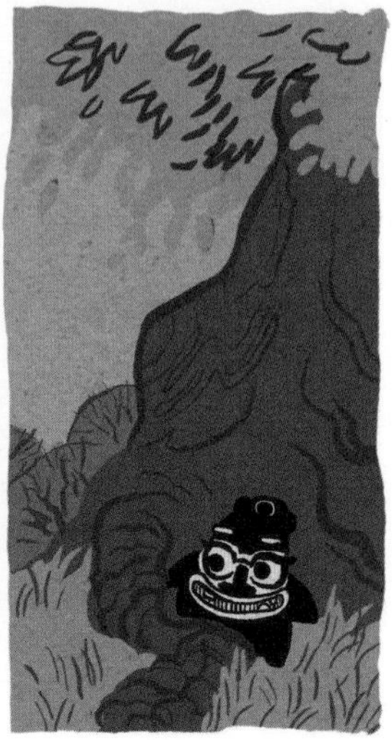

IN THE DAYS OF YORE, THERE WAS AN IMAGINATIVE LITTLE GIRL WHO LIKED TO TELL STORIES.

HER FAVORITE WAS A TALE SHE TOLD OF A LITTLE DJINNE WHO, LIKE ALL HIS KIN, WAS AFRAID OF BLACK DOGS. THE CHILDREN OF THE CITY WOULD GLADLY GATHER AROUND HER TO LISTEN TO HIS LATEST ADVENTURES...

...AND SO DID I. FOR YOU SEE, TO A FRETFUL, LONELY DJINNE, THESE STORIES FELT LIKE THEY WERE ABOUT ME!

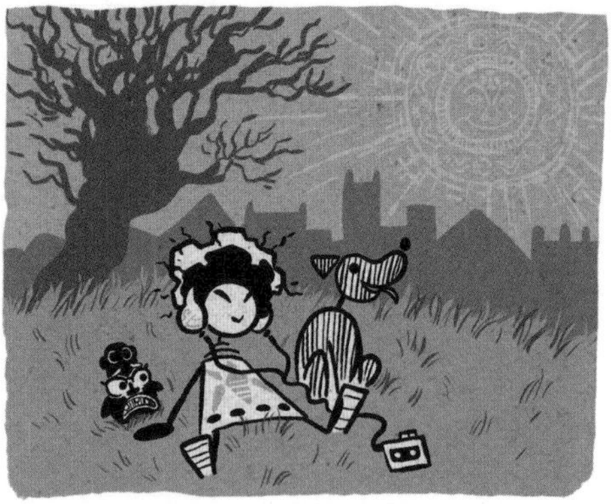

AND THAT IS WHY, FOR THE FIRST TIME, I LET A HUMAN SEE ME. SO WE COULD BE FRIENDS! EVEN THOUGH I WAS INDEED VERY SCARED OF HER FURRY MONSTER!

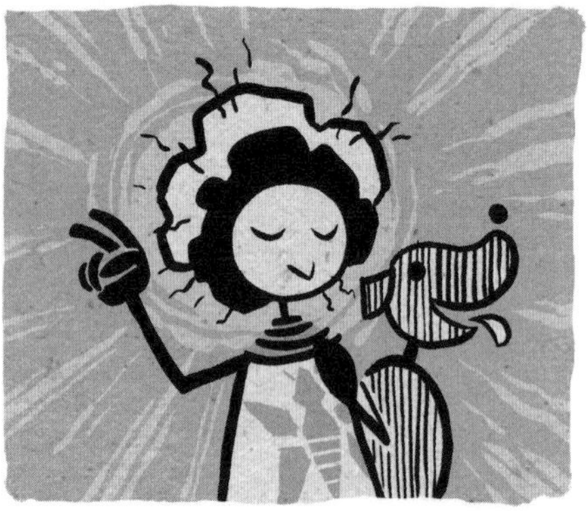

– *BUT DOGS ARE SO SWEET!* SAID AWA.

– *I WILL HELP YOU FIND OUT WHY YOU ARE SO SCARED, AND THE FEAR WILL GO AWAY!*

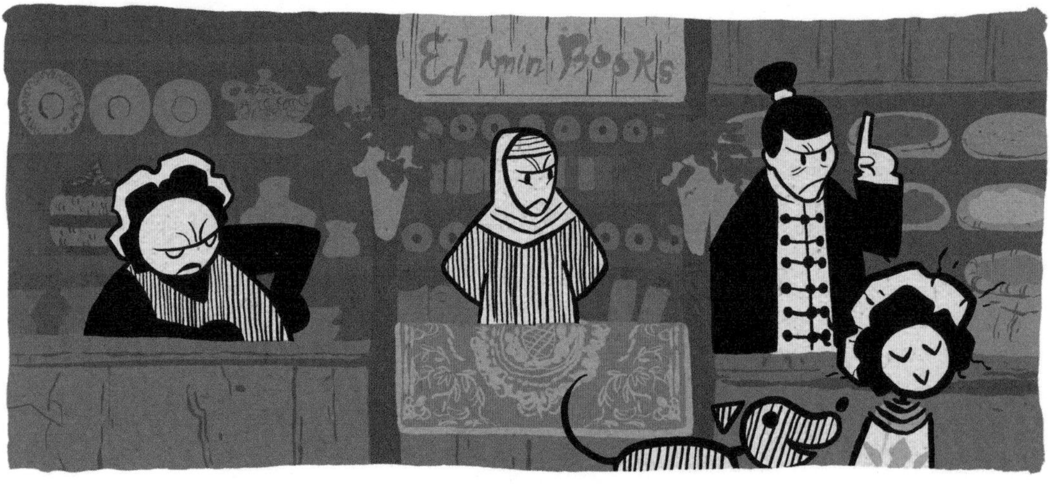
El Amin Books

SHE WOULD ASK THE JAR SELLER FROM THE SOUTH, THE SCROLL TRADER FROM THE NORTH, AND EVEN THE SPICE MERCHANT FROM THE FAR EAST, BUT ALL SAID:

WHAT A PECULIAR GIRL! ALWAYS TALKING TO HERSELF AND NOW EVEN ASKING QUESTIONS ABOUT HER IMAGINARY FRIEND!

– BAH! SHE'LL GROW OUT OF IT. LIFE IS HARD, AND THESE DARK TIMES WILL MAKE HER WISE UP!

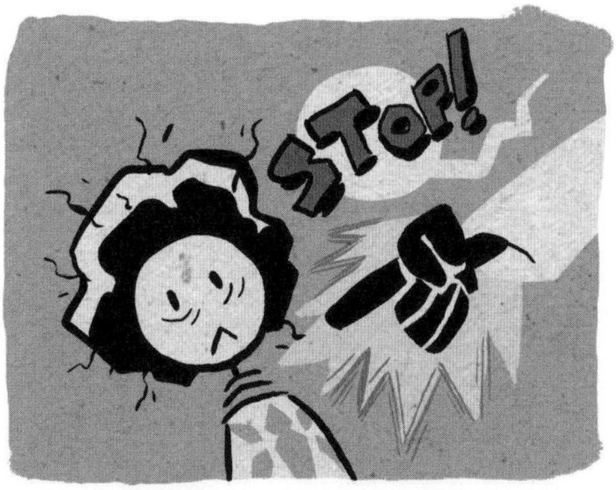
STOP!

WORD CAME TO HER PARENT'S EARS,
WHO LECTURED HER HARSHLY!

– A DJELI'S TALENTS SERVE TO COUNSEL AND EDUCATE,
NOT TO SPREAD NONSENSE,
AND HAVE YOUR HEAD IN THE CLOUDS!

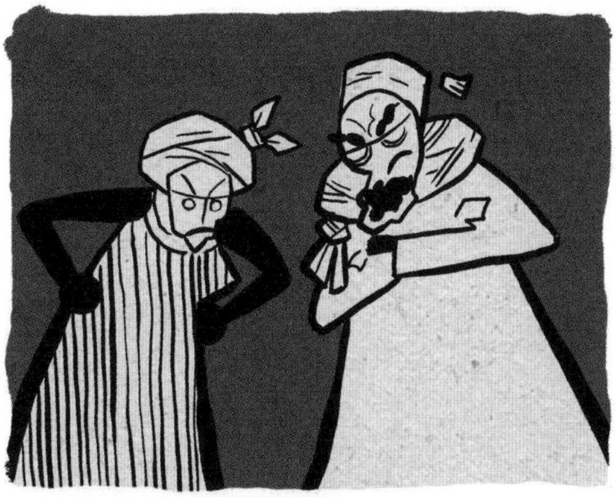

– DJINNES DON'T EXIST, AND DAYDREAMING
DOESN'T HELP ANYBODY!

– KEEP YOUR FEET ON THE GROUND, AND START
BEING MORE PRACTICAL!

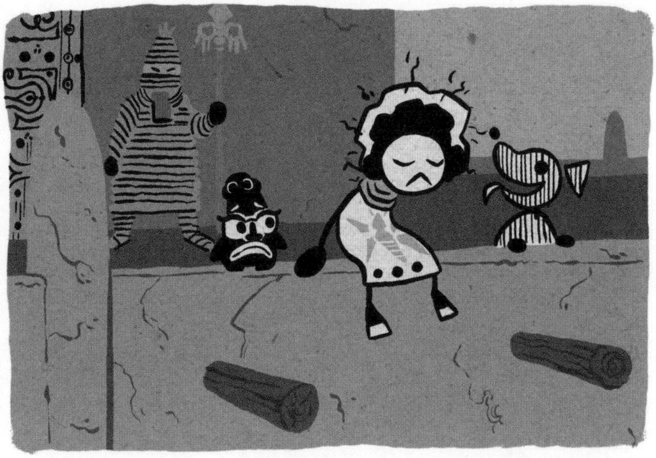

AWA WAS DEVASTATED! SOON SHE WOULD HAVE TO SAY GOODBYE TO HER
FRIENDS AND SPEND HER TIME TAKING LESSONS, ALL TO ONE DAY TAKE OVER
AFTER HER FATHER...

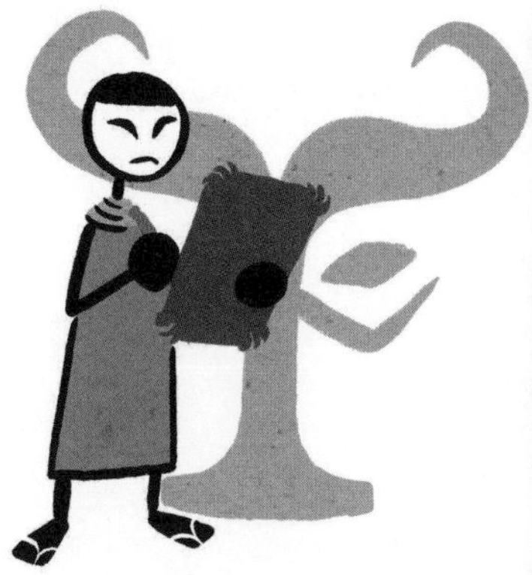

...JUST LIKE PRINCE MANSOUR,
WHO DIDN'T EVEN LEAVE THE
PALACE ANYMORE.

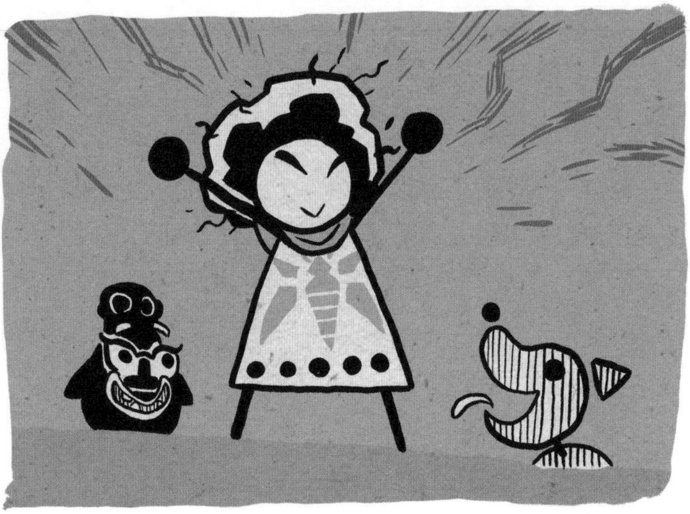

– THEY'RE JUST LIKE YOU, XOGNE! UPSET OVER THINGS THEY DON'T
UNDERSTAND. I'LL SHOW THEM THAT YOU EXIST, AND THAT MY STORIES
BRING JOY TO PEOPLE! THAT THEY'RE NOT A WASTE OF TIME!

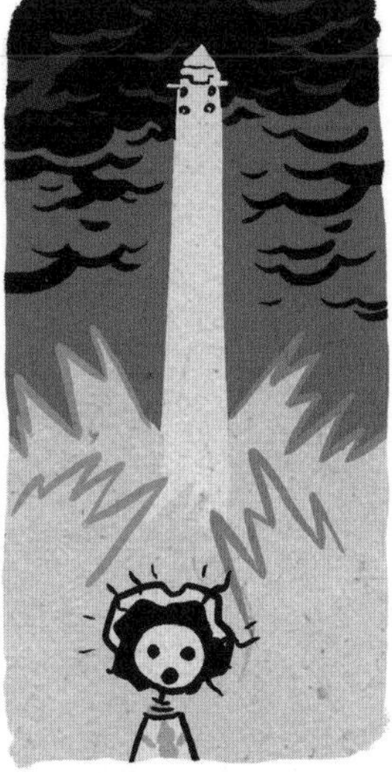

BUT THAT'S WHEN
THE TOWER CAME...

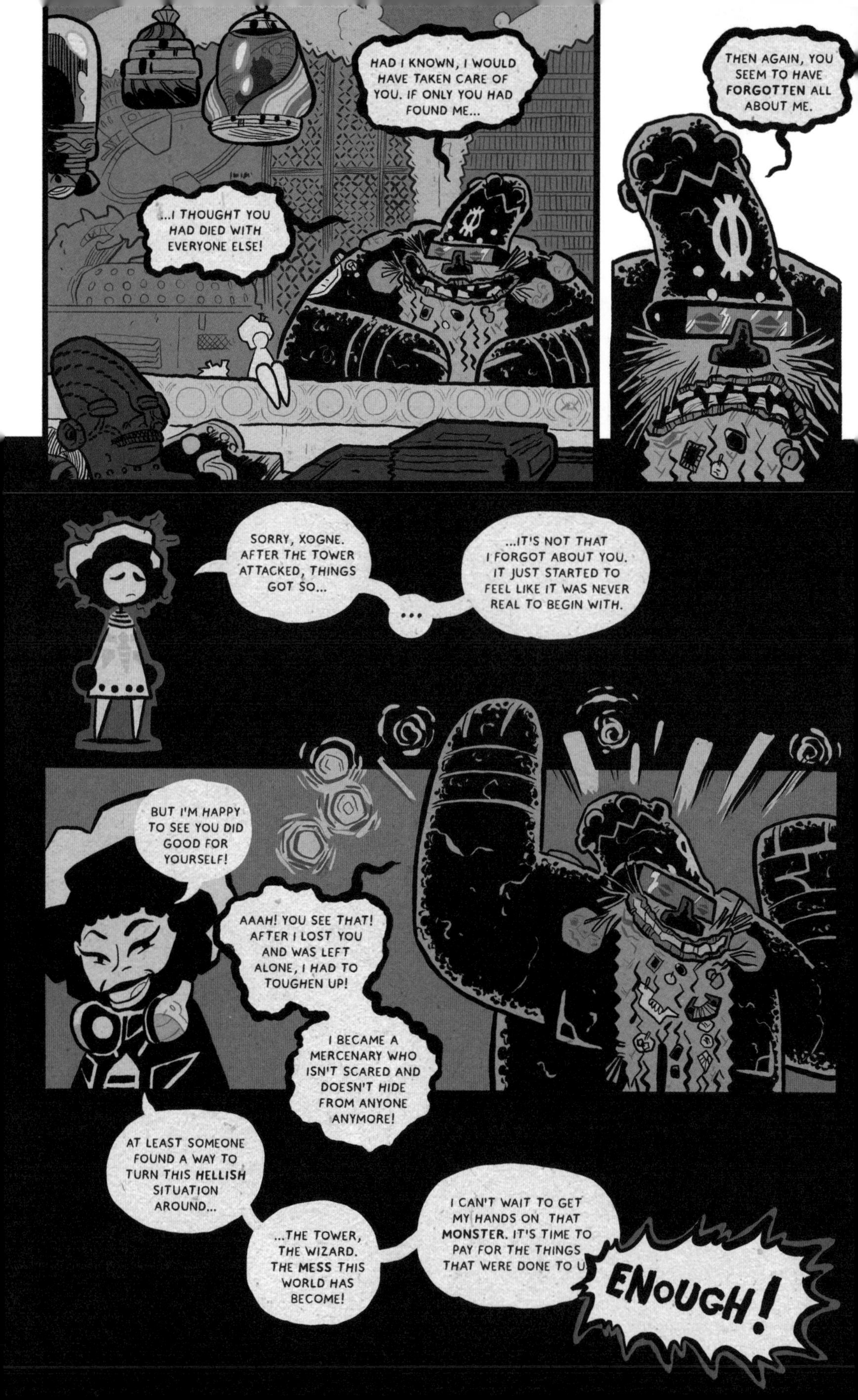
HAD I KNOWN, I WOULD HAVE TAKEN CARE OF YOU. IF ONLY YOU HAD FOUND ME...
...I THOUGHT YOU HAD DIED WITH EVERYONE ELSE!
THEN AGAIN, YOU SEEM TO HAVE FORGOTTEN ALL ABOUT ME.
SORRY, XOGNE. AFTER THE TOWER ATTACKED, THINGS GOT SO...
...
...IT'S NOT THAT I FORGOT ABOUT YOU. IT JUST STARTED TO FEEL LIKE IT WAS NEVER REAL TO BEGIN WITH.
BUT I'M HAPPY TO SEE YOU DID GOOD FOR YOURSELF!
AAAH! YOU SEE THAT! AFTER I LOST YOU AND WAS LEFT ALONE, I HAD TO TOUGHEN UP!
I BECAME A MERCENARY WHO ISN'T SCARED AND DOESN'T HIDE FROM ANYONE ANYMORE!
AT LEAST SOMEONE FOUND A WAY TO TURN THIS HELLISH SITUATION AROUND...
...THE TOWER, THE WIZARD. THE MESS THIS WORLD HAS BECOME!
I CAN'T WAIT TO GET MY HANDS ON THAT MONSTER. IT'S TIME TO PAY FOR THE THINGS THAT WERE DONE TO U
ENOUGH!

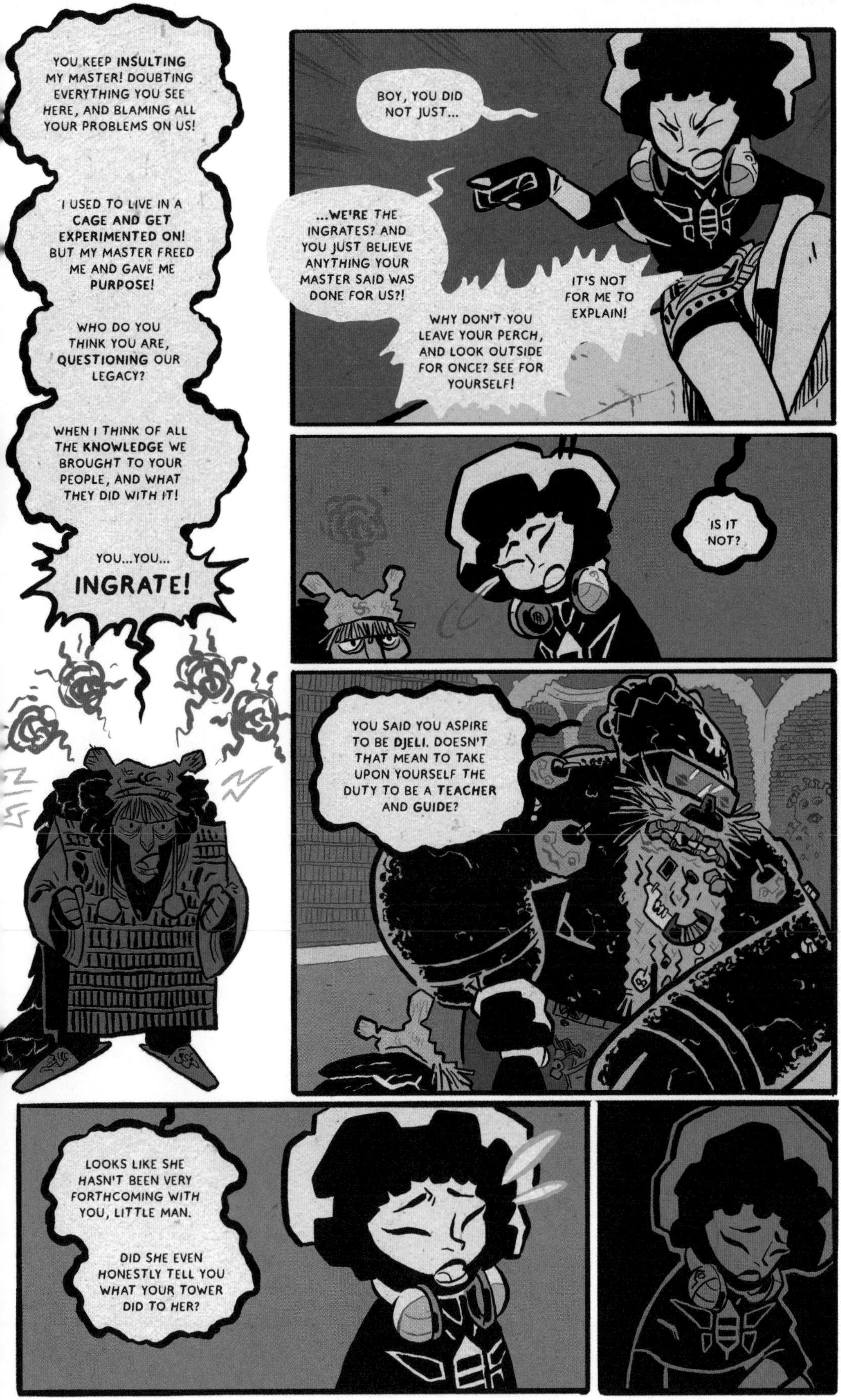
YOU KEEP INSULTING MY MASTER! DOUBTING EVERYTHING YOU SEE HERE, AND BLAMING ALL YOUR PROBLEMS ON US!
I USED TO LIVE IN A CAGE AND GET EXPERIMENTED ON! BUT MY MASTER FREED ME AND GAVE ME PURPOSE!
WHO DO YOU THINK YOU ARE, QUESTIONING OUR LEGACY?
WHEN I THINK OF ALL THE KNOWLEDGE WE BROUGHT TO YOUR PEOPLE, AND WHAT THEY DID WITH IT!
YOU...YOU... INGRATE!
BOY, YOU DID NOT JUST...
...WE'RE THE INGRATES? AND YOU JUST BELIEVE ANYTHING YOUR MASTER SAID WAS DONE FOR US?!
WHY DON'T YOU LEAVE YOUR PERCH, AND LOOK OUTSIDE FOR ONCE? SEE FOR YOURSELF!
IT'S NOT FOR ME TO EXPLAIN!
IS IT NOT?
YOU SAID YOU ASPIRE TO BE DJELI. DOESN'T THAT MEAN TO TAKE UPON YOURSELF THE DUTY TO BE A TEACHER AND GUIDE?
LOOKS LIKE SHE HASN'T BEEN VERY FORTHCOMING WITH YOU, LITTLE MAN.
DID SHE EVEN HONESTLY TELL YOU WHAT YOUR TOWER DID TO HER?

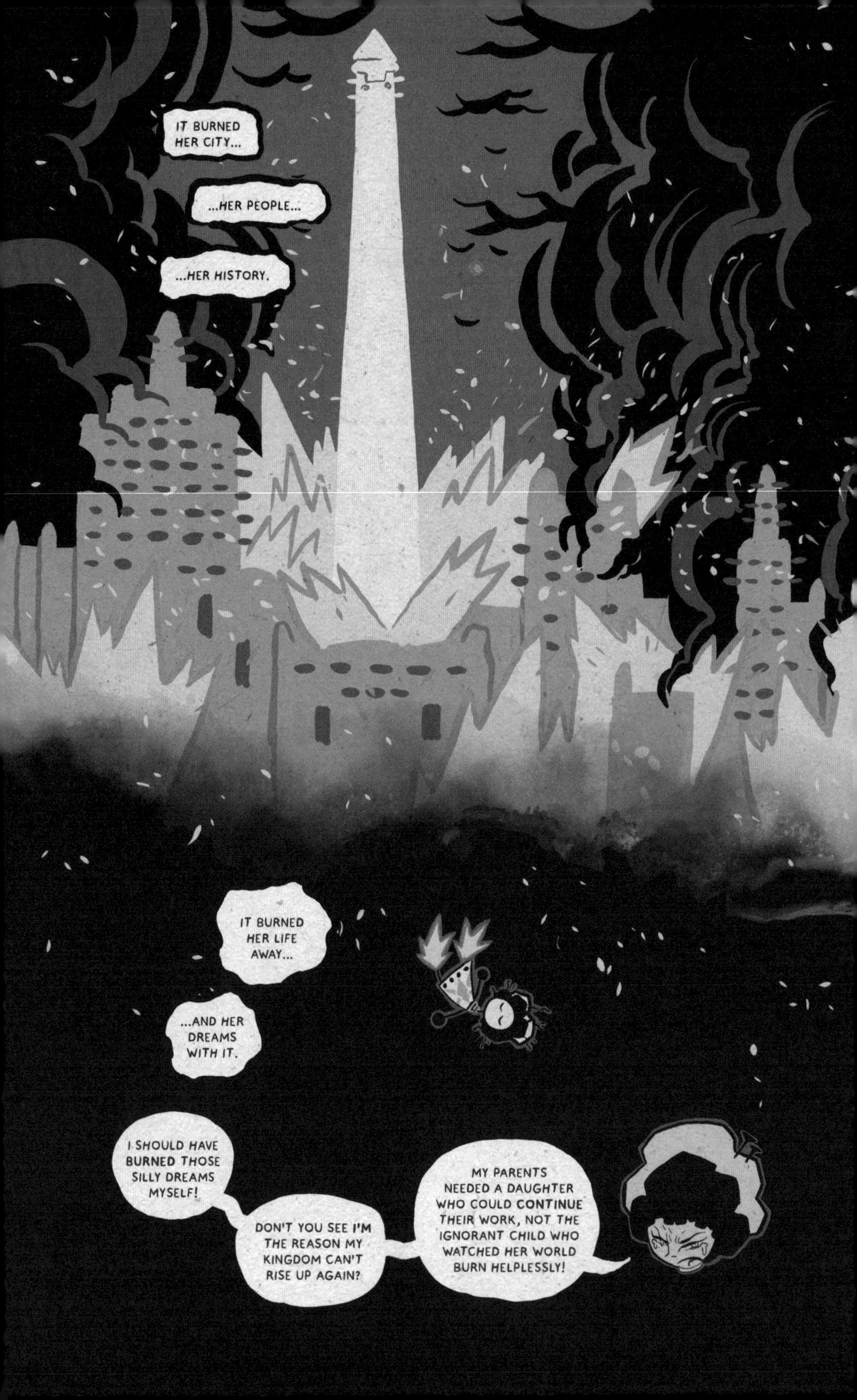
IT BURNED HER CITY...
...HER PEOPLE...
...HER HISTORY.
IT BURNED HER LIFE AWAY...
...AND HER DREAMS WITH IT.
I SHOULD HAVE BURNED THOSE SILLY DREAMS MYSELF!
DON'T YOU SEE I'M THE REASON MY KINGDOM CAN'T RISE UP AGAIN?
MY PARENTS NEEDED A DAUGHTER WHO COULD CONTINUE THEIR WORK, NOT THE IGNORANT CHILD WHO WATCHED HER WORLD BURN HELPLESSLY!

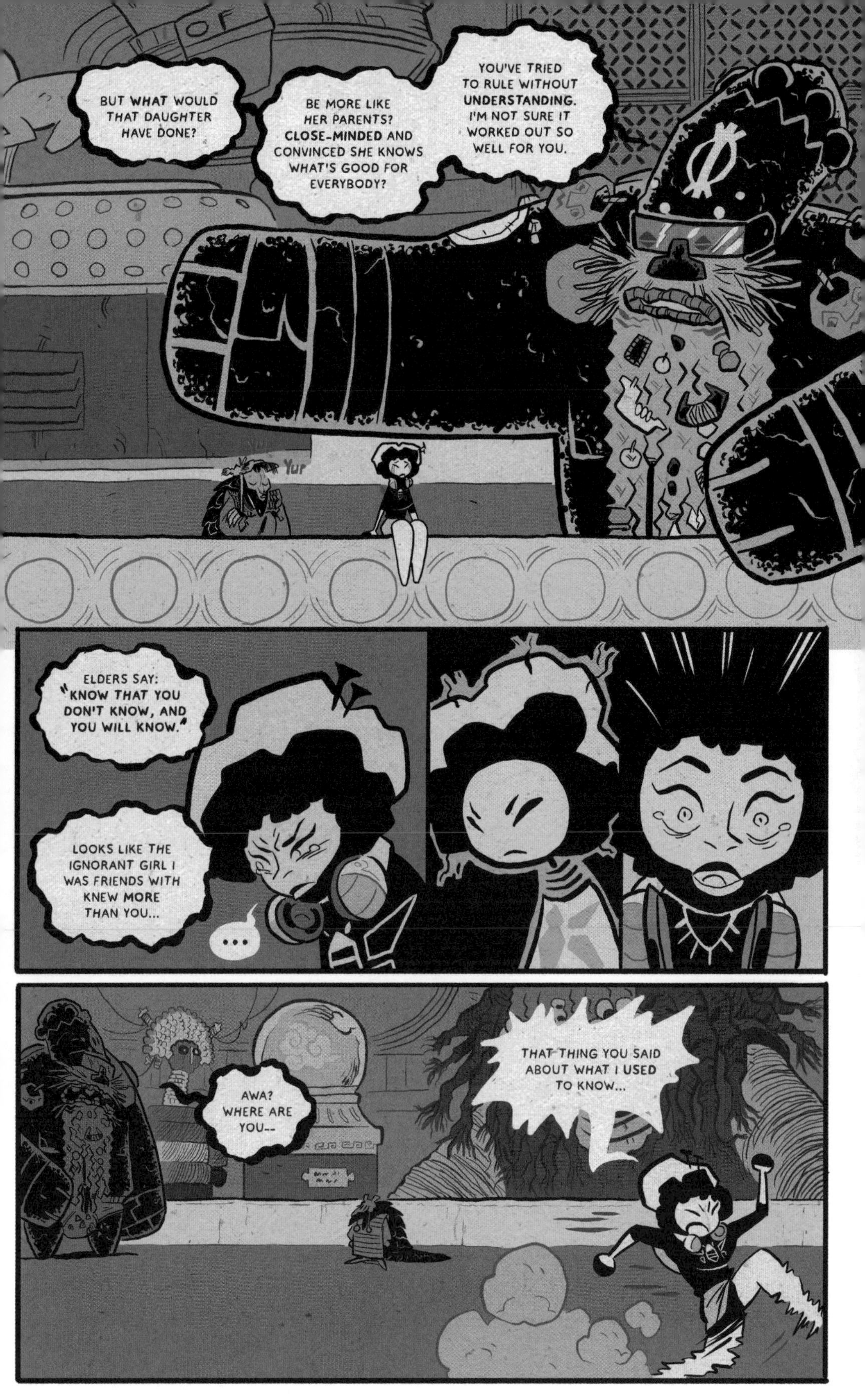

BUT WHAT WOULD THAT DAUGHTER HAVE DONE?
BE MORE LIKE HER PARENTS? CLOSE-MINDED AND CONVINCED SHE KNOWS WHAT'S GOOD FOR EVERYBODY?
YOU'VE TRIED TO RULE WITHOUT UNDERSTANDING. I'M NOT SURE IT WORKED OUT SO WELL FOR YOU.
YUP
ELDERS SAY: "KNOW THAT YOU DON'T KNOW, AND YOU WILL KNOW."
LOOKS LIKE THE IGNORANT GIRL I WAS FRIENDS WITH KNEW MORE THAN YOU...
...
AWA? WHERE ARE YOU--
THAT THING YOU SAID ABOUT WHAT I USED TO KNOW...

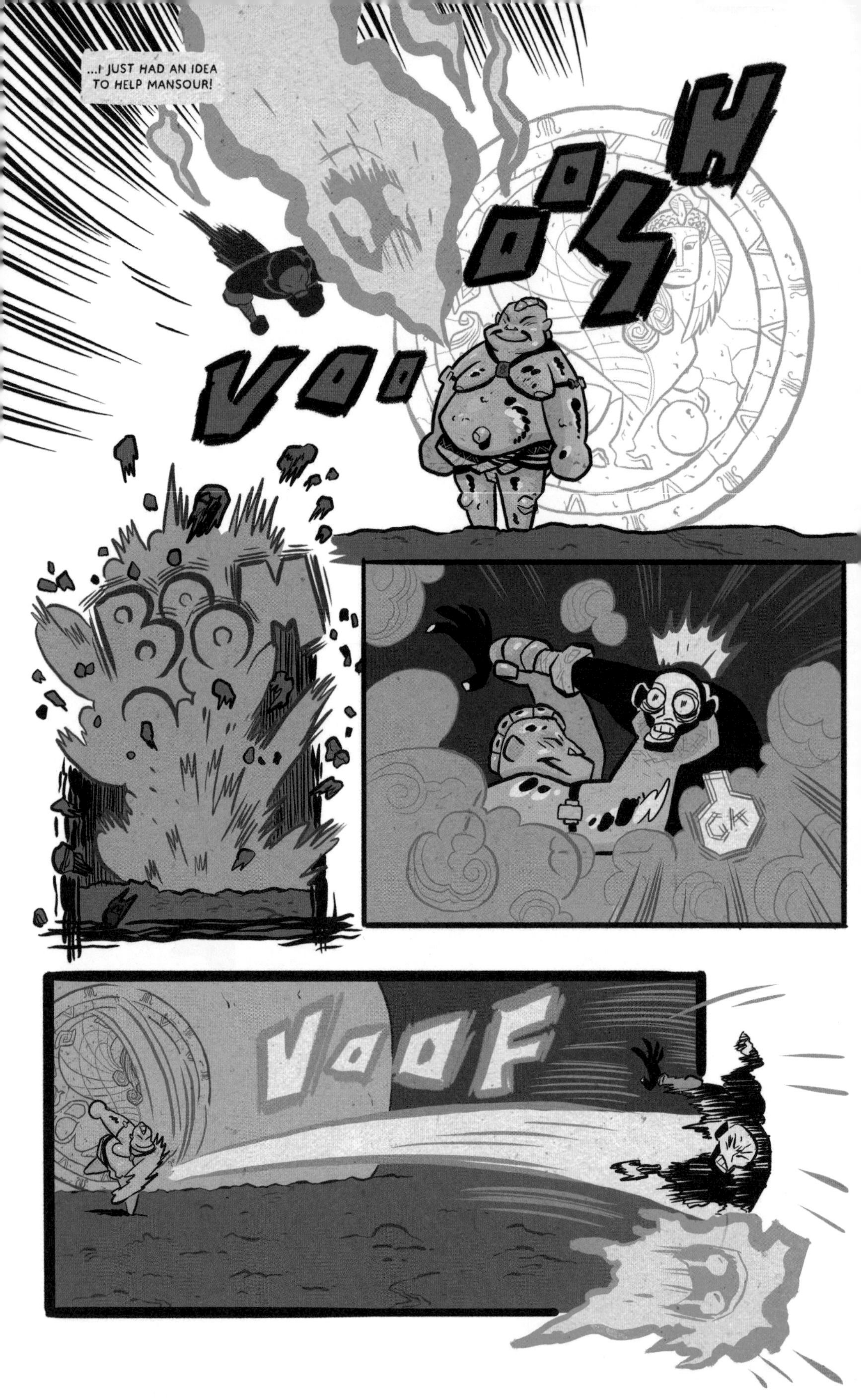
...I JUST HAD AN IDEA TO HELP MANSOUR!
VOOOSH
BOOM
GAK
VOOF

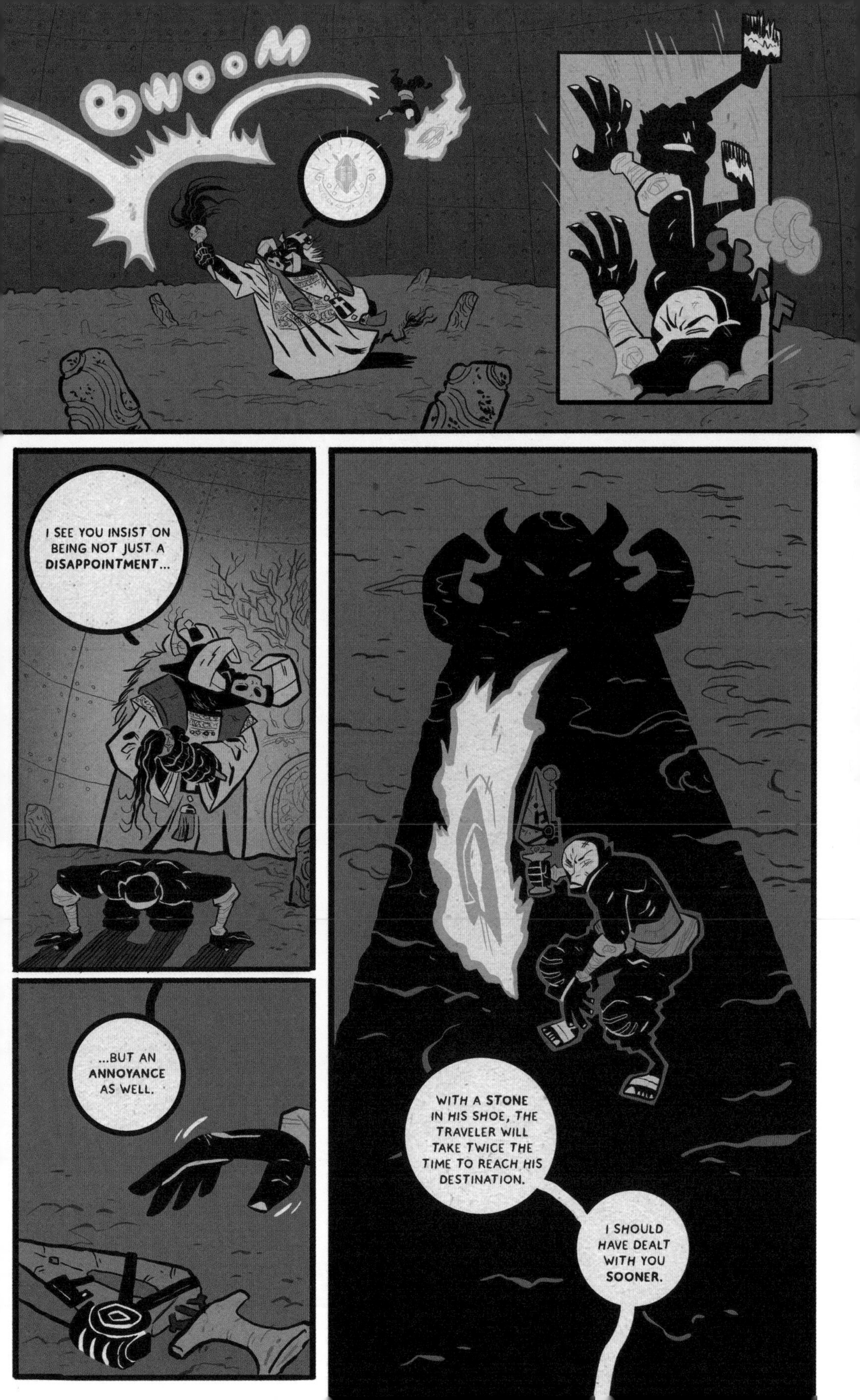
BWOOM
SBRF
I SEE YOU INSIST ON BEING NOT JUST A DISAPPOINTMENT...
...BUT AN ANNOYANCE AS WELL.
WITH A STONE IN HIS SHOE, THE TRAVELER WILL TAKE TWICE THE TIME TO REACH HIS DESTINATION.
I SHOULD HAVE DEALT WITH YOU SOONER.

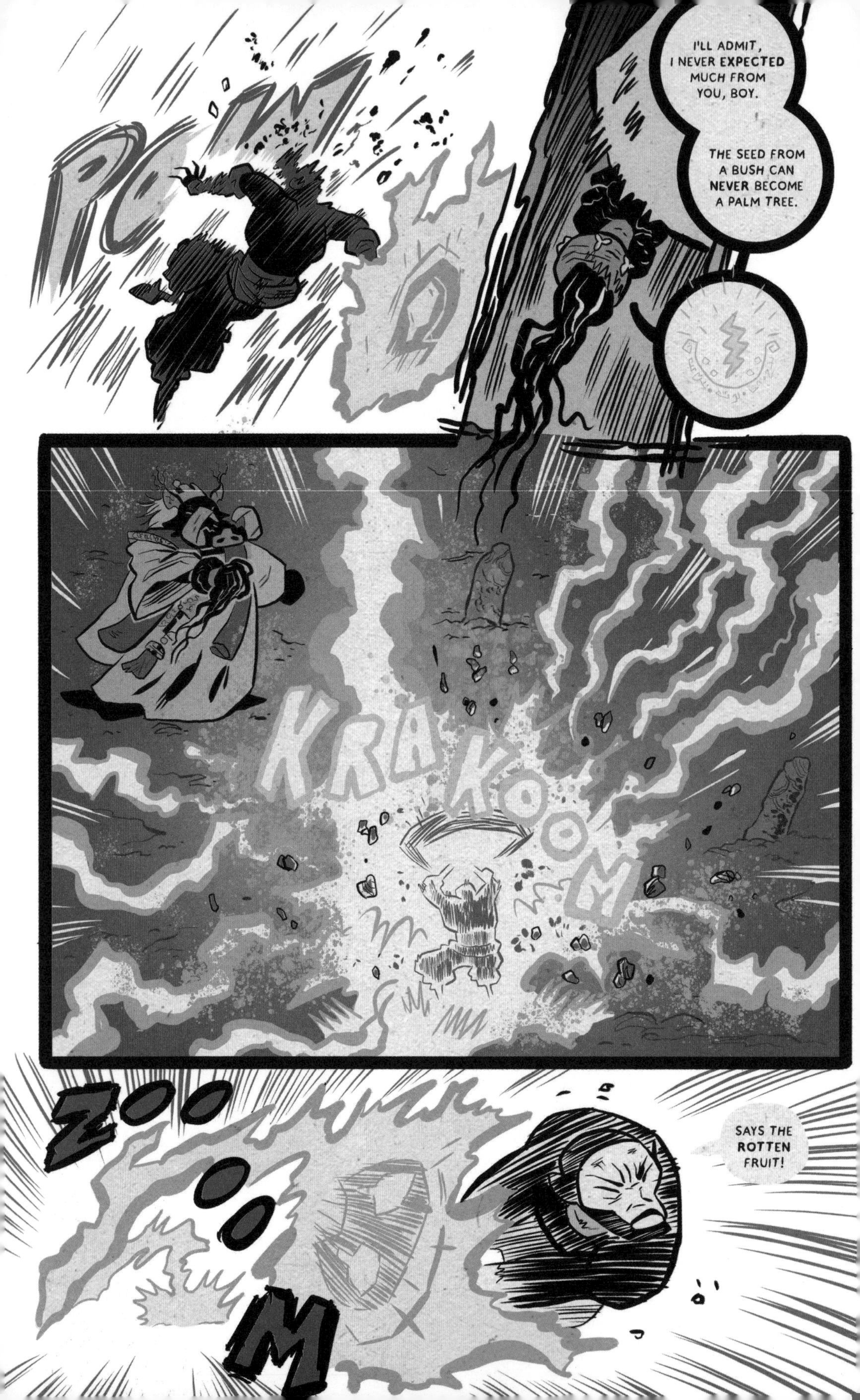
POOM
I'LL ADMIT, I NEVER EXPECTED MUCH FROM YOU, BOY.
THE SEED FROM A BUSH CAN NEVER BECOME A PALM TREE.
KRAKOOOM
ZOOOOOM
SAYS THE ROTTEN FRUIT!

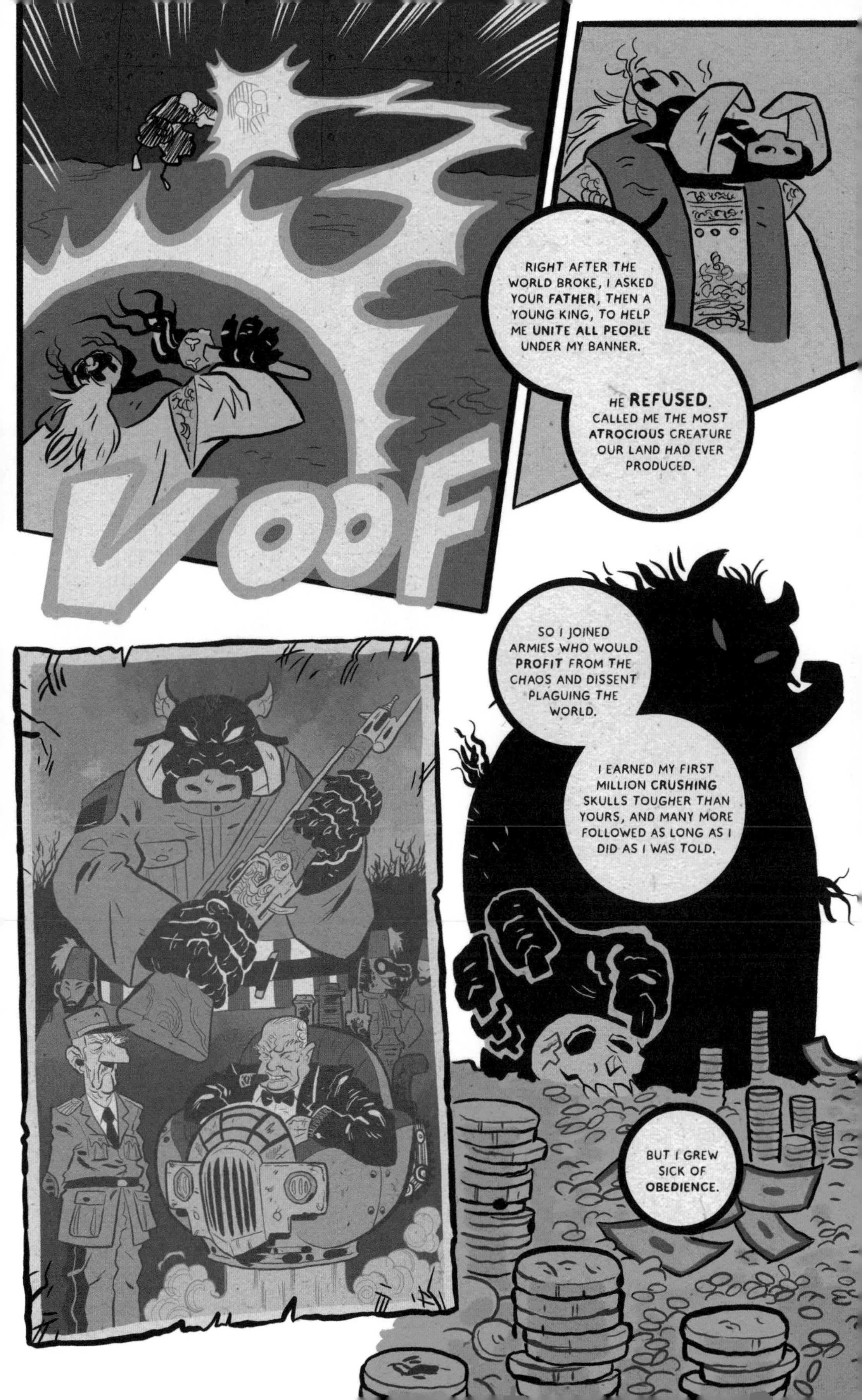
VOOF
RIGHT AFTER THE WORLD BROKE, I ASKED YOUR FATHER, THEN A YOUNG KING, TO HELP ME UNITE ALL PEOPLE UNDER MY BANNER.
HE REFUSED. CALLED ME THE MOST ATROCIOUS CREATURE OUR LAND HAD EVER PRODUCED.
SO I JOINED ARMIES WHO WOULD PROFIT FROM THE CHAOS AND DISSENT PLAGUING THE WORLD.
I EARNED MY FIRST MILLION CRUSHING SKULLS TOUGHER THAN YOURS, AND MANY MORE FOLLOWED AS LONG AS I DID AS I WAS TOLD.
BUT I GREW SICK OF OBEDIENCE.

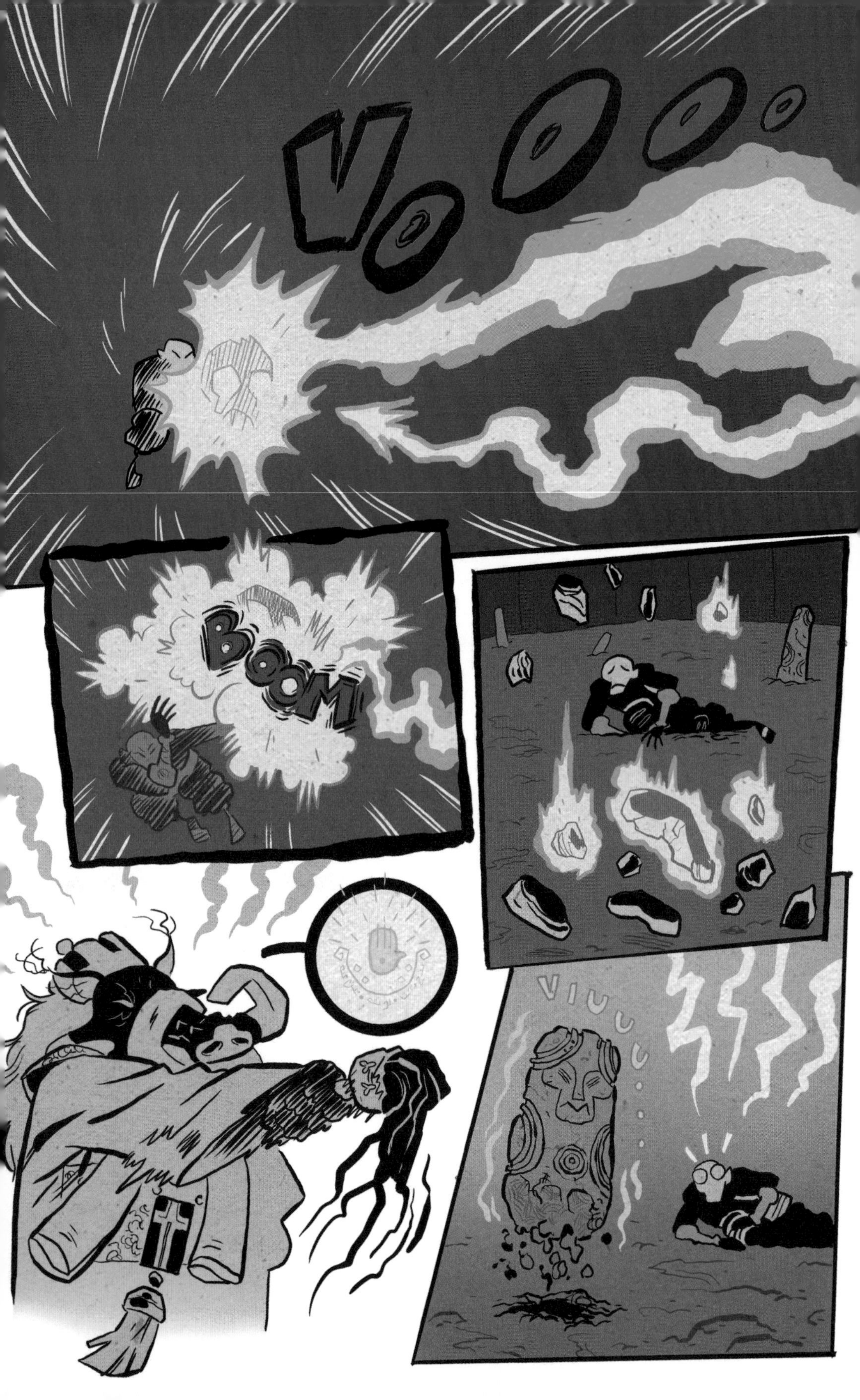
VOOOOO
BOOM
VIUUU...

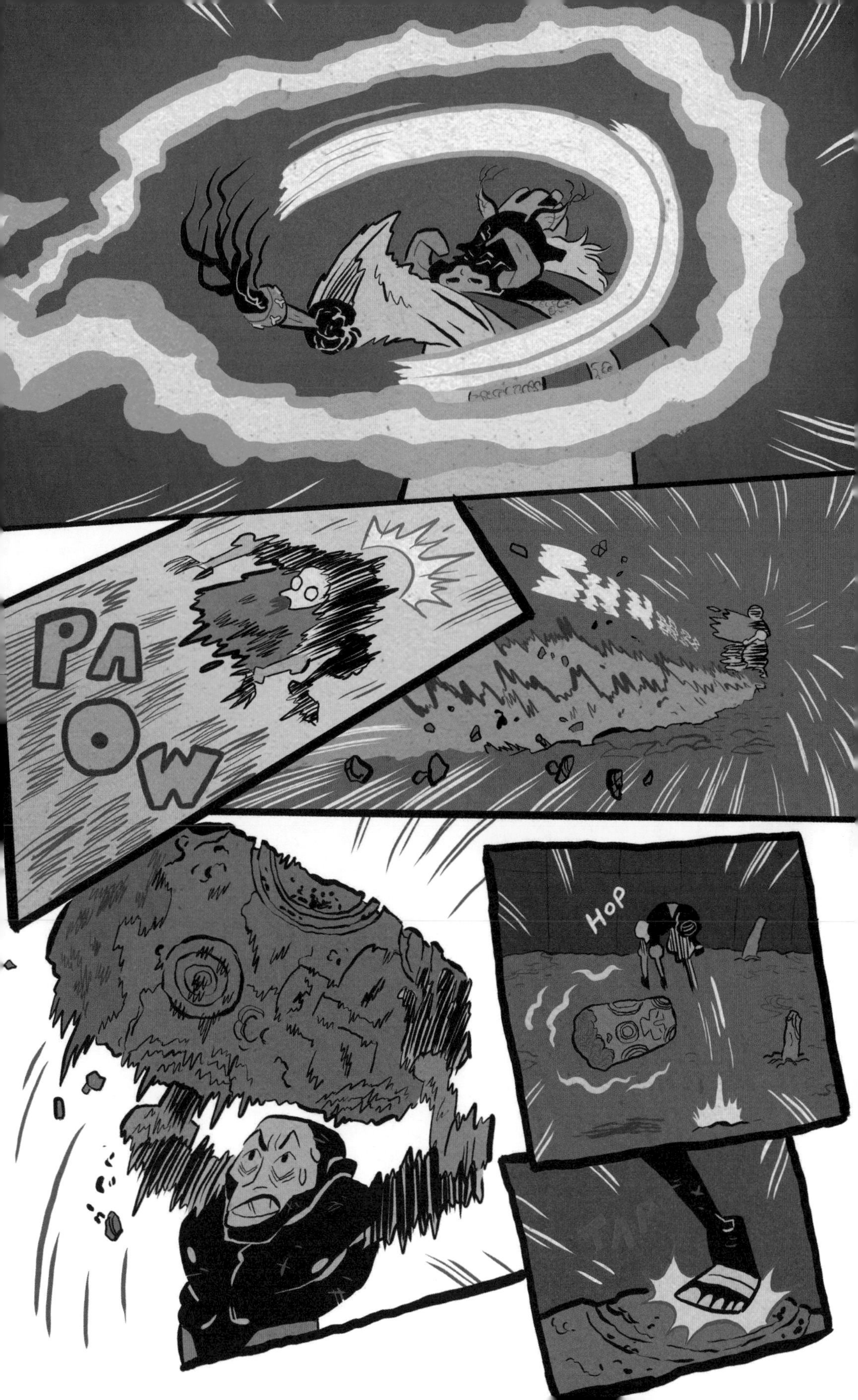
PAOW
HOP

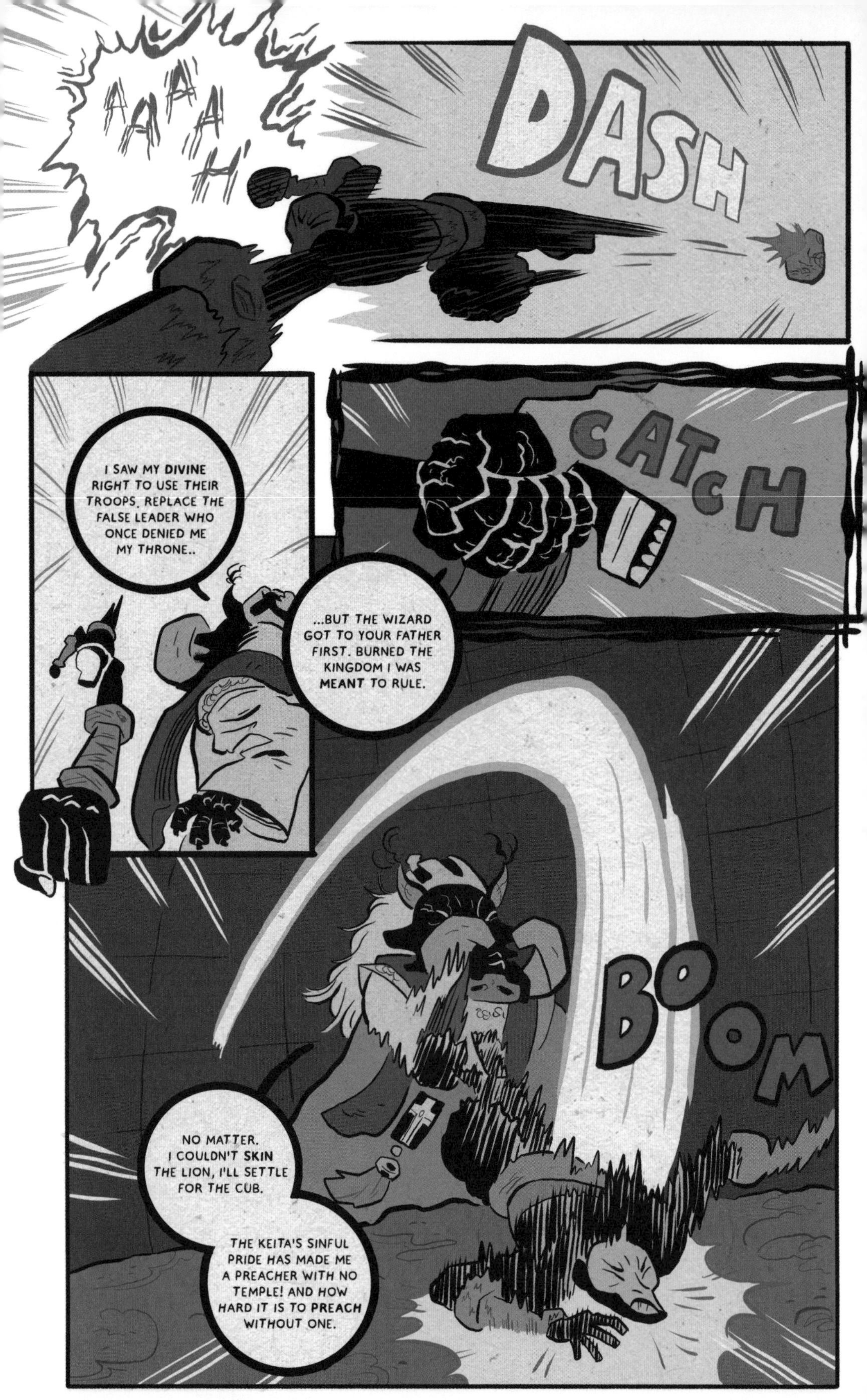
AAAAH
DASH
CATCH
I SAW MY DIVINE RIGHT TO USE THEIR TROOPS, REPLACE THE FALSE LEADER WHO ONCE DENIED ME MY THRONE..
...BUT THE WIZARD GOT TO YOUR FATHER FIRST. BURNED THE KINGDOM I WAS MEANT TO RULE.
BOOOM
NO MATTER. I COULDN'T SKIN THE LION, I'LL SETTLE FOR THE CUB.
THE KEITA'S SINFUL PRIDE HAS MADE ME A PREACHER WITH NO TEMPLE! AND HOW HARD IT IS TO PREACH WITHOUT ONE.

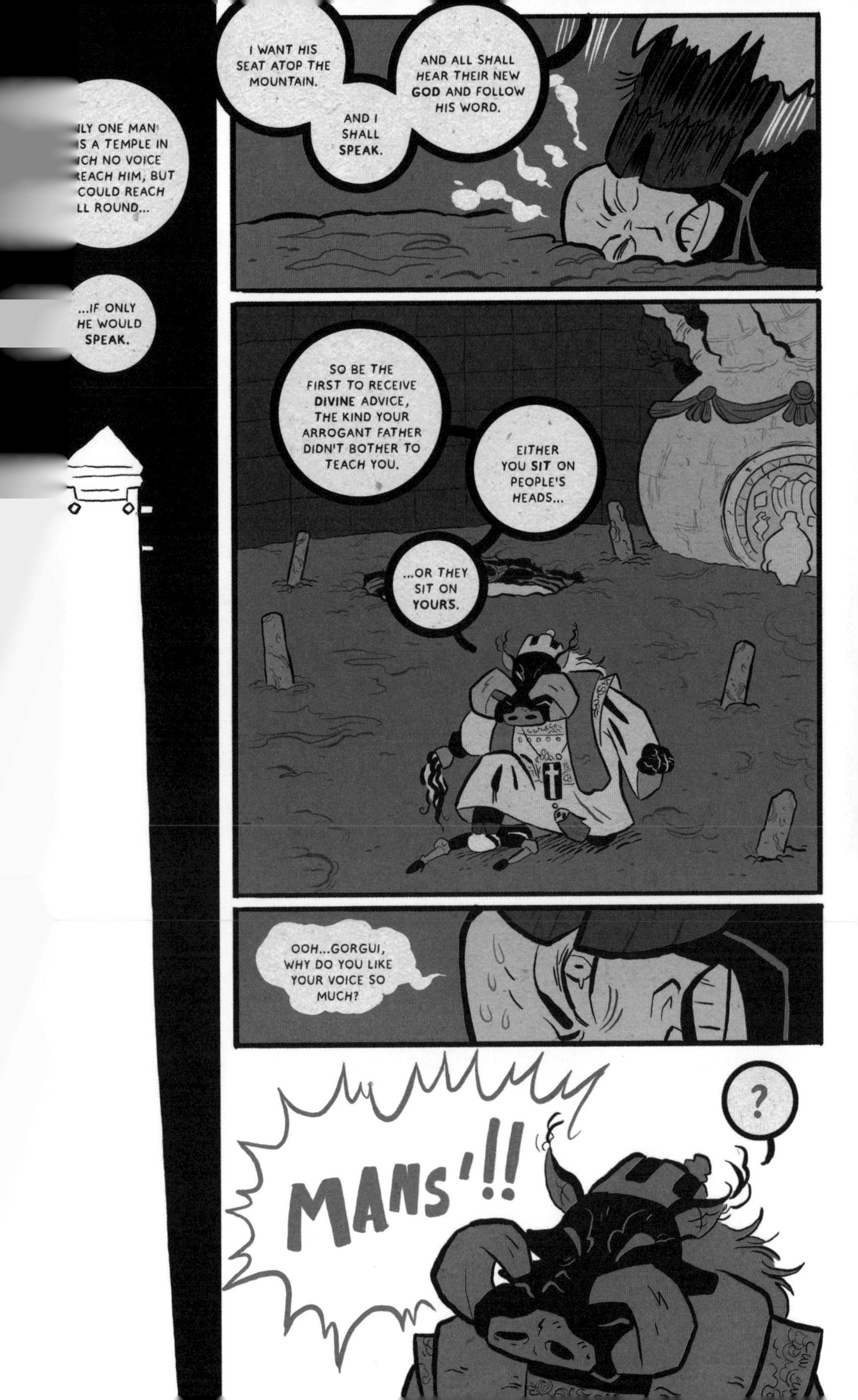
...IF ONLY HE WOULD SPEAK.
I WANT HIS SEAT ATOP THE MOUNTAIN.
AND I SHALL SPEAK.
AND ALL SHALL HEAR THEIR NEW GOD AND FOLLOW HIS WORD.
SO BE THE FIRST TO RECEIVE DIVINE ADVICE, THE KIND YOUR ARROGANT FATHER DIDN'T BOTHER TO TEACH YOU.
EITHER YOU SIT ON PEOPLE'S HEADS...
...OR THEY SIT ON YOURS.
OOH...GORGUI, WHY DO YOU LIKE YOUR VOICE SO MUCH?
MANS'!!
?

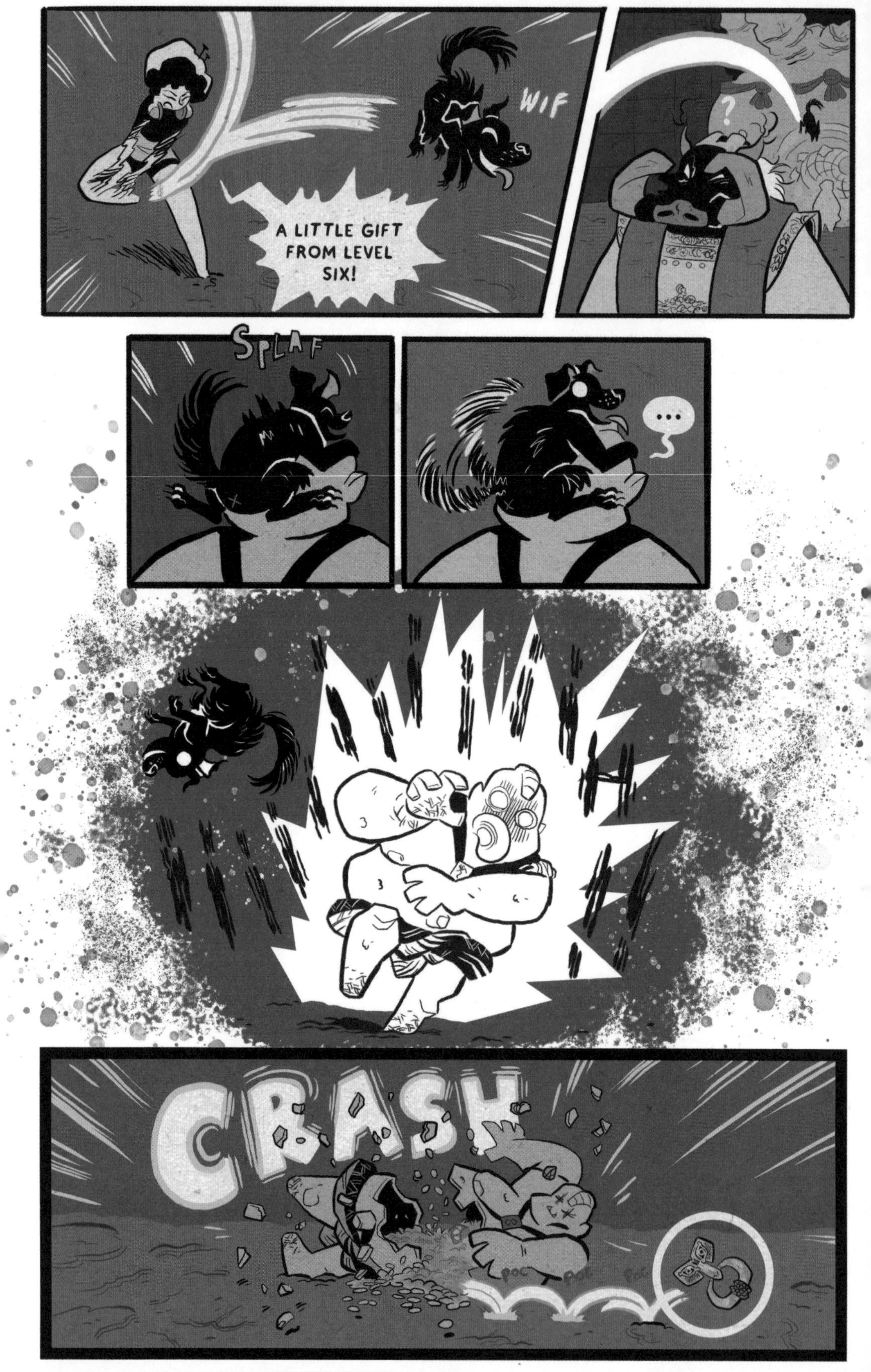
WIF
A LITTLE GIFT FROM LEVEL SIX!
?
SPLAF
...
CRASH
POC
POC
POC

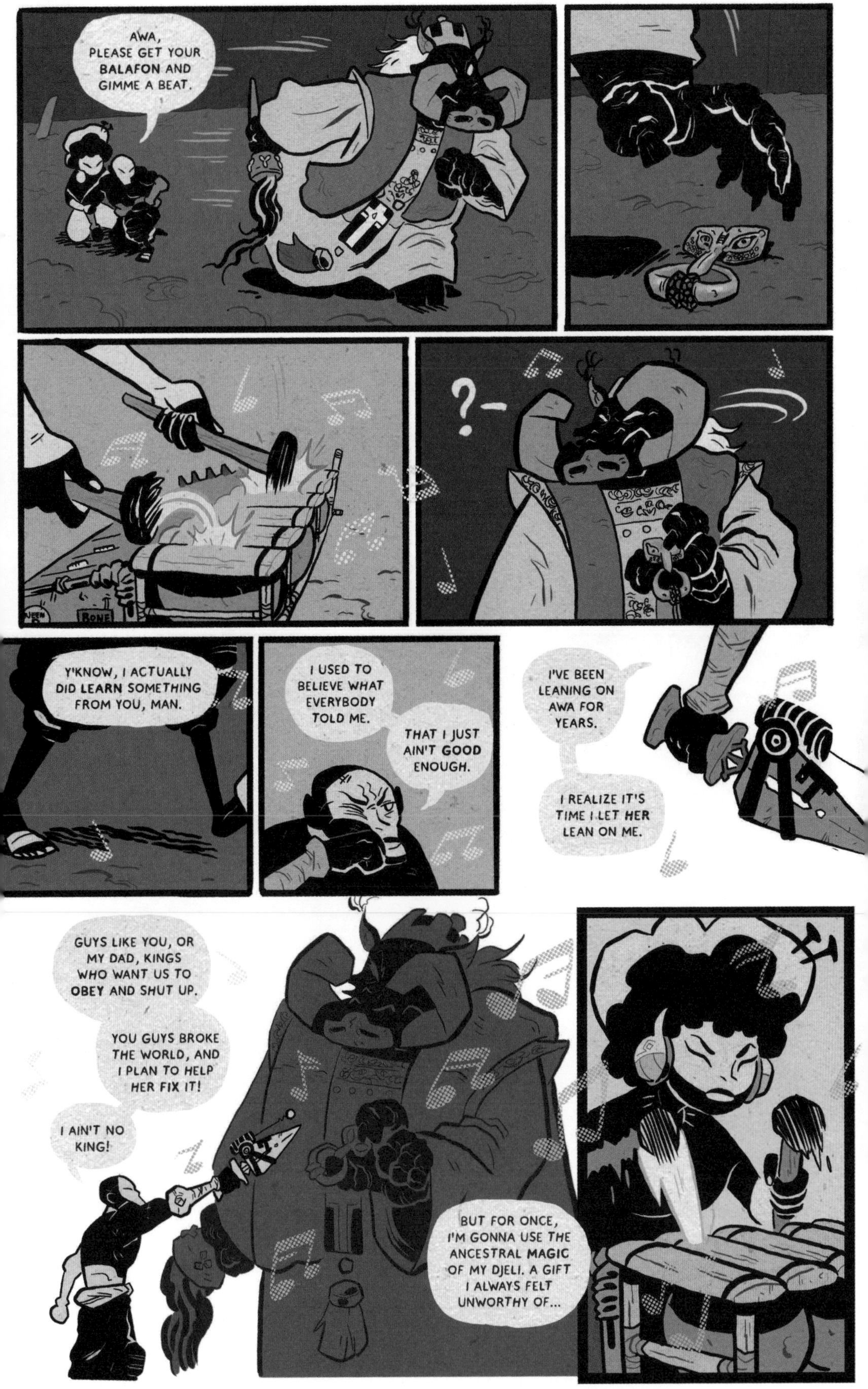
AWA, PLEASE GET YOUR BALAFON AND GIMME A BEAT.
?-
Y'KNOW, I ACTUALLY DID LEARN SOMETHING FROM YOU, MAN.
I USED TO BELIEVE WHAT EVERYBODY TOLD ME.
THAT I JUST AIN'T GOOD ENOUGH.
I'VE BEEN LEANING ON AWA FOR YEARS.
I REALIZE IT'S TIME I LET HER LEAN ON ME.
GUYS LIKE YOU, OR MY DAD, KINGS WHO WANT US TO OBEY AND SHUT UP.
YOU GUYS BROKE THE WORLD, AND I PLAN TO HELP HER FIX IT!
I AIN'T NO KING!
BUT FOR ONCE, I'M GONNA USE THE ANCESTRAL MAGIC OF MY DJELI. A GIFT I ALWAYS FELT UNWORTHY OF...

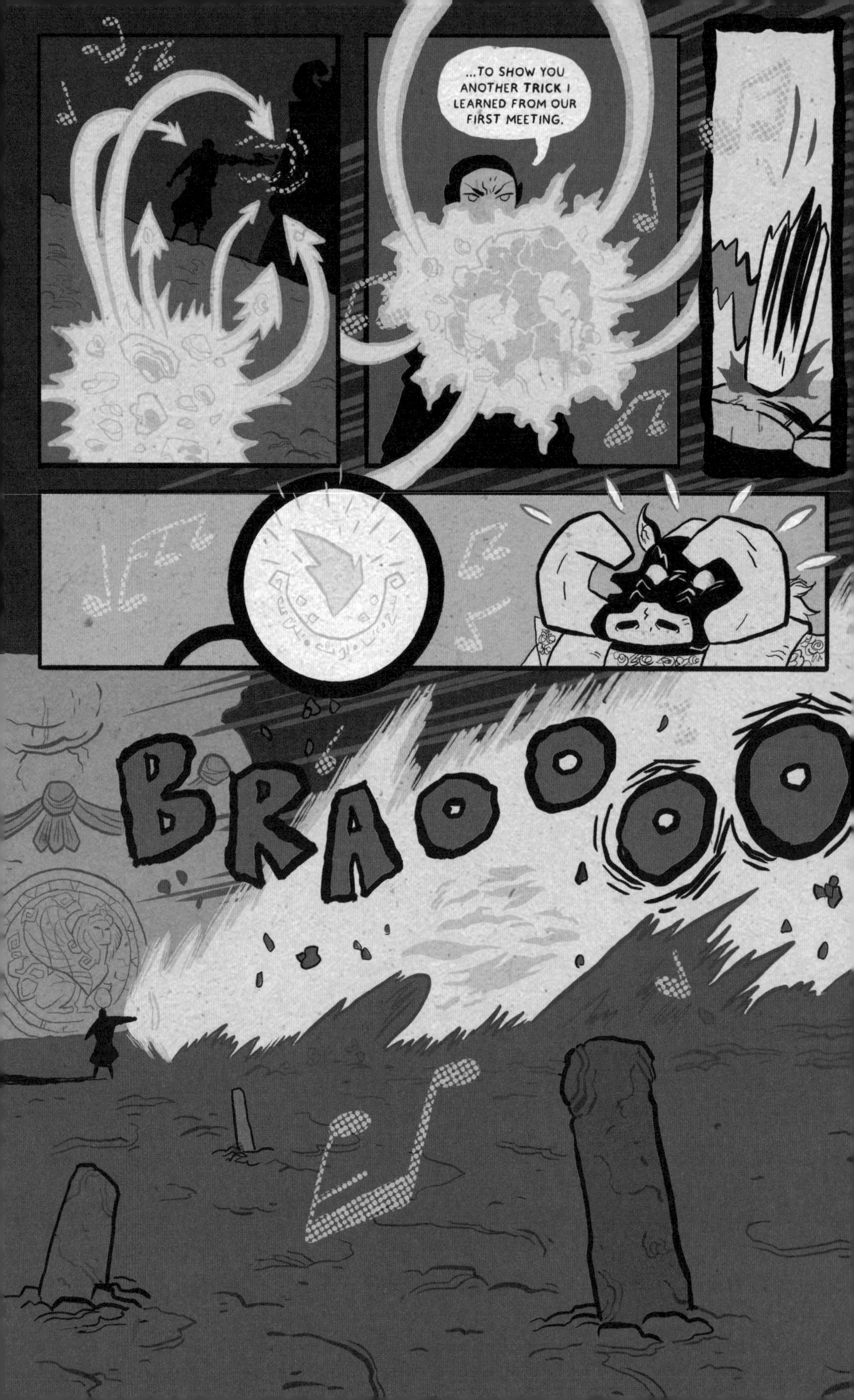
...TO SHOW YOU ANOTHER TRICK I LEARNED FROM OUR FIRST MEETING.
BRAOOOO

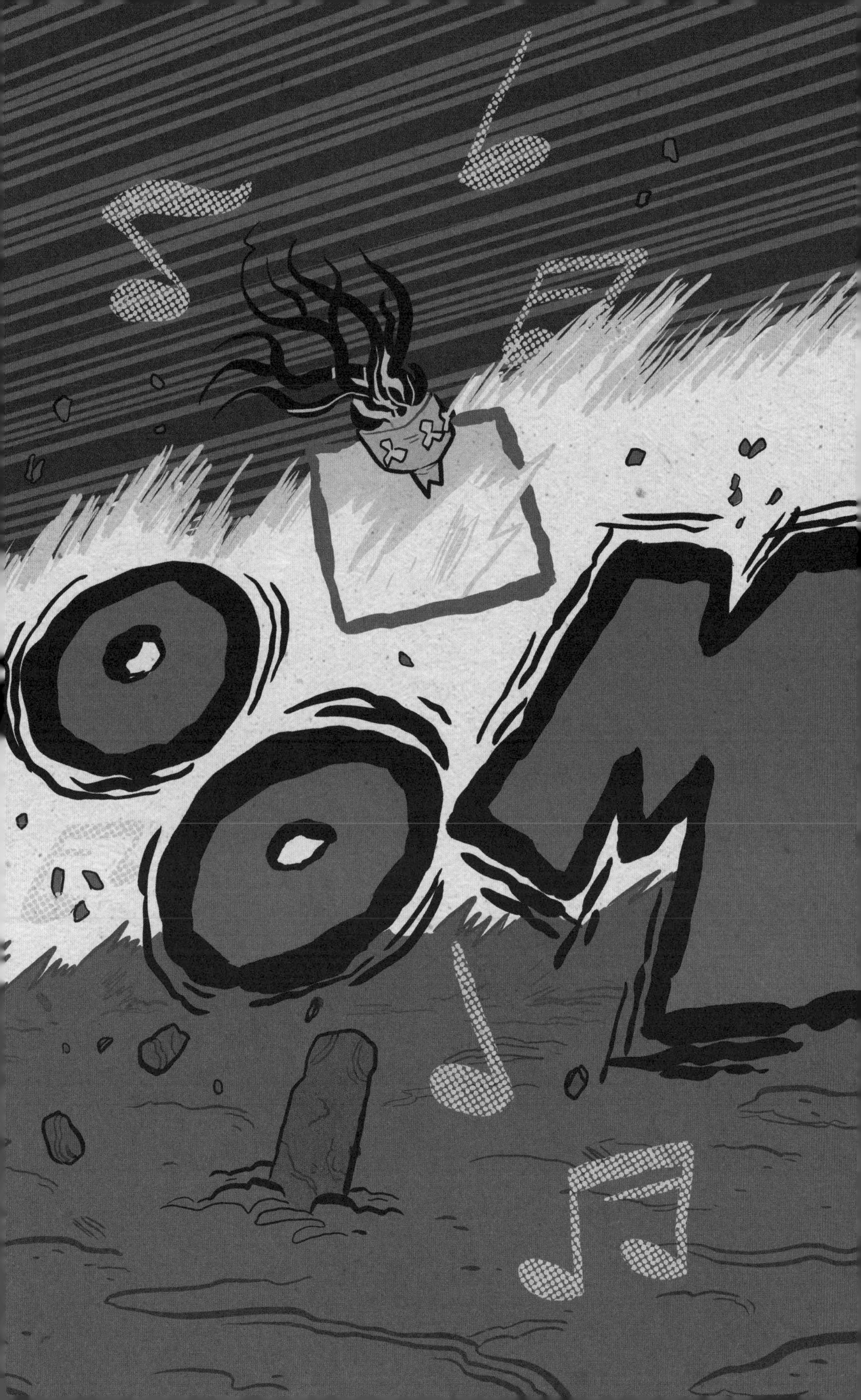
OOM

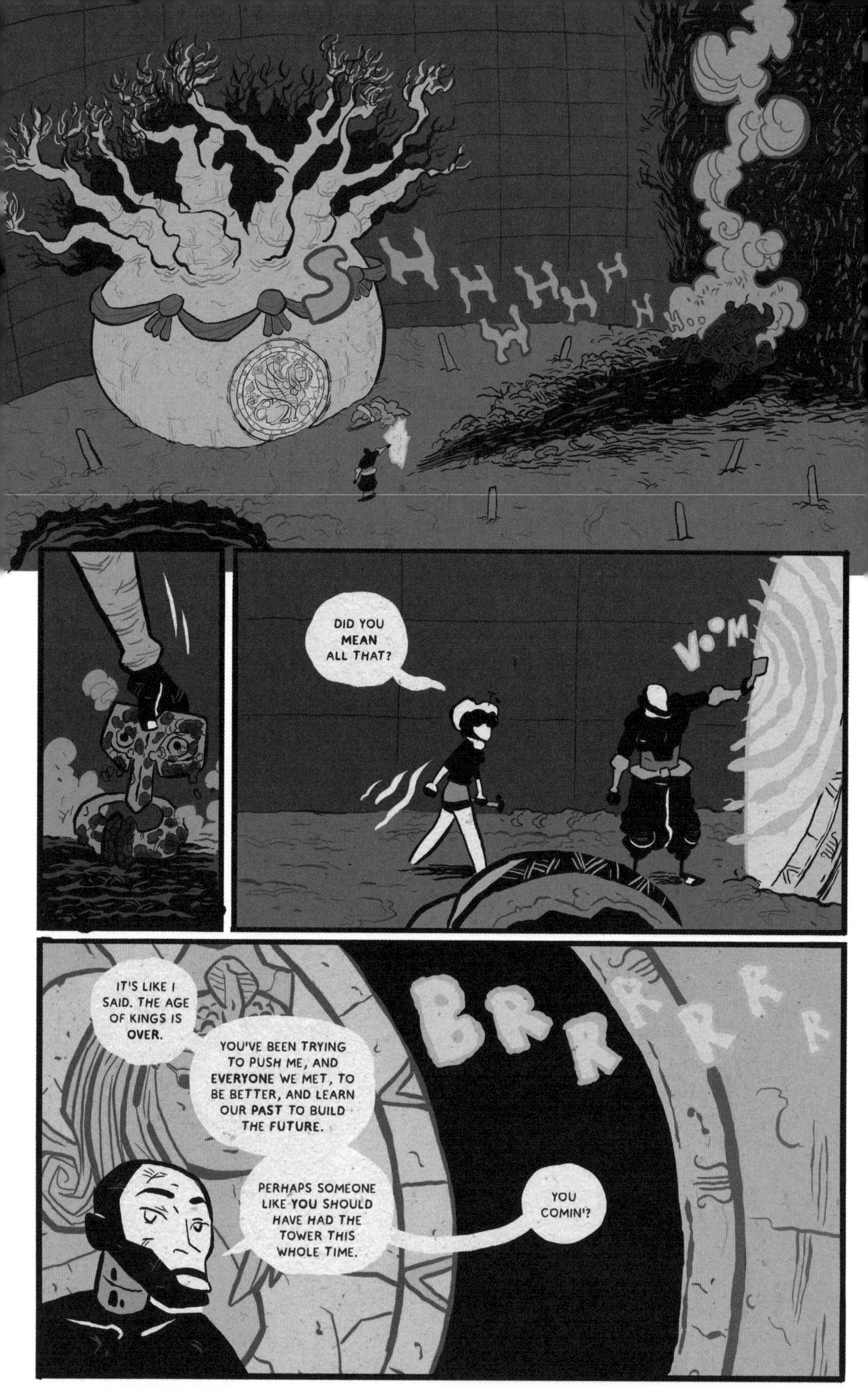
SHHHHHHHHH
DID YOU MEAN ALL THAT?
VOOM
IT'S LIKE I SAID. THE AGE OF KINGS IS OVER.
YOU'VE BEEN TRYING TO PUSH ME, AND EVERYONE WE MET, TO BE BETTER, AND LEARN OUR PAST TO BUILD THE FUTURE.
PERHAPS SOMEONE LIKE YOU SHOULD HAVE HAD THE TOWER THIS WHOLE TIME.
BRRRRRR
YOU COMIN'?

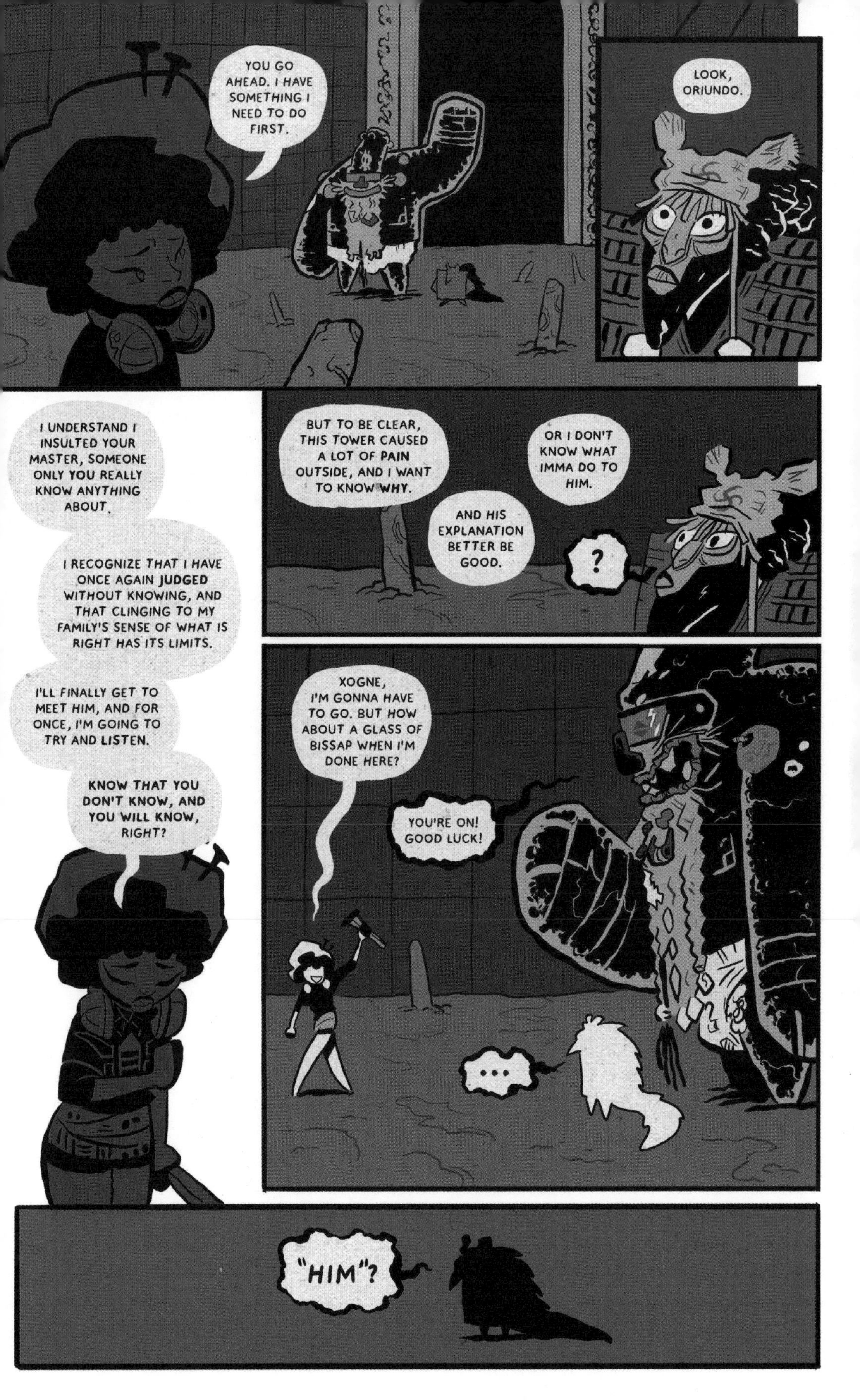
YOU GO AHEAD. I HAVE SOMETHING I NEED TO DO FIRST.
LOOK, ORIUNDO.
I UNDERSTAND I INSULTED YOUR MASTER, SOMEONE ONLY YOU REALLY KNOW ANYTHING ABOUT.
I RECOGNIZE THAT I HAVE ONCE AGAIN JUDGED WITHOUT KNOWING, AND THAT CLINGING TO MY FAMILY'S SENSE OF WHAT IS RIGHT HAS ITS LIMITS.
I'LL FINALLY GET TO MEET HIM, AND FOR ONCE, I'M GOING TO TRY AND LISTEN.
KNOW THAT YOU DON'T KNOW, AND YOU WILL KNOW, RIGHT?
BUT TO BE CLEAR, THIS TOWER CAUSED A LOT OF PAIN OUTSIDE, AND I WANT TO KNOW WHY.
AND HIS EXPLANATION BETTER BE GOOD.
OR I DON'T KNOW WHAT IMMA DO TO HIM.
?
XOGNE, I'M GONNA HAVE TO GO. BUT HOW ABOUT A GLASS OF BISSAP WHEN I'M DONE HERE?
YOU'RE ON! GOOD LUCK!
...
"HIM"?

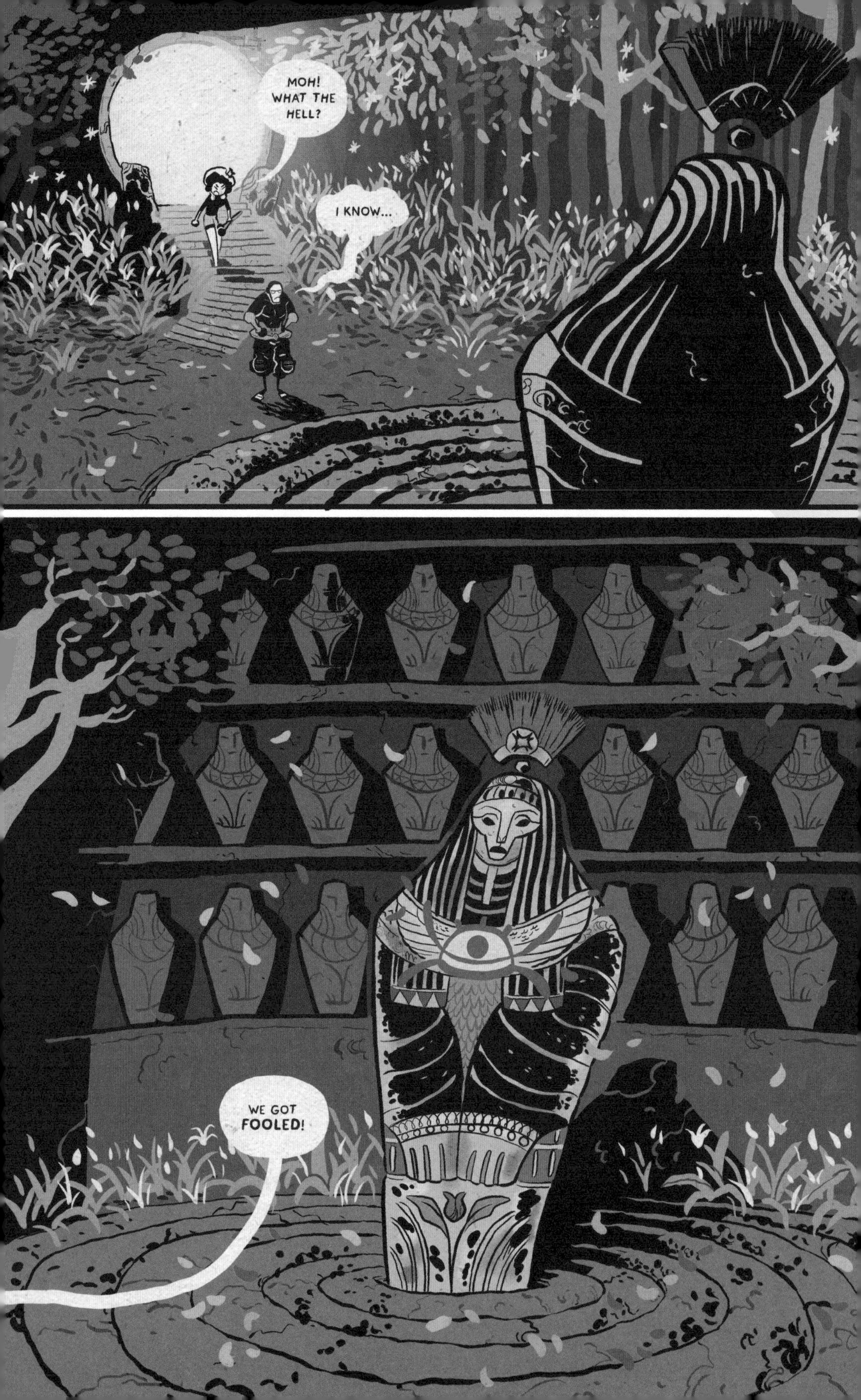
MOH! WHAT THE HELL?
I KNOW...
WE GOT FOOLED!

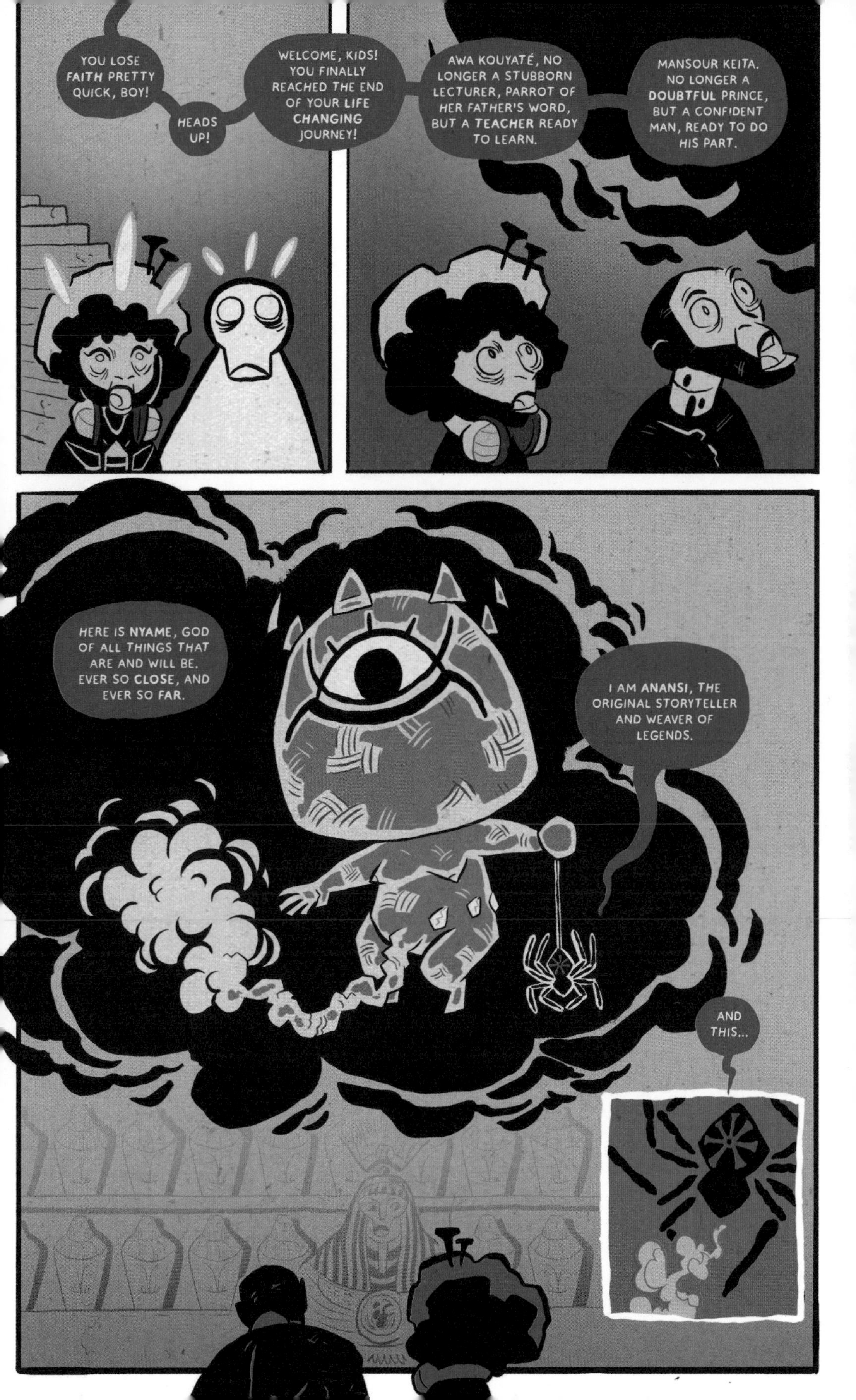
YOU LOSE FAITH PRETTY QUICK, BOY!
HEADS UP!
WELCOME, KIDS! YOU FINALLY REACHED THE END OF YOUR LIFE CHANGING JOURNEY!
AWA KOUYATÉ, NO LONGER A STUBBORN LECTURER, PARROT OF HER FATHER'S WORD, BUT A TEACHER READY TO LEARN.
MANSOUR KEITA. NO LONGER A DOUBTFUL PRINCE, BUT A CONFIDENT MAN, READY TO DO HIS PART.
HERE IS NYAME, GOD OF ALL THINGS THAT ARE AND WILL BE. EVER SO CLOSE, AND EVER SO FAR.
I AM ANANSI, THE ORIGINAL STORYTELLER AND WEAVER OF LEGENDS.
AND THIS...

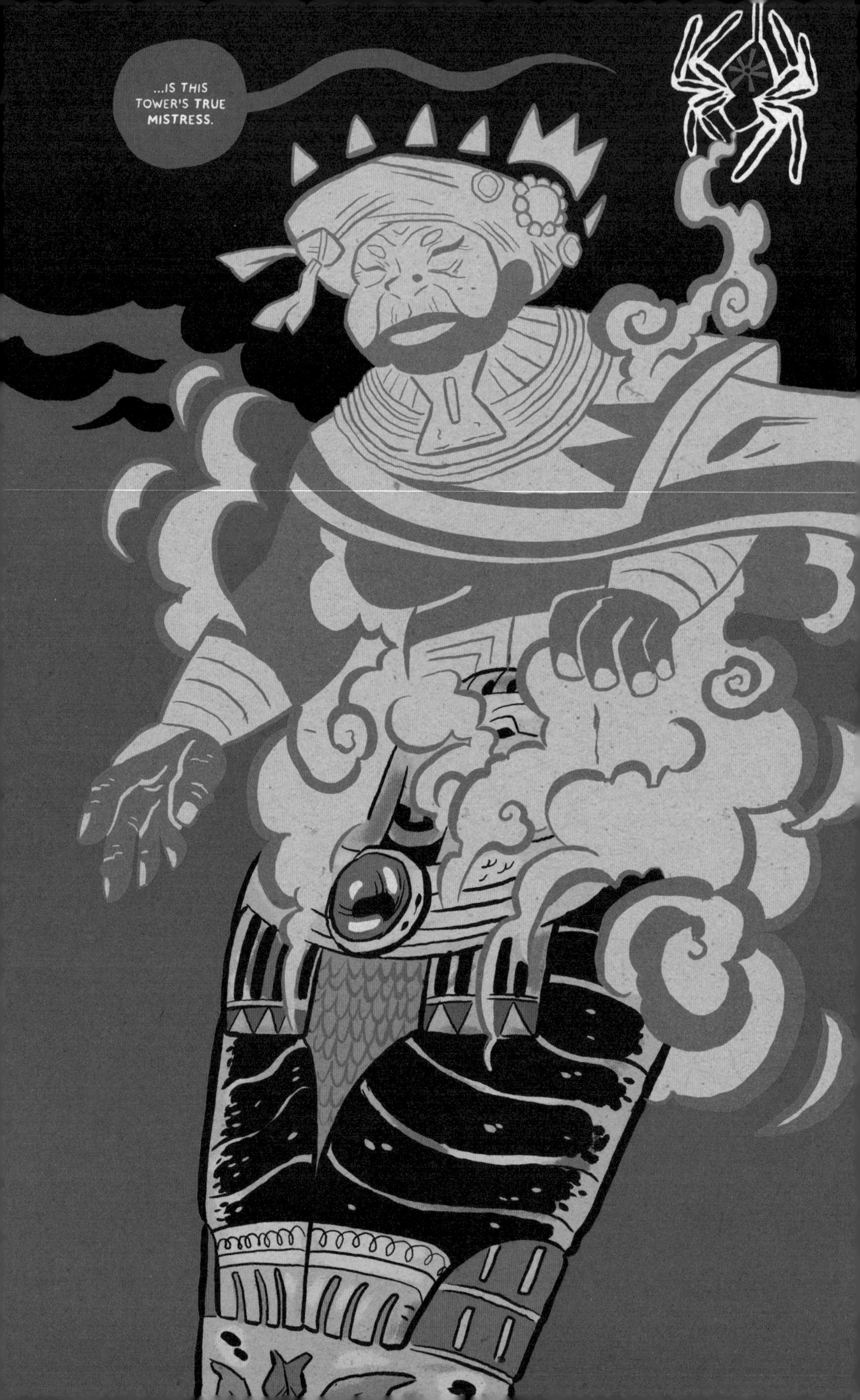
...IS THIS TOWER'S TRUE MISTRESS.

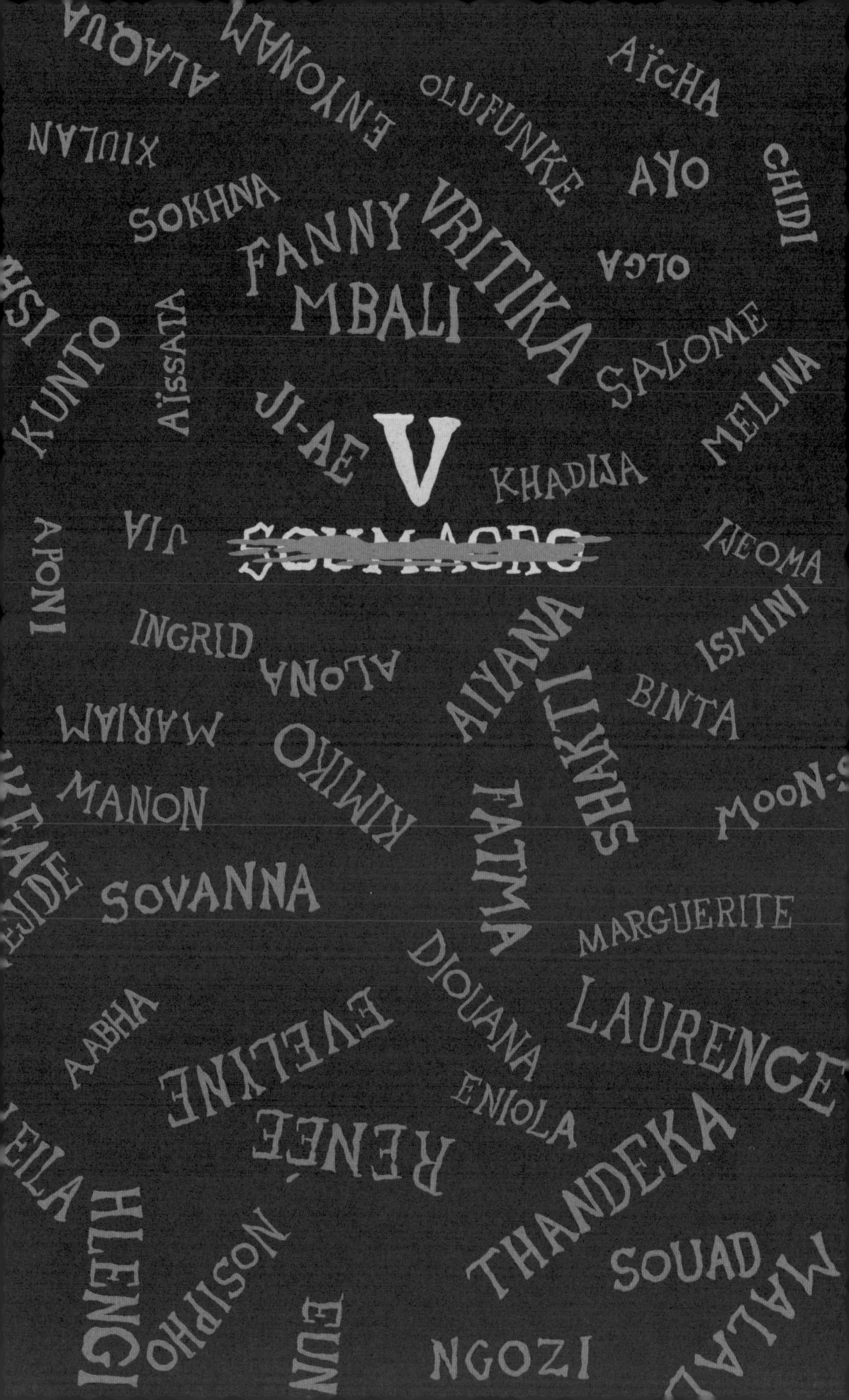
V
ALAQUA
ENYONAM
AÏCHA
OLUFUNKE
XIULAN
AYO
CHIDI
SOKHNA
FANNY
VRITIKA
OLGA
MBALI
AÏSSATA
KUNTO
SALOME
MELINA
JI-AE
KHADIJA
JIA
APONI
IJEOMA
ISMINI
INGRID
ALONA
AIYANA
SHAKTI
BINTA
MARIAM
KIMIKO
MANON
MOON-
FATIMA
SOVANNA
MARGUERITE
DJOUANA
AABHA
EVELYNE
LAURENCE
ENIOLA
RENÉE
THANDEKA
HLENGI
SOPHISON
SOUAD
EUN
NGOZI

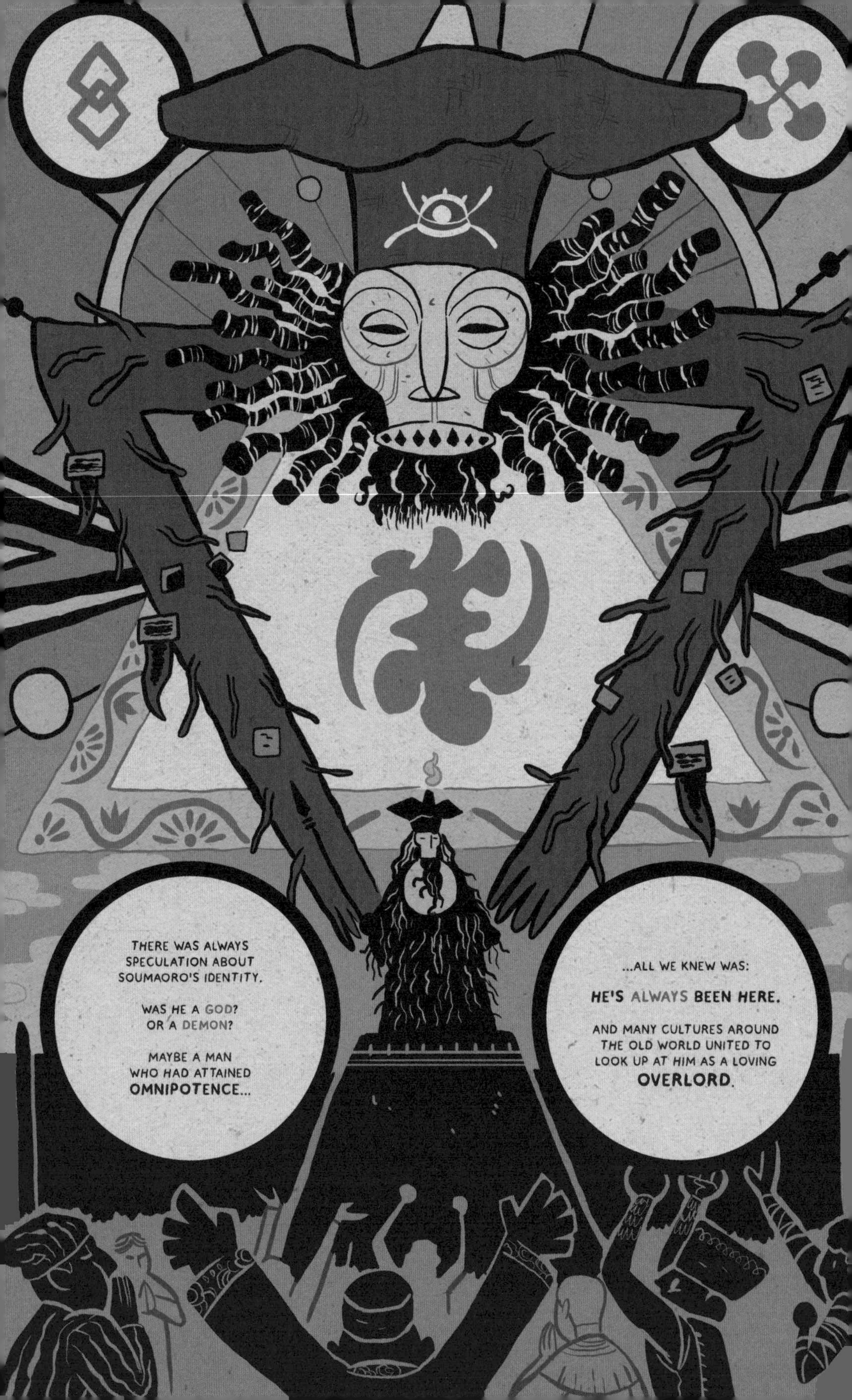
THERE WAS ALWAYS SPECULATION ABOUT SOUMAORO'S IDENTITY.
WAS HE A GOD? OR A DEMON?
MAYBE A MAN WHO HAD ATTAINED **OMNIPOTENCE...**
...ALL WE KNEW WAS:
HE'S ALWAYS BEEN HERE.
AND MANY CULTURES AROUND THE OLD WORLD UNITED TO LOOK UP AT HIM AS A LOVING **OVERLORD.**

HOW SURPRISED THEY WOULD BE,
IF THEY KNEW WHAT HE WAS **REALLY** LIKE.

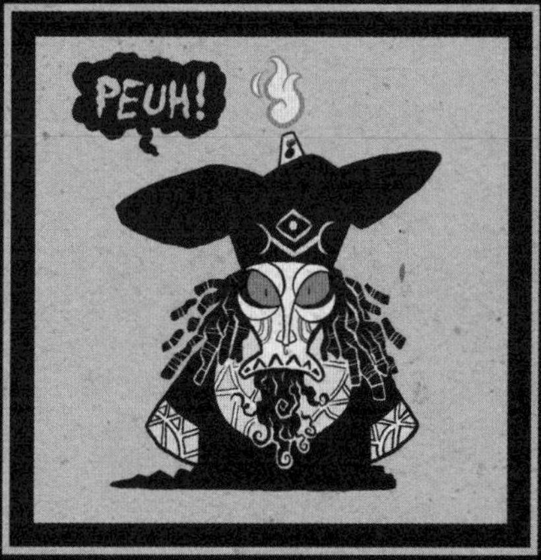
PEUH!

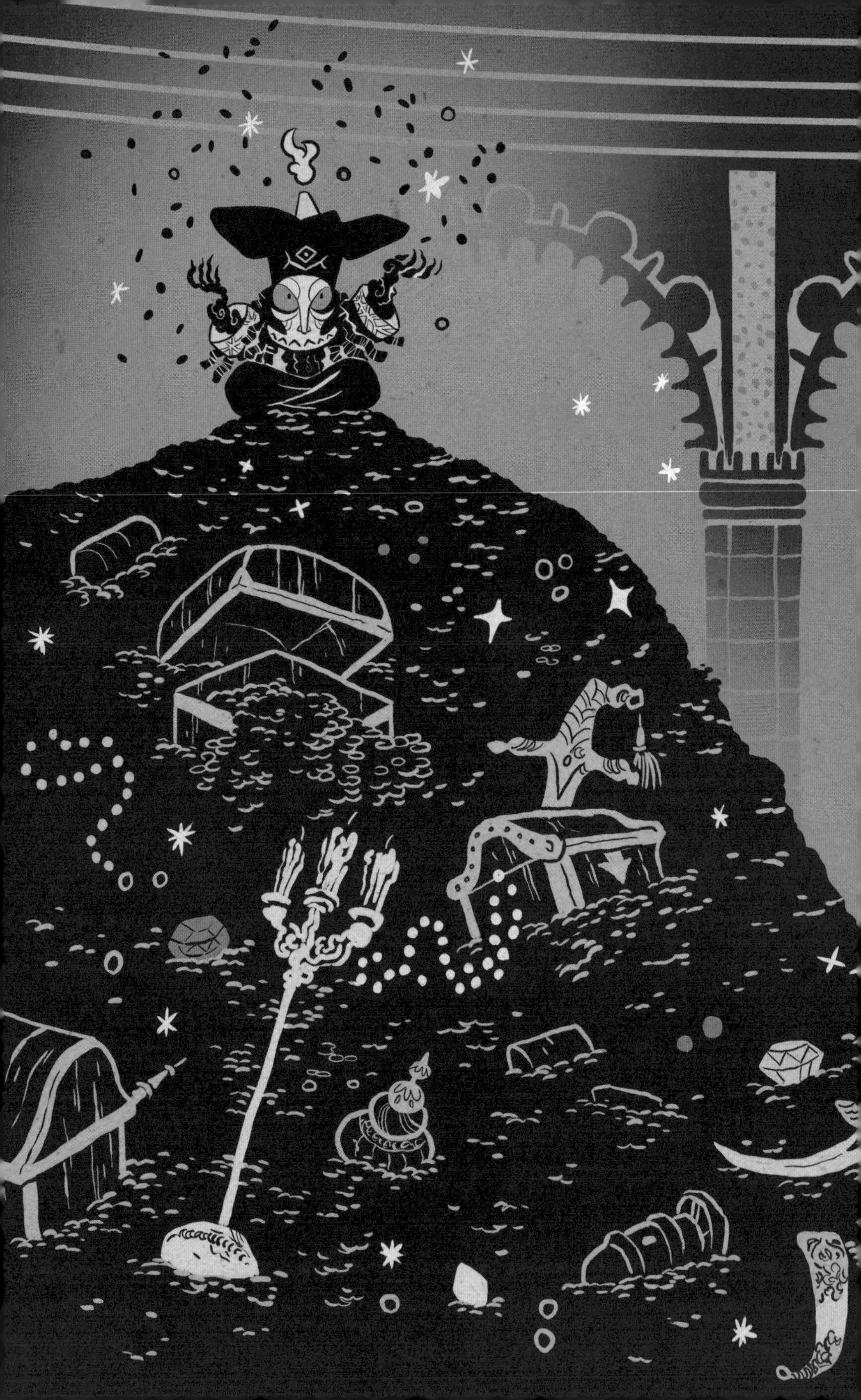

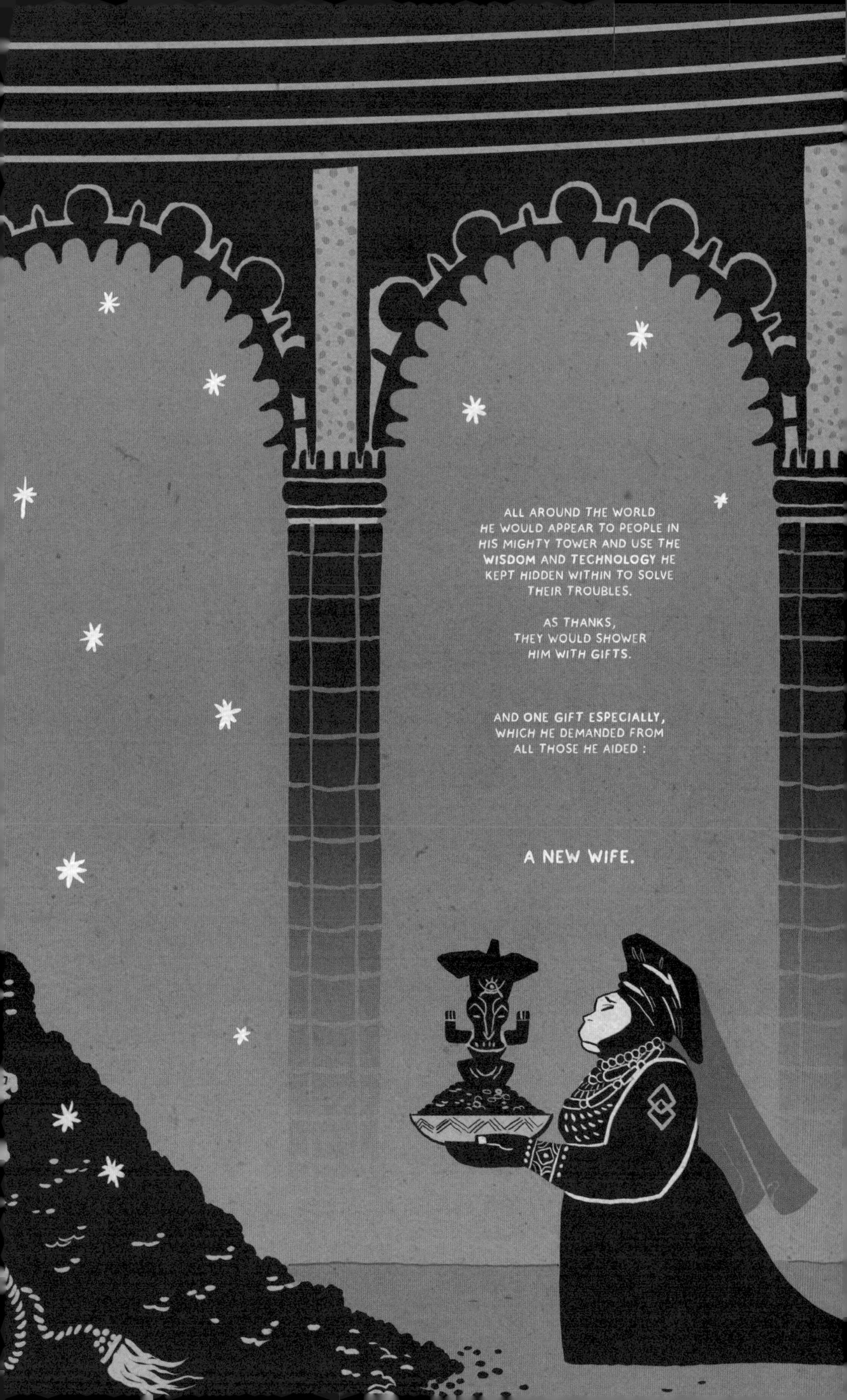
ALL AROUND THE WORLD HE WOULD APPEAR TO PEOPLE IN HIS MIGHTY TOWER AND USE THE WISDOM AND TECHNOLOGY HE KEPT HIDDEN WITHIN TO SOLVE THEIR TROUBLES.
AS THANKS, THEY WOULD SHOWER HIM WITH GIFTS.
AND ONE GIFT ESPECIALLY, WHICH HE DEMANDED FROM ALL THOSE HE AIDED :
A NEW WIFE.

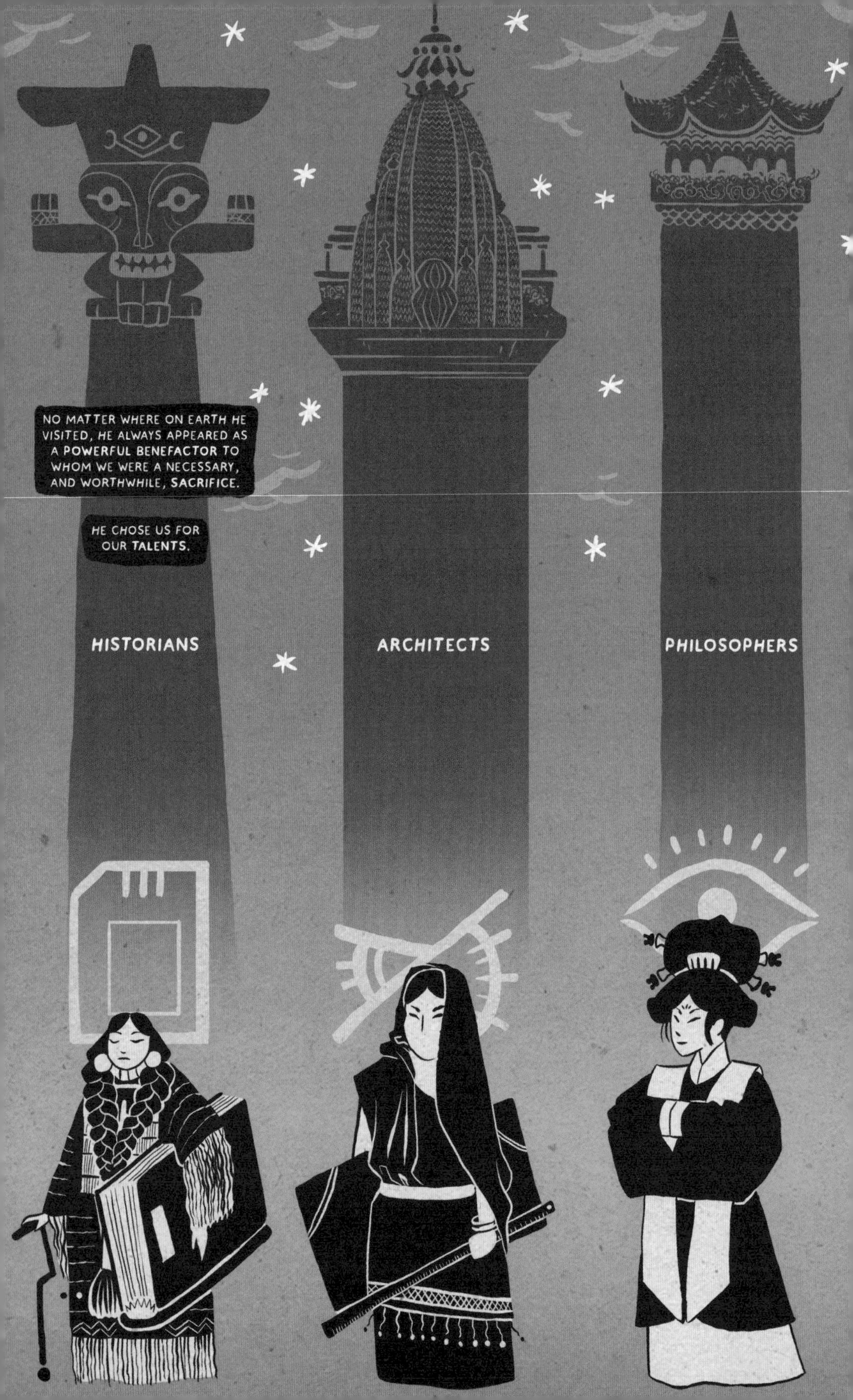
NO MATTER WHERE ON EARTH HE VISITED, HE ALWAYS APPEARED AS A **POWERFUL BENEFACTOR** TO WHOM WE WERE A NECESSARY, AND WORTHWHILE, **SACRIFICE**.
HE CHOSE US FOR OUR **TALENTS**.
HISTORIANS
ARCHITECTS
PHILOSOPHERS

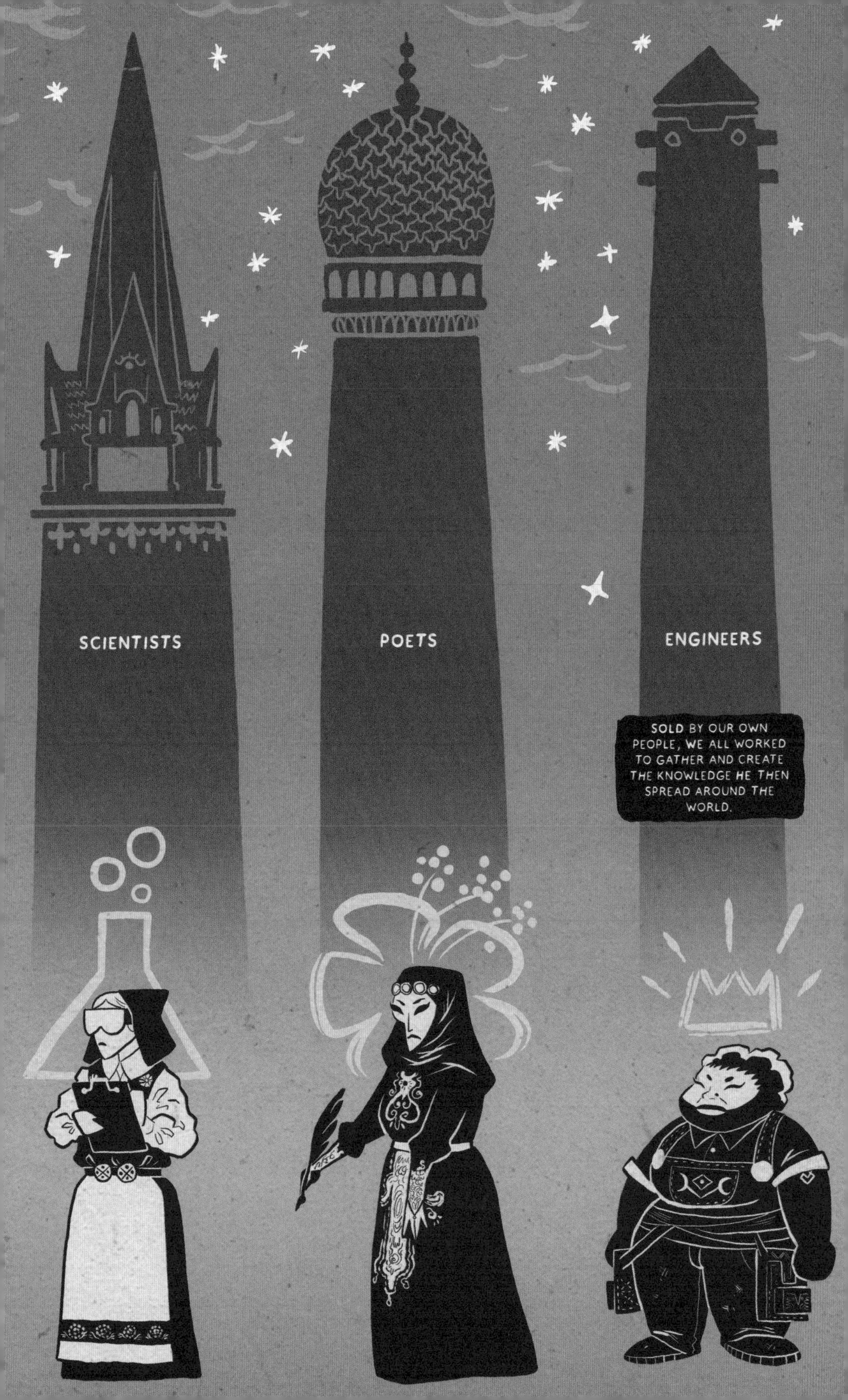
SCIENTISTS
POETS
ENGINEERS
SOLD BY OUR OWN PEOPLE, WE ALL WORKED TO GATHER AND CREATE THE KNOWLEDGE HE THEN SPREAD AROUND THE WORLD.

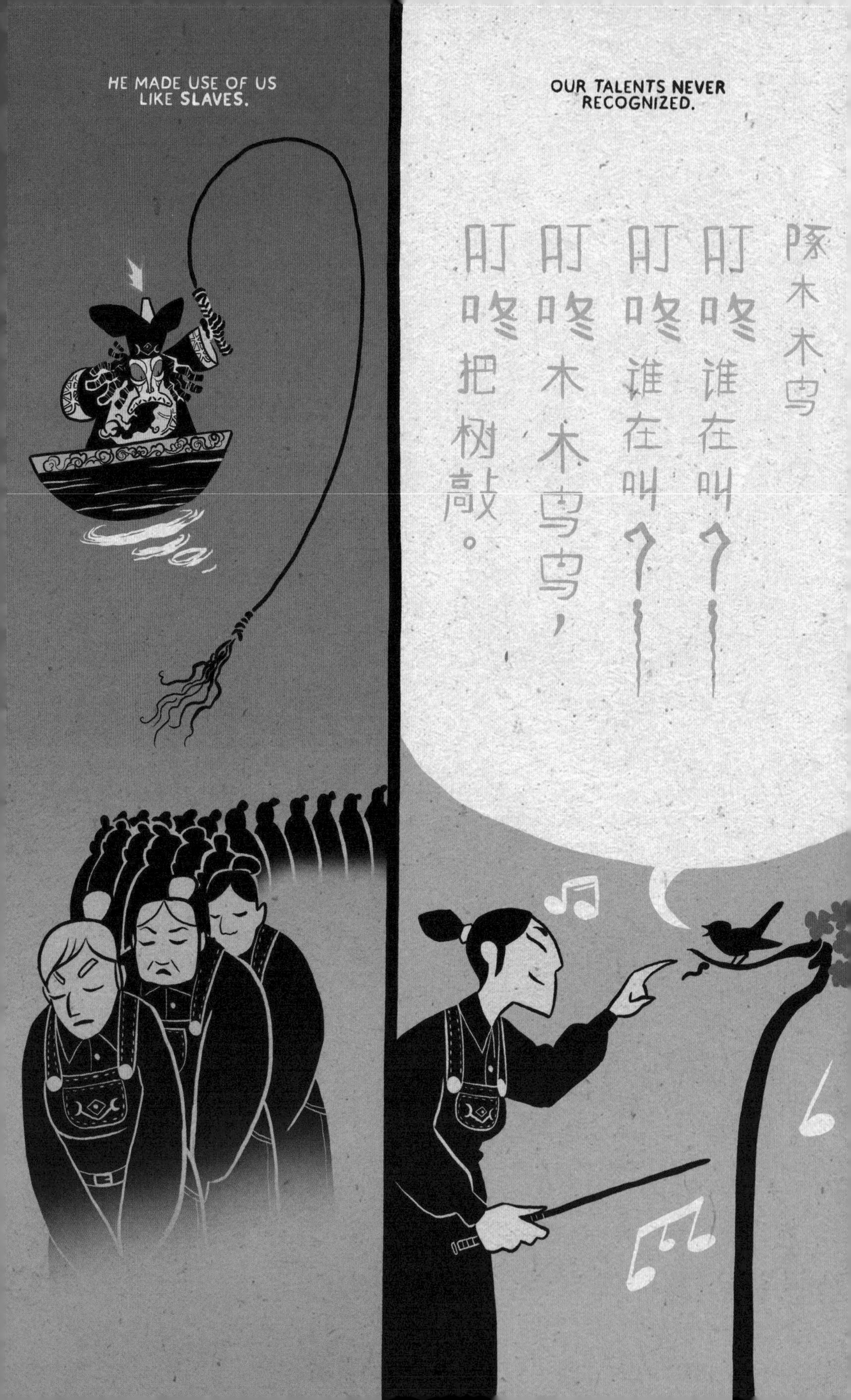
HE MADE USE OF US LIKE SLAVES.
OUR TALENTS NEVER RECOGNIZED.
啄木木鸟
叮咚谁在叫？——
叮咚谁在叫？——
叮咚木木鸟鸟，
叮咚把树敲。

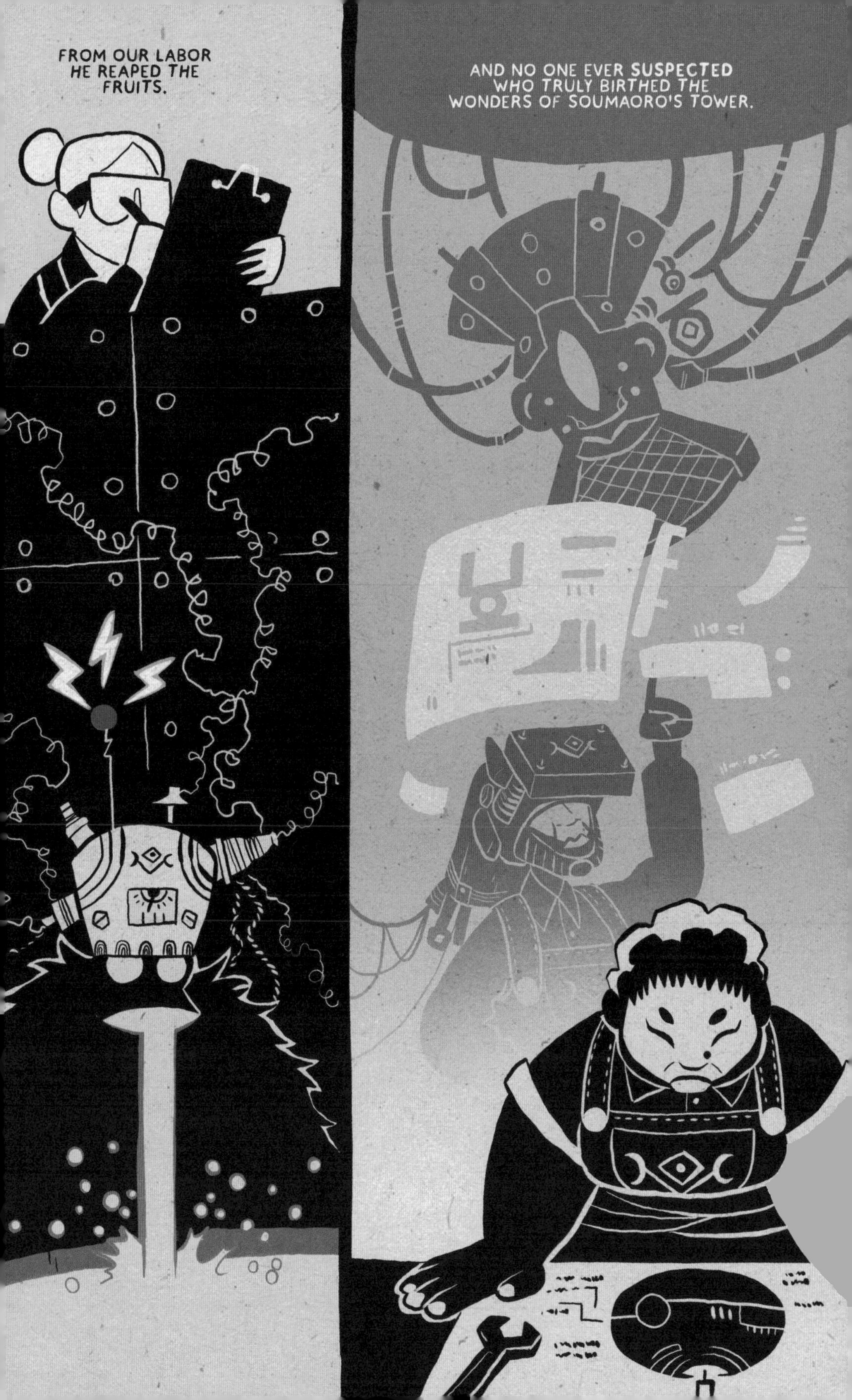
FROM OUR LABOR HE REAPED THE FRUITS.
AND NO ONE EVER SUSPECTED WHO TRULY BIRTHED THE WONDERS OF SOUMAORO'S TOWER.

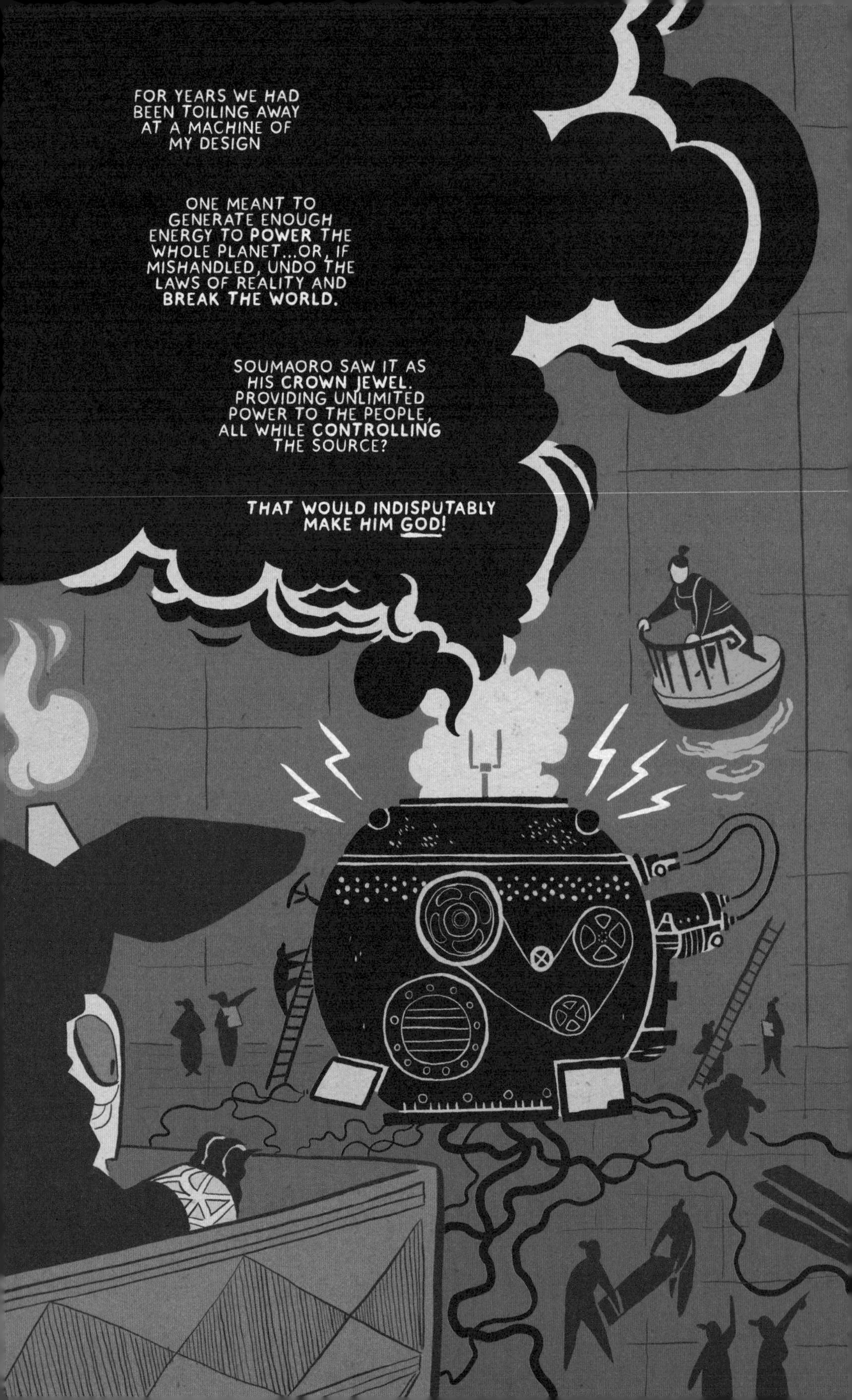
FOR YEARS WE HAD BEEN TOILING AWAY AT A MACHINE OF MY DESIGN
ONE MEANT TO GENERATE ENOUGH ENERGY TO POWER THE WHOLE PLANET...OR, IF MISHANDLED, UNDO THE LAWS OF REALITY AND BREAK THE WORLD.
SOUMAORO SAW IT AS HIS CROWN JEWEL. PROVIDING UNLIMITED POWER TO THE PEOPLE, ALL WHILE CONTROLLING THE SOURCE?
THAT WOULD INDISPUTABLY MAKE HIM GOD!

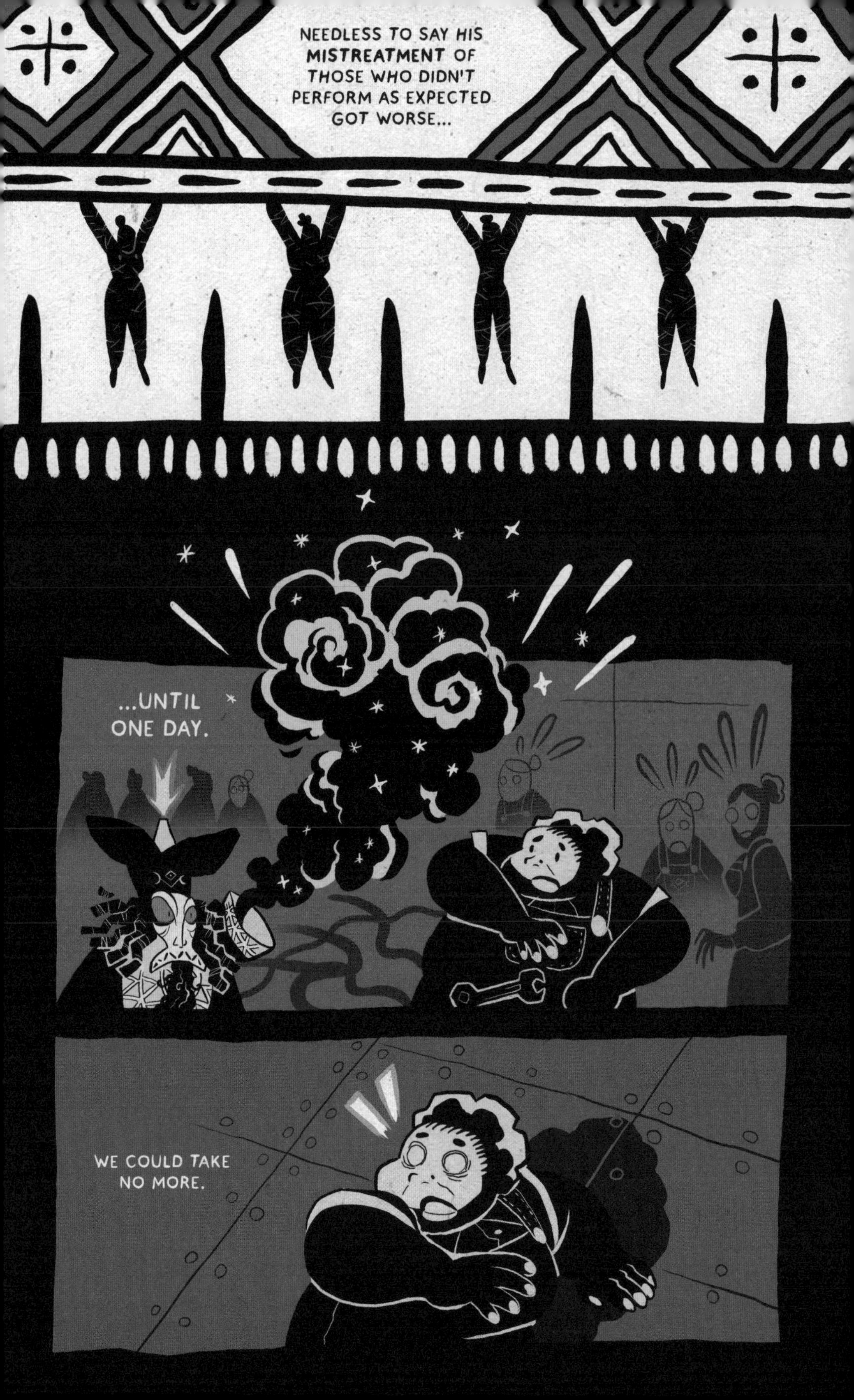
NEEDLESS TO SAY HIS MISTREATMENT OF THOSE WHO DIDN'T PERFORM AS EXPECTED GOT WORSE...
...UNTIL ONE DAY.
WE COULD TAKE NO MORE.

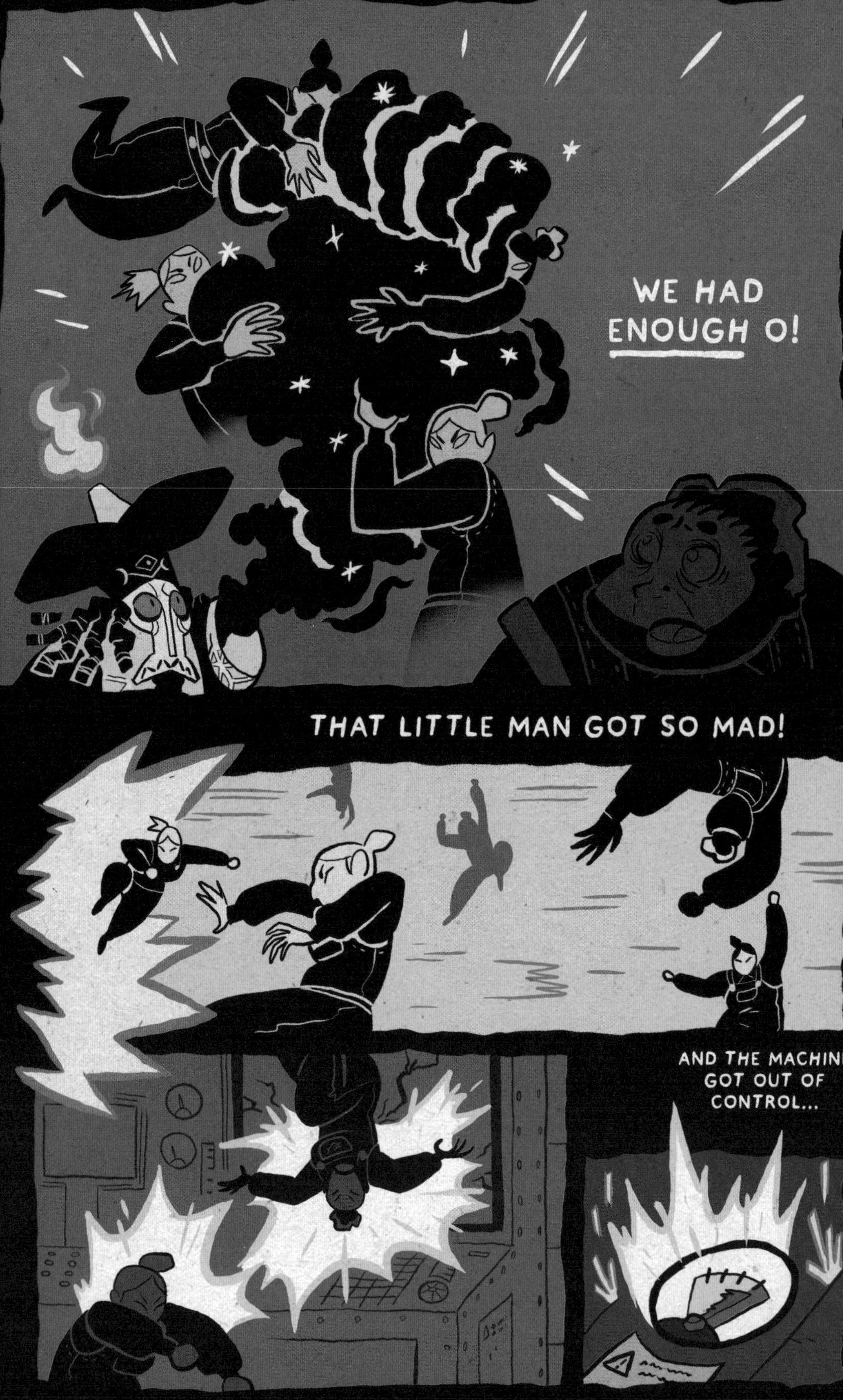
WE HAD ENOUGH O!
THAT LITTLE MAN GOT SO MAD!
AND THE MACHINE GOT OUT OF CONTROL...

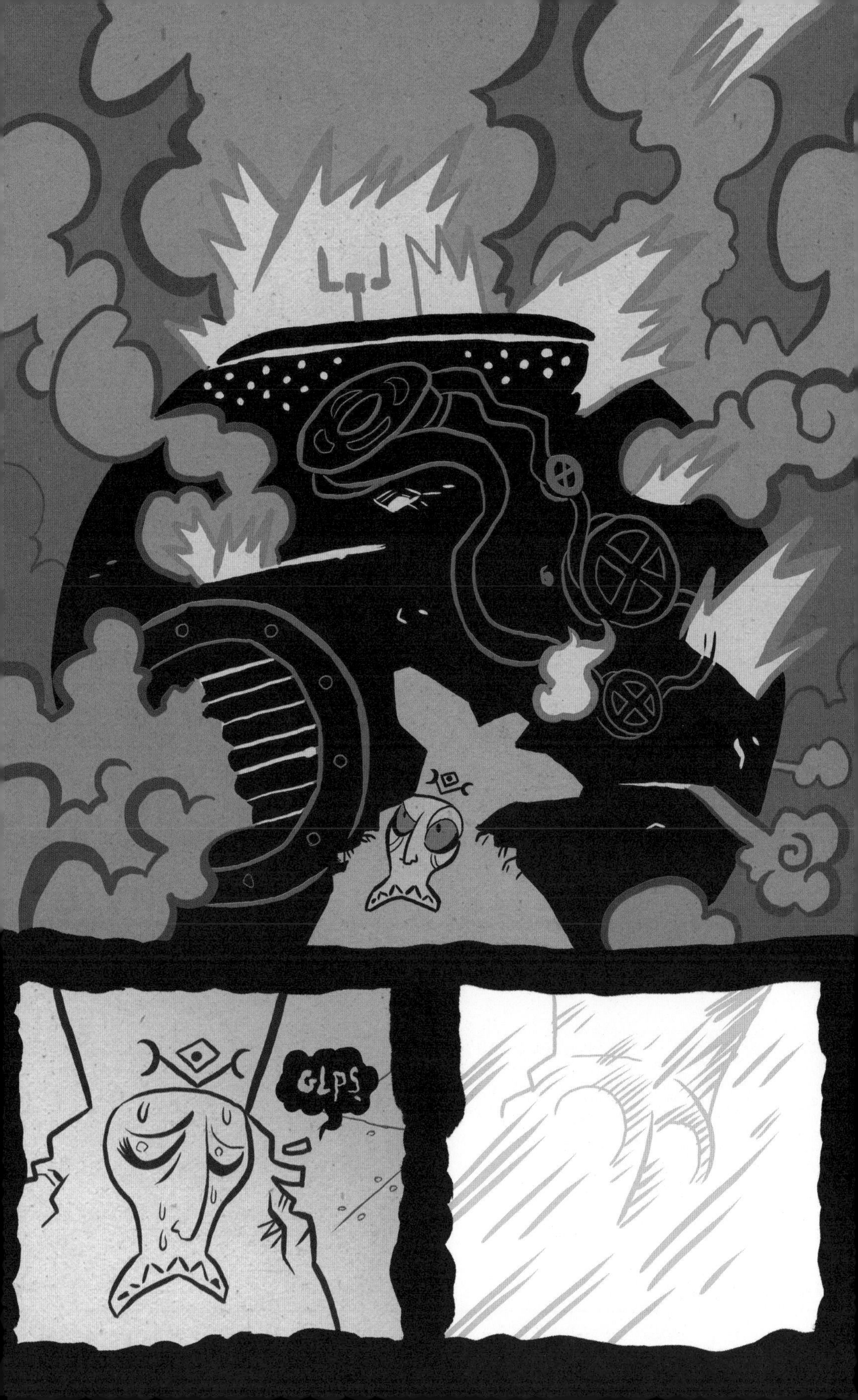
GLPS

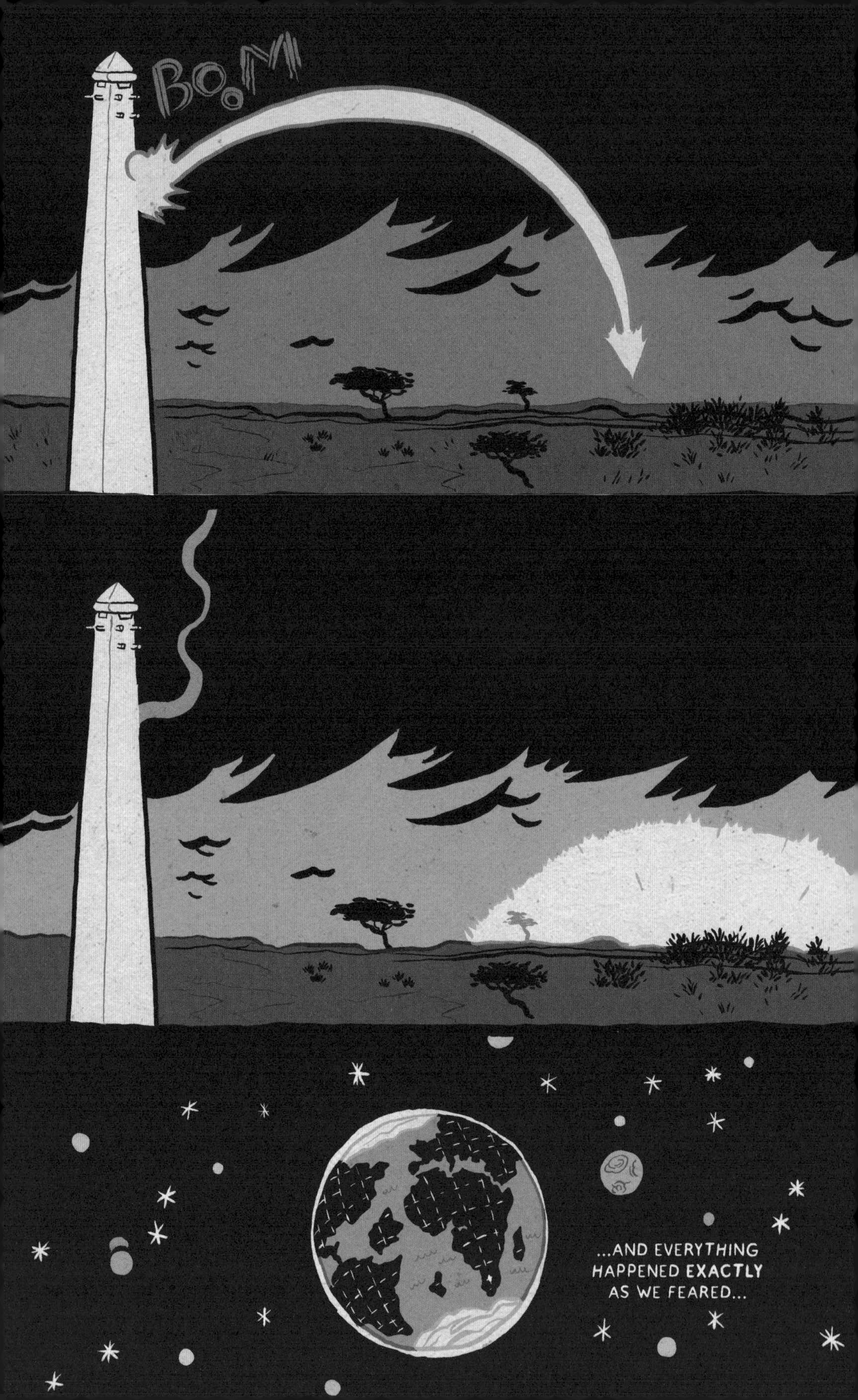
BOOM
...AND EVERYTHING
HAPPENED EXACTLY
AS WE FEARED...

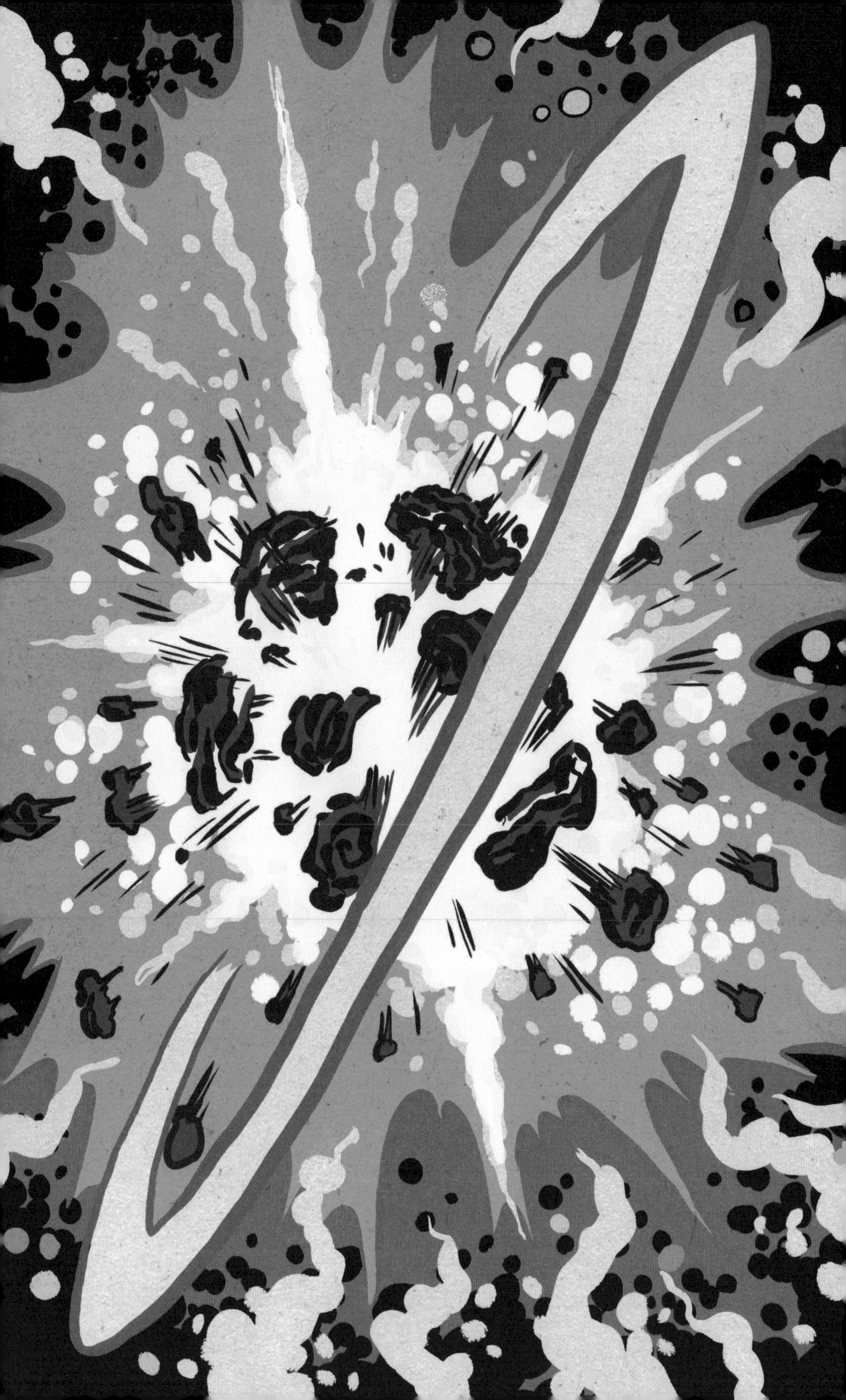

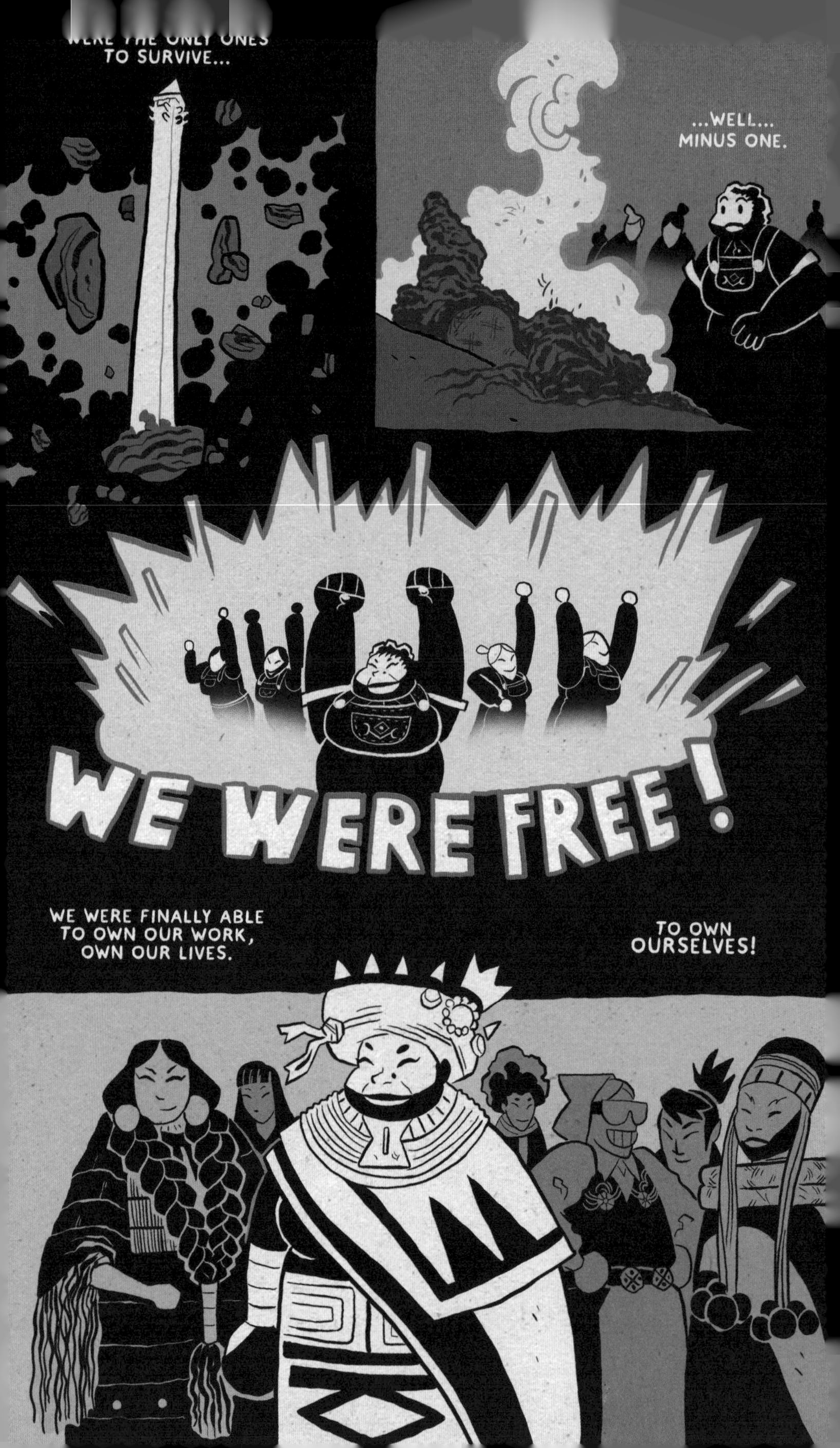
TO SURVIVE...
...WELL... MINUS ONE.
WE WERE FREE!
WE WERE FINALLY ABLE TO OWN OUR WORK, OWN OUR LIVES.
TO OWN OURSELVES!

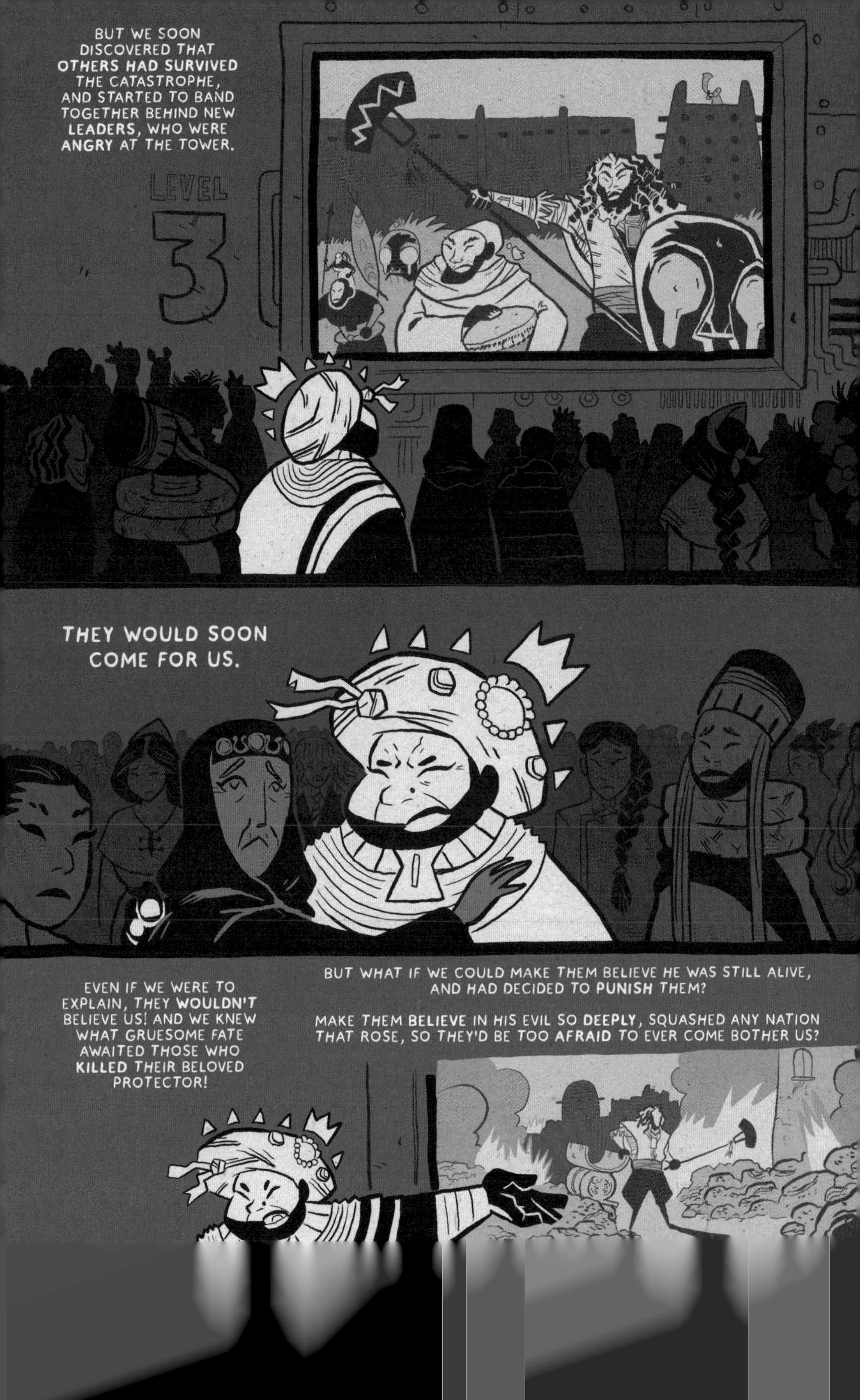
BUT WE SOON DISCOVERED THAT OTHERS HAD SURVIVED THE CATASTROPHE, AND STARTED TO BAND TOGETHER BEHIND NEW LEADERS, WHO WERE ANGRY AT THE TOWER.
LEVEL
3
THEY WOULD SOON COME FOR US.
EVEN IF WE WERE TO EXPLAIN, THEY WOULDN'T BELIEVE US! AND WE KNEW WHAT GRUESOME FATE AWAITED THOSE WHO KILLED THEIR BELOVED PROTECTOR!
BUT WHAT IF WE COULD MAKE THEM BELIEVE HE WAS STILL ALIVE, AND HAD DECIDED TO PUNISH THEM?
MAKE THEM BELIEVE IN HIS EVIL SO DEEPLY, SQUASHED ANY NATION THAT ROSE, SO THEY'D BE TOO AFRAID TO EVER COME BOTHER US?

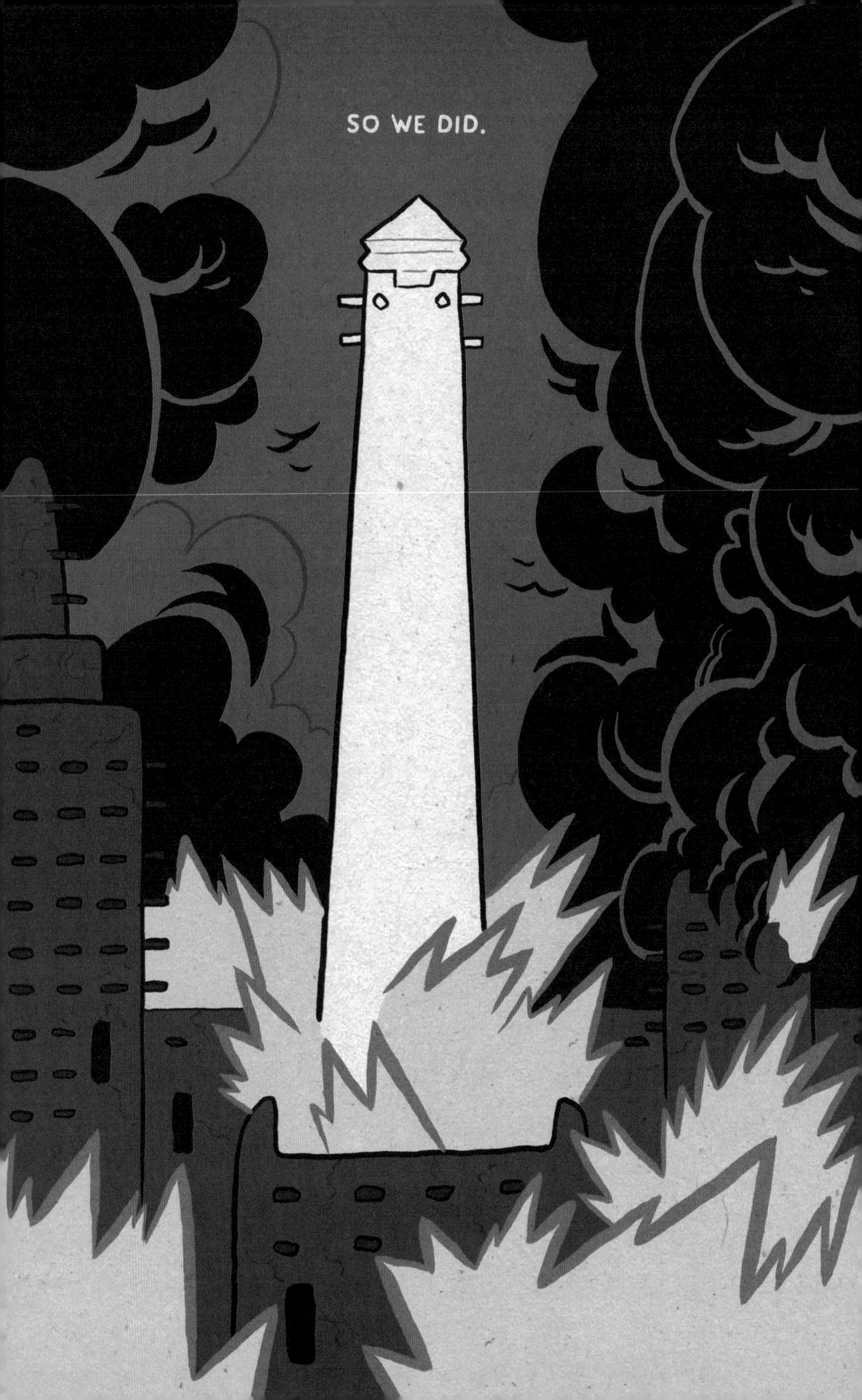
SO WE DID.

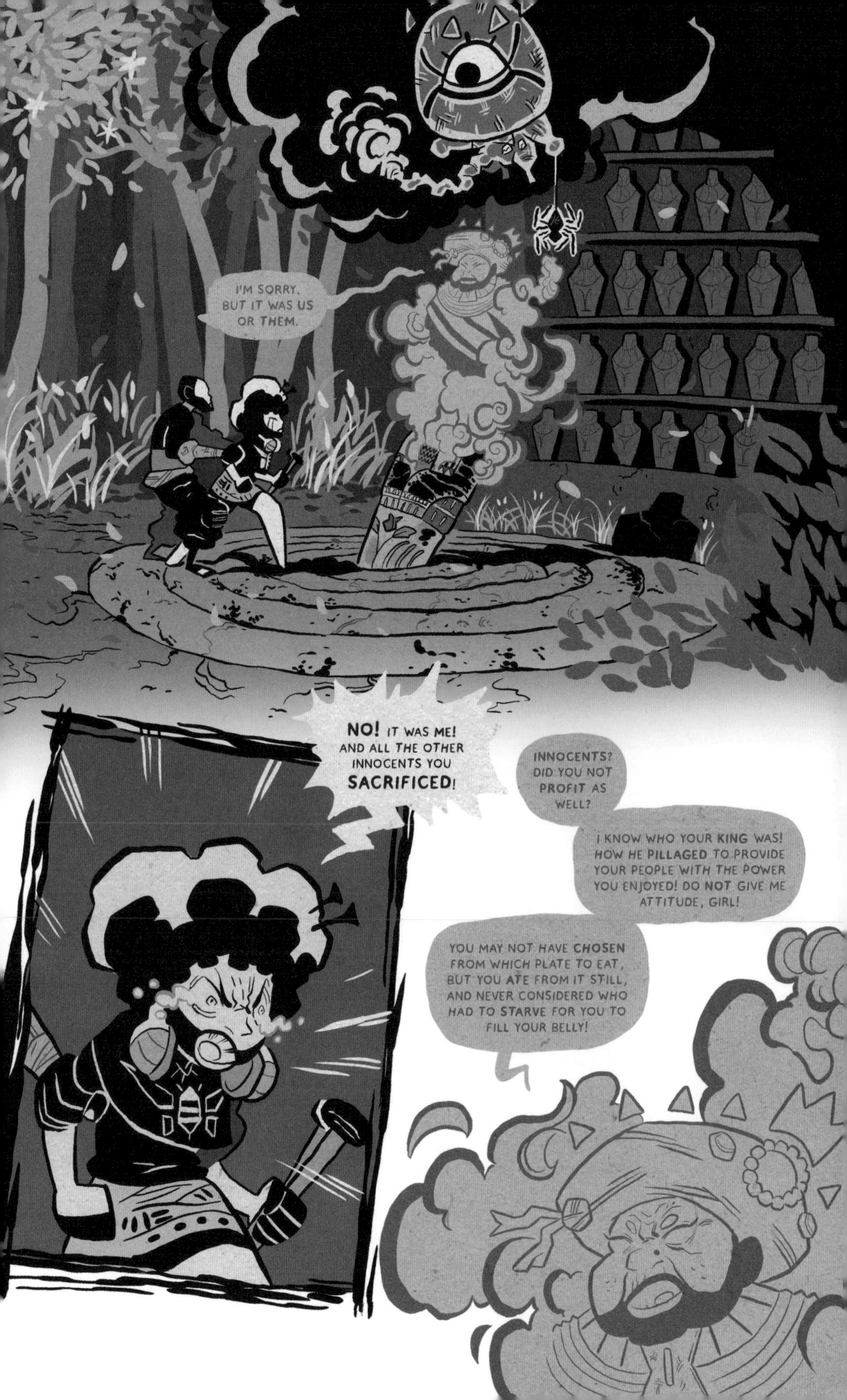
I'M SORRY. BUT IT WAS US OR THEM.
NO! IT WAS ME! AND ALL THE OTHER INNOCENTS YOU SACRIFICED!
INNOCENTS? DID YOU NOT PROFIT AS WELL?
I KNOW WHO YOUR KING WAS! HOW HE PILLAGED TO PROVIDE YOUR PEOPLE WITH THE POWER YOU ENJOYED! DO NOT GIVE ME ATTITUDE, GIRL!
YOU MAY NOT HAVE CHOSEN FROM WHICH PLATE TO EAT, BUT YOU ATE FROM IT STILL, AND NEVER CONSIDERED WHO HAD TO STARVE FOR YOU TO FILL YOUR BELLY!

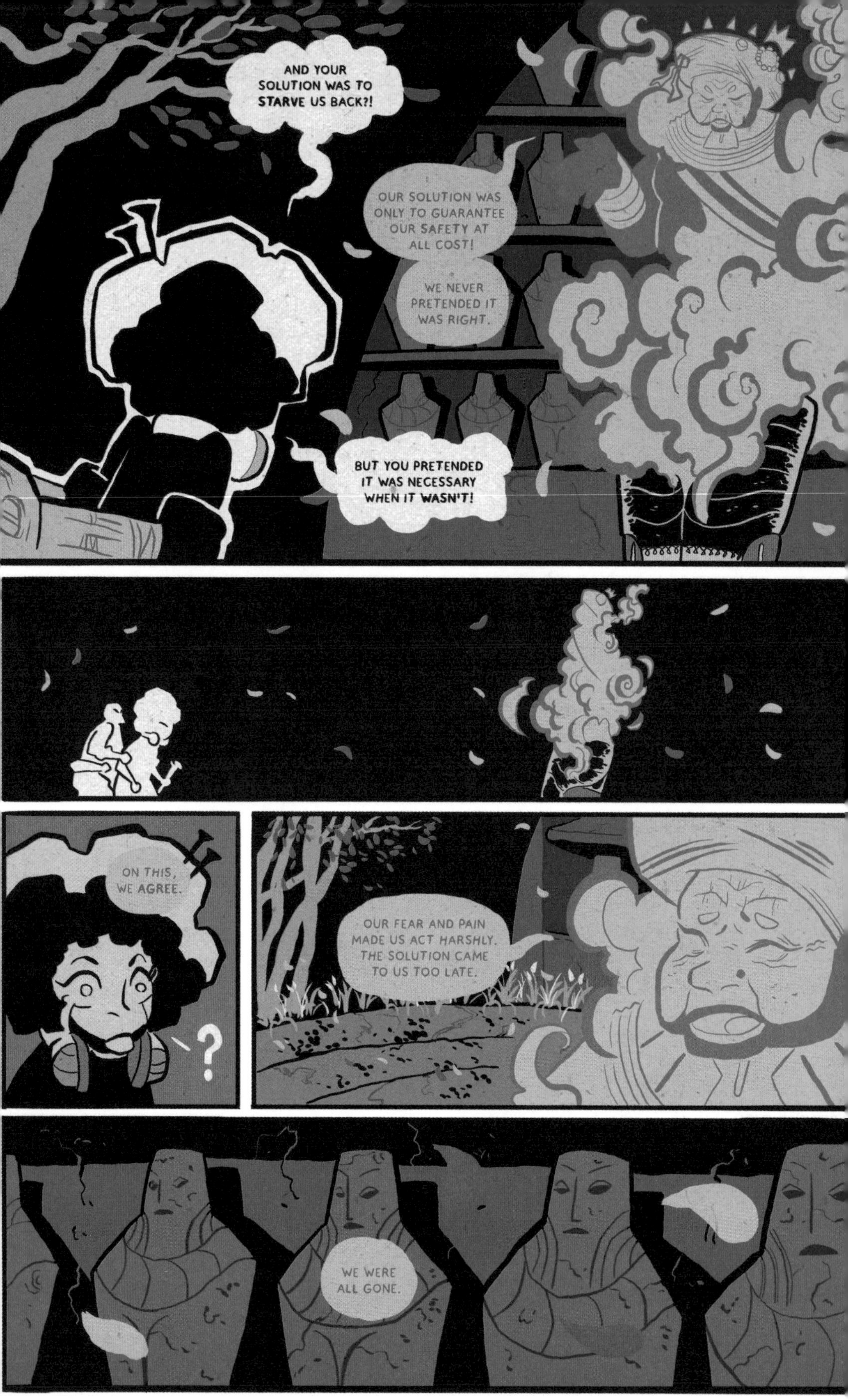
AND YOUR SOLUTION WAS TO STARVE US BACK?!
OUR SOLUTION WAS ONLY TO GUARANTEE OUR SAFETY AT ALL COST!
WE NEVER PRETENDED IT WAS RIGHT.
BUT YOU PRETENDED IT WAS NECESSARY WHEN IT WASN'T!
ON THIS, WE AGREE.
?
OUR FEAR AND PAIN MADE US ACT HARSHLY. THE SOLUTION CAME TO US TOO LATE.
WE WERE ALL GONE.

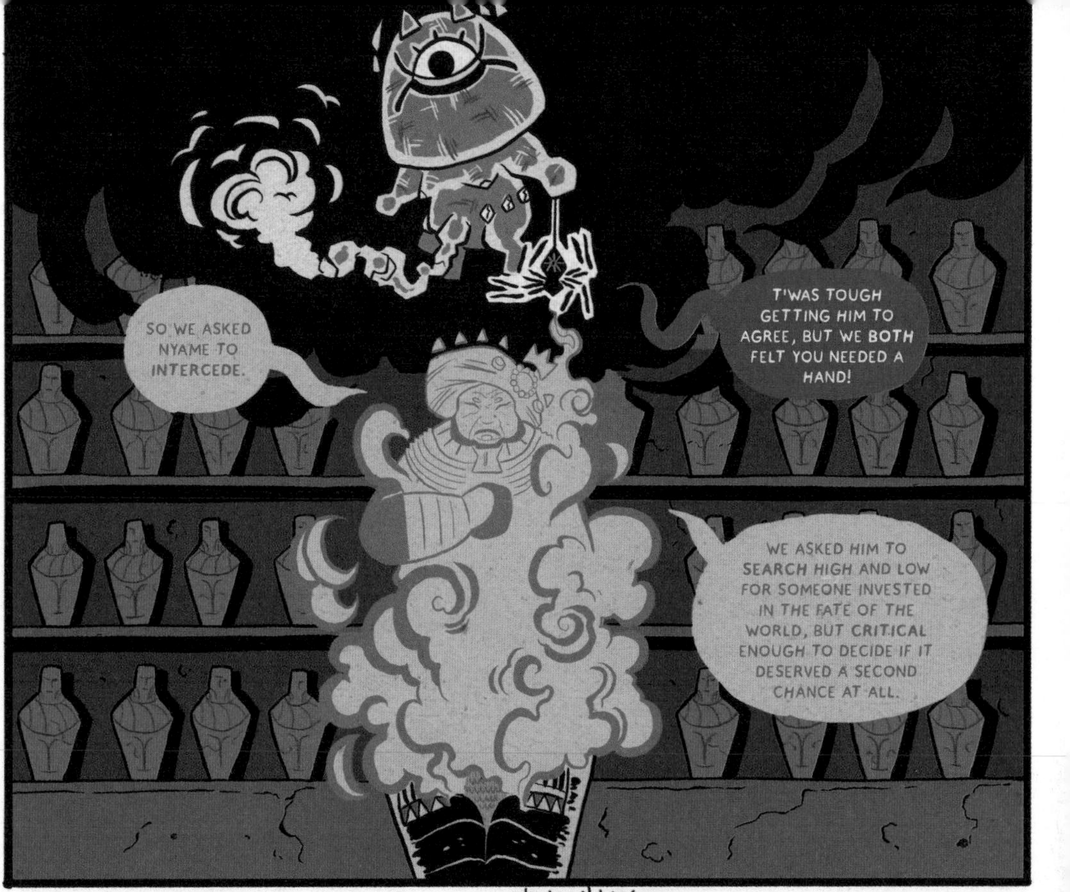
SO WE ASKED NYAME TO INTERCEDE.
T'WAS TOUGH GETTING HIM TO AGREE, BUT WE BOTH FELT YOU NEEDED A HAND!
WE ASKED HIM TO SEARCH HIGH AND LOW FOR SOMEONE INVESTED IN THE FATE OF THE WORLD, BUT CRITICAL ENOUGH TO DECIDE IF IT DESERVED A SECOND CHANCE AT ALL.

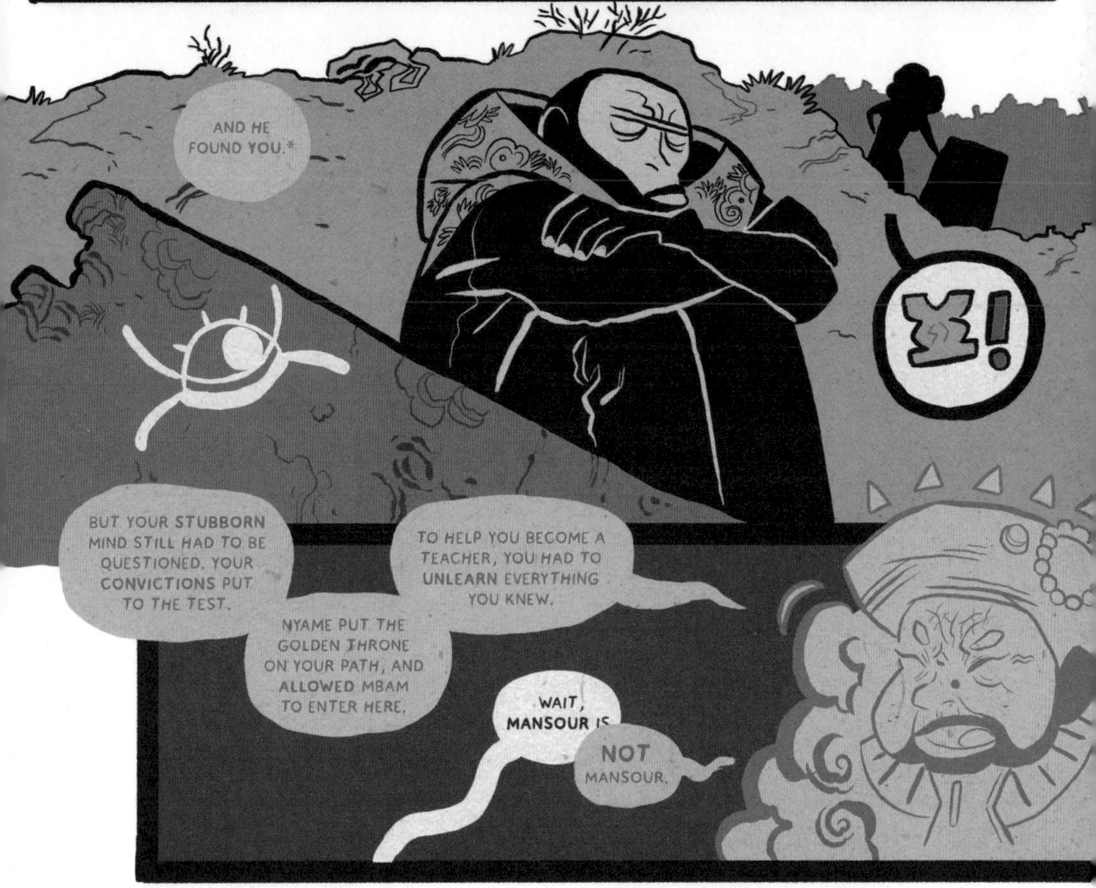
AND HE FOUND YOU.*
BUT YOUR STUBBORN MIND STILL HAD TO BE QUESTIONED. YOUR CONVICTIONS PUT TO THE TEST.
TO HELP YOU BECOME A TEACHER, YOU HAD TO UNLEARN EVERYTHING YOU KNEW.
NYAME PUT THE GOLDEN THRONE ON YOUR PATH, AND ALLOWED MBAM TO ENTER HERE.
WAIT, MANSOUR IS
NOT MANSOUR.

*GO BACK TO TRY AND FIND THE ICON OF NYAME THROUGHOUT THE STORY!

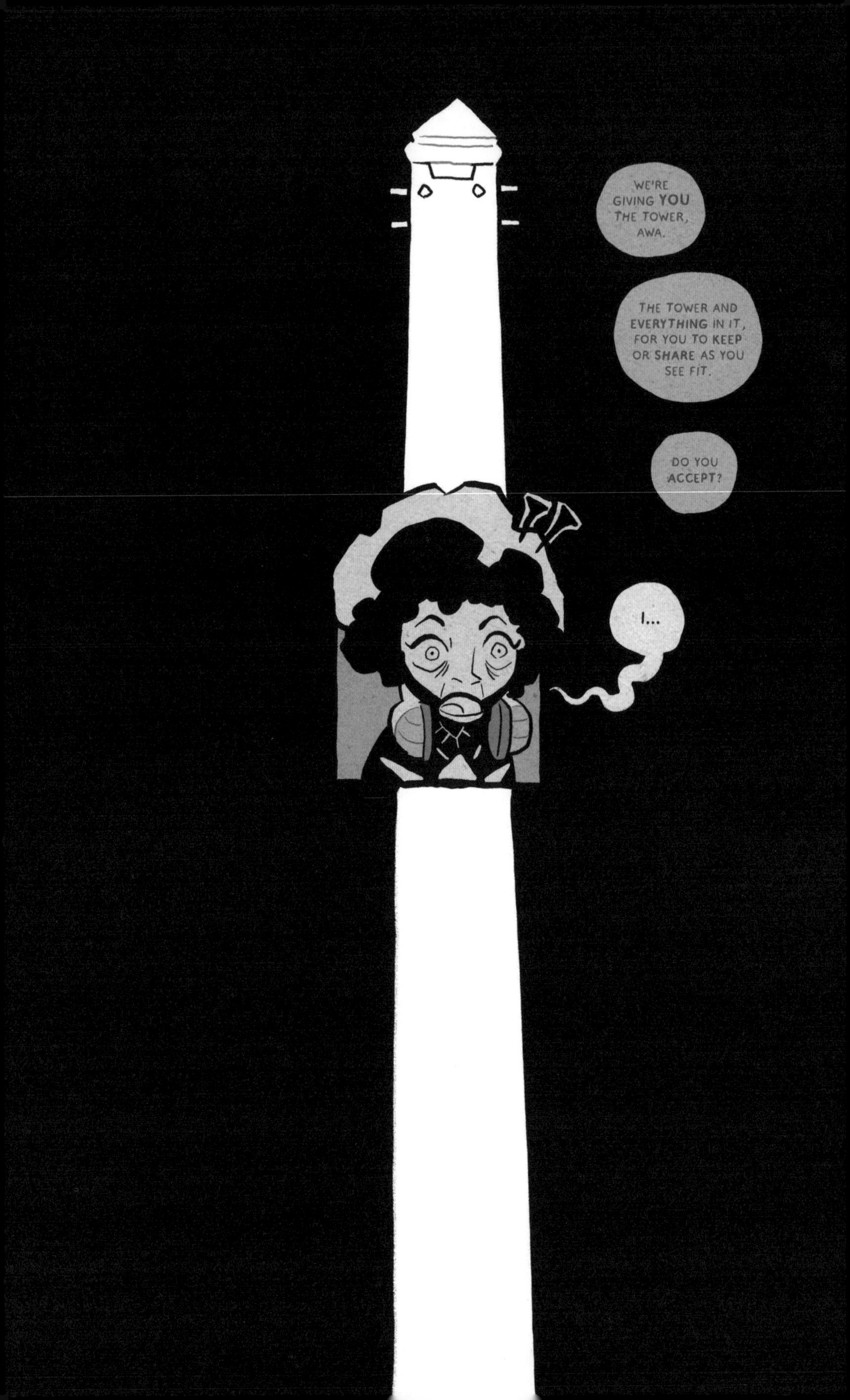
WE'RE GIVING YOU THE TOWER, AWA.
THE TOWER AND EVERYTHING IN IT, FOR YOU TO KEEP OR SHARE AS YOU SEE FIT.
DO YOU ACCEPT?
I...

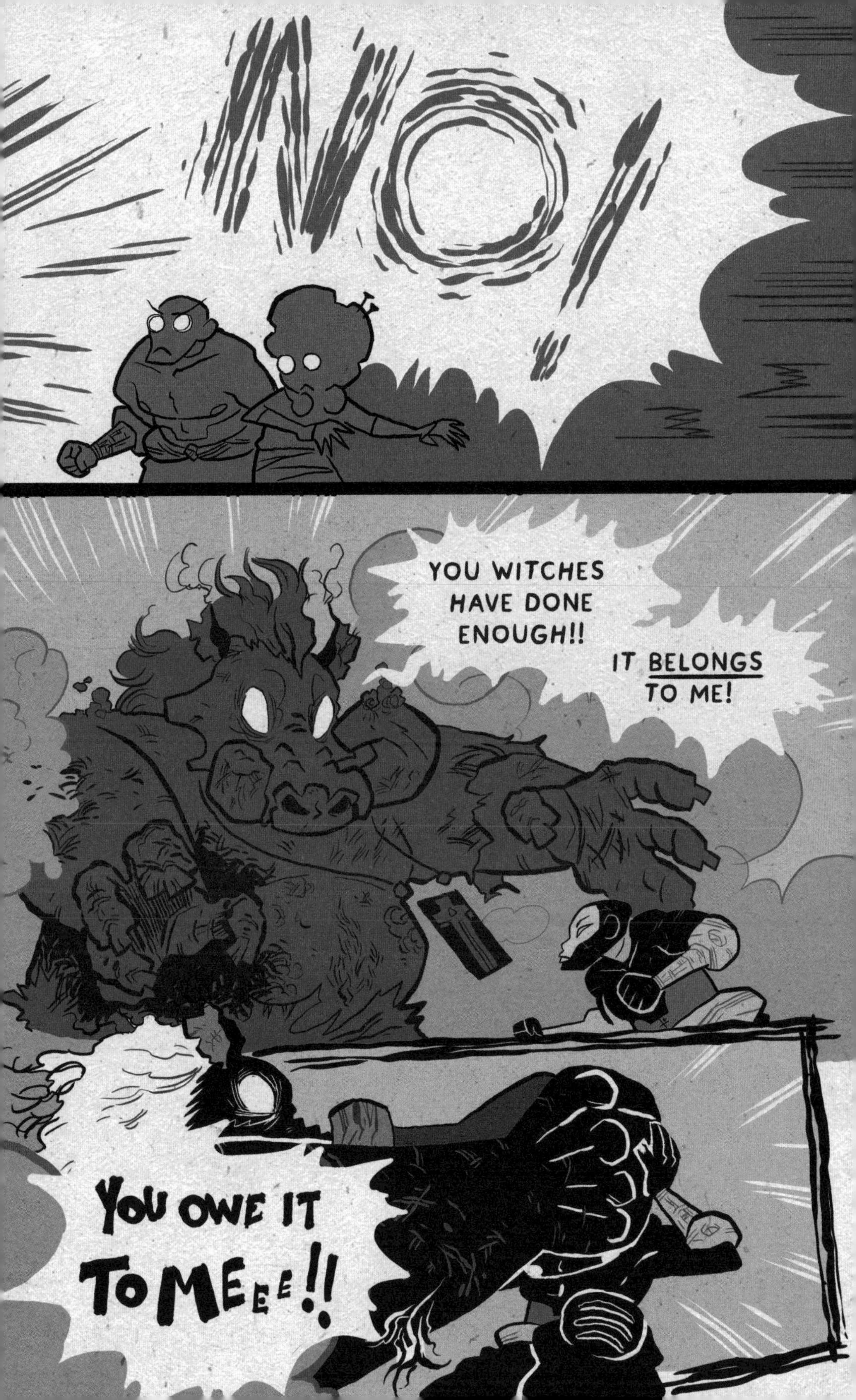
NO!
YOU WITCHES HAVE DONE ENOUGH!!
IT BELONGS TO ME!
YOU OWE IT TO MEEEE!!

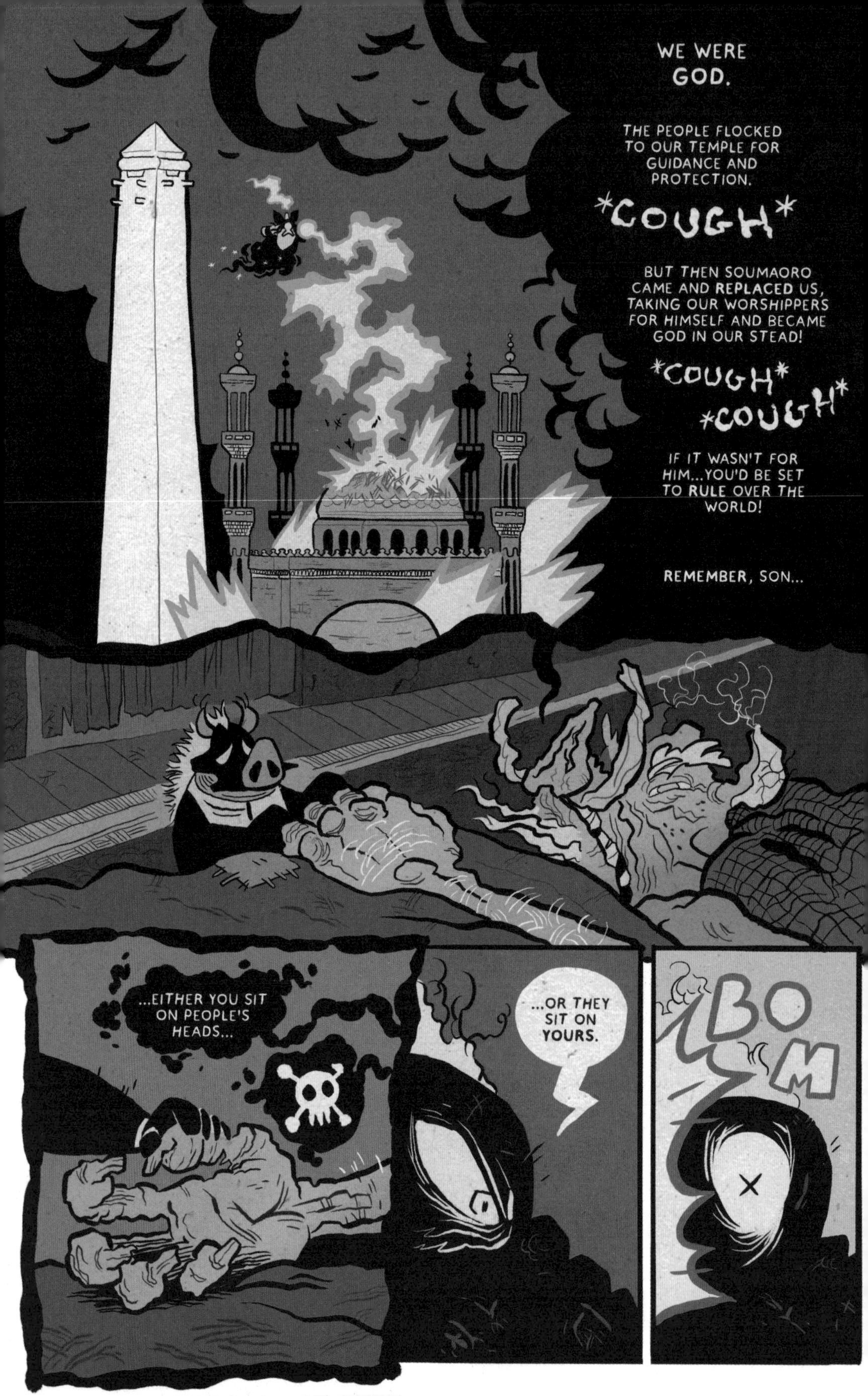
WE WERE GOD.
THE PEOPLE FLOCKED TO OUR TEMPLE FOR GUIDANCE AND PROTECTION.
COUGH
BUT THEN SOUMAORO CAME AND REPLACED US, TAKING OUR WORSHIPPERS FOR HIMSELF AND BECAME GOD IN OUR STEAD!
COUGH
COUGH
IF IT WASN'T FOR HIM...YOU'D BE SET TO RULE OVER THE WORLD!
REMEMBER, SON...
...EITHER YOU SIT ON PEOPLE'S HEADS...
...OR THEY SIT ON YOURS.
BOOM

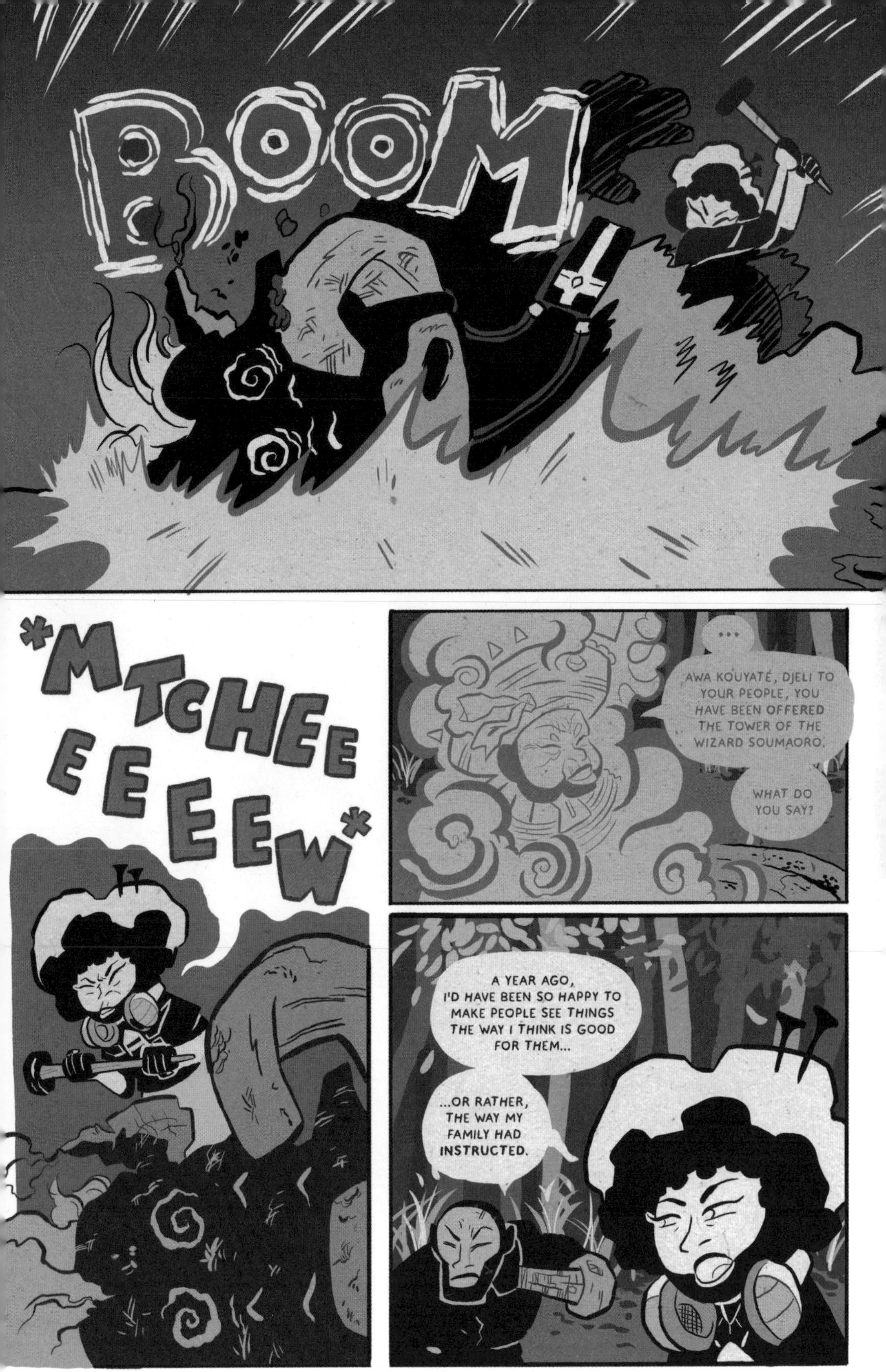
BOOM
MTCHEEEEEEW
...
AWA KOUYATÉ, DJELI TO YOUR PEOPLE, YOU HAVE BEEN OFFERED THE TOWER OF THE WIZARD SOUMAORO.
WHAT DO YOU SAY?
A YEAR AGO, I'D HAVE BEEN SO HAPPY TO MAKE PEOPLE SEE THINGS THE WAY I THINK IS GOOD FOR THEM...
...OR RATHER, THE WAY MY FAMILY HAD INSTRUCTED.

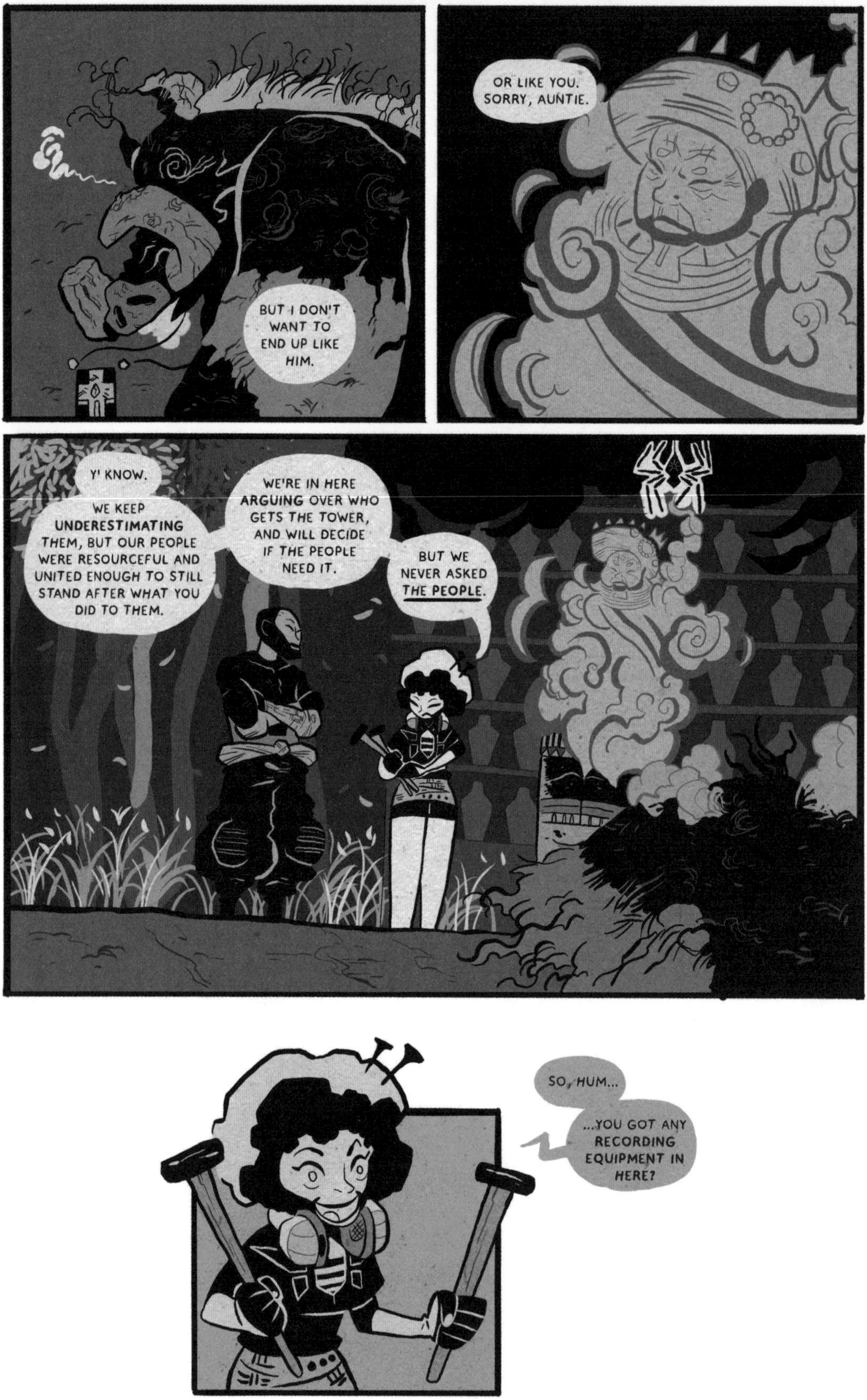
BUT I DON'T WANT TO END UP LIKE HIM.
OR LIKE YOU. SORRY, AUNTIE.
Y' KNOW.
WE KEEP UNDERESTIMATING THEM, BUT OUR PEOPLE WERE RESOURCEFUL AND UNITED ENOUGH TO STILL STAND AFTER WHAT YOU DID TO THEM.
WE'RE IN HERE ARGUING OVER WHO GETS THE TOWER, AND WILL DECIDE IF THE PEOPLE NEED IT.
BUT WE NEVER ASKED THE PEOPLE.
SO, HUM...
...YOU GOT ANY RECORDING EQUIPMENT IN HERE?

EPILOGUE

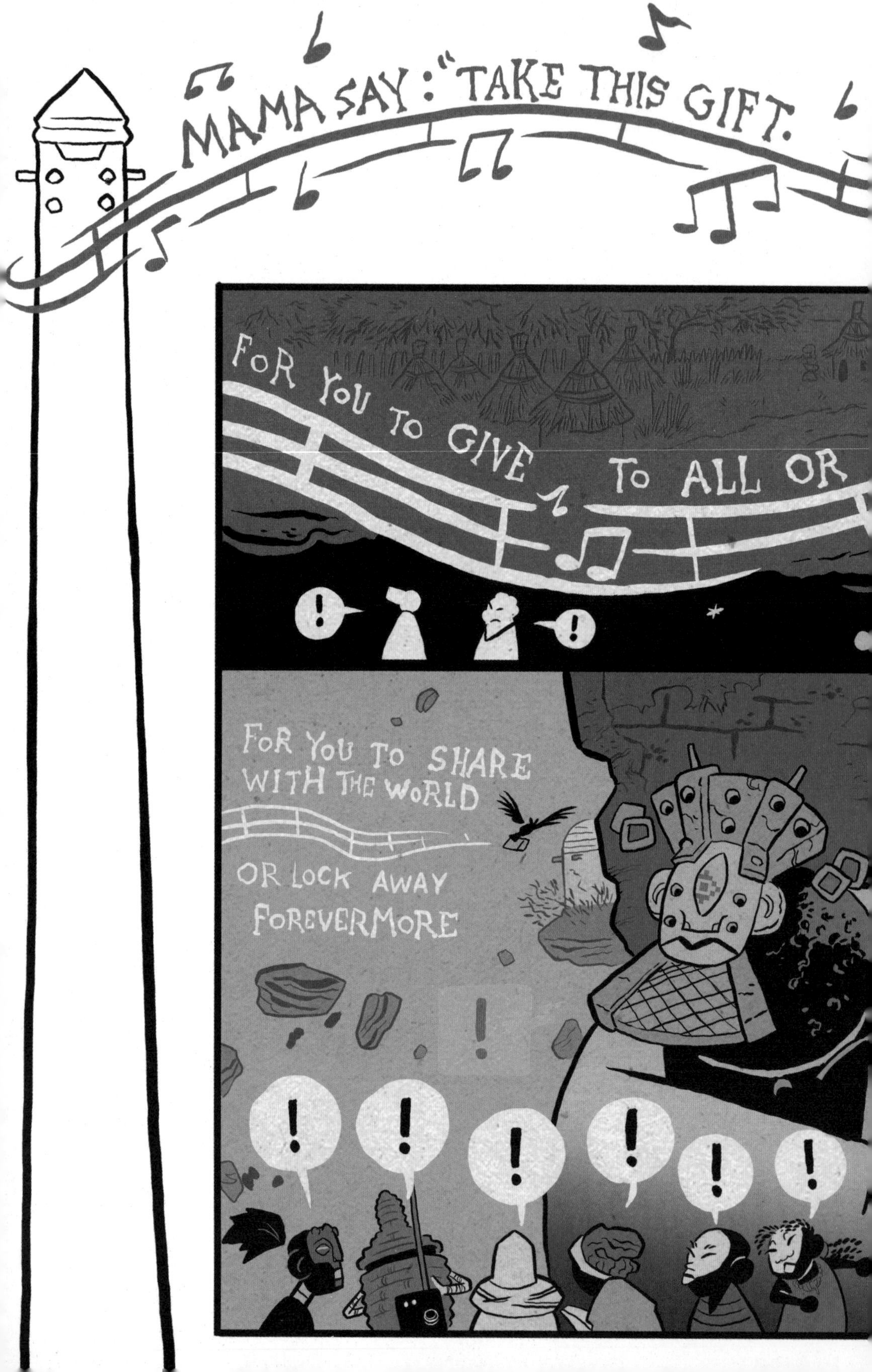
MAMA SAY: "TAKE THIS GIFT.
FOR YOU TO GIVE TO ALL OR
!
!
FOR YOU TO SHARE WITH THE WORLD
OR LOCK AWAY FOREVERMORE
!
!
!
!
!
!
!

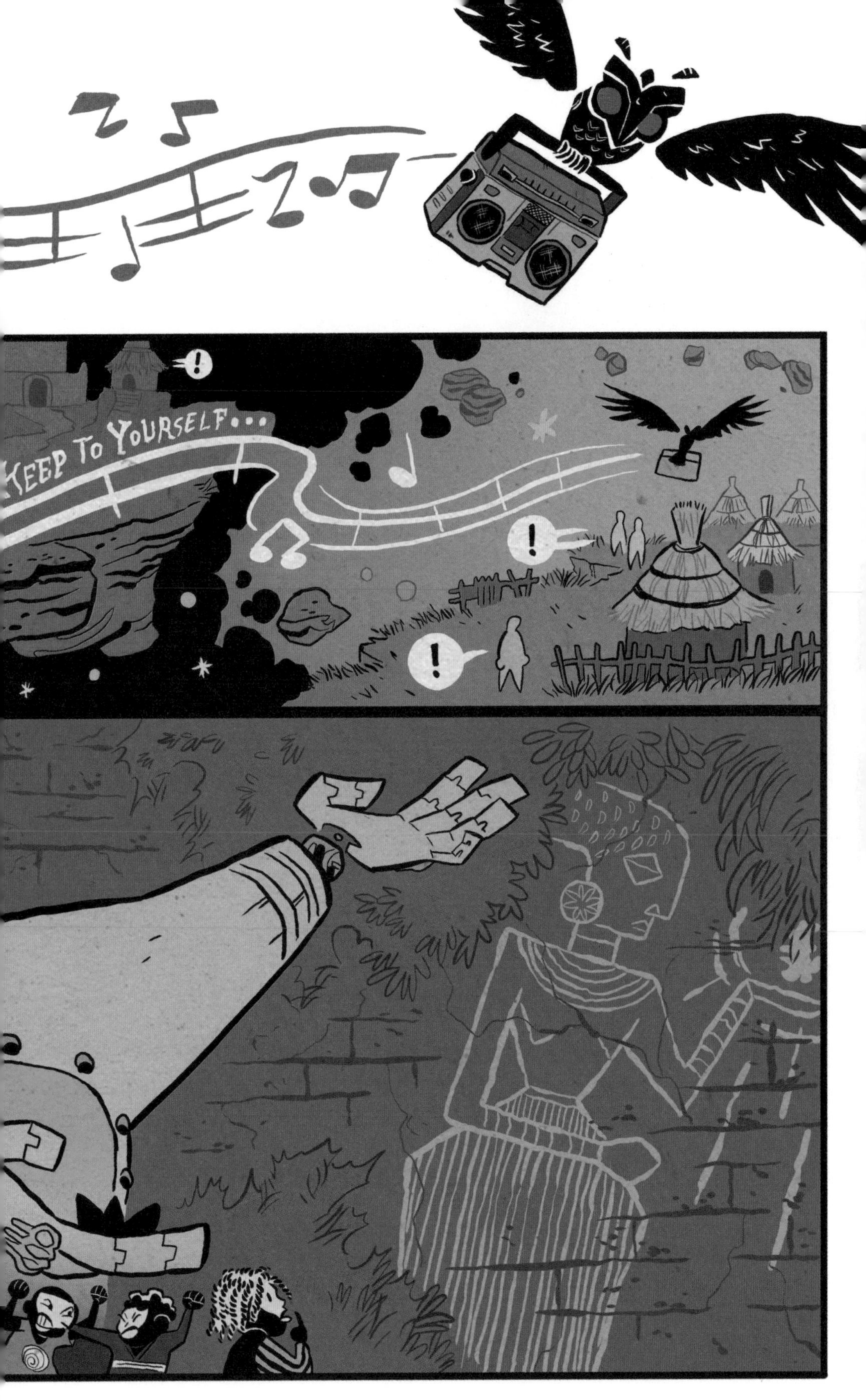

KEEP TO YOURSELF...
!
!
!

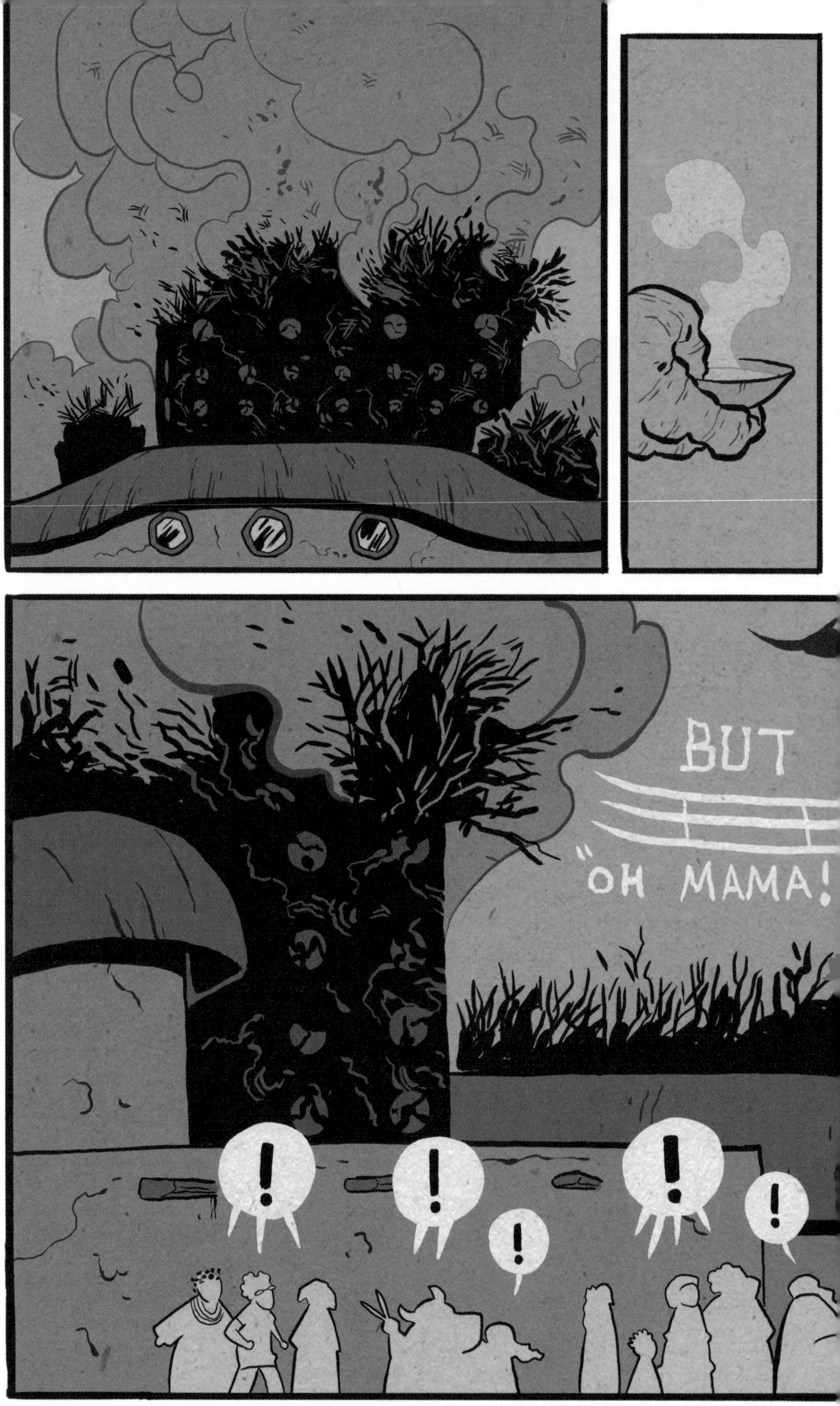
BUT
"OH MAMA!
!
!
!
!
!

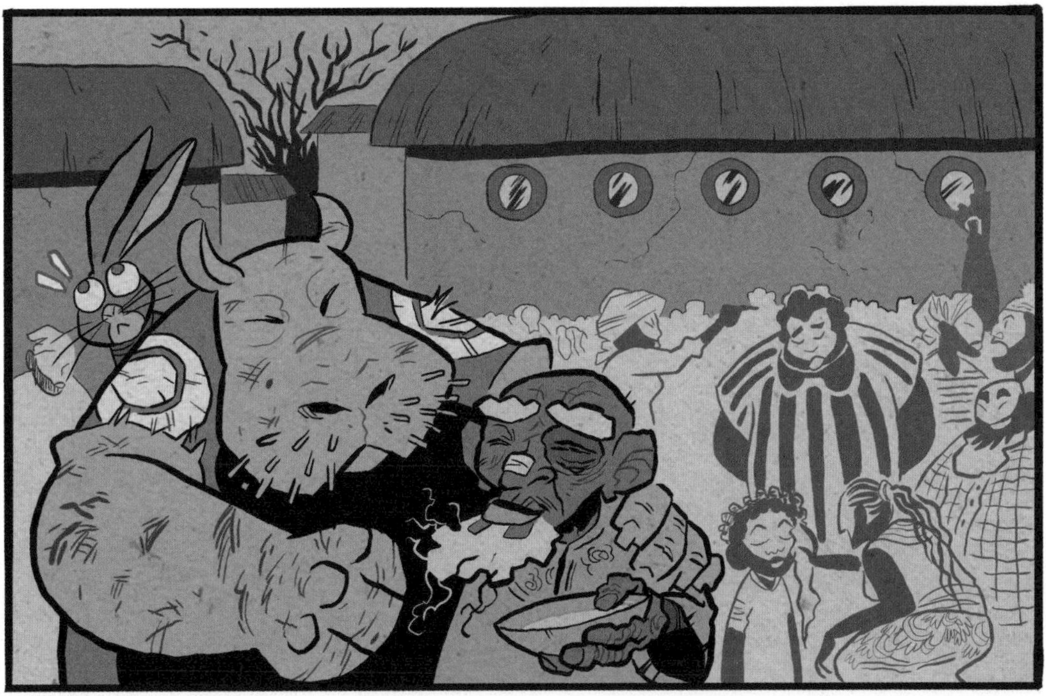

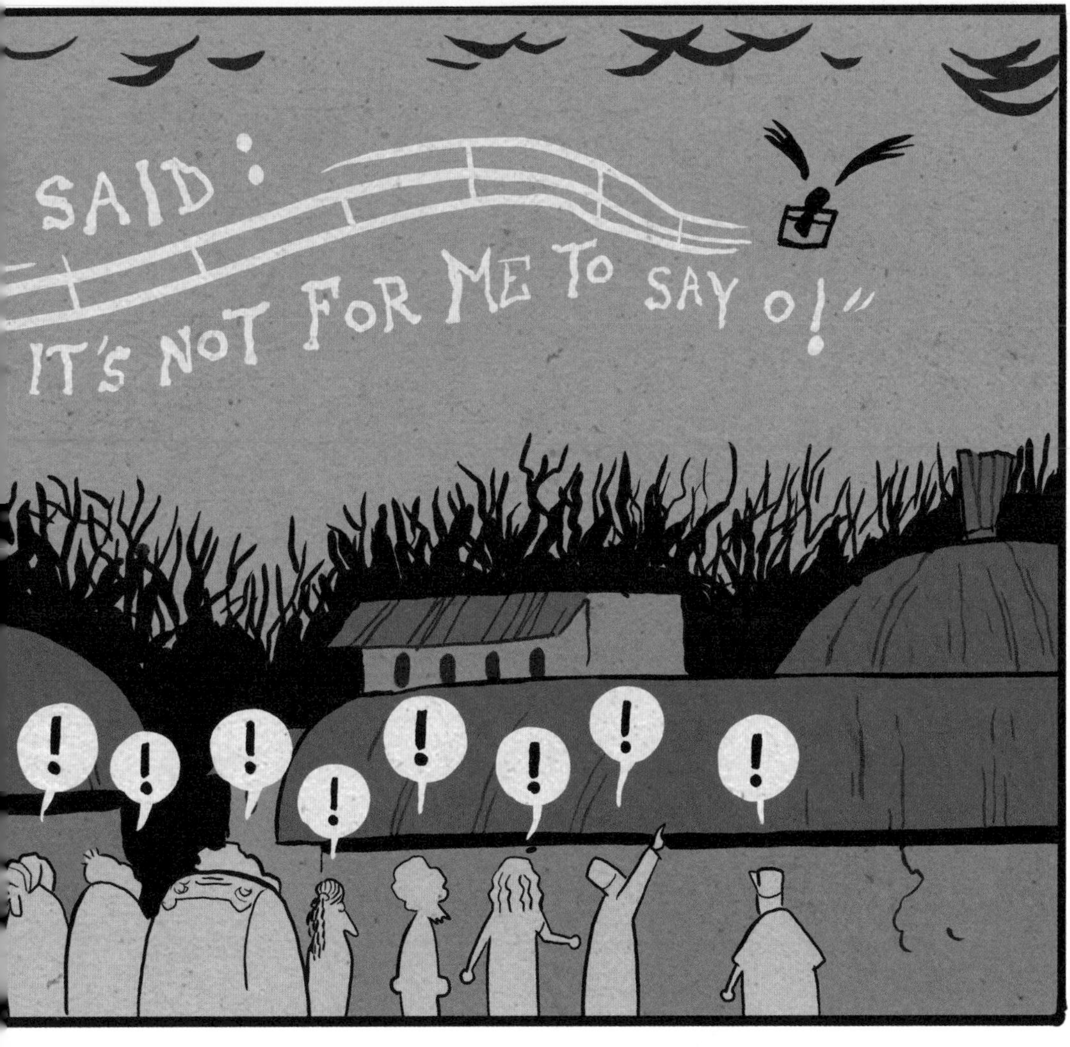
SAID:
IT'S NOT FOR ME TO SAY O!"
!
!
!
!
!
!
!
!
!

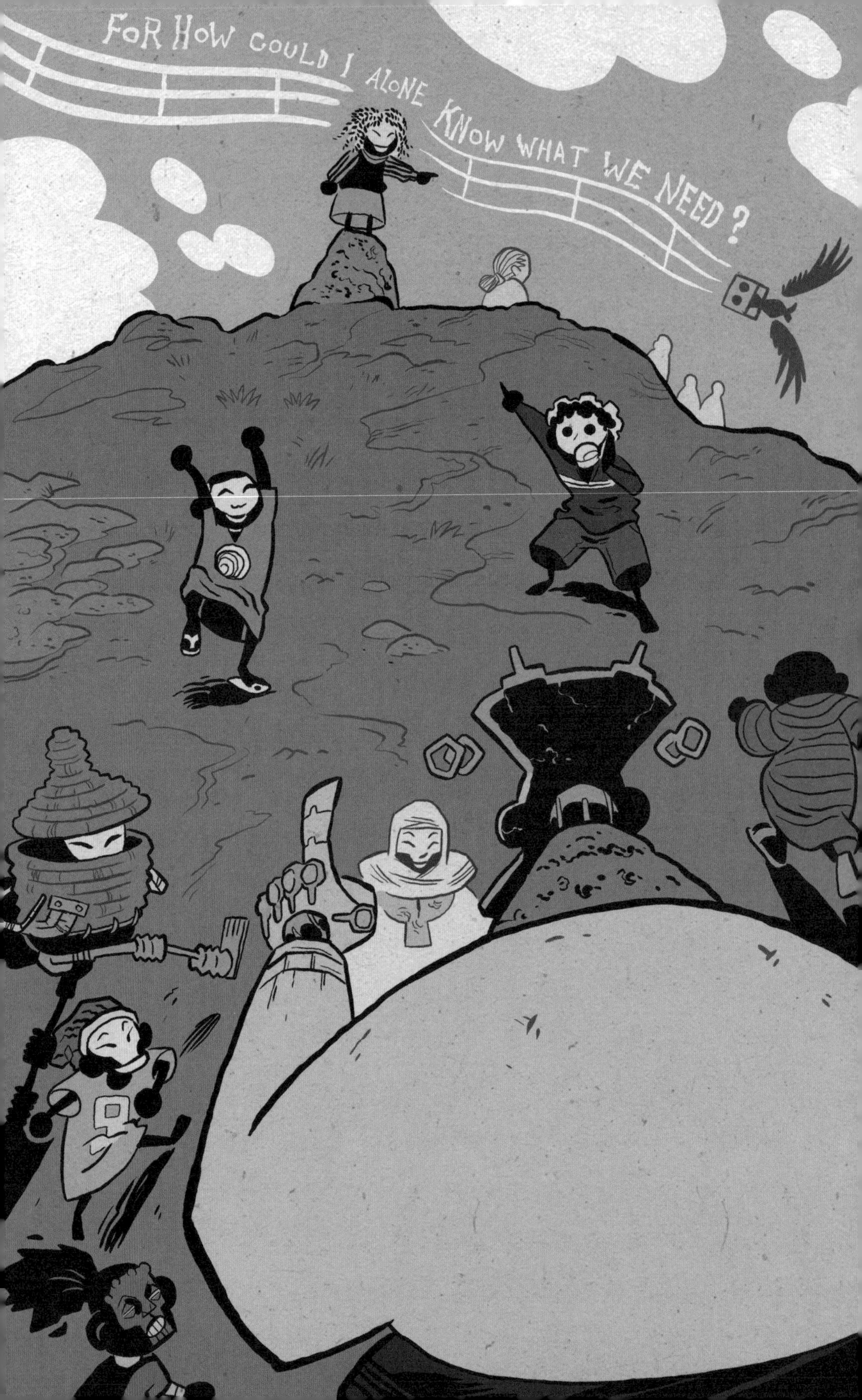
FOR HOW COULD I ALONE KNOW WHAT WE NEED?

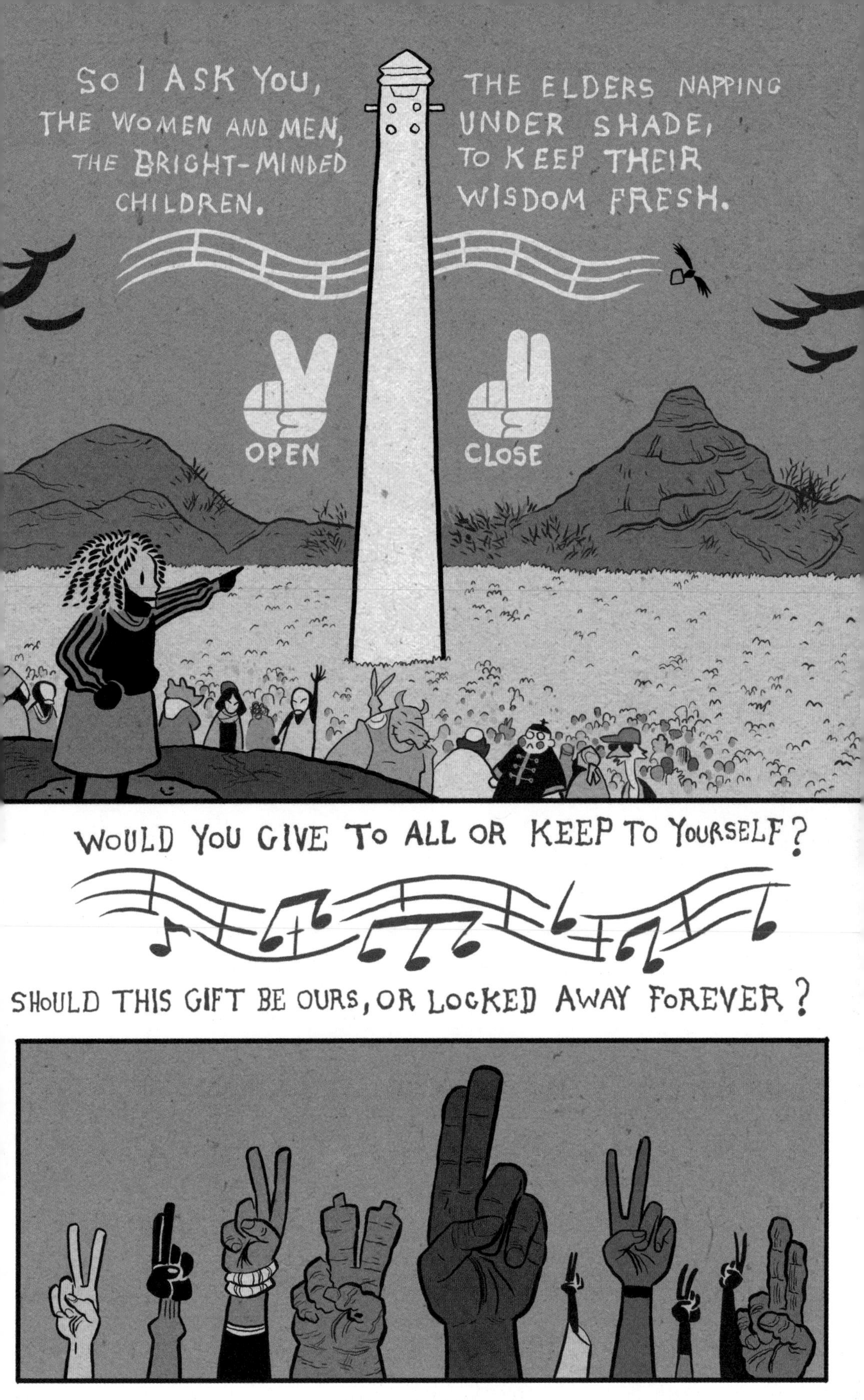
SO I ASK YOU,
THE WOMEN AND MEN,
THE BRIGHT-MINDED
CHILDREN.
THE ELDERS NAPPING
UNDER SHADE,
TO KEEP THEIR
WISDOM FRESH.
OPEN
CLOSE
WOULD YOU GIVE TO ALL OR KEEP TO YOURSELF?
SHOULD THIS GIFT BE OURS, OR LOCKED AWAY FOREVER?

AND I

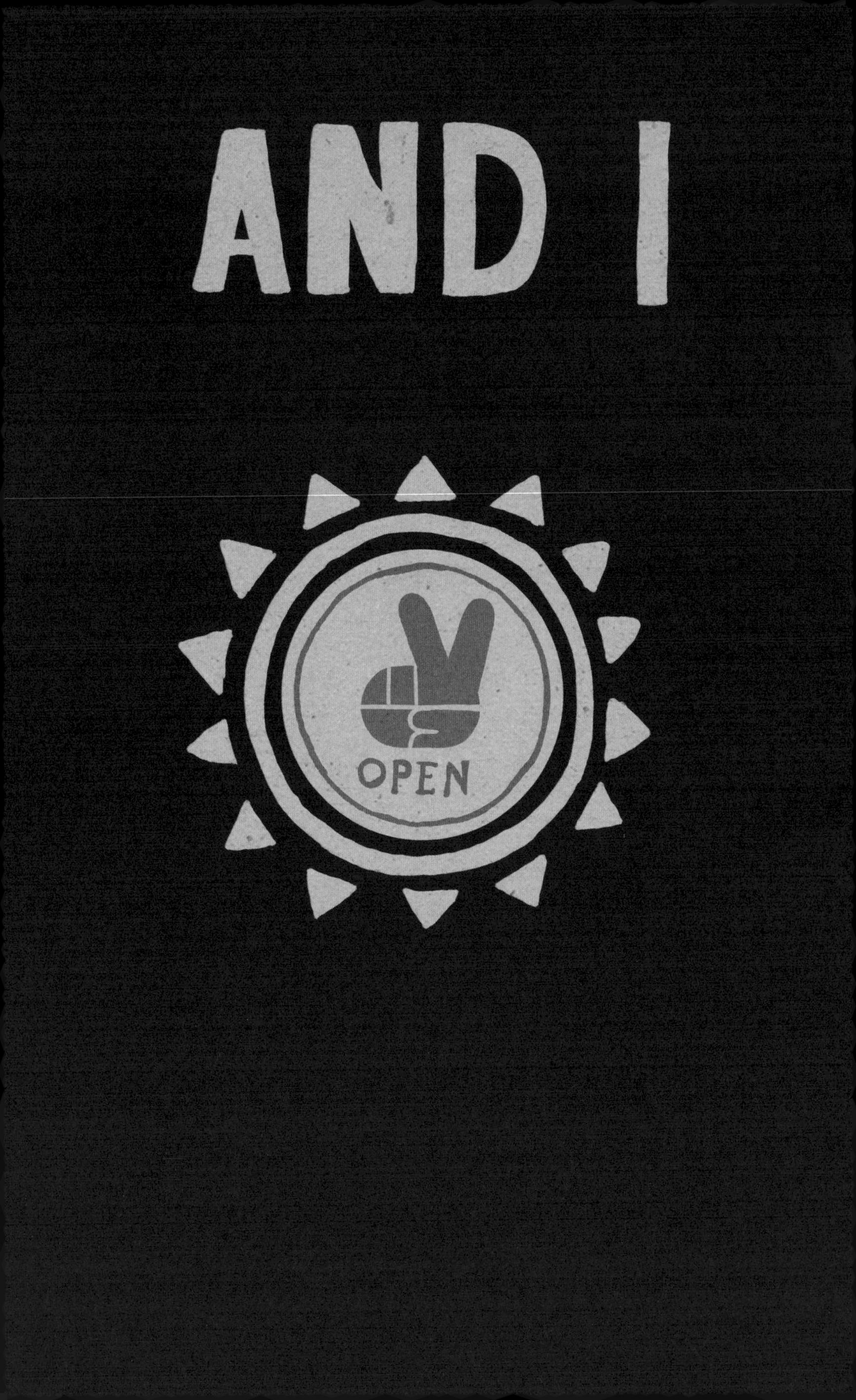
OPEN

ASK YOU

CLOSE

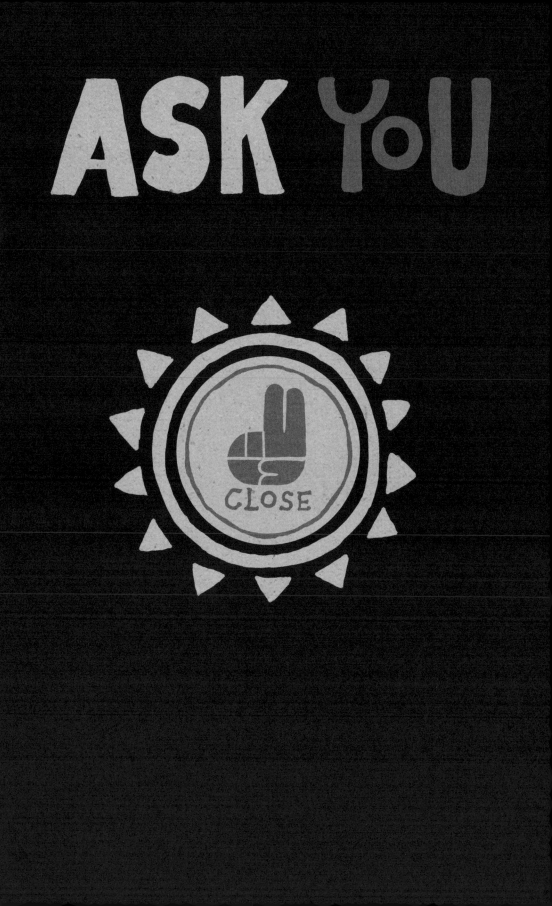

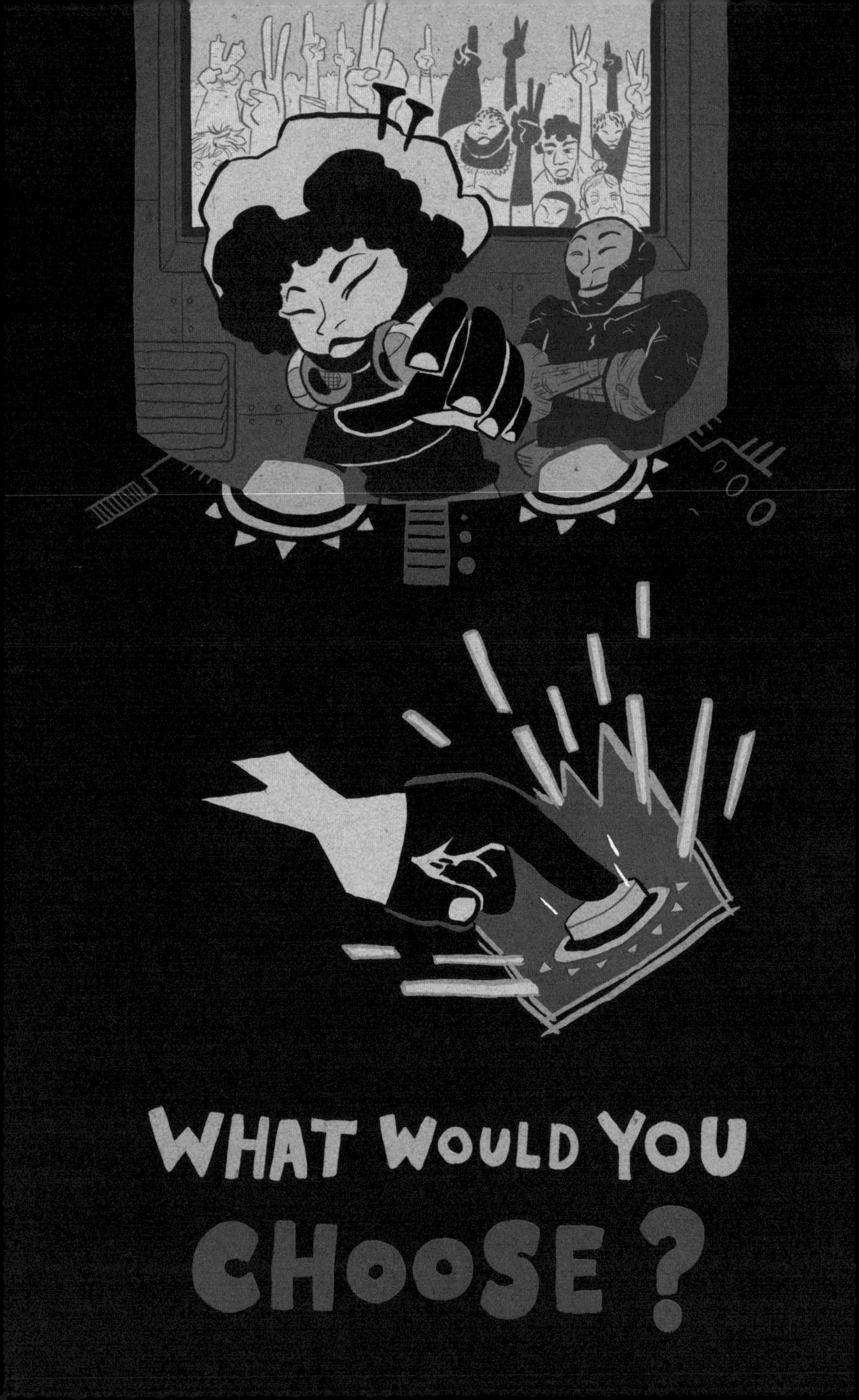
WHAT WOULD YOU
CHOOSE?

THE END

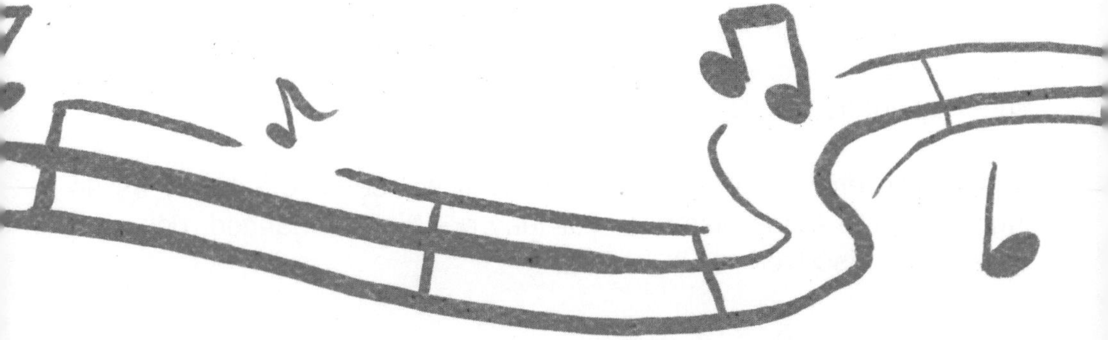

THE INSPIRATION FOR *DJELIYA*: AFRICAN FOLKLORE AND ORAL HISTORY

While *Djeliya* is a work of fiction, it is based on very real, very old, and very beloved folklores, cultures, and history passed down from (mostly Western) Africa. The back matter is compiled here for you reader, no matter your age, creed, and origin, to delve into the aspects of Africa you may not be aware of.

It is not an encyclopedia, but we hope it will serve effectively as an introduction to these histories. For they are plural, nuanced, rich, and quite fun to discover!

NAME PRONUNCIATIONS

Here is a list of the foreign names whose pronunciation may not be evident to readers and a guide to help you say their names right. These come from Wolof, the language of the ethnic group of the same name (prominent in Senegal), and from Twi, the language of the Asante people of Ghana, whose myths and culture inspired the second chapter.

Mbam (Wolof for "pig"): Pronounced as written. "Mb" being pronounced together and not as "EM-BAM," as some may assume.
Bouki (Wolof for "hyena"): "BOO-KEE"
Xogne (Wolof): "HROGNE," "HR" being a gravely exhaling sound. It sounds like what it is named after, the crunchy burned rice at the bottom of the pot. The same pronunciation applies to "Xalis," which means "money."
Maame (Twi for "mother"): "MAA-MEH"
Nyame (Twi for "God"): "NEE-AH-MEH"

Djeli: A Malinké term referring to the griot, a central figure in traditional West African cultures. They are a counselor, but most of all a keeper of his people's history, thanks largely to his tremendous memory.

The term *djeli* itself means "bloodline," highlighting how this knowledge is passed from father to son (or daughters in some cases). The end of the bloodline would spell the end of the practice and knowledge itself.

As a skilled wordsmith and musician who spreads lessons and knowledge through folktales and recounted history, a *djeli* is also the keeper of mystical and ancient knowledge that only their fellow *djelis* can possess.

The oral tradition remains a very strong and important one in West Africa, though it is challenged by the modernization of countries that are, let's not forget, just around 60 years old.
It is easy to discard their oral history as unreliable (as if the written word couldn't lie), but archeological research tends to prove that this form of historical recording is to be considered with respect.

Though the practice may disappear as time goes on, it is important to gather as much knowledge from its practitioners as possible, before they all pass and the knowledge dies with them.

ANTHROPOMORPHIC ANIMALS
The presence of anthropomorphic animals in this book is inspired by the many folktales from West Africa, often featuring talking animals that are characterized by very defined traits pertaining to their species. The hyena, for example, is portrayed as crafty but of questionable morality. The hare is intelligent but constantly mindful of danger. Like many storied cultures in the world, these archetypes serve to entertain or give lessons to the young and old.

The two main inspirations for the story you have read are the book "Belle Histoire de Leuk-le-Lièvre," by Léopold Sédar Senghor and artist Abdoulaye Sadji, and the Fulani folktales transcribed by Amadou Hampâté Bâ. As is tradition, the names used for the animals in this book are literally the name of their species in the Wolof language. The only exception being Tchoki (which means "to fight" in Wolof).

SOUMAORO AND THE KEITA CLAN
The epic of Sundiata Keita is a piece of oral history passed on since the early days of the Mali Empire in the 1200s, all the way down to today. It tells the adventure of Sundiata Keita, the first king and founder of the Mali Empire, as he unites the peoples of the region against the tyrannical rule of King Soumaoro Kante.

The characters in Djeliya are thus loosely inspired by this epic, and are in no way a faithful representation of any historical figures.

For any music lovers reading this, Sundiata's descendant Salif Keita is a renowned and very talented musician, whose work I recommend you discover for yourself.

ADINKRA SYMBOLS

Adinkra is one of the most recognizable written languages on the African continent. The Adinkra (meaning "goodbye") stems from the Akan peoples of Ghana and the Ivory Coast. Each symbol represents an idea, a historical event, beings, a proverb, or words of wisdom. Usually printed on cloth or pieces of architecture, they are a visual representation of the wisdom of the Akan peoples. All symbol translations here are taken from Twi ("tchwi"), the language of the Akan.

Here is a chart presenting each symbol used in this book, in order of appearance, then followed by two original symbols and their meaning. (Translations taken from *"Afrikan Alphabets, the Story of Writing in Afrika,"* by Saki Mafundikwa).

All Seeing Eye,
God's omnipresence.

Talons of the Eagle, Loyalty,
devotion to service.

Home security,
one way in or out.

King's stool, royal authority.

War horn,
call to arms.

"I fear none but God,"
omnipotence of God.

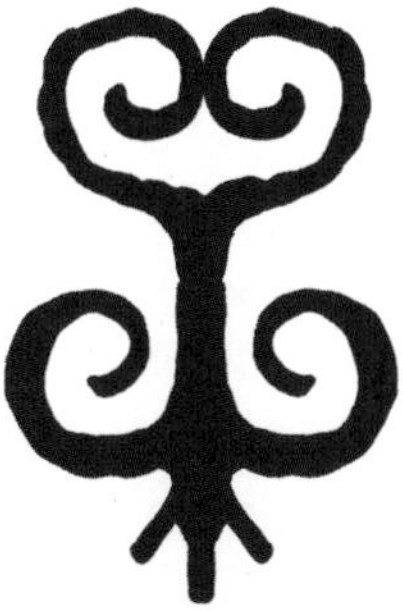

"Return and Get it," learn from the past

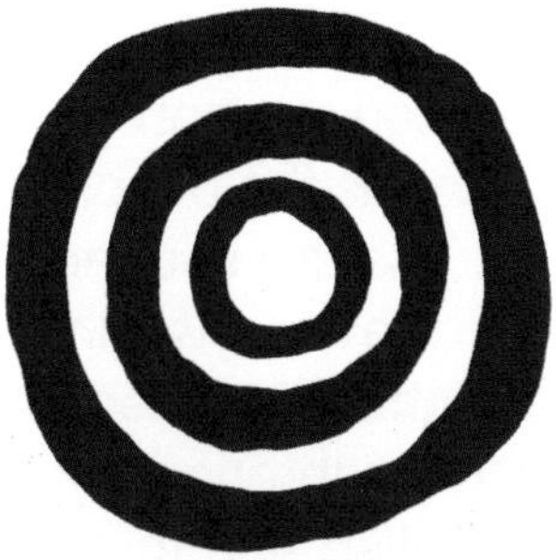

Chief of Adinkra signs, leadership, greatness, and charisma.

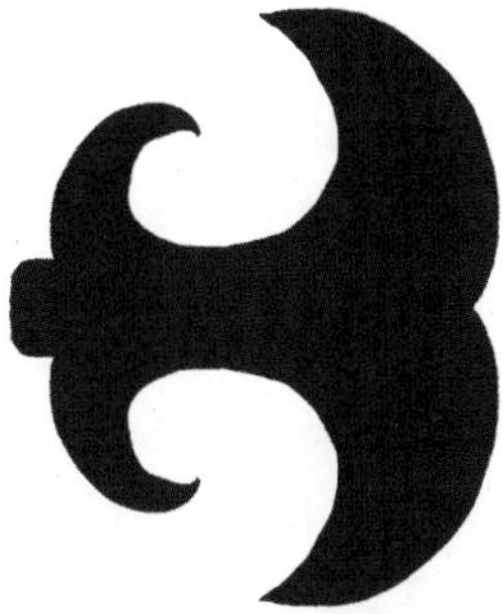

Notion to feed and discipline children. To raise them without overprotecting.

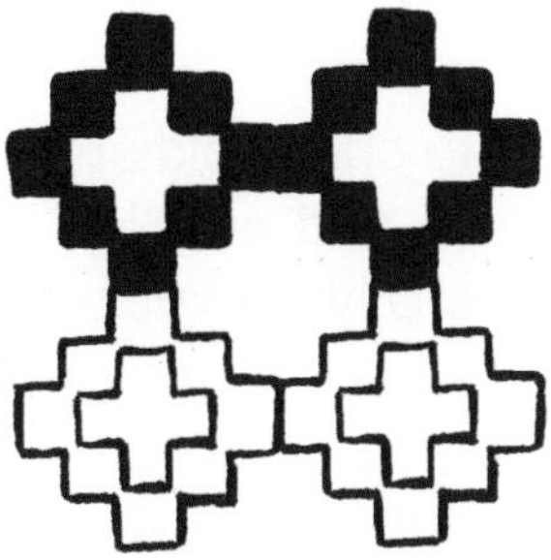

Seat of Government.

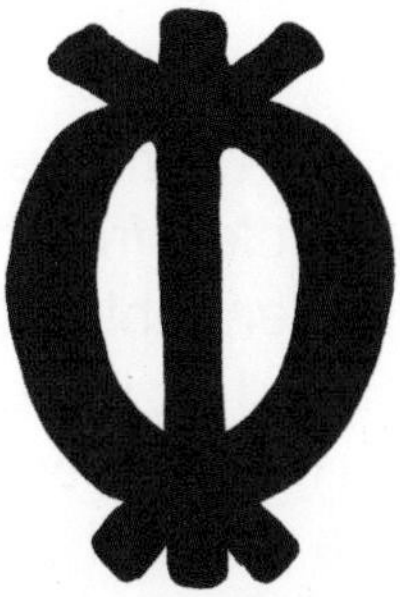

Wawa Ba, a hard wood used in carving. Strength.

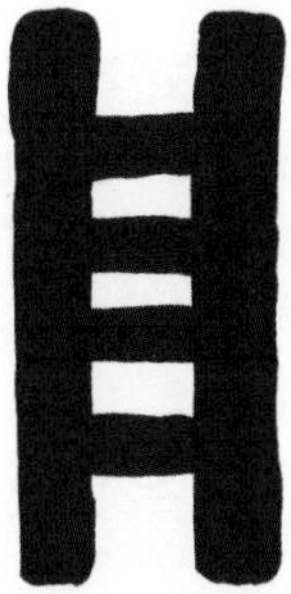

"The Ladder of Death will be climbed by all." Mortality.

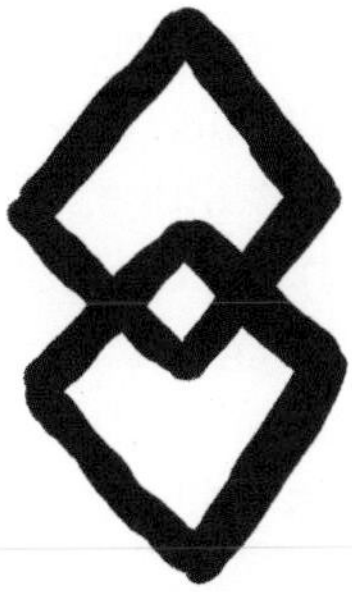

"You are the slave of him whose handcuffs you wear." Servitude.

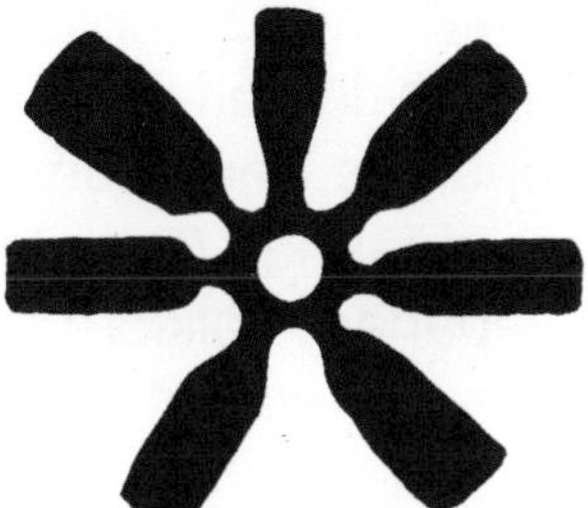

Symbol of Anansi. Creativity and wisdom.

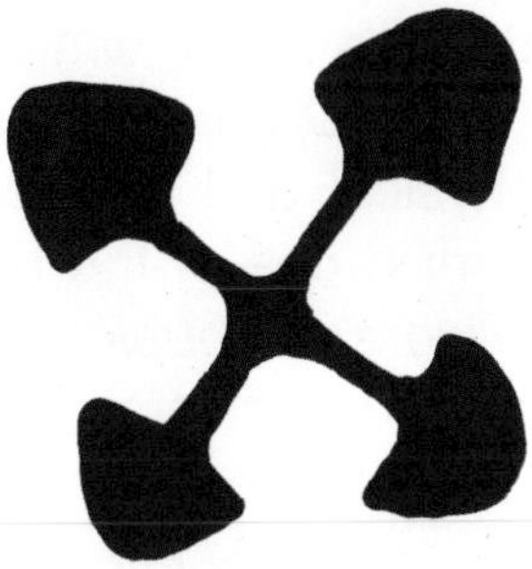

Linked hearts. Understanding, agreement.

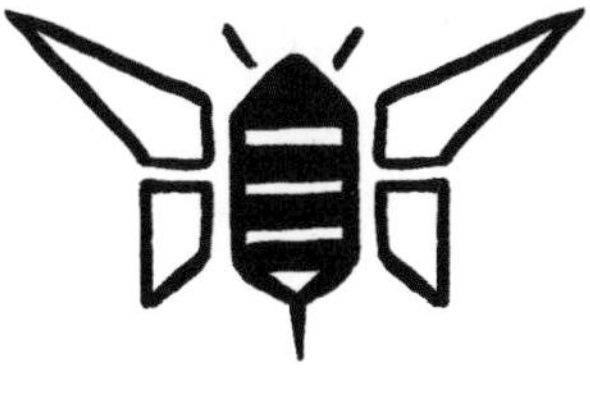

A bee. In Fulani culture, it represents wisdom. (Also low-key represents Beyoncé.)

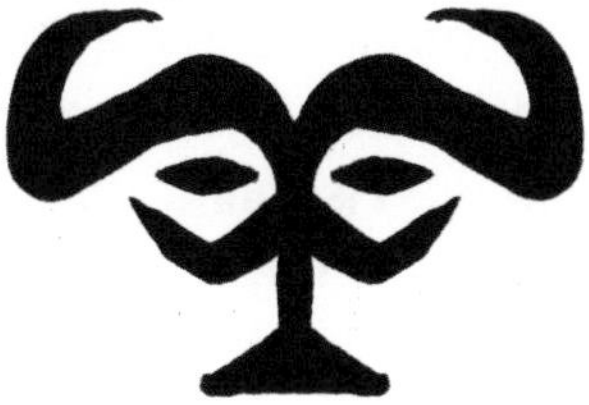

Water buffalo, designed after the role the animal has in the birth of Sundiata Keita in the original epic.

THE ASANTE THRONE

Called Sika Dwa, the most prized symbol of the Asante people of Ghana. This throne is said to be as old as the people themselves, given by God to their first king Osei Tutu. It is the soul and unifier of the Asante. An artifact so respected that not even the king is allowed to sit upon it, and it benefited from the highest-level security possible, even better than the king himself. In fact, the throne remained protected and hidden by its people, even as the British and their African forces invaded the country. The queen in Chapter 2 is named after the Asante people (and a childhood icon of mine, the RnB singer Ashanti!)

KADOGOS

Swahili for "small ones." It is the term used to refer to child soldiers in places like the Congo. Often stolen from their homes and enrolled in militias, as they constitute an expendable, cheap, and easily manipulated "workforce" that are kept subdued by undue influence, drugs, and peer pressure. Sadly, many will join of their free will, as they seek protection, community, and belonging to a group that will protect them in the face of poverty, war, or discrimination in unstable regions.

DJINNES

Sharing many similarities with the Djinn of Arabic folklore, the West African *Djinne*, a ghost, spirit, or demon, is a mysterious creature whose physical and mystical properties vary from culture to culture. They remind one of the bestiary of faeries (from Welsh, Irish, and Scottish folklore) or *obake* (from Japanese folklore): living all around us, yet hidden, each creature with its own way of living and peculiar traits. They have inspired many stories, including this one, as well as, for example, the book "My Life in the Bush of Ghosts" by Amos Tutuola.

NYAME AND ANANSI

Nyame (or Onyamekopon) is the omnipresent and omnipotent God of the Akan people of Ghana. His representation in this book is reimagined. Here he is accompanied by a fabled hero in West Africa: Anansi, the spider man, a trickster and adventurer whose deeds are the subject of many tales, and who is intimately connected to the art of storytelling. This character especially enjoys great popularity, and his stories have survived even the forceful and relentless attempts at keeping enslaved Africans from their culture. Today he appears on tv shows, in books, and comics by Africans, African-Americans, and even the works of a certain famous British author. He is a testament to the power and resilience of storytelling.

BIBLIOGRAPHY

Hale, Thomas A. *Griots and Griottes: Masters of Word and Music.* Bloomington, IN: Indiana University Press, 1998.

Niane, Djibril Tamsir. *Soundjata ou l'Epopée du Manding*. Paris: Présence africaine, 1960.

Senghor, Léopold Sédar and Abdoulaye Sadji. *La Belle Histoire de Leuk-le-Lièvre*. Paris: Hachette, 1953.

Tutuola, Amos. *My Life in the Bush of Ghosts*. New York, NY: Grove Press, 1954.

Mafundikwa, Saki. *Afrikan Alphabets: the Story of Writing in Afrika.* West New York, N.J. : Mark Batty, 2004.

Lallemand, Suzanne and François-Victor Équilbecq. *Contes populaires d'Afrique occidentale. Précédés d'un Essai sur la littérature merveilleuse des Noirs*. In: *Cahiers d'études africaines*, vol. 13, n°52, Paris: EHESS, 1973.

As well as:
The Oral Epic of Sundiata Keita

Fulani folktales transcribed by Amadou Hămpaté Bă

The works, speeches and interviews of Chimamanda Ngozi Adichie

And my family's eternal well of knowledge

JUHI
BA

JUNI BA is what happens when the influences of 2000s era Cartoon Network enter the brain of an average Senegalese boy. Since growing up in Dakar, he has come up with several works including the *Monkey Meat* comics, the *Kayin and Abeni* miniseries with co-writer Keenan Kornegay, as well as being featured in the publications of the Nigerian house Kugali.

DJELIYA is his first graphic novel, but hopefully the first of many, to tackle subjects in and out of Africa.